PERSON/A

PERSON/A

A Novel by
ELIZABETH ELLEN

Short Flight / Long Drive Books
A DIVISION OF Hobart

SHORT FLIGHT/LONG DRIVE BOOKS

A division of Hobart Publishing

PO Box 1658

Ann Arbor, MI 48106

www.hobartpulp.com/minibooks

ISBN: 978-0-9896950-6-0

Printed in the United States of America

Inside text set in Georgia

Cover design by Chelsea Martin

Author photos by Elizabeth Ellen

Layout by Alban Fischer

PERSON/A

Dear Elizabeth,

Thank you for sharing PERSON(A). I'm so pleased that [ ] made this introduction, as I've long admired your voice from afar. I found your novel to be startling in its emotional complexity, clarity and voice. I was so intrigued by your experimental storytelling and found that the mixture of poetry, prose passages and collected quotes presented such a fascinating lily-padding roadmap of this woman's journey. There's a unique language of pain in your prose that is so evocative and moving.

That said, despite my deep admiration of your ambitious novel, I'm afraid that I had some hesitations that make me think I might not have the best vision for you here... As intrigued as I was by your unconventional story-telling, I often felt that the voice and narration felt disjointed as a result of the non-linear style. I found some of the passages where she laments the loss of her lover(s) to be so repetitive that I lost the forward thrust of the narrative. The narrator is clearly obsessive, but I wanted the emotional stakes to feel slightly more tailored and story-driven. The inventiveness of the prose, which you have in spades, needs to be hinged on something, even if the form is played with.

At this point, despite my admiration for the risk and movement of this book, I'm afraid I just don't think I'm the best advocate for you here. With your best interests at heart, I will step aside so that you may find an agent who will offer you the passionate representation you deserve. I wish you the best of luck, and look forward to seeing your name on shelves soon.

All best,

[ ]

Hi Elizabeth,

Thank you so much for sending me these pages. PERSON(A) has a heartbeat that I can feel on every page, and a narrator who is ruthlessly exacting in her self-analysis—she is so honest and candid, and even as she treads that very fine line between fact and fiction, she does so consciously, never letting herself off the hook, never flinching at the implications or consequences of her choices (e.g. "Am I acting like a monster in order to get to the place I need to be to finish this book or have I become a monster? / Have I become 'Elizabeth Ellen'? Have I become my persona? And what would that mean, anyway? What is my persona? Who am I? (I am a monster)" (372)). Despite this rigorous self-examina-tion, though, she can also be wryly funny (e.g. "In their presence I felt inadequate and uncool and desirous of feeling myself included in their group, though I did not feel that I was, and because of this I overcompen-sated by talking too much and nervously, so that by the time I left the area I felt I had come off as even less cool than I might have had I not been so aware of trying to be cool" (110))—which is another interesting facet of her personality: she holds herself accountable, but she isn't afraid to poke fun at herself, too. I won't keep quoting your own lines back to you, but this is all to say that there's just so much in these pages that I love, so much that is working so well.

In the end, though, and even with all there is to celebrate here, I'm very disappointed to say I don't think I'm your guy for this. One of the major successes of this novel is its vivid depiction of the narrator's anxiety, and this also created an almost physical closeness for me. This is brilliantly executed, but for me it intensifies over the course of the novel, and even-tually I felt so close—to the narrator, to the anxiety—that I began to have trouble seeing past her: she seems, ultimately, to occupy too much nar-rative space, and as such there doesn't seem to be quite enough oppor-tunity for the other characters to really come alive for me, or for the rest of the novel to grow around her. I don't at all think that this suggests the novel isn't working as a whole, or even that this closeness is something that should change—again, I think this is a brilliant element of the novel. Rather, I think it suggests very simply that I might just not be the book's best reader. And with that in mind I think the best thing, unfortunately, is for me to step aside here. I'm so glad you thought to send this my way, Elizabeth, and so grateful to be trusted with your pages. I will be wishing you all the best with PERSON(A) and with all else going forward.

Best,

█

to me

Hi Elizabeth,

Thank you again for allowing me to consider your novel. I understand why ▌ had such nice things to say about it — it's clear you're a talented writer. But I'm afraid, for reasons that boil down to simple personal taste, I didn't fall quite enough in love with this project. I hope you find a great home for this book and please know I'll always be happy to read more from you.

Best,

PERSONA

Dear Elizabeth,

Thank you for the chance to consider PERSONA and for your patience waiting to hear back from me. I love the honesty, the humor, and the voice in this book. This narrator can pull in the reader by baring all, but then hold herself at an ironic remove, a skill that feels acutely controlled in your authorial hands. That control feels wonderfully contemporary, of-the-moment. However, I struggle with what it all adds up to, and in particular, its aim to be a novel. Though I was voyeuristically intrigued by the material here, at times I felt that I could open the book at any page and somehow know both everything I needed to know, and yet also, not enough. In the end, I desired more of a traditional narrative arc and a throughline that felt cumulative and propulsive. I'm sorry to say that I don't think this is right for my list at the moment, and I would not be its best advocate—as fully convinced of your talent as I am. I'm sorry to step aside, but look forward to seeing where this lands. Thank you again for the opportunity to consider PERSONA.

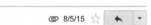

to me ▾   🔗 8/5/15 ☆ ← ▾

i'll be v curious what you think...

I liked it a lot. I was extremely interested throughout, all until the parts that began to seem made-up.

abt what i can do to improve it....

I don't like telling people how they can improve their writing. I think you'll never be satisfied if you keep looking to people for advice on it. I would just spend a long time looking at it yourself, using books you like as models or for guidance, and then when you're done, view it as done and then just try to get it published until it is published. Then whoever your editor is will look at it and offer whatever suggestions, and you can take or leave them, then it's done.

I don't want to read your book with a lot of other input on it from other people, even me. I want to read your book with only your own input on it.

i know i want to disguise ppl more.

While reading it, I didn't understand the characters that wanted you to disguise other characters in it. I feel like you didn't reveal anything about anyone that will reflect badly on anyone. You didn't use real names. Outside of like 10 people, or something, no one will know who is who, and it didn't matter to me. Disguising things could lead to other problems, for example if you changed the writer to a musician, that would mess with things in subtle ways that would make the book seem less real, I feel.

One thing that distracted me was the writer being featured in Rolling Stones in a 4000(?) word article. If that happened, the writer would be extremely, insanely famous and it wouldn't fit with the rest of the details about him, I felt immediately.

and i had a lot of repetition.

i sent it to yr agent and he wrote me back a VERY NICE email passing on it.
and that's all i've done.
re any attempt to publish it.

still conflicted...
(but maybe i would be less so if i edited it in a way i felt more comfortable w it?)

I would just work on it on your own, and not ask for other people's opinions, especially for such a personal book. I 'cringed' at all the advice the characters were giving the narrator throughout volume 2.

I'm meeting my editor on Thursday to discuss my 100 pages and according to my agent my editor wants to offer his advice on how to change my novel, like he wants to change it to third person and some other stuff. I'm going to tell him I want to work on it on my own and that I already have my vision for it. Ideally I would finish all my novels THEN turn it in, but I need money. My first two novels were written alone and without input, and I liked that best.

In terms of whether the book will hurt anyone if you publish it...I feel like you obviously aren't writing to maliciously denounce anyone, and the character that conventionally would be viewed as most denounced is the narrator, in my view, so I wouldn't worry about that. It's a novel, so people have to deal with that, they have to view it as fiction and they have to view every character in the book as a character, and not connect information about those characters to people in real life. If they don't do that, that's a defect and problem THEY have, a problem with which they are hurting people—by conflating characters and people—not YOU, in my view. By using your memory as source material, you have written the deepest, most intense, most interesting thing you can write, I feel. Everyone should be able to use their memory as source material to create moving, relevant, interesting, complicated fiction. Everyone should also learn to distinguish fiction and reality, characters and people, but almost no one else, which makes it difficult and why you even have these doubts, I think.

I feel pressure not to write autobiographically, from the literary world and from my editor, and I don't like it. I want to write MORE autobiographically, to examine the purposes of autobiographical fiction, the differences between people and characters, the relationship between people and books, not less. It always on some level feels like I'm doing something bad when I write autobiographically, like I'm being self-centered or narcissistic, but I'm becoming more and more confident that it's just a temporary thing in the culture that is telling me I'm bad for doing it. I think in Japan there's a much longer history of what's called "auto-fiction" and they probably have a more sophisticated view of it. The "romantics" also wrote autobiographically and all these other people. But today there seems to be pressure against writing autobiographically, and I don't like it.

I liked your book a lot. I would just look at it again in September, and work on it more if you want to, then when you feel it's done, try to get it published.

Sorry I couldn't offer direct advice on the book. I've never done that to anyone, it completely defeats the purpose of writing a novel to me, I want your personal vision, not a lot of different people's.

You have my support in and encouragement in publishing it and in not worrying about hurting people. It seems ridiculous to me that people would even be thinking about you hurting people with it. It's an exciting, moving, intense novel to me.

Hey Beth,

I did read your book this weekend. I know that reality TV is in, so I'll bet reality books are in. My personal opinion though is that it was so self-absorbed and so self-serving that frankly it was boring. After about 20 pages, I started anxiously looking to the next page and the next page and the next page to see if this was all it was, was it going somewhere, did it involve anyone else. The answer was no and the only others involved were stick figures, one-dimensional people.

I feel sorry that at 40 you seem to be stuck. I would think you'd wake up every morning with your head thrown back in laugher, but instead it seems you greet each day by scratching that old itch of what you "deserve" and then you wallow in your self-righteousness. I was astonished to be at your house and see you stomp off from playing cards to go sit in your room because someone or everyone didn't anticipate your every need and fulfill it. To see you stomp off from a family outing because someone or everyone didn't say the exact right thing to meet your needs. To see you stomp off from my mother's because I wasn't meeting your every need. I'm so sad that this is your life and you just don't seem to get it. It's up to you to be happy or sad every day, to make your life what you want it to be. You seem to be drowning in this philosophy of "I'm not getting what I deserve so I'm going to withdraw and that'll show 'em."

Now you're writing about stalking someone because you had a fling with him and now he's not interested? And you're sending him nude photos? How demeaning to yourself. You have everything going on for yourself. If you don't think so, why don't you go volunteer at a homeless shelter, at the guardian at litem for children, at the literacy program, at the department of children and families, at a women's shelter, see what people have to deal with on an everyday basis, see what you think they deserve, see how your life measures up.

Your mom

A LETTER FROM THE EDITOR[1]

Dear Reader,

A couple of years ago, I purchased a book written by a woman that was garnering a fair amount of attention for its "controversial subject matter." What I found most surprising and shocking and even somewhat "offensive," if such a word is to be thrown around as casually and as perhaps gratuitously as it seems to be currently, about the novel was not its "controversial" subject matter, which, honestly, didn't seem all that shocking (an eight year age difference between lovers, though the younger of the two was as we used to say, "jailbait," fourteen, and the older of the two was *a woman*), but the letter from the editor that opened the book and an interview with the author that closed the book, both of which seemed to serve the dual purpose of explaining the history of unlikable literary and cinematic characters and to encourage any uncomfortable moral finger-pointing to be at the novel's protagonist, rather than at the editor or author. (Neither the editor nor the author seemed to trust the reading public (i.e., the non-academic reader) to distinguish between the art and the artist, or, between entertainment (i.e., a novel) and real life (i.e., *real life!*).)

The editor and the author went to great lengths to be certain we understood just how evil they believed the protagonist of this novel to be, going so far as to name the "real life woman" on whom the novel's protagonist was based (so we would know it wasn't based on the author, herself once a young teacher?), and to use a series of vilifying words to describe her, the most notable of which was used by both editor and author: *sociopath*, as in "You are about to read the story of a real life *sociopath*!"

I should admit here I have always been made uncomfortable by that term, *sociopath*, in the same manner I have been made uncomfortable by the term, mostly out of fashion currently but still very much used in my coming-of-age years: *nymphomaniac*.

I have a hard time believing either—the sociopath or the nymphomaniac—exists. Just as I would hope there existed one or two brave pre-1970 souls who did not conform to the notion that homosexuality was a mental

---

[1] *the editor of this book is Elizabeth Ellen*

disorder, who did not believe homosexuals to be depraved or amoral or mental defectives, who did not view the act of sodomy as a crime.

The letter by the editor of the book I began this letter mentioning, used the letter to introduce to readers a "new literary monster."

All that being said, and with that in mind, I write this letter to you, dear reader, as both editor and author of this novel, with full awareness and with full admission that *if there is* a "Monster at the End of This Book," that monster is I. I am that monster.

Let this then serve as our introduction.

Most sincerely,

Elizabeth Ellen

For Elizabeth Ellen

Also, For Chloe

At last I understood that the way over, or through this dilemma, the unease at writing about 'petty personal problems' was to recognize that nothing is personal, in the sense that it is uniquely one's own. Writing about oneself, one is writing about others, since your problems, pains, pleasures, emotions—and your extraordinary and remarkable ideas—can't be yours alone.

—DORIS LESSING,

from her Introduction to *The Golden Notebook*, 1971

Bukowski was a fairly well known, underground figure in Los Angeles at the time because he wrote a column at the *LA Free Press* called "Notes of a Dirty Old Man." One week he wrote this article in there about going to San Francisco to read and having these punk asshole stupid filmmakers along and he was trying to kind of help them along and organizing this and that . . . it was quite an entertaining kind of funny piece. So I read it and I saw him later and I said, 'Hank, I read that article,' and he says, 'Yeah, baby, what'dya think?' I said, 'Well, I thought it was full of shit, man.' I said, 'You forget, I have the film. You're the guy who's drunk on the plane making a fool out of yourself and you made me . . . '

He says, 'Hey, baby, when I write, I'm the hero of my shit.'

—TAYLOR HACKFORD,

documentary filmmaker, on Charles Bukowski

VOLUME ONE.

Although I was with other men after him, some who mattered only a little to me and others who mattered more, my feelings for him did not change as quickly as I would have thought. Where did I keep them during those years? Did they sit intact in a group in my brain somewhere? Did I have only to open the door to that small area of my brain to experience them again?

—LYDIA DAVIS,

The End of the Story

He says he's lonely, horribly lonely because of this love he feels for her. She says she's lonely too. She doesn't say why.

—MARGUERITE DURAS,

The Lover

I would like for this to be a road novel. I often read novels that involve the road—navigation of unknown highways, in particular—and am envious of their narrators. It is decidedly harder to alleviate feelings of restlessness while confined to one's home. In the morning I often sit in the chair nearest the window and close my eyes and imagine what it would be like to be driving in my car in some far off state such as Iowa or Tennessee or Nebraska. Occasionally on such mornings, when the desire for movement is strongest and I am unable to set it aside in order to begin my day, I leave my chair and drive off in one direction or another away from my house. I find roads that pass cornfields and lead away from the town in which I live toward other towns, towns with which I am unfamiliar. The names of these towns are unimportant and I do not note them on signs or if I do note them, I do so only momentarily and forget them again as soon as I have passed into the next one. When I set out on these drives it is usually with the intent of being gone a matter of minutes, long enough only to momentarily quell my feelings of restlessness, though almost always I am gone much longer than I intended. I either become lost and have to keep driving until I find my way again or I become so intoxicated by the road and the navigation of it that I procrastinate turning onto the roads I know will lead me home and instead continue to turn onto the roads I know will lead me farther away. Always there is the desire to keep making the turns that lead away so that I will eventually end up in one of the far off states. Most of the time now I no longer think of driving to the state in which he resides. It is only the signs on the highway—denoting the number of miles between our cities—that reminds me how close to me he is physically, 229 miles, though it is something other than miles that separates us, and in that regard my restlessness cannot be alleviated with driving anymore than it can be alleviated by the writing of this novel during the day or the drinking of small or large amounts of alcohol in the evening. These feelings of restlessness preceded him and will very likely outlast him and I have become in some ways accustomed to them so that in their absence I would likely not know how to feel or would feel nothing at all, which would be, in many ways, unpreferable to the feelings of restlessness.

TWICE I drove to see him without telling him and twice he did not see me once I arrived. Two times before that I had driven to see him with his knowledge and each of those two times he had seen me. The two times he had seen me were a week apart and toward the beginning of our relationship, though in this case phrases such as "in the beginning" and "at the end" feel interchangeable and equally accurate, given that it seemed we were ending almost from the beginning. Even then he was somewhat reluctant to see me the second time. The night before I made the second drive I called him to let him know I was coming. It was a last minute decision on my part. I had made plans to fly to New York City for a friend's reading but had decided for reasons involving my general tiredness, and tiredness when it came to feelings of sociability in particular, not to go. It was merely coincidental that his twenty-sixth birthday fell on the same evening. We were talking on the phone about me coming for a second visit when he made the comment that I was trying to control him. The comment was disguised as a joke and we both laughed but I knew even then there was some truth to it, in his mind, at least, though I did not believe it myself. At the time I attributed a phrase like "trying to control me" as strictly a negative assessment of a situation and since I did not feel that what I was trying to do was negative in anyway, I could not accept that what I was doing was trying to control him. I have thought of this phrase many times since, however, and have come to the conclusion that if by "trying to control me" he meant I was trying to force him to see me again when he felt uncomfortable seeing me and was fearful that seeing me would result in increased feelings of anguish and heartache once we parted, then I admit he was correct in his usage of the word control and I was in fact guilty of trying to control him.

I have real feelings.

I HAVE tried to control him many times over the last seven months and not once has he tried to control me when what I want most is to feel his control thrust down on top of me like a weighted blanket on a child with Asperger's. If only! I think. Then I would finally be able to sleep!

Real feelings are staples inside my brain that itch and remind me of my ineffectualness.

IT OCCURRED TO ME TODAY that though nine months have passed since our initial meeting, I still do not know very basic information about him, such as his address, the names of his friends, the number of serious relationships he had prior to me and the duration of these relationships and reasons for their ending. I know he has two younger brothers, though I do not know their names. I know where he went to university though I do not know when. I know he was prom king at his high school but I do not know which high school or its location.

By contrast, he knows the names of all my close friends, the names of my daughter's close friends, and a general sense of the length of time I dated the man before him, as well as the length of my marriage. He knows my address, has been to my house, though he has not been inside my bedroom.

I remember once, early on, during a phone conversation, commenting on the lack of things I knew about him. I told him this made it awkward for me when friends of mine asked me basic questions with regard to him. I told him I had to keep answering, "I don't know," which seemed to invalidate our relationship in their eyes. In response to this he told me I could ask him anything and that he would answer. But put this way I was too embarrassed to ask him the questions I wanted to ask. Suddenly the questions seemed silly and clichéd, as though the answers were merely inconsequential facts and would not offer me a better understanding of him or who he was.

Now I question everything he told me, as though the things I do not know about him somehow cancel out those I do. I am skeptical, for instance, of something as basic as his name. The name I first knew him by was a pseudonym he used for his writing but the name he gave me as his "real" name does not feel any more real to me. When I asked once to see his driver's license he told me he did not have it with him. "I don't carry a wallet or a driver's license," he said. I once tried to find his "real" name on the Internet but was unsuccessful, which only justified my theory that it was yet another pseudonym and his actual name was still unknown to me, along with so much else.

And yet, I do not think anything would be different now if I knew these things about him. I do not think I would feel I know him any better than I do or that our relationship would be more or less validated by this missing information.

THE SECOND time I drove to see him without telling him I did not tell anyone I was going. I was bored of talking about him with my friends and was embarrassed that I had not managed to overcome my feelings for him. Several of my friends had mentioned the word "therapy" which I thought of in a similar vein and with similar seriousness as the words "murder" and "online dating service." I.e., I couldn't take any of them seriously, though of the three, "murder" felt the least offensive and also the most likely to succeed.

I am considering becoming better friends with the high school kid who lives three houses down in order to procure the drugs that will alleviate these real feelings.

IT BOTHERS me that I cannot remember if it was he or someone else who attempted to lie over those of us in the backseat of the taxicab that night. I have spent a considerable amount of time envisioning the group of us standing on the sidewalk outside the bar, the taxi pulling up to the curb, two or three people getting in front, four or five of us getting in back, the last person still on the curb . . . it would fit with his personality to be the last person on the curb. It would also fit with his personality to think he could lie across our laps in the backseat even though he was the tallest one in the group. Maybe if I had not become claustrophobic and asked to be let out of the cab I would be able to remember if he was the last person on the curb. I was against the door. Either his head or his feet would have been in my lap. Instead they were in someone else's and now someone else has the memory I want.

I spent the first year of my marriage convincing my husband that I loved him and this feels not dissimilar to that.

THAT HE WAS SO MUCH YOUNGER than I did not seem to affect the way I felt about him, though I wonder now how much of how he felt about me, specifically how resistant he was to progression with regard to our relationship, could be attributed to our age difference and his fears with regard to it. I was uncomfortable addressing it with him then, as I am uncomfortable addressing it now. For a while I believed I did not want to address it out of embarrassment or ashamedness at being so much older than he. But now I see that I did not want to address it because it was something over which I had no control and I wished to only address those things we could control and not give any thought to those things we could not.

Also there is the fact that I am commonly mistaken for someone his age and am drawn to people his age, both for friendships and romantic involvements. It is unclear to me if I am drawn to people his age precisely because I look more their age than my own or if I would be drawn to them even if I looked the age I am. When I am in the company of people younger than me I am seldom aware of the age difference. I am easily deluded into thinking I am of similar age unless something specific reminds me I am not, such as the purchasing of alcohol or questions regarding my daughter. More often, when in the company of people my age, I think to myself how much older than me they seem. I am more likely to feel out of place with these people than with those younger than me, though certainly this wasn't always the case and I am unsure when I began to feel differently and why.

I was never conscious of feeling older when I was with him. He was a great deal smarter and had read so much more that if anything I felt younger and intimidated by his knowledge and his intelligence in the way I might have if he had been much older than me instead of the other way around. The subject of my age came up only once, in the beginning, when he made a comment about believing me to be younger than him. It was in the same conversation that he asked the age of my child and something he said gave me the impression he believed her to be very young, a baby or a toddler, and I knew he thought this because he thought me so much younger than I was. He never asked directly my age and so I did not reveal it. I told him my daughter's age instead as I knew then he would have a general idea of my age and a general idea was all I was comfortable revealing.

I want to have meaningful moments with friends who are like brothers to me in order to exact revenge upon people I am incapable of exacting revenge upon.

THINGS I THINK about sometimes while listening to a single sad song on repeat and smoking cigarettes in my basement: what is the least amount of minutes two people have spent in each other's presence that have resulted in the most days spent writing that person's name on the wall in their mind? How am I more or less whacked?

THE LAST TIME WE SPOKE on a regular basis was toward the end of August, three months after I'd last seen him and four months prior to the time in which I am writing this section of the book. I had taken my daughter to New York City for a week to celebrate her thirteenth birthday and the first afternoon we were there we spent three hours walking through Central Park and during those three hours I took many photographs with the camera on my phone with the intent of sending him one. Each time we made a turn around a corner or another interesting landscape presented itself I stopped and took three or four pictures and then deleted all but one. After we had made our way through the majority of the park and I had a number of pictures on my phone I sat on a rock and looked through the pictures I had taken. I had taken pictures of the skyline and pictures of the various lakes and ponds and a few of a statue of Romeo and Juliet that sat outside a theater in the middle of the park, as he had referenced this play in the past and identified at times, I thought, with Romeo. But the photographs of the statue were unclear and I did not think you could tell from looking at them who the figures in the statue were so I did not send him one of those. Instead I chose one of the pictures of the pond with the tall buildings visible in the background because he seemed to hold a special affinity for water and had responded positively when I'd sent him photographs of my friend's lake or the river that ran through my town. I did not expect him to respond and if I did expect him to respond I did not expect him to respond for a while, a couple of hours at least. I put my phone back in my purse and tried not to think about whether or not he would respond or to listen for the sound my phone makes when someone texts me. It had been a cool summer overall, with temperatures rarely making it into the eighties, but the week we were in New York was an exception, and that afternoon it was in the mid-nineties and during our walk we had to keep stopping to rest or buy flavored ice or a cold drink or to sit in the shade. We were sitting on a bench resting and watching people skate or jog or push strollers by when I somewhat absently took my phone back out of my purse to check the time. Only five or ten minutes had passed since I had sent him the picture and put my phone away and already there was a response from him, a picture he had taken of his foot, and I laughed out loud and showed the picture to my daughter and the happiness I felt in that moment was similar to the happiness I had felt in the past when a lover had unexpectedly brought me flowers or written me a love letter or held me in their arms and told me how much they loved me. I sent him many more pictures that week we were in New York and each time I did so he responded with another text and in the evenings, as I sat on the concrete ground of the patio outside our hotel room to have a cigarette and listen to music before bed, I texted him about things we had done that day, museums and restaurants we had gone to and plays we had seen, and he responded as he had at the beginning of our relationship before we were in the prolonged state of ending. And each night we said goodnight to each other as we had every night before I'd gone to Jamaica and everything had changed and I became accustomed again while in New York to communicating with him as though we were in a real relationship with a real future so that it was twice as hard once I returned home and he suddenly stopped responding to my texts and emails again, or answered only intermittently and unreliably in the days and weeks following. I could not understand why he had responded the way he had in New York and then not responded once I was home. I could not pinpoint what the difference was in his mind, though he had acted similarly a few weeks earlier when I had gone to Atlantic City for a weekend to take part in a reading with other writers who were friends of ours. Then, too, there was a period before the weekend in which he rarely answered my texts and emails and I had begun to lose faith in us. And then again suddenly while I was in Atlantic City he began regularly texting me and sending me pictures on my phone and texting me for hours as I lay in my motel room at night. And in Atlantic City, as in New York, when I texted him that I was with a person he knew, he would tell me to tell that person something and I was surprised by this, by his seeming to want our mutual friends to know we were in contact with one another. And now I wonder if this was partly the reason he was so consistently communicating with me during each of those trips; that despite the general failings of our relationship, despite repeated attempts on each of our parts, but his part more often, to break things off, he remained invested in people knowing we were still a couple.

I cried for forty nights. It felt like a decent number; biblical and shit.

THE SECOND time I drove to see him without telling him I bought a new pair of shoes and painted my nails red, which does not coincide with my assertion that I was 99% sure he wouldn't see me. Either that or an amount of hope as insignificant as 1% can motivate me to prepare for something I know is very unlikely to happen.

ONCE, WHEN I WAS TALKING on the phone with him, I attempted to tell him about my phobia of using the bathroom in front of people but was too embarrassed to say it outright to him. Instead I made him hang up so I could text him and when he called me back afterward I was still embarrassed to the point that I almost didn't answer the phone. And when I finally picked up on the last ring before it went to voicemail, he said, "That's interesting. Because I have this fetish . . . " And then I laughed and forgot about my embarrassment and it was due to moments such as this that I was so fond of him and endeared to him despite the difficulties he presented at other times.

Sometimes I wonder if you find me interesting only because I find you interesting.

And no, it's not the same thing

I AM A SENTIMENTAL MOTHERFUKKER

The playing cards you shoved inside the empty pack of Camel Lights is still sitting on the counter where you left them. Sometimes when people come over now they ask when I started smoking Camel Lights and I laugh really hard. Then when they go to open the pack I take it from their hands and make a mean face because only I can touch it now.

Everyone I have ever wanted to love me now does and I no longer care.

SOMETIMES I attribute his unwillingness to see me to the breaking of the lucky horseshoe necklace I was wearing each of the times we were together. It is hard to think of a better reason. I have tried, but so far I have failed to come up with anything I consider more plausible. Currently the necklace is in a plastic baggie in a drawer in my kitchen. I keep meaning to take it out of the drawer. I have the address of a jeweler downtown written on a sticky note on the fridge. Some part of me must know it won't make a difference, however, which is why it is still in the drawer and not around my neck.

I go to my hometown and don't tell anyone I'm there. I drive by the houses of my relatives and look in their windows and keep driving.

THE FIRST time I drove to see him without telling him was two days after I got back from Jamaica. I think of our relationship now in terms of before Jamaica and after. I was gone six days. I often wonder if I hadn't gone to Jamaica if things would have turned out differently. I think it's a fair thing to wonder.

I would be embarrassed for you to see the stack of books in my bathroom. I am uncomfortable with you knowing the influence you have already had on me.

IN THE MOMENT, it felt insignificant. I was unaware of memorizing particular details, such as the amount of distance he was standing from me, or the manner in which his fingers found his mouth as I looked in his direction. Similarly, it is impossible to know what details about that moment I have forgotten. Later he told me he had repeatedly asked the person standing next to him what type of tequila was in the flask they were sharing. I had not remembered anyone standing next to him or the presence of a flask. In my memory he is standing alone. I am thinking now of all the movie moments in which one person sees another person from across a room and everyone else around them disappears. Previously I had thought this strictly an effect of cinema. I wonder now how his memory of this moment looks: if I am standing alone or with my friend who had approached the table with me. I will try to remember to ask him if he ever decides to speak to me again.

I have been trying to figure out how long I am obligated to remain on this planet now that I have procreated. (I don't want to be an asshole, but come on!)

I AM BOTHERED BY the longevity of top forty songs. Lately I have been unable to turn on the radio without a certain song coming on. This song was just beginning to be played on the radio the second time I drove back from seeing him. I remember turning the volume on the radio very high and singing along whenever the song came on that day. I was conscious of the fact that he would not like the song. It amused me to think of him feigning annoyance with the song and with me for singing it. I thought of feigned annoyance as something akin to endearment. This song should not still be on the radio. I would like to believe a great deal of time has passed since the second time I drove back from seeing him. I do not like being reminded that not that much time has passed at all. The lack of time passing reminds me that he never really gave us a chance. Now when this song comes on I quickly turn the station. There is nothing endearing about a brokenhearted women singing loudly to herself.

I want to drive my car at 100 mph past cornfields at sunset and wield my computer and phone into them.

I DO not consider myself the jealous type, just as I do not consider myself the murderous type or the suicidal type or the adulterous type. I do not think most people would think of themselves in these terms, and yet every day people commit murder and suicide and adultery and behave in a manner that could be construed by others and themselves as jealous. The first time I drove to see him without telling him he told me he could not see me due to an ankle injury he had sustained the previous night. He did not tell me then but revealed to me a few days later that he had been with a certain woman the night he sustained the ankle injury. I have never met this woman though I have known of her for some time. One of the things I know about this woman is that she has very large breasts. I am aware that there exist people who would like to sleep with this woman due in part to her very large breasts. My breasts are large but not very large. It is not, however, the size of her breasts that made me jealous. I do not think a thing like breast size matters all that much to him. What made me jealous of this woman was the fact that he spent the night drinking in the park with her. I would very much like to spend an evening drinking in the park with him. I am painfully aware that I am now the only person he would refuse to drink in a park with and I am jealous of every person with whom he would or will, regardless of breast size.

I am running out of ways to make you love me.

IT OCCURRED to me today how much my current life resembles the life I led as a sixteen-year-old. Then I lived with my mother and her boyfriend in a small two-bedroom apartment in Arizona. We lived there only one year and I did not make friends easily and spent the majority of time alone in my bedroom reading and listening to music and wondering why my mother did not love me in the manner in which I wanted to be loved (i.e. with the same volatile, intensity with which she loved the boyfriend who dented our walls with her awkwardly splayed body parts and tolerated me in varying degrees based on the amount of alcohol/cocaine/crank he had consumed on any given day). I slept on a mattress on the floor and decorated my walls with photographs torn from fashion magazines. I did not know the names of the people in the photographs but their beauty served to remind me to keep quiet and remain indoors. Currently I live in a large house with my daughter. The large house was purchased at a time when I lived with a man and knew a number of people in town and believed a house of this size was warranted for the entertaining of the man and the number of people we knew. Since then the man and I have broken up and other people have moved away and I no longer need a house of this size. I spend the majority of my time in this house alone in my bedroom reading and writing and staring at the walls onto which I have hung various photographs. On the wall over my computer I have hung, side by side, photographs of him and me because I do not have a photograph of the two of us together. I suppose in hanging these photographs side by side I hoped that my mind might weld them together into one photograph and produce some sort of happiness on the subconscious level that might trickle into my conscious. Though if I have been successful in this regard, I am unaware, and if I am unaware, have I really been successful? Most of the time I find myself focusing on the picture of him that I found by searching his name on the Internet. The photograph was taken at a reading he did two months ago. The night before the reading he and I were talking and I made a joke about coming to the reading. He must have been unable to tell I was joking because he replied that he would be angry with me if I came. Now whenever I look at this picture I am reminded of this and wonder how he would have reacted had I actually gone, if he would have been angry or if seeing me would have produced within him another emotion altogether. It is impossible to know and I would have been too frightened to test his warning. In the photograph he is wearing the same chain I wrapped around my fingers each time we were together. The chain holds what I believe are dog tags. I was never comfortable enough to ask him if they were his or someone else's and if they were someone else's, who that someone else was to him. Every time I look at this photograph I am reminded there is something very significant about him that I do not know.

I am never drinking Red Stag whiskey again.

AT SOME point during the day or night we met I turned to a mutual friend and said, "The last time I felt like this I ended up married a month later." I cannot recall if I said this five minutes after being introduced to him, while still in the conference center, or later that evening in the taxi-cab on the way to see him a second time. It is possible I said it both times, to two different acquaintances. I remember being unable to stop talking about him, which did not go unnoticed by the man I was seeing at the time. My thinking was that if I was honest about my feelings from the get go I would hurt people less. I no longer believe this to be true. I have hurt many people with my honesty and been hurt equally by others who have been honest with me. Perhaps this is why he refuses to tell me this is over.

Don't ever tell me goodbye again ever.

I HAVE become a logger of numbers. I have committed to memory the dates of significant moments and am constantly calculating how much time has passed since they occurred. I can tell you how long it's been since he told me he loved me ( ), how long it's been since he texted me without me first texting him ( ), the number of days that have passed since I last saw him ( ), the number of days since I last emailed him ( ), how long it's been since he admitted to still being in love with me ( ), the last time we talked on the phone ( ). Every day that I do not talk to him these numbers increase and I feel farther from him. I wonder how much time will pass before I no longer remember to make these calculations and how I will feel when I do. I think perhaps I will feel better, though it is hard to know for sure.

Every hotel room is the same without you in it.

I AM constantly reminded of him, though he was here only three days and the man I lived with before I met him was here three years. There are remnants of the man I lived with littered throughout the house. I see these remnants but do not make an emotional connection to them. Instead I walk through the house and visualize the places he stood and the things he said. I walk from my car to the house and he is standing there, holding the birdseed I keep on the shelf in his hand. He took inventory of everything that weekend. He asked why I had tropical birdseed on a shelf in my garage and I said to feed the birds at the park. My answer made him laugh. I do not live in a region of the country considered tropical. It amused him that I would feed the local birds tropical food. When I see the birdseed there now I am unsure whether to laugh or cry. I have not fed the birds since he was here. I have not done much of anything, really. I am considering moving to a region of the country where tropical food would be appropriate for the feeding of local birds. Such a region would be more than a day's drive from him. I would like to think I would use the bag of tropical birdseed he pointed to that day in my garage but probably I wouldn't. Probably I would buy a new bag and leave that one on the shelf as a reminder.

I think I have to go away for a while.

ALWAYS NOW there is the feeling that I've irrevocably screwed this up. I email him and he doesn't respond and I read my email over to myself and think how I've emailed the wrong thing. I think that if I'd said something else or not said anything at all he'd still be talking to me. I am always unsure whether I should say more or less, if I should be withholding of my feelings or express myself more. I spend too much time attempting to analyze his personality and react in the way I think will cause him to react in the way I'd like for him to react. I am aware that thinking in this manner indicates it is likely irrelevant how I react or what I say. In the beginning everything was easy. I did not need to censor what I said or when I said it. In the beginning everything I said was met with enthusiasm and answered in a timely fashion. In the beginning it was he who censored himself. In the beginning he said that if he wrote me without self-censoring I would be frightened by the magnitude of his feelings and turn away from him. I cannot imagine that he could have said anything to make me turn away, though I do remember once or twice feeling surprised by the intensity with which he seemed to love me then. The last time I felt I had irrevocably screwed this up was a week ago. It had been a month since he had texted me without me first texting him. I had begun to feel hopeless with regard to him and with regard to "us." I emailed him that I thought I needed to go away for a while. I turned my phone off before going to bed to prevent myself from texting him. It had been a while since he had texted me back and I didn't think I could bear the sadness that would follow another unanswered text. I had been sleeping with my phone for weeks. The next morning when I turned my phone on there was a text from him. "How are you" was all it said but reading it and seeing his name on my phone I felt first elated and then after the elation wore off, a tremendous sense of regret and sadness at the lost opportunity to speak with him. I tried to imagine what we might have talked about and how things might now be different between us. It's been a week and though I have texted him three of the last seven nights, he has yet to respond. I now feel more hopeless with regard to him and "us" than I felt the night I turned my phone off. I would like to believe things would be different had I left my phone on, but that is a hard thing to believe.

I wonder about the things he would have written me in the beginning had he not censored himself. I would like to have been offered the opportunity to turn away.

THOUGH HE HAS COME to know me quite intimately over the last nine months due to my writing him as though he were a diary or a long lost friend, I know very little about him. When I have pointed this out in a text or email he has responded that this is because there is little interesting about his life and what there is is depressing. Most of what I know about him I have read on his blog or in his published pieces and books. I have had to try to discern what is fiction and what is fact, though I suppose he could say the same of what I have told him in my letters and emails and texts.

I am never really embarrassed by anything I tell you because I know deep down you're as retarded as I am.

OTHER WAYS IN WHICH I HAVE COME TO PHYSICALLY
UNDERSTAND THE DEFINITION OF THE WORD "REGRET"

The second night he was here we went for a walk and then stood in the driveway until all the cars that did not belong had returned to a place in which they did. I was hosting a party inside the house I no longer wished to attend. We had spent an hour in various configurations around the living room not talking to each other or anyone else. Sometimes to amuse myself I watch this hour in my mind as though it is part of a movie played on fast forward. In the movie our bodies move from bar stools to floor to kitchen counter, always within reach of one another but never touching. In the background people talk and drink alcoholic beverages. Ours are the only two bodies in motion. In the driveway time sped up similarly. I asked the last person to leave the party what time it was and was surprised by his answer. I had been expecting it to be considerably earlier than it was. It was very late. All the lights inside the house had been turned off. I cannot remember now what we talked about though we talked for several hours. I remember dropping my chin to my chest in avoidance of his eyes at several points during the conversation. Whatever we were discussing must have caused me a considerable amount of embarrassment. Either that or I still felt generally bashful in his presence. I remember he told me I had a good personality and I must have made a face when he said this because he followed it by saying that this was the highest compliment he could give me. At the time I had thought of the cliché manner in which men typically say this to women or about women to whom they are not attracted. Now that I know him better I think he was sincere when he complimented my personality and wonder if he still feels the same about it or if his opinion of my personality has changed significantly. I worry that it has. I am aware that I have changed as a person in the months since that night we spent in my drive, though I am unclear to what extent. I feel equally the same person as then and a different person entirely. Too, I feel that the forms in which he has chosen to continue communicating with me (email and texts) must skew my personality to a degree and severely limit the manner in which he views me so that I appear at times two dimensional. Perhaps this has been his intent. I would imagine it would be easier to let go of a two dimensional person than a whole one. Perhaps this is at the heart of his refusal to see me or even to talk to me on the phone, either of which would humanize me in a way that would make him uncomfortable or from which he would be less able to disassociate.

After we had been made aware of the time by the last person to leave the party we could no longer stand in the drive as though not much time had passed. Suddenly I was aware of the cold and the numbness of my toes. Inside the house I was oddly surprised by the darkness and quiet. Though I had been able to see the darkness from the outside it still surprised me once we were surrounded by it, as the last time we had been inside the house it had still been lit up and noisy and full of people. It did not seem we had been outside long enough for all of them to have gone home or to bed and I half expected one or two to reappear at any moment, as though they had merely gone to the bathroom or outside to smoke.

The previous night we had also been the last two awake. We had sat outside on the porch talking and smoking at several different points in the evening and at one point we had gone back inside to find everyone else had gone to bed. It was three thirty or four or four thirty and it could have been any hour and we would not have been tired. In the kitchen I stood still in front of the counter as he reached around me to grab bottles and empty them into the sink. My in-the-wayness was a conscious move on my part and we were both aware that it was. The raised fibers of his flannel shirt-sleeve brushed my bare arm and I felt a lightheadedness that I attributed to a combination of his touch and the alcohol I had consumed earlier in the evening when consuming alcohol felt the only way I would be able to talk to him. After he had emptied all the bottles and wiped the counter he left me and went and sat in a nearby chair. I followed and stood a while by the chair and then suddenly, with the suddenness of one who has no explanation for her subsequent actions, I was in his lap with my cheek pressed to his and the warmness of his body all around me. If I were asked currently to pick the single most contented moment of my life I would probably point to this one, though it is hard to tell if that would be because of how things have unfolded since then. If, say, the subsequent months had not been filled with anguish and heartache and diminishing hope, would I still feel as strongly about this moment? It is impossible to know. We remained still like this for an unknowable amount of time, though time at that point felt infinite and I desperately wanted it to be so. I would have been content to have made a home in that moment and were I to define love I would point to the warmth I felt there in that chair with my mouth so close to his, knowing it would soon be warm with mine, but in no hurry for it to be. And then there was the slightest movement from each of us, my chin upturning toward his, and our lips not yet parted but resting gently against one another for another length of time that could be described as infinite in feel, infinite in our desire for it to remain exactly so. It occurred to me the next day that at any moment someone — e.g., the man I was still, for the next two days at least, living with — could have walked into the kitchen and found us, though I did not once think of this then, nor would it have deterred me if I had. I became very selfish in his presence in a way I did not realize until much later. At some point, however, he must have been aware of this, or aware of the lateness of the hour or aware in a way I wasn't that this could not continue on indefinitely (how close this word is to infidelity) and he broke his mouth from mine and pressed it instead to my ear and whispered warmly into it. He called me by my name and then he called me a number of words I had been called before by other men in similar situations but which had meant less coming from their mouths. The words felt new and deeply meaningful coming from him and each one felt like the softest blanket against my skin. He asked if he could carry me to my bed but the man I was living with was already there and so I told him he could not. I instead pushed my face under his chin and shook my head against his collarbone, resisting his desire to tell me goodnight. "Come on, sweetie-baby," he said. He said there would be plenty of time for us in the future. I see now that this was likely the first time he lied to me. Our time, as it would appear now, was very limited. But I allowed him first to pull me to a righted position in his lap and then, after his hand had very quickly, almost imperceptibly, traveled up under the shorts I was wearing to my inner thigh, to pull me to my feet. We walked hand in hand to the hall outside my room and mouthed a goodnight before he went down the stairs into the basement and I went into my bed beside the man with whom I was living.

That second night, however, we entered the house and did not go into the kitchen but walked swiftly to the hall. Or perhaps it was I who walked swiftly to the hall and he merely followed. I was unaware until after we parted that my bed was empty. The man I lived with had taken a pillow and a blanket to the garage and was already asleep in the back of his car. It would not have altered the outcome of our evening had I known this earlier, however. Though I was behaving selfishly, I was not selfish enough to sleep with him while the man I lived with slept in the garage. More than that, I had an uncharacteristic desire to prolong having sex with him. There was something otherworldly and somnambulistic about our interactions thus far and having sex would have grounded us in a way I did not wish yet to be grounded. Instead we stood awkwardly in the hall. His eyes, as I see them now, were pleading. Later he told me he had hoped I'd follow him downstairs into the basement, slept on the floor beside him. Instead I mouthed another silent goodnight and walked without him into my room. Here now is another moment I feel I would go back and undo; act out differently. I would have liked to take his hand, allowed him to lead me down the stairs to the floor beside him. He would have removed his shirt and placed it under my head in lieu of a pillow. He would have draped his body over mine in place of a blanket. He would have whispered more familiar words into my ear, which would have sounded unfamiliar coming from his mouth. And I now would have eight more hours in which to seek comfort, in which to return to him, when alone in my bed at night.

Maybe if you hadn't choked on a carrot that time we were talking on the phone this would all be okay.

WEEKS LATER I said something to him like, "What are the odds?", meaning, what were the odds we'd be the last two people still awake in the house, to which he replied the odds were very high, given that we'd intentionally stayed awake until we were the last two in the house who weren't asleep. I had not looked at it that way, though it seemed obvious to me once he pointed it out. I had been looking at it from the standpoint of someone who prior to that night had hoped to be left alone with him but had not felt it very likely that I would be, in part, I suppose, because until that night I was still unsure of his feelings for me or what exactly his intentions were. And now, months later, I am again equally unsure of both.

Who told you to try and eat a carrot while we were talking on the phone anyway?

I HAVE begun to wonder if I should be writing this now, while I am still so deeply in love with him, though I am not at all sure anymore that what I am feeling is in fact love or that it ever was. I am beginning to wonder if what I have felt these last few months would be more accurately defined as obsession. But whether it is love or obsession, the question is equally valid: should I be documenting this now or should I have waited until I had more distance from these events and from him and my feelings for him? I think most people would advise me to wait, to garner objectivity, before attempting such an undertaking. I am aware I am likely unable at present to write with any real semblance of objectivity but I am equally interested, if not slightly more interested, in writing about this unobjectively. I am interested in comparing how I felt when I first began this document with how I will feel when I finish it, assuming this will take several months and assuming I will feel differently after those several months have passed. I would hope, for instance, that several months from now I will be able to keep the computer downstairs at night instead of making sure it is safely hidden away in my daughter's bedroom. I would like to think I would be able one day to turn on the computer and not first go to his blog and then to my email account, hoping to find his name in my inbox and feeling deflated and sad when I do not. I would like to think I would be able to move on sooner rather than later. I welcome a time in which I will be able to look at these events unemotionally, as though they happened to someone else, a friend of mine, or a character in a novel. Partly that is a lie. Partly I feel preemptively sad for a time in which his name evokes no emotion within me, though when that times comes I will likely not feel sad at all, which is precisely what makes me sad now thinking of it. It has happened before. A man I thought myself greatly in love with three years ago, no longer invokes within me feelings other than friendship, though the man now regularly confesses to feelings of love for me. I do not feel sad that I no longer love this man as I once did. I feel relieved and in control of my emotions. I am also slightly amused by the jealousy the man I loved three years ago has expressed toward the man I love currently. I once wrote many poems and short stories about the man I loved three years ago. I think he took for granted that I would go on writing about him indefinitely and now that I am writing about someone else he feels slighted, though at the time I was writing about him, he did not mention the things that I wrote, if he liked them or didn't like them. At the time I wrote them I was not even sure he was aware of them or that they were about him. This man is still a very good friend of mine and I wonder what he will think when he reads this. Probably he will wish it were about him. If I were to write about him now I could write very objectively but in many ways this objectivity would not interest me, which is why I don't.

The part of me that keeps asking for this to end is the part that knows it never will. Not without a massive lie on both our parts.

A FRIEND of mine accused me yesterday of being self-centered and I could not argue her accusation. I was already aware of my self-centered-ness before she accused me of it. I have developed an addict's one-track mind. I don't know if this is actual self-centeredness or an inability to talk/think/care about anything other than the source of one's addiction, in my case: him. I wanted to tell her I was less self-centered than him-centered but I did not think she would recognize the distinction. Also, I worried that discussing it further would only serve to strengthen her accusation regarding my self-centeredness. Instead I ended the conversation saying I was busy and then turned on my computer and searched his name for a half an hour on the Internet.

This will end us both.

THE FIRST time I drove to see him with his knowledge was two days after he left my house. I had planned weeks before to make this trip for a reason other than seeing him, though now the other thing I had to do was done quickly and without excitement and seeing him felt like my real reason for being there. I was nervous as I prepared for the evening, as it would be the first time we would be alone in a room without the threat of other people walking in and without my feeling as though I belonged to someone else and I was unsure what might happen or what I wanted to happen or what he did. I had been with the same man for six years and there were things about myself, which made me insecure, physical attributes of course, but also the way in which I acted in certain situations. I did not think I wanted to sleep with him that night, for one, though I wasn't sure why I thought this. In the past I had slept with men the first or second night I was with them and had gone on to see them for a period of months or years. I was not fearful that my sleeping with him would result in an abbreviation of our potential relationship. There had been an unsureness to our interactions up until then that I found disconcerting in an intoxicating way and I did not want to disrupt this unsureness just yet. I wanted to prolong the feelings of unfamiliarity and unknowingness. Also I did not want to disenchant him of whatever romantic ideals he held of me. I worried that undressed and in the act of lovemaking he would recognize my common-ness. I did not want to disappoint him.

I was sharing a hotel room with another woman. I had reserved a small room when I booked it weeks in advance but when I checked into the hotel that afternoon I had asked how much more it would be to upgrade to a suite, and when the woman told me the amount and it wasn't consider-ably more, I had asked her to make the change. When I thought of a suite, I thought of a bedroom with a door and a small living room with a couch. I was only interested in the door. I wanted to make sure I would have time alone with him. Also, the other woman was a friend of the man I had lived with and I did not want to be aware of her judging me for beginning something new with someone else so soon. When the woman and I got to the room we were surprised by its largeness. There was a bedroom with two beds, a bathroom, and a TV, and a living room with another bathroom, two couches, a TV, a full sized dining room table and a small kitchen with a wet bar. The room was much larger than I had pictured and I worried that he would think I was accustomed to staying in rooms of this size and that this would give him the idea that I was spoiled and indiscriminate when it came to money and the spending of it. He did not have much money and I didn't want money to be an issue between us. I made such a big deal about warning him of the size of the room that when he finally came up he was not surprised by its size at all and said he had actually thought it would be much bigger, given that I had gone on about it so.

The woman was already in the bedroom watching TV when he arrived. He had walked an hour in the rain to get to the hotel and said he did not feel well. I pressed the palm of my hand to his forehead as I do with my daughter and it felt fevered. He complained of a headache and I offered him an aspirin, which at first he was reluctant to take, saying he avoided all medicines, but eventually swallowed at my urging. He lay down on the couch and I lay down beside him. His clothing was damp from the rain and beneath his clothing his body was sweaty with fever. I wanted to take off his clothes and then take off mine and spread out atop him for as long as I could stand it in the same manner in which a person holds their hand over an open flame. He was quiet for a while and I attributed his quietness to his not feeling well. I rested my head on his chest and looked up at him and he was looking up at the ceiling. "Do you ever get the feeling you're disappointing people?" he said. I didn't and I said so. "I do," he said. "I have that feeling a lot." I was quiet, waiting for him to elaborate but he didn't say anything else for a while after this and the silence did not bother me. I was content to lie beside him and be quiet and contemplate the meaning of what he had said. There were many things I wanted to talk about with him but I felt no rush to do so. I wanted to learn things about him slowly, just as I wanted the stages of our physical interactions to occur in a deliberate, unhurried manner so that I would be mindful of every undoing.

After a while his skin cooled slightly and he began to talk more. It is hard for me to remember specific details of what we talked about that night on the couch, just as it is hard for me to recall what we talked about two nights before in the driveway of my house for three or four hours. I remember the conversation being interspersed with long moments of silence and my undressing, though he remained fully clothed throughout the eve-ning and on into the next morning. I remember at some point during the night telling him I had not planned on having sex with him, though by the time I said it I had changed my mind and wanted to have sex with him very badly. I had thought he would find my admission amusing, that we would share a laugh at my expense, after which we would proceed to sleep together. Instead he said he had thought the same thing and now that he knew I had thought it too, he was sure we were making the right deci-sion to not have sex. I then spent the rest of the night trying to get him to change his mind and have sex with me but his resolve was unwavering and finally I gave up and turned my back to him and fell asleep with his arms wrapped around me, and was as content as though we had.

We were only asleep a couple of hours before the woman in the bed-room appeared with her suitcase in hand on her way to the airport. There was a hurried goodbye from the couch. I was in my bra and underwear and did not want to get up. As soon as she closed the door we rose and walked to the bedroom and lay down atop the made bed and I resumed my efforts to seduce him. I had never been unclothed with a man and not slept with him. I cannot remember now if I removed my bra and underwear or if he did. I would say that I did except that I was still shy about him seeing me completely undressed. I was insecure about the parts of me contained by the bra and underwear. Some parts of me seemed to me too large and other parts too small and it had been so long since anyone but the man I'd lived with for six years had seen them and when I had voiced my insecu-rities to him he had made jokes meant to deflect my concerns but had not relieved them.

I lay reclined on the bed and he sat near my left hip, bent over at the waist. My face was turned away from him toward the wall. I did not want to be aware of the exact location of his gaze. I had never been inspected so thoroughly and I found his closeness disconcerting. He looked silently for a moment and then began to offer me an animated oration of his findings. This is the body that contained your child, he said, and there was a mixture of awe and respect in his voice when he said it so that I felt pride rather than shame with regard to the physical attributes that attested to this fact. I kept my eyes safely on the wall, though my mouth opened into a grin it could not contain. I began to feel a comfortableness with my body as he saw it and slowly turned my head from the wall. I wanted to study his face as he studied me. I had forgotten my embarrassment. I was believing of what he told me.

When he had satisfied himself with his visual inspection of me he began to inspect me in other ways. He was still clothed but this did not bother me. I liked the idiosyncratic nature of his handling of me. I was no longer concerned with rushing toward a predictable outcome.

He asked if he could bathe me and I laughed but I could see by his face he was serious. I have to stop momentarily as I'm writing this, as the regret of this moment is so great within me that it demands my full attention. He wanted to wash my hair. That sentence and the image it produces wounds me in a way no other sentence I will ever write will. **He wanted to wash my hair** and I laughed and did not let him. I was uncomfortable with the intimacy the act implied. I thought there would be time for such acts of intimacy in the future. I find myself envious now of the women before and after me who were not uncomfortable and did not laugh. I stand in the shower and pour shampoo in my palm and think about the lack of emotion I feel doing so.

We were aware of the time in a way that made us detest the telling of it but appreciative of every minute. We lay on the bed and he wrapped his clothed body around my nakedness and I thought of the famous photograph of John and Yoko and wished someone were around to take our picture and at the same time was happy that no one was. He was teasing me about something. He was trying to coax words out of me. This teasing and coaxing had begun in the middle of the night, after my failed seduction, before we fell asleep. I had interviewed him for a website in the weeks between our initial meeting and the weekend he came to my house and in the last email exchange for that interview he had thanked me and then made an additional comment regarding the way he felt about me and I was unsure if this additional comment were part of the interview, and thus insincere, or a personal note to me and thus genuine. When I had inquired about this prior to submitting the interview he had told me those words were for me only and so I had deleted them from the interview but still did not believe they were meant sincerely. Now he was trying to get me to say to him the words he had said to me, either sincerely or insincerely, two months earlier under the guise of an interview and I knew that I would say them and that they would be sincere. I knew also he would say them back to me and that I would believe in his sincerity this time when he said them.

I hate you most for the stupid moments we're not having on the couch in front of the TV.

LATELY I HAVE been wondering how many accidental car crashes are misdiagnosed suicides. It seems that if your intent is to kill yourself without afterward being thought an asshole by your friends and family, running your car into a tree or telephone pole would be the way to do it. Nobody gets hurt and everyone chalks it up as a "freak occurrence." Of course now that I've posed the question in this form, I have eliminated it as a possibility for myself. I mean, I could still do it, but everyone would know for sure I am an asshole.

Cavemen don't have real feelings.

AT THE TIME, I refuted his claim that it would be harder to part if we made love and I stick with my refutation. There are no parts of me left unfilled by anguish. I cannot speak for him. Perhaps the anguish that resides within him is less compact and more malleable, capable of condensation. It is possible there are hidden cavities within him of which I am unaware. But I would be highly suspect of such a claim. I would need to see them for myself. I do not believe this could be harder.

TWO MONTHS AFTER my trip to New York City, I drove to Buffalo for a writers' conference. I was not participating on any panels or doing any readings and I decided at the last minute to go mainly to see other writers I knew who were friends of mine and to get out of the house, and consequently, away from myself. He and I had not spoken or had any communication with one another in almost a month and I was feeling overwhelmingly lonely and isolated because of this. Before I left I had asked another writer to go with me. Most of the writers I knew who were going were male and this writer was female and I thought it would be nice to have another female writer there and offered her my room to share. I had never met this female writer in person and had not even so much as exchanged an email with her until a couple of weeks before the Buffalo trip when she emailed me to say she liked a particular story of mine. Prior to her emailing me I knew very little about her except that she was a good friend of his and that she had been the person he had spent the day with the night he hurt his ankle and did not see me the day following. At the time I had blamed her for his not seeing me and believed there to be some sort of romantic interest on her part or both of their parts, though he had sworn she was like a sister to him and that nothing had happened between them. In the months between the day they spent together and the trip to Buffalo she had published a story I read about a day she had spent with a male friend of hers and I had wrongly attributed the male character to him and had torn up the story upon reading it as it had inferred a romantic interest in the male character. Later she told me it was not about him but about another male writer I knew and I laughed and felt silly for my instinct to think everything was about him and my assumption that because I felt so strongly about him, every other female must as well.

I do not like to admit so, but a large part of the reason I invited this woman to Buffalo was because of my knowledge that she was a close friend of his, though I felt conflicted about inviting her for the same reason. I was worried I would drink and become loose lipped and divulge information I did not want to divulge or ask questions I did not want to ask and that the particular questions I chose to ask would divulge as much about me and him and about my feelings for him as any answers I could give. Also, I still felt deeply loyal to him and did not want him to think I was betraying him by telling her things we had talked about and done or not talked about and not done.

At the time I invited this woman it was very late at night and I had been drinking, and she had been drinking as well. I asked her to come to Buffalo with me on a whim and on a whim she said yes and before either of us could change our minds I had bought her a plane ticket and reserved us a room. Even though he and I were not speaking, I emailed him to tell him she was going to be joining me in Buffalo and he did not respond and I had not expected him to but I seemed to want him to know all the same.

On the drive to Buffalo a few days later I began to have reservations about having asked her but also I was excited to meet her and hopeful we would get along and become friends. I knew that she drank and smoked and I figured we had that much in common and that that much would be enough to bond us in a way that would see us through the weekend. When I had told my daughter about my reservations with regard to meeting this woman, my daughter had said, "If she's a friend of his, she must be okay," and I had laughed when she said this but at the same time felt somewhat melancholy in the face of my daughter's continued admiration for him, knowing she might never see him again, and that I might never see him again either.

Once in Buffalo my nervousness with regard to meeting this woman became amplified to the point that I changed our reservation from one room to two adjoining rooms. I was aware of the fact that the woman would likely view the adjoining rooms as an unnecessary expense and I did not want her to think me spoiled or careless with money, but at the same time I did not want to put myself in a situation in which I might feel claustrophobic and uncomfortable for an entire weekend. I wanted my own bed and my own bathroom and I did not want to be aware of when she used the bathroom or for how long, just as I did not want her to be aware of the same things with regard to me.I only had an hour between the time I checked into the hotel room and the time in which I had to pick up the woman from the airport and I wanted to have a drink, to calm my nerves, but I did not want to drive after having even one drink because I was unfamiliar with the area and unaccustomed to driving after drinking.

The woman had texted me from the airport before she got on the plane to say she had already had two Bloody Mary's and would probably have two more in the air and therefore would likely be drunk already when I picked her up. I did not mind her being drunk. Generally, when meeting someone for the first time or meeting someone alone for the first time, I am grateful to them for drinking or being drunk because I rarely drink more than one drink when out and only truly feel comfortable drinking in my own house, most often, when alone. I prefer other people, however, when they are drinking or drunk, as it makes me feel they are paying slightly less attention to me and therefore I feel more comfortable being myself and do not feel as much of a need to censor what I say.

When I picked her up she did not, however, appear to be inebriated. She was smoking a cigarette and threw it on the sidewalk and got in the car and immediately she began to talk, and I was comforted by her chatter, as I would have been by her inebriation, and I knew that everything would be all right and that I had not needed to book two rooms, but the rooms were booked, and this is how we would live for two nights.

There are people you meet in life whom you know for years but never really feel you know and people you feel you know right away, the first night you speak with them, and she belonged wholly to the latter category and I was mesmerized by her and quite taken with her because of this. Weeks later, after the conference had ended and people were talking about it and the people they had met while there, I realized I had met no one new, despite there having been people present I wanted to meet and I attributed this to my inability to focus on anyone but her while in her presence. Partially this was due to the person she is and partially this was due to my strong need to feel belonged to by someone after so long feeling not belonged to by him. For the majority of both nights we sat close together so that the sides of our bodies met and often she had her arm draped over the back of my chair or my shoulder and I liked the way it felt to be so close to someone and was reluctant to move away from her toward someone else, and consequently I remained still beside her, listening to her talk, to me or another person, it didn't matter which. And halfway through the first night, after I'd had two drinks, which was more than I was used to having when out, she began questioning me about the man I had alluded to being in love with. Part of me wanted to tell her everything, because I

had told only one or two people anything and because the one or two people I had told did not know him and therefore had an impression of him
that was based only on my side of the story, which was admittedly unfavor-
able, and I wanted someone who knew him and had a good impression of
him to listen to my account and offer me a less biased opinion of what had
happened and of him. At the time I did not think she knew who it was and
I was torn between giving her the information she needed to figure it out
and not giving her this information and leaving it a mystery. But she was
persistent and I found her persistence and interest in what I was saying
and, consequently, her interest in me, flattering and I found myself telling
her more and more until finally she guessed his name and I let out a long
sigh and looked at her with guilty eyes and she knew that she had guessed
correctly. Later, after I had returned home and had a chance to replay our
conversation over in my head many times, I was more confident that she
had known all along, or at the very least had guessed, based on things he
had told her. She told me he had confessed the day he hurt his ankle to
being torn up about a particular woman, and though he did not tell her my
name, he described the woman as tall and thin and blonde, and said she
was a woman she knew of but did not know personally, and of the female
writers in our circle, I was the only one I knew of who fit this description.

Before she guessed his name I had felt myself almost bursting with
wanting her to know and immediately after I was overcome with regret
and felt I had told her too much and been disloyal to him. It was at this
time that the party moved from the bar where we had been sitting for
many hours back to the hotel where we were staying. Most of the people in
our group were going to a hotel room on a different floor from ours and I
said I was going up to the room for a minute and then would be back down
but once I was in the room, I no longer felt like being around people and
changed out of my clothes and into my pajamas and got in bed. A half an
hour or so later she returned to the room also and came and sat on the bed
next to me. I had been crying but I wasn't sure she was able to tell because
she was so intoxicated and I was appreciative of the fact that she was too
intoxicated to tell or that she would not remember in the morning even
if she were aware of it then. She sat only for a few minutes and then she
said she was tired and was going to bed and we did not speak of him in
the morning or again that weekend and I was relieved not to be speaking

of him. I did not like feeling that the only reason I had asked her to come was to garner information about him and did not want her to think this either. I had come to like her independent of her friendship with him and found over the course of the next day and a half that we had much more in common than him and that I was desirous of continuing this friendship after we had each returned home. Most of my friends had moved out of the town in which I lived in the past year or two and I missed the easy conversations I had had with my female friends over coffee or drinks and was thus hungry for and all the more appreciative of any time I spent in the company of women.

The morning of our departure we sat in the hotel restaurant and had brunch and she ordered two Bloody Mary's and afterward, as we stood close together on the sidewalk in front of the hotel and had a final ciga-rette, I was conscious of the tomato juice on her breath and emanating from her skin, and already I was sad for a time in which that smell would not be available to me and she would be gone.

I can't tell if all the things that make me insecure would make you love me more or less, but mostly I just think it doesn't matter.

I WAS READING a book about the poet John Keats today after seeing a movie about his life two nights ago. The movie concerned the love affair he had with a woman he was unable, due to his poor financial circumstances and ill health, to marry, and naturally I paralleled their love story with my own, which made watching the movie more interesting for me. I was reading the book primarily to read the letters he wrote this woman but also to feel a sense of comradeship with a person equally anguished and undone by love. An academic in the book is quoted as saying that the mistake John Keats made was pouring his heart out to this woman in his letters, the insinuation being that if he had been more reserved, he might have married her despite all the other obstacles seeming to prevent their marriage. Reading this I again thought of my own story, of the many letters I have written him over the last two months. I cannot help but wonder now if I too did not make a misstep in writing so candidly about my love for him. I did not stop to think while writing them how they would be received or what effect they would have. At the time I wrote them I was incapable of thinking in such a manner. I felt compelled to write the letters as though out of a necessity as basic as eating or sleeping or breathing, as though without choice, just as I felt compelled to love him, just as I still do, though what I would give for a choice!

He wrote me a single letter in return, in response to the first letter I sent him, though its beauty and honesty are such that his one letter equals all that I have sent him, and I carry it with me, neatly folded in a hidden pocket of my wallet, so that I might take it out at any time and read it again and confirm there was a time when he loved me with equal fervor and regret and anguish and longing. And I am reminded it was not a misstep I made in writing him these letters. If there was a misstep, it was somewhere else, in meeting his glance that first time I saw him, perhaps. But even then, there is the question of free will for which I do not have an answer.

If you pick me up, I'll never let you put me back down.

MY PHONE IS TRYING TO BREAK MY HEART

Though we spoke on the phone nightly the first month of our relationship, he left me a single voicemail. I remember playing it for a friend of mine soon after he left it. This friend had not met him and hasn't met him since but she commented after listening to it that his voice was full of love for me. "He is really smitten," she said, smiling, and I felt the heat rise to my cheeks as I smiled bashfully back. I had not listened to it myself. He had warned me after leaving it that his message was unremarkable, that he would leave a better one next time, and I was preemptively embarrassed for him, as though it was I who had left him a message. I waited almost two weeks to listen to it and when I finally did I understood what my friend had meant. There was a vulnerability in his voice, the same vulnerability I recognized in his eyes every time he looked at me. I did not listen to the message but that once. I waited too long and when I finally decided to listen to it again, it was gone, erased from my phone as he was slowly erasing himself from my life. Though we had spoken every night on the phone prior to my going to Jamaica, though he had written me emails telling me that he looked forward to our nightly conversations, that every day was a countdown to the time when we would talk, we inexplicably never spoke again once I returned. At first there were excuses (bad moods), apologies, promises always to call the following day. I teased him, threateningly once, at which point he reprimanded me again for attempting to control him ("You're being disrespectful. I'm trying to work."). But we never again spoke and I came to miss his voice as much as I missed the warmth of his body. I had become attached to his voice, the depth of it, the mixture of vulnerability and masculinity, the playfulness and randomness of our conversations that was often absent from other forms of communication. His voice had made me swoon such that I typically had a glass of wine or a shot of whiskey before he called to quell my nervousness. Recently I discovered a video on his website in which he recites one of his poems as he walks through a field at night. He is holding the camera and is not seen in the video but his voice is the same as I remember it and listening to him speak I felt my cheeks flush and my stomach overturn as they had when we talked on the phone and after watching it I poured myself a drink to steady myself from the feelings his voice had awakened. I have not watched this video again, in part because watching it made me feel uneasily voyeuristic, and in part because I did not know what to do with the feelings once they were awakened, and the rest of the evening there was a lingering sadness within me I have not wished to revisit.

After losing his voicemail I was conscious of not wanting to lose anymore of him. Though we were no longer speaking on the phone we were still engaging in hours of nightly texts and I began to go through them after we'd finished, deleting the more frivolous of the bunch and locking those that I knew I would want to read again. I wish that I had done this from the beginning as then he had written me texts that read like Shakespearean sonnets and I remember struggling to answer them similarly, though it was obvious to myself and must have been to him as well that his knowledge of language and the ease with which he wrote far surpassed my own. Of course I had no way of knowing then that the writing of sonnets was a finite act. He had told me he would woo me forever and like a fool I believed him. How quickly things turned, almost without my noticing, and for a long while it has felt as though it is I who am trying, and failing miserably, to woo him. Even, I suppose, to some degree, now, in writing this, I am making an attempt, a last, perhaps, at wooing him.

Every text I send him, every email, every word contained within these pages, is a carefully constructed attempt at returning him to me. I pick and choose words for their potential ability to reach him, to awaken within him a desire so strong he will be unable to reason it away, even as I hold little faith any word or combination of words are capable of overriding his will power and stubbornness which have proven themselves time and again more powerful and unwielding than any other I have ever known. I take photographs with my phone of train tracks and rivers and cornfields at dusk and send them with the same hope.

Once he sent me similar photographs, of lakes and city skylines and empty subway cars, but overtime my phone has deleted all but a precious few. I am afraid now to look at the picture album on my phone, as it seems every time I do, I have one less photograph, one less piece of him remaining.

The first time I was aware of missing a photograph was during our first attempt at saying goodbye to one another (there have been many such attempts since) and the loss was immediately devastating and had the feeling of a bad omen, particularly because the photograph in question was of him, the only one he ever sent. He'd taken it shortly after the last time I'd seen him, while at a wedding we'd both wished I could have attended. He'd texted me from the reception, told me what he was wearing, and I'd asked him to send me a picture of himself, though I had not really believed he would. Half an hour later there he was, reflected in a bathroom mirror, dressed in a white suit, just as he had described, and I stared at him, at his handsomeness, and was endeared to him anew, so moved was I by this act that did not fit with his personality. And even as I write this I am moved to tears thinking back to what this gesture meant to me and how far it feels we are from ever knowing such a gesture again. And still I carry that image with me, though it is no longer a physical entity on my phone. And still I am endeared by the gesture, though the gesturer is no longer a physical presence in my life, and wasn't even then, really.

Don't be a bitch, I know you can carry me, no problem

THE SECOND TIME his mouth found mine was in the afternoon as we stood in my kitchen. Because we shared only a handful of such moments, I can remember each instance with exact detail — date, time, location, duration, position of bodies, conversations leading up to and after — in a way I would be unable to had we been afforded the opportunity to make a habit of them. This was the day after the night we stood in my drive. We had gone to lunch with a woman who was also staying at the house and the woman had gone upstairs to work or watch TV on the Internet or catch up on email. It's hard to remember now which, as her reasons were uninteresting to me then and continue to be now; my mind was some place else. We had continued to sit on the balcony a while after she left but very quickly the sun became too hot and we went inside. We walked into the kitchen and I stood in front of him, leaning against the counter for support. We kissed for a minute or two and then suddenly he broke from me and took a step back. When I asked him why he'd pulled away from me, he answered that he'd felt like he was going to pass out. I've never felt like this before, he said, and at the time I believed him because I had felt and thought similarly, but now I wonder if he really meant what he said or if this was something he's said to others in the past or since. I have become more cynical in the months since he left. I do not like this side of me. I would prefer to believe everything he has told me, even if some of what he told me is not the truth. I suppose it's possible it was the heat from the sun or the fact that neither of us could eat our lunch that dizzied us in the kitchen. This is another explanation that does not require my believing he was being dishonest, though I still prefer to believe he was telling the truth.

Crying in the rain is similar to crying in the shower, you smile and no one can tell the difference.

A WEEK ago I had a dream about him. In the dream a mutual friend of ours emailed me to tell me he had seen him walking through a Wal-Mart in Ohio with his dad. The mutual friend added that I should not let on that I knew, and I was unsure if this was because he thought he'd be ashamed to have been seen with his dad or at Wal-Mart or in Ohio. I remember being happy when my friend told me this and one of the reasons I was happy was because I'd made certain assumptions based on this information and one of the assumptions I'd made was that he was living in Ohio, which in my dream felt somehow closer to me, though in reality it is a similar distance.

I told the mutual friend about this dream the other day. The mutual friend said I need to get out more. The mutual friend has never been a fan of our being together, even though the mutual friend is responsible for our having met. I agree, I said. I do need to get out more. The problem is, I have little interest in going out. I remember a time when the mutual friend mentioned his name a lot and whenever he did I would become bored and anxious for another topic of conversation to present itself. His name then was a series of flat letters. I could not have cared less. I wonder if I had the opportunity to return to that level of ignorance and disinterest regarding him if I would take it. If I knew what was good for me, I would. The problem is, most of the time I do not.

Crying in the shower is good but I prefer right before bed.

ALL MY BFFS ARE 13

I bemoan loneliness even as I laze round with it. Last night and this morning both I have recoiled from invitations to dinner and lunch. You are becoming a recluse, my friends say in texts because I won't speak to them on the phone or in person. Do I have some vested interest in being perceived as such? Do I think he would be impressed? Is that what this is about? It's hard to analyze. Getting dressed, putting on makeup, smiling... these activities feel like a lot of work to me in my current state. Which is...? I make an exception at three in the afternoon. My daughter brings boys home with her now. I used to fear I harbored pedophile-like inclinations. I found I had more in common with those under eighteen. I was relieved to discover I had no interest in fucking these boys. Perhaps, I thought, what I am feeling is maternal. Perhaps I am thinking of these boys as the sons I never had. I had wanted to have a son with him. Hence the dream I told him about. Gahhhh, he said when I told him. Such a beautiful dream. I flirt with them from time to time. I've witnessed other mothers behaving as such. It feels par for the course. Or whatever that antiquated golf term means.

If you think I'm conceited, this just proves how little you really know me.

I HAVE BEEN telling myself for some time now that I will no longer attempt to contact him. Whenever I write him an email or send him a text I circle the date on the calendar and tell myself it is the last time. There are five or six days around which I have made a circle this month. I think about making some sort of other shape, a square or triangle, maybe. It's not that I believe it will make a difference, but something needs to change and it seems unlikely this something will be me.

I HAVE NEVER BEEN A SUICIDAL PERSON but after knowing him for some time I began to view suicide differently. In the past when I'd thought of suicide, I had either thought of it as an act of desperation or one of self-violence, believing the person committing the act to be one wanting to separate him or herself from either great physical or emotional pain or from a self-loathing of equal greatness. I had experienced only minor physical pain in my lifetime and what I consider to be a normal amount of emotional pain and self-loathing. He had experienced a great deal more emotional pain and self-loathing in his life already, and though he did not speak of suicide as an option he was considering presently, I was aware of his past suicidal tendencies and did not believe he had entirely overcome them. I don't think I was suicidal, though I had become increasingly aware of feelings of indifference toward living. I had no great desire to become any older, for instance. Nor did I have a desire to become any more distanced from him, physically or emotionally. There were weeks we once again spoke and during those weeks my desire to lie down beside him with a mouthful of sleeping pills was greatest, so that I viewed ending our lives not as an escape from pain so much as a perpetuation of closeness. Of course I never mentioned this outright to him, only hinted at it vaguely, and am unsure I ever considered it seriously, i.e. as something I was prepared to do if he suddenly came to me and asked, or if suicide was merely something I romanticized as I did so many other ideas I had about he and I, for instance, having a baby, which would seem to be in direct contrast to the idea of killing ourselves.

Yesterday I spent the entire day writing him a letter and did not work on my book at all. Oddly, it did not feel to me a waste of time, as I was sure it would.

THE SECOND TIME I drove to see him and he did not see me I had contemplated driving to see the man I had been living with when we met instead and had brought with me a bottle of alcohol that man and I had bought on our last vacation together in case I did. I lived with this man for six years and in the last year of our relationship we had swung from periods of discussing marriage and children to periods in which we both believed we would be better off apart. During the period in which we discussed marriage and children I had gone so far as to make an appointment to have my IUD removed but had cancelled the appointment at the last minute. I cannot remember now what reason I gave for doing so but I must have held lingering doubts regarding this man and the idea of creating a family with him. I have never been happier than I was during the six years I lived with this man and yet always something within me kept me from committing to him fully. I worry now that I will never again be as happy as I was during those six years. A large part of me regrets not marrying this man. It is this same part of me that does not want to grow old without him. I cannot remember a time in which this man and I fought or a time in which he caused me pain or suffering of any kind. This man was consistently good to me in a way no one else in my life has ever been and I am ashamed of the shabby manner in which I treated him and the swiftness with which I left him for someone else.

Alone in the hotel that night I opened the bottle the man and I had bought during a period in which we were discussing marriage and children. We had been saving the bottle for a special occasion, such as a wedding or an anniversary, and I drank from it and became melancholy knowing now there would be no such occasion and that I alone was responsible for this fact. I drank for an hour and then called the man with whom I had purchased the bottle. I did not tell him I had opened the bottle, nor did I tell him I was in a hotel or a city other than the one in which he believed me to be. We talked for an hour and while we talked I continued to drink from the bottle so that by the time we hung up I was sobbing uncontrollably and could not even manage to say goodbye. I have talked to this man several times since, both on the phone and in person, and each time I do I end the conversation in tears and am as confused as he is by my emotions, both the presence of them now and their absence a few months ago when I left him for someone else.

In the morning the bottle was where I'd left it on the table by the bed. It was a large bottle and still three quarters full and I left it for the house-keeper rather than packing it as I no longer wished to be reminded of the occasions it had once represented or the shitty manner with which I had treated the one person in my life who had loved me the way I wanted to be loved.

I have effectively rid my life of every hopeful distraction.

THE FIRST TIME I met him was also the first time I read anything by him. Prior to this I had been aware of his name but believed it a pseudonym for someone else and was disinterested in his writing because of this. The day I met him I was at a book fair and a mutual friend handed me his book and told me to buy it. This same friend had told me several times before to buy his book and each time I had smiled politely and not bought it. This time, however, my friend added that the author of the book was standing a few feet from us and I did not want to be impolite or hurt the man's feelings. After I had paid for the book my friend said I should get it signed and called the man who had written it over. I had glanced in the man's direction when my friend first pointed him out to me and the man had seemed to recoil another foot or so from us as though he were embarrassed by his book or by the fact that our mutual friend was trying to guilt me into buying it. Now the man walked toward us, though he remained still at a distance so that I had to stretch out my arm as far as it would go in order to hand him the book. He was tall and everything about him felt large but at the same time there was a vulnerability to the way he held himself as though he worried he would reveal too much if he did not keep carefully guarded and it was this mixture of bravado and uneasiness that intrigued me and drew me to him. I stood still and waited as he signed the book, then thanked him and carried on walking around the book fair with my friend. A few minutes later we stopped at another table and he was there, too, sitting against a wall with his knees raised in front of him and his arms resting on his knees, and as I talked to the friend at the table I was conscious of him in a way I am typically conscious of men for whom I have developed an attraction, though I was not yet aware that I had, mainly because I had not stopped talking to people since I met him and had not had time alone with my thoughts, or time to digest them. I was conscious only of feeling inadequate in the face of this group of young, mostly male, writers whom I associated with a sort of coolness I did not believe I possessed. In their presence I felt inadequate and uncool and desirous of feeling myself included in their group, though I did not feel that I was, and because of this I overcompensated by talking too much and nervously, so that by the time I left the area I felt I had come off as even less cool than I might have had I not been so aware of trying to be cool.

Later that night there was a reading on a train to which he and I had both been invited to read. I had read only a handful of times in the past and was uneasy about reading in general, and uneasy about this reading in particular. I worried I would be unable to project over the noise of the train and that I would be the sort of reader people in the audience pitied because they seem nervous and unsure of themselves, and I was both.

There were six or seven readers in total and I can't remember if he read first or second but when they called out his name there was a palpable energy in the car and I remember being concerned that I would be unable to see him because the train was so full of people, some of whom were tall or standing on seats. I was pleased then when the person in charge of the reading brought him to the middle of the car and stood him directly in front of me. I had not had time to look at his book and so was still unfamiliar with his writing and unprepared for it in the same way I had been unprepared for meeting him earlier. He began reading and though he had been quiet and unassuming both of the times I had come into contact with him that day, the moment he began reading his voice and posture changed such that he was immediately in charge of the audience and it was impossible to look away or think of anything else while he read, as I almost always do at some point while listening to people read, even people whose writing I hold in high esteem. He read two poems from his book, both of which were marked with violence and romantic longing and a sense of self-awareness and humor not typically found in poems that incorporate violence and romantic longing and I found myself equally attracted to the writer and his writing so that put together I was completely undone by them. Much later, after I'd returned from the book fair, I came across a video someone had made of the reading. In the video I am visible behind his right shoulder and watching myself I was horrified by the wide range of facial expressions I made and the general enthusiasm I seemed to exude for both him and his reading, neither of which went unnoticed by commenters to the video.

The next morning I was alone in my hotel room and after I got up and made a pot of coffee I got back in bed and began to read his book. I read half of it in an hour and made notes in the margins of the book as I read.

Later I told him about the notes I'd made in his book and he asked to see it so he could read them. When he first asked I was still too embarrassed by my notes and shy about my feelings for him to show him and later when I was ready to show him he would not see me. Currently I have two copies of his book. One is unmarked and this one I keep on the bookshelf in my living room. The one in which I made notes I keep in a drawer under my bed. I would mail it to him but I do not have his address and he would not give it to me if I asked.

I have a large bruise on my right shin from hitting it on the corner of my bed every night when I get up to use the bathroom and I blame you for this because you are not here to steer me around it.

ONE OF THE THINGS I remember him saying when we stood in my driveway that night is that he would have broken up with anyone for me. This was on the eve of the night I broke things off with the man I was living with for him, though that is not an entirely accurate statement. The man I was living with and I had almost broken up two weekends prior to this and I do not think then that he would have been the reason if we had. If he was, I did not consciously think of him as being the reason. There had only been our brief initial meeting and then a handful of emails, but it is possible my subconscious mind was preemptively clearing room in my life for him, as though it already knew the influence he would have on my life, negative or positive and mostly a mixture of both.

I want the last heart I break to be my own.

THE SECOND TIME I drove to see him and he saw me we met in the same hotel as the first time though I had no one else with me and no other purpose for being in his city other than seeing him. When I arrived in the city it was early evening and immediately I felt anxious to see him. He said he would be a couple hours and then a couple hours turned into a few and I became more anxious though I did not worry that he would not come, I just wanted him to come sooner rather than later. I turned on my computer and tried to write but could not concentrate. I turned on music and tried to lie on the bed and remain calm but every minute or two I got up and looked in the mirror or brushed my teeth or in some manner prepared for him though I'd already prepared some hours before so that now I was merely fiddling with things which were already ready. Finally he texted me that he was in the lobby and I said that I would come down and get him. I had been given a room on a floor that required a room key to access so he could not come up without me. And here again is a moment that is painful for me to write about in a way I did not expect. Some parts of this I think will be painful to recollect and then they are not so painful and I get through them without having to stop and cover my eyes with my hands and say his name aloud and others, which I don't anticipate being painful, take me by surprise, such as this one, and then I am overcome with the urge to communicate with him in some manner, to tell him that I am writing about this moment and how painful it is. But we are not currently in communication and so I sit here at my desk and close my eyes and see him as he was when I stepped out of the elevator to him. And there he is, sitting in a chair waiting for me and looking lost and melancholy in the way he always looked when we parted and it is seeing his face like that again that causes me to stop where I am and check my email and otherwise distract myself until I can see his face without covering my own and then I can continue.

I walked over to the chair where he was sitting and he slowly stood and followed me back to the elevator. I pushed the button and we waited standing next to each other but not touching. I wanted to take hold of his arm or hand but something about the moment, about being in public with him or in that particular environment, felt awkward, as though our touching were something that required privacy, and I resisted. We weren't speaking and this too felt awkward and then he said something about the lobby of the hotel making him uneasy and I felt guilty about bringing him into an environment that made him so uncomfortable. Finally the elevator door opened and we stepped inside. Once the door had closed and we were alone, I reached out and touched his shirtsleeve and then his hand. He still had a pained look on his face and I felt hurried to get him to the room where I thought he would feel more comfortable and where I could distract him from his surroundings.

In the room he asked if he could remove his boots as they were wet and I said of course he could. It moved me that he had thought he needed to ask my permission or that he wanted to be polite and not presume too much. In my presence he was always very considerate and thoughtful in a way that was often in contrast to how he seemed to be when we were apart, and there in the room with him I did not feel insecure or anxious or unsure of his feelings for me as I would when I was not with him. It was because of this that I later drove twice to see him without telling him. I believed then as I believe now that he would be unable to deny his feelings for me were I standing in front of him as I was the first time we met, though perhaps that is egotism on my part and he would be able to deny his feelings for me anywhere, in my presence or out of it. It is possible too that he has overcome his feelings for me altogether. I cannot be sure of anything now, though I was sure of it then, which just happened to be the last time I saw him, though I did not know it would be the last time then, though I believed it to be the beginning.

It is hard to remember the middle parts of these encounters. The parts that stick with me, that I can view as though I am watching a video of the moments in slow motion, are the parts that came at the beginning and the end. Perhaps this is because the beginnings and endings were so rapt with emotion that they cannot be forgotten whereas the parts that came in the middle were merely euphoric and pleasurable in a way that runs them all together. I remember the removal of clothing and the songs that were playing on my computer as we removed them. I remember at some point during the night being vastly hungry and having only a single bag of peanut M&Ms and eating them one at a time off the bed and the way he looked at me as I ate them. I remember fighting sleep, not wanting to lose a single minute to it, but finally becoming so tired that we gave into it, though neither of us slept well, in part because of the awareness of time but also due to the temperature of the room which seemed to fluctuate from one extreme to the other. When we'd first fallen asleep we'd been cold and pulled both of the blankets up around us and shivered together under them, but at some point during the night I awoke and his skin was moist with heat but I did not want to move away from him so I pushed the blankets off of us and lay with him wrapped around me and did not mind the moistness as much as I would have minded being disjoined from him.

I do not know how many hours we slept, three or four, but then very quickly again it was morning and we were trying once more to fill every minute with as much of each other as possible, as though each of us sensed this would be the last time we would see each other and be in each other's arms. Outwardly we were making plans for the future and speaking as though this were still the beginning and there would be an indefinite amount of similarly spent times in the weeks and months to follow, but inwardly we seemed to know otherwise. I remember making him promise me he would come to see me as soon as possible and him saying he would, though the fact that I made him promise seems to imply some part of me did not believe him or did not believe that he would.

At eleven there was a knock on the door and then a woman's voice. We had not looked at the clock for a while and were unaware what time check out was and the woman's voice surprised us. One of us answered that we'd be a few minutes, though I cannot remember which one of us it was, and the woman said she would come back. When she'd gone I got out of bed and began to fold my clothes and put them in my suitcase, while he walked around the room opening drawers and searching papers. I asked him what he was looking for and he said something that would tell us what time check out was. It seemed obvious to me that check out was at eleven but I found it endearing that he seemed to want to believe otherwise. Here again is another way in which his actions when with me were in such stark contrast to his actions when we were apart. It had been he who had fought our meeting that night and who when he had come, had arrived late though I had begged him to come earlier, and now here he was, desperate for another hour with me and less wanting to part. I, however, was in a rush. I do not like to keep people waiting and, though it seems silly to me now, was more concerned in the moment with vacating the room in a timely fashion than I was in spending a few more minutes with him. He had only to put on his shirt and pants and was ready much sooner than I was. I was still undressed and brushing my hair which was full of tangles and he asked if he could brush it for me. Had I been able to foresee the future, I would have let him brush my hair then just as I would have let him bathe me the time we met prior to this. Instead I said no, thinking it would be quicker if I brushed it myself. I was anxious now for him to leave, just as the night before I'd been anxious for him to arrive. He offered to stay and wait for me. He wanted us to leave together. He mentioned the possibility of our sharing lunch before I left town. I was uncomfortable with him watching me get ready. I was also uncomfortable with telling him goodbye in public, and perhaps, being with him in public in general. I have tendencies toward shyness and my shyness is amplified when in the company of someone who exhibits similar tendencies, as he did. The one time we had gone to get something to eat together we had both been quiet and awkward in our actions and neither of us had eaten more than a couple bites of our food or talked because of this. I did not think I'd be able to chew my food with him sitting across from me. It was for similar reasons that I had not suggested we get something to eat the night before though I had been already starving when he arrived.

I feared the awkwardness of a shared lunch and so I made a joke about him waiting for me in the lobby instead, half hoping he would. I desperately wanted him to defy the soundness of both our minds and act in a manner that was unsound. I hugged him goodbye with the brush still in my hand and again made him promise to come see me, as though hearing his promise a second time somehow meant more than hearing it just the once. He left me with the same look on his face as he'd had when he arrived. It was similar to the look a child gives his mother when she leaves him on the first day of kindergarten. It was a look of abandonment and I pushed it aside as I got ready, as thinking of it would have made it impossible for me to leave.

I made a last check of the room before I left and on a pad of paper beside the bed I found a sheet of paper on which he'd written, "Elizabeth is b-a-d." I tore it off and stuck it in my purse. It is the only handwritten note he wrote me and I've hung it over my desk where I can look at it whenever I want tangible proof of his having once existed in my life. Without it, I could easily disbelieve. I did not notice when he wrote it and still do not know if he wrote it just before he left or at some point during the morning or night. It made me laugh when I found it. Now when I notice it I have the feeling I've abandoned someone, though I think my feelings with regard to him are often backwards. I think I should feel as though someone has abandoned me. I can't figure out, then, why I feel it the other way around.

Nuh uh. Yuh huh.

AFTER I RETURNED from Jamaica everything felt different. For a long time I did not know to what to attribute this change. I was gone only six days. Initially I thought it had something to do with his ex; that he'd seen her or gotten back together with her. Now I believe six days was all it took for him to talk himself out of moving forward with our relationship. In situations such as this it is often the unknown that drives a person craziest and I have driven myself crazy many times wondering if he would have been able to talk himself out of this had I not gone to Jamaica. Before I went to Jamaica we talked on the phone nightly. It is possible, I suppose, that he would have at some point stopped calling me had I not gone to Jamaica, though it seems less likely. Actually, I think that is an unfair statement. Even before I left for Jamaica there were signs I chose to ignore predicting this sort of premature ending. We had been arguing on the phone almost nightly in the days leading up to my trip about his coming to see me when I returned. The arguments were marked by playfulness and humor given that we were new to each other and each being careful not to offend or hurt the other, but looking back I think he was more serious about the arguments than I. I could not understand then the conflict he felt about visiting me. He had promised me when we parted in the hotel that second time that he would come to see me when I returned from Jamaica but in the days leading up to my trip he was still unwilling to set a date for his visit. This was the subject of our arguments, though in the beginning it had just been playful nudging on my part. The more nights we discussed it however, always at my urging, the more he seemed to respond with something like anger in his voice so that a couple of nights I hung up the phone and immediately broke down crying due to the stress of our conversations. And yet still I did not believe he would not come and still I did not understand his reluctance to set a date. I had been in long distance relationships before and was used to traveling to see the person I was in the relationship with. It did not seem such a big deal to me as I see now it did to him and I overlooked the stress it was causing him or that my continued nagging regarding it caused him. I thought of his visit as something that should be easy, a four-hour bus ride, and not much money. I did not view our seeing each other as causing or perpetuating anguish but of relieving it. He, however, I learned later, viewed it oppositely.

The night before I left for Jamaica he said he was too tired to talk. The previous night's phone conversation had gone badly and I think he felt a lingering sense of hopelessness regarding us because of it, though I did not think this way at the time. At the time I boarded the plane I was still quite hopeful about us in general and seeing him in particular. It wasn't until I returned and his communications with me became more sparse and intermittent that I began to share in his hopelessness. For the six days I was in Jamaica I was still under the delusion that everything was fine or would soon be fine, and I see now that I haven't felt the same since.

On the moon with red wine and weed!

THINGS FELL APART QUICKLY AFTER THIS. Or perhaps they fell apart slowly. It was two days after my return from Jamaica that I first drove to see him without telling him and he did not see. It was after this that we first started talking about ending things, though each time we tried, one or the other of us would pull the other back in so that we were continuously falling apart and coming back together and this part of our relationship lasted three months, which was a good deal longer than any other part of our relationship.

BEFORE FLYING TO JAMAICA I had sent him the novel I was working on. It was my first attempt at a novel and I didn't think it was very good and had been reluctant to show it to him. He had recently finished a book of plays and wanted me to read them (he never seemed anything less than a hundred percent self confident when it came to his writing, which was in direct contrast to how I felt about my own writing and in contrast also to how he seemed to feel about the other parts of himself). I was eager to read his plays but insecure about showing him my novel and told him so. In the days leading up to my trip he wrote me emails in which he talked about trust and trusting one another enough to share our work and I wanted, of course, to trust him, for us to trust each other. It wasn't a matter of trust, however, I assured him, but a matter of belief. He believed in his plays in a way I didn't believe in my novel, so that it was far easier for him to share his work with me than it was for me to share mine with him. Still, he kept urging me to send him my novel and in the end I did. I sent it the morning I left for the airport, which was the last email I sent before getting on the plane. Part of me, I think, hoped I was wrong about the novel, that he would see something in it I didn't, and that he would admire me more because of it. Later, after I was back, all he would say about the novel was that it wasn't for him to comment on, but that maybe I was meant to be a writer of short fiction, and I knew then that it wasn't any good, as I had suspected all along, and I began to wonder, as it became apparent he wasn't going to take the bus to come see me, if things would have turned out differently if my novel had been better, if he had admired me more as a writer, and more specifically, as a novelist. While in Jamaica I had read his book of plays in the sun at the pool and in bed at night and while they hadn't made me love him more, I wonder if I would have loved him less had they not been very good. I wonder similarly sometimes if he loved me less because of my novel or if it just seemed that way at the time and to a certain extent now. I think it is fair also to wonder if I produced a novel he felt was good in the future, if he would love me more again, and if he would love me enough to see me.

IT WAS AROUND THIS TIME that the writing group I had been a part of reformed. Two of the original members had moved to different states to attend graduate school, leaving only myself and one other member and he and I had waited a number of months before finding another writer we liked and asking him to join. The first night we met as a new group was the same night I was aware of him doing a reading in his city with a mutual friend. I had purposely scheduled this night to meet in hopes of distracting myself from the fact that I was not at his reading, which was where I wanted to be. I was hyperaware of the time throughout the evening, and checked my phone periodically and thought things like, "Okay, now they are most likely meeting for a pre-reading dinner" and "Now is the time in which he would be reading" and "Now they are probably drinking in a bar." I was aware from reading his blog earlier in the day that a female friend of his was going to the reading also and so I was picturing her drinking in the bar beside him. I had looked at the blog of this female friend and knew from looking that she was an artist who had gone to school in another state and recently moved back to the city in which he lived. There was one photograph of her on her blog and I had studied it many times and carefully, so that I could envision her short, black hair and petite, pixie face. Physically, she was the exact opposite of me and partially I found this comforting and partially I found this discomforting, as I knew he had dated artsy girls in the past and thought he might find comfort in that type, if only because he was used to it.

Because this was our first meeting we did not yet have work to critique but were discussing the work we would be sending after this initial meeting. The new member of the group said he had part of a novella he needed help with but also he said he was working on a project with another writer which he also was interested in getting comments on and then he mentioned the other writer's name and I was taking a drink when he said it and very nearly choked because it was the name of the man I was in love with, the man whose reading I wished I were at, the man I had been trying not to think about the entire evening. And I went in the bathroom and texted him, despite the fact we weren't currently speaking, and told him what the man had said. "It is impossible for me to escape you," I added. And after I hit send and went back out to the table and sat with the two men who were the members of my writing group, I thought about him receiving my text. I wondered if he would read it then or wait until later, when he was alone, perhaps, walking home from the bar, or if he would read it while sitting at the table with her. I was unsure how good of friends he was with the pixie woman, if he had known her before she went away to art school in Oregon or if they had met online during the time she was away and only recently met in person. Likewise I did not know if she was interested in him in a romantic way or merely as a friend. I went home that night and tried not to think of the two of them walking home together. I waited a little while for him to text me back, even though I was all but sure he would not, and fell asleep with the phone in my hand and woke up similarly.

The next time we met we first discussed the new member's work, which was the collaboration with him, and then after that we discussed some of the pages of my novel, which was about him, though they did not, to my knowledge, know it was about him, or if they did, they did not let on that they knew, so that the bulk of the evening we were talking about him in one way or another, about his writing or his person. By this time he and I had begun communicating again, though intermittently, and he texted me later that evening to ask how the meeting had gone, as he knew we were discussing both his collaboration and sections of my book, and I wasn't sure which he was more curious to hear back about, my work or his, though he had formed the question as though he were only interested in mine and so I answered only about it.

At this time I was still hesitant in my correspondences with him since there had been the long chunk of time in which I didn't hear from him at all, a month or longer, so that receiving emails and texts from him now made me uneasy and disconcerted and I was unsure how to precede. I had just gotten to the point where I was beginning to accept that I might never hear from him again and had stopped checking my email and phone every two minutes with the hope of finding an email or text from him and I was weary now of falling back into a routine with him, of becoming dependant again on talking to him, as I was certain he would eventually turn away from me and there would be nothing I could do or say to change this when it happened. At the same time, I felt somewhat less anxious about the time in which he stopped speaking to me as I'd been through it once already and now I knew that just as the time in which we were in communication didn't last, neither did the time in which we weren't. I felt that the cycle would continue ad infinitum as long as I allowed it to.

It was around this time, or a little later, too, that I began a campaign to convince myself that this was a viable option; that this, too, was a form of a relationship, however odd or limiting it might seem to outside eyes, or myself even, if I allowed myself to look at it as an outsider, which I tried not to do. A. was with a new woman and if I couldn't be with A., if I couldn't marry A. and live a normal, happy life with him, as half of me desperately wanted to do, I would live the lonely, eccentric life of an artist, which was how he lived already, and he and I would be one another's sole confidant, and in that way, we, too, would be a great love.

I had been aware of this sort of duality in my nature for some time and attributed it to my breaking with A. for him. I wanted two different lives at once and quite often I felt as though I were two different people, or one person in need of two ways of living.

In the beginning everything was easy: brush hair, eat M&M's.

THE FIRST TIME I sent him nude photos of myself was two weeks after I got back from Jamaica and a week after I wrote him the first three-page letter. Since then I have written him fourteen more. But it was only the first he responded to in any real manner. I wrote the first letter at five in the morning. We'd stayed up until four thirty talking first in a series of emails and then texts and I couldn't sleep thinking about all the things we'd said as well as some of the things we hadn't. I'd been writing him the letter in my head for half an hour already and finally I got up and turned on my computer and typed the letter into a Word document. This took me some time, as I wanted to get all my thoughts right for him and not leave anything out or anything open for misinterpretation. I was trying to convince him I was sturdier than he believed me to be. I listed hardships I'd been through as though filling out work experience on a resume. He seemed to take a protective stance with regard to me and I worried this protectiveness would be the reason he offered himself when he ended things. I was asking him to give me a chance. He seemed to want to imagine my life as cloudless and carefree and his own as seeped in misery so that he could in good conscious separate himself from me, so that he could view doing so as an act of benevolence rather than one of abandonment. I wanted to rid him of any such delusions. Later he claimed to a mutual friend or myself, I can't remember which, that I had made our relationship more serious than it needed to be and I'd laughed inwardly to myself when I heard this as I held the opposite view, that is, I felt I had been the one pleading to let things unfold in a more natural state whereas I saw him as over thinking every step and offering every word and action more weight than it was warranted, so that we could not make one move forward without him attempting to talk us both out of it.

The letter seemed in the days immediately following to have the effect I'd sought in writing it. He wrote back that it'd offered him a better understanding of me and that there was a sort of comfort in that understanding and for a short time I thought he might give us a real chance. But very quickly, after only a few days, he again allowed his mind to regress and began posing all the same arguments he'd posed before with regard to us. I was worn out from the arguments and more desperate than ever to see him. I felt powerless across so many miles, just as he'd admitted to feelings of powerlessness in my presence, which was, I suppose, the main reason he would not allow us to meet.

I was running out of ways to reach him. His mind was already set against me. I wanted to remind him of my physical self in a way I couldn't on paper. I also wanted to offer a gesture of trust, in hopes that he would open himself to me more fully in return. The reason I'd never taken nude photos of myself or allowed anyone else to take them of me was because I'd always thought ahead to a day when I was no longer with the person who'd asked to take them. I worried where they might end up or that the person would hold on to them after we'd parted, and I did not like the idea of that person continuing to have them and look at them or sharing them with people I either did not know or knew but did not want to know me in that way. With him, however, I did not seem to have the same worries. Either I trusted him in a way I'd not trusted the people I'd been with before him or the idea of him continuing to have and look at photographs of me after we parted did not bother me. There is also the possibility that I was simply so desperate to have him love me that I viewed these fears as unimportant or failed to view them at all.

The first photographs I sent him had a similar effect as the first letter I wrote and the effects lasted a similar length of time. After that I wrote more letters and sent more photographs but each time I did so, the letters and photographs had less of an effect and he returned more quickly to his arguments, or to the main argument, which was that he did not want to hurt me and the only way to prevent this from happening was to not see me at all. And yet still I continued to send the letters and photographs because there was nothing else left to do and I could not do nothing. Some-times now I wonder what he has done with all the letters and photographs, if he deleted them immediately upon viewing them or if he has them saved somewhere on his computer and takes them out from time to time or on a daily basis. I think about what his face looks like when he reads my letters or looks at my photographs. I would like to think it looks similar to the way I remember it looking when I ate M&Ms one at a time off the bed or stood a foot from him that first time we met. I do not think he reads or looks at them daily for the same reason he has refused to see me since that last time we met in the hotel. I do not think he likes the way he feels when his face looks the way I remember it or the way I want it to look when he thinks of me now.

I *wonder* about the existence and location of the letters and photographs but I do not worry about them. My trust in him is implicit. Also, if he were to betray my trust I would be so distraught that I would no longer care who saw my photographs or read my letters. His betrayal would be viewed as evidence of a lack of protectiveness on his part with regard to me and because of this I would no longer feel protective of myself or of us.

I want only slightly more than you are capable of offering anyone else.

THE LAST TIME I heard his voice was on my daughter's phone when she called to tell him a joke. I had called him two times since my return from Jamaica and neither time had he answered his phone or returned the call. My daughter and I had been walking the dogs and she had told me a joke that reminded me of something he would find funny. I told my daughter she should call him and tell him the joke, though I did not actually think that she would or that he would answer his phone if she did. I was standing beside her in the kitchen when she called him and when I heard his voice on the speakerphone I had to run upstairs and hide my head under a pillow until I could not hear it anymore. It was the sort of joke in which the person being told the joke has to repeat certain words at certain intervals and when I'd heard him repeating the words, his voice had sounded soft and vulnerable in a way I had not heard it before. When my daughter was finished telling the joke I came back downstairs and stood beside her while she instructed him on what to do next. My daughter liked him as an individual and us as a couple, though she did not always like the way I as an individual acted with regard to him. She thought I should act more like her, i.e. instructive, and less like I did, i.e. compliant.

She had instructed him not to answer his phone the next time she called and he had said okay, he wouldn't. She wanted to hear his voice-mail (which I had told her was humorous) and leave him a message. When she called back the first time he answered his phone before the voicemail could pick up, even though he had said he would not, and we had laughed because we thought he was being dumb or forgetful and either way it was funny. The second time she called back he again answered and we again laughed though this time we were less convinced of his being dumb or forgetful and more convinced that he was having fun at our expense. The third time she called he did not even speak but laughed loudly and uproariously and my daughter feigned annoyance and hung up. Finally, the fourth time she called he did not answer and when he did not answer it felt a little like disappointment as we had gotten used to his answering and to his laughter and now the game was up and we would have no more reason for calling.

After she hung up this last time my daughter turned to me and shrugged her shoulders as if to say, what was so hard about that. Have you even tried calling him?, she wanted to know. She did not understand why the man she thought of as my boyfriend would talk to her and not me and I shrugged my shoulders and held my palms flat in the air as if to say, I don't know either. When I walked into my bedroom my phone was making the sound it makes when I receive a text and I looked at my phone and it was from him and I lay down on my bed to text him back but did not call him.

You like me best five minutes after I've told you goodbye.

YESTERDAY I HEARD from him for the first time in weeks. It had been ten days since I had attempted to communicate with him. The last time I had contacted him was the night he was doing a reading with a mutual friend. I had contacted him more than usual in the days leading up to the reading because I wanted to go to the reading but believed he would be angry with me if I did. The last time he and the mutual friend had read together I had been at the reading with my daughter and before he read he had come over and asked if he could sit with us. After the reading I had to leave before everyone else to take my daughter home and he had left with us. Later he told me he would have been sad if we had left without him.

When I contacted him yesterday it was to tell him about something sad that had happened. I had not planned on contacting him for another week or two, but then the sad thing happened and I knew he would be empathetic about the sad thing, though this did not mean I believed he would respond, only that he would feel empathy. He had not responded the last ten or so times I had contacted him. I thought that if he did respond it wouldn't be for a day or two or even longer. I wrote him about the sad thing and then went to smoke a cigarette and by the time I returned he had already written me back. When I saw his name I felt an immediate sense of gratitude toward him and I thanked him for his response, which was thoughtful and compassionate, and then turned off my computer so as not to ruin the moment by waiting to see if he would respond again or if his responding was limited to a single email. I felt contented and hopeful in a way I had not felt in a long time and I wanted to continue to feel this way a while longer.

And every time I tell you goodbye I mean it.
And one day I will tell you goodbye and really, really mean it.
And that day you will like me best.
You will like me for a long time after that.

TWO NIGHTS AGO I emailed him another goodbye. Or rather, I emailed him the proposition of a goodbye. I.e., something along the lines of: *I can't do this anymore. We should stop. It's too painful. You're killing me. Blah, blah, blah.* I'd said the same thing two or three or ten times before. It was doubtful he took me seriously anymore. I want to believe that the first time I said goodbye I meant it. It's hard to know for sure but I remember crying for three days after, which would seem to indicate that I did. I turned off my phone and computer and gave them to my daughter. I told her I couldn't be trusted not to contact him anymore. On the third day I lied to my daughter. I told her I was strong enough to use my phone and computer and she believed me or was tired of dealing with me or both. She gave me back my computer and phone and we did not talk about him for a long while after that.

THE FOURTH OR FIFTH TIME I told him goodbye he responded by asking me which of the two universities near me he should apply to. I did not include this sentence in the original version of this document my mother read three years ago. I realize now I seem to have left out the majority of ways in which he contacted me or said things to me each time I tried to stop talking to him so that I have presented myself as the woman in the movie who has an unfounded obsession when in reality it was more a mutual obsession, a mutual inability to cease communication. I don't know why I have chosen to write it this way. Perhaps I felt it was unfair to speak for him. Or perhaps this was, as my mother accused in her email, all about me after all.

AFTERWARD (2013)

It's been three and a half years since I've had any communication with him and I am still aware how long it's been.

I love you so much that nothing can matter to me—not even you...only my love—not your answer. Not even your indifference.

—AYN RAND,
The Fountainhead

VOLUME ONE.

One of the problems with people in Chicago, she remembered, was that they were never lonely at the same time. Their sadness occurred in isolation, ...

—LORRIE MOORE,
"Willing"

I try to talk to people about how much acting goes into music. How much of a character goes into what you put on stage. You ever sit down with Jay[-Z]? He's not the guy he is on stage. I'm not the guy I am on stage. I am a performer. It's an elevated idea.

—JUSTIN TIMBERLAKE,
New York Times Sunday Styles, September, 2013

To the Editor[2]:

Your issue on love and death is very interesting, but it omits the theme of illness from love. The pain of love, once present in treatises and medical textbooks, has disappeared from the medical vocabulary. But is there still lovesickness nowadays? In poetry and in ancient Egyptian writings, as well as in the works of classical Greek antiquity, the symptoms of the disease are described in detail. The lovesick change color, suffer insomnia and burn with fever; their tongues stick to the palate; they even become crazy and die from love. In the medical tradition, lovesickness led to general dryness of the body, rashes, dry eyes, worn appearance and so on. And what about today? In some forms, the passion of love, unrequited love, is a real disease, underestimated by mental health experts.

Having a "broken heart" consumed with love can translate into a real physical and mental disease accompanied by a constellation of symptoms leading to a typical picture of "major depression," according to the severity: delusion, depression/elation, crisis crying, insomnia, mood swings, loss of appetite, inability to concentrate and obsessive-compulsive disorders like dependency on email and smartphones.

Love can also be folly. From Hippocrates to the Persian Avicenna to Galen up to the Montpellier School, there is frequent mention of the link between love and madness, to the representation of a specific morbid picture, lovesickness or insane love, unbridled or erotic melancholy.

EUGENIA TOGNOTTI

Sassari, Italy

The writer is a professor of the history of medicine and human sciences in the department of biomedical sciences at the University of Sassari.

---

[2] *The New York Times Book Review,* February 28th, 2016

Once, while in Mexico, I had gone to an Internet café to see if Ian had emailed me. It was toward the end of the trip and I had become increasingly anxious to talk to him. It had been nearly a month since I had last seen him, five or six days since I had heard his voice on my phone, four days of listening almost nonstop to his new songs on my iPod, of loitering in his voice, in song lyrics that did not seem to be in any fashion about me, but sometimes seemed to reference another woman, one I was unfamiliar with, an ex, or perhaps, someone he was still seeing currently, while I was away in another country. I had no way of knowing anything with regard to him and his 'personal life,' as strange as that sounds now to myself and perhaps to you here.

The air conditioning in the small café did not work or did not work well. It was crowded and I sat at what appeared to be an older model computer and attempted to navigate it first to his blog and then to my email. I had not thought to buy a bottle of water. I was likely dehydrated from the walk in the midday sun to the café. I was lightheaded and dizzy. I was most likely suffering from heat exhaustion as well as claustrophobia-like feelings brought on by the smallness of my immediate surroundings as well as the claustrophobia of being alone in a foreign city and of being alone away from a new lover, being unable to speak to him or to ascertain details regarding his life and his life as it did or didn't pertain to me.

There was no mention of me on his blog (I did not expect there to be; there had been only mentions of me months earlier, before we really knew one another, before we had interacted in any real fashion and my name was still a form of mystery (and likely a from of fantasy) to him) and no email from him either, and I began to feel more undone by the heat and bodies within close proximity to me, as well as by the thought of the length of the walk back to my hotel.

I contemplated writing an email to him or posting something on his blog, a comment under my own name or "anonymous," but instead did nothing. I sat staring at his blog posts, the ones he had made since I had left the country. They were not telling in any way, were very general, about his upcoming concerts and events, music he was listening to, books he was reading. There were already several comments by women I did not know, or by persons with fictitious female sounding names, and I did not like any of these women because they seemed to be flirting with him some-how, even if their comments were not outright flirtatious, even if they were merely asking for more details regarding a concert or congratulating on his music or so on and so forth. I did not like how he responded to them, in a timely fashion and with politeness and often gratitude. I did not want him to ignore them or to treat them badly, but I did not like seeing him treat them well or address them at all either. I took every one of their com-ments, and each of his responses, as coded messages, as hints at meeting up in person at some future event, or as a nod to a time in which they met up at an event in the past. There was so much I did not know with regard to him that I was forced to interpret everything I read and saw in numer-ous ways, to act suspiciously and with suspicion, to act as a woman who is crazy or obsessed or has tendencies for stalking, which I did; to make things up.

I finally turned off the computer and hurried out of the café, out into the sun where I thought I would finally be able to breathe, but where, on a broken sidewalk, I stumbled and fell and had to raise myself back upward or remain fallen: a choice it took me some time to make. I was, by then, no good at making decisions, where once making decisions had been my strong point. I think I must have remained in a state of falling as long as possible. I can't remember getting back to the hotel, I only know that eventually I did.

Prior to my going to Mexico, we talked every night. We spoke on the phone for hours. Ian would always be outside, walking, during these phone conversations and often he would complain of mosquitoes biting him or he would have to let me go for five minutes because a policeman was harassing him. I pictured him walking down an urban street like an actor in a movie because I had no way of imagining his setting otherwise.

During the day he wrote me long, manic emails with strings of excla-mation points. He would quote from philosophy books or plays he was reading or songs he was listening to or writing. Sometimes he would text me when he finished an email. He was often impatient for my reaction. I would be at the mall, eating dinner with my son, and Ian would text me, "Where are you? I just wrote you the funniest email! You have to read it right now!"

But I took my time eating. I did not rush. I smiled at my son.

There is a video of us on a train the day we met. You can watch it on You-Tube if you search Ian's name and "train" and "2009." In the video I am standing behind Ian in a grey wool coat. I had another coat on underneath it but you cannot tell this from watching the video. You can only see the one. Ian is wearing an army jacket and underneath the jacket he is wearing another jacket with a hood. When he raps, the hood is over his head. He is wearing the sort of boots my college boyfriend wore, the kind you wear if you want people to think you are punk rock or a skinhead and his head is shaved on the sides like a skinhead but I don't think he is a skinhead. He raps first or second, I forget which. I am worried I won't be able to see him but someone brings him to the center of the train right in front of me. I am unaware we are being filmed. I have no idea my facial expressions are being recorded, that aside from Ian, I will be the most visible person in the video. I will be embarrassed when I watch the video for the first time at home on my computer three days later. I will try to focus on Ian's face and ignore my own. I will feel something like embarrassment watching either.

The train was full of people I barely knew at the time, other writers and musicians. Some of the people have since become good friends of mine and also good friends of Ian's. This was the first time any of us had seen Ian perform. I had been introduced to him earlier in the day by a mutual friend who had produced his first mixtape. The indie literary world and underground music scene collided that spring and summer in small Mid-western cities. We traveled together. Did shows together. It was not uncommon for young writers and musicians to tour together or to do drugs together or to sleep together. I was not young but everyone surrounding me seemed to be.

The morning after the night I met Ian, I found myself alone in the hotel room in Iowa City. L. was already gone, having breakfast with friends or wandering the city, and had left me to sleep. I got up and made myself a pot of the cheap hotel room coffee and got back in bed. I pulled Ian's CD from my bag and put it in my laptop. I listened to every song and took notes as I listened and then listened again as I showered and dressed and blew dry my hair. Weeks later, after he'd come to my house, I told Ian about the notes I'd made. He asked to see them. He was curious what I had thought of his songs and indirectly, I suppose, what I had thought of him. But I was too shy about my feelings for him then to show him and since then I have thrown away that notebook and the CD he signed to me. For a long time after that, I listened to his songs by searching his name on the Internet, typically late at night, alone and intoxicated.

Before flying to Mexico I had sent Ian the novel I was working on. It was my first attempt at a novel and I didn't think it was very good and had been reluctant to show it to him. He had recently finished a new batch of songs he'd been working on when we met and wanted me to listen to them (he never seemed anything less than a hundred percent self confident when it came to his music, which was in direct contrast to how I felt about my writing and in contrast also to how he seemed to feel about the other parts of himself), and offer advice on the lyrics in particular and on the music in general. I was eager to hear his new songs but insecure about showing him my novel and told him so. In the days leading up to my trip he wrote me emails in which he talked about trust and trusting one another enough to share our work and I wanted, of course, to trust him, for us to trust each other. It wasn't a matter of trust, however, I assured him, but a matter of belief. He believed in his music in a way I didn't believe in my novel, so that it was far easier for him to share his work with me than it was for me to share mine with him. Still, he kept urging me to send him my novel and in the end I did. I sent it the morning I left for the airport, which was the last email I sent before getting on the plane. Part of me, I think, hoped I was wrong about the novel, that he would see something in it I didn't, and that he would admire me more because of it. Later, after I was back, all he would say about the novel was that it wasn't for him to comment on, but that maybe I was meant to be a writer of short fiction, and I knew then that it wasn't any good, as I had suspected all along, and I began to wonder, as it became apparent he wasn't going to take the bus to come see me, if things would have turned out differently if my novel had been better, if he had admired me more as a writer, and more specifically, as a novelist. While in Mexico I had listened to his songs in the sun at the pool and in bed at night and while they hadn't made me love him more, I wonder if I would have loved him less had they not been very good. I wonder similarly sometimes if he loved me less because of my novel or if it just seemed that way at the time and to a certain extent now. I think it is fair also to wonder if I produced a novel he felt was good in the future, if he would love me more again, and if he would love me enough then to see me.

In the moment, it felt insignificant. Later Ian told me he had repeatedly asked the person standing next to him what type of tequila was in the flask they were sharing, evidence of his nervousness. I had not remembered anyone standing next to him or the presence of a flask or him seeming nervous. In my memory he is standing alone. In my memory he is alternately standing with his hood up over his head, obstructing my view of his face, or sitting on the ground, his hood pushed back, the sides of his head shaved and cut, the middle section formed into a mohawk. There is a cover of a Minor Threat album on the wall in my basement and often when I am smoking down there my eyes find it and always when this happens I am reminded of Ian, the young punk singer, the young angry man sitting alone on the pavement or sidewalk. This was my first impression of him and it remains the most lasting.

There's nothing as significant as a human face. Nor as eloquent. We can never really know another person, except by our first glance at him. Because, in that glance, we know everything. (Even though we're not always wise enough to unravel the knowledge.) — Ayn Rand, The Fountainhead

I see now, if I didn't then, that my tendencies toward obsession date back to my childhood, to my worship of my mother, my obsession with her, which has led, in more recent years, to my feelings of hurt and anger toward her, to my feelings of abandonment, which were similar to my feelings regarding him.

My mother was nineteen when she became pregnant with me, twenty when she divorced my father, twenty-six when she divorced the man after that, thirty when she divorced the man after that . . . I was always waiting for these small windows of time in which my mother and I could be alone together . . .

I was always waiting in my room for my mother.
I was an only child.
There were no distractions from myself or from my waiting.
Things were similar after L. left in 2009.
I spent nine months waiting on Ian.

The thing I couldn't say upfront in 2009, the thing I was afraid for Ian to know, for him to find out, was that I was forty years old . . . he was twenty-six. We had each had a birthday shortly after meeting. I was quite conscious of mine, of not wanting him to find out how old I was, of letting my age remain a mystery, as so much about him did. It was the one thing about myself I was unwilling to share, and there were so many things about him of which he was unwilling . . . It did not seem unfair.

Twice I drove to see Ian without telling him and twice he did not see me once I arrived. Two times before that I had driven to see him with his knowledge and each of those two times he had seen me. The two times he had seen me were a week apart and toward the beginning of our relationship, though in this case phrases such as "in the beginning" and "at the end" feel interchangeable and equally accurate, given that it seemed we were ending almost from the beginning. Even then he was somewhat reluctant to see me the second time. The night before I made the second drive I called him to let him know I was coming. It was a last minute decision on my part. I had made plans to fly to New York City for a friend's reading but had decided for reasons involving my general tiredness, and tiredness when it came to feelings of sociability in particular, not to go. It was merely coincidental that his twenty-sixth birthday fell on the same evening. We were talking on the phone about me coming for a second visit when he made the comment that I was trying to control him. The comment was disguised as a joke and we both laughed but I knew even then there was some truth to it, in his mind, at least, though I did not believe it myself. At the time I attributed a phrase like "trying to control me" as strictly a negative assessment of a situation and since I did not feel that what I was trying to do was negative in any way, I could not accept that what I was doing was trying to control him. I have thought of this phrase many times since, however, and have come to the conclusion that if by "trying to control me" he meant I was trying to force him to see me again when he felt uncomfortable seeing me and was fearful that seeing me would result in increased feelings of anguish and heartache once we parted, then I admit he was correct in his usage of the word control and I was in fact guilty of trying to control him.

A month later I began to take photographs of myself to send to him.

In the first photographs my hair is unclean. He had commented the last time I had seen him on wanting to wash it and I suppose I was trying to show that it was still dirty for him . . . that I was unclean . . . to provide him with a motivation for coming to see me, a job he might be able to do, an occupation.

In a weird way, I think my mother instilled this need for both independence and domination in me. My mother was a contradiction of political agendas: marching for women's rights in the '70s and staying in a physically and emotionally abusive relationship for the last five years of the '80s. I was caught between asserting myself as a fiercely independent woman (with L.) and craving male domination (with Ian).

I remember a mutual female friend, a woman, saying to me, "Ian is better read in Women's studies and feminist books than I am."

This was saying something because our mutual friend was highly educated and often cited the names of books and authors I had never heard of, almost all of them female.

I never made it past my first year of college.

I don't know if I have ever read a feminist text.

Only *The Bell Jar*. Or *The Color Purple*. If either counts.

How funny then that Ian has been labeled a misogynist by critics and the media, that his lyrics, his songs, have been so misunderstood, misinterpreted, misconstrued (perhaps in a similar way to how I am misconstruing him here), while I am written to by young women who praise my writing for its strength, its strong female characters . . .

I do not feel particularly strong. I have never felt like a strong female anything.

I had married my first husband, Jared, a month after we met. I was still living with another man at the time. Jared had just turned eighteen and I had just turned twenty-five. We would have married sooner but there was a two-week waiting period to get a marriage license in Ohio.

I tell you this so that you will understand the level of disbelief I underwent when Ian didn't marry me, when he didn't drop everything for me, when nothing about his life changed in any significant manner, outwardly at least. I cannot speak for what may or may not have changed inwardly. I have no way of knowing this. I have as much was of knowing as you do.

The first time I spent any significant amount of time with Ian was at a party at my house. This was three months after we'd been introduced at a festival in Iowa City. There were seven or eight people in town staying at my house also. Forty or so people at the party. A male friend of ours — the same man who had read with Ian and me on the train the day we met — sat beside me on the pool table, legs swinging, as Ian paced in front of my bookshelves, making witty comments about Bukowski and Nabokov and Keroauc. He had read everything and had something funny to say about everyone. This was the performative side of him, the side he showed on stage. He could have been a comedian as easily as a musician. Later the friend disappeared, or more likely, we disappeared from our friend as we managed to disappear from everyone else that evening, and it was just Ian and I sitting on the cold concrete of the front porch, our backs resting against the house, smoking cigarettes together like a pair of teenage outcasts, our first attempt at being alone together. I remember I was wearing jeans shorts — it was April or May in the Midwest, warm during the day, still chilly at night — and he offered to remove the flannel shirt he was wearing to cover my legs. I refused politely, tried to downplay the cold, despite the bumps that had broken out over my thighs. I wasn't yet comfortable with any form of intimacy between us (though two hours later I would be sitting in his lap in my kitchen, his hand up my shorts, perfectly okay with him feeling the damp cotton between my legs). We sat like that a while, smoking and occasionally smiling awkwardly at one another, but otherwise staring straight ahead and not talking much. At some point the friend who had sat beside me on the pool table peeked his head out to take a picture of us, a photograph I later asked him to email me, and months after that, once it was apparent Ian and I were not going to become anything, deleted from my computer. There exist no other photographs of Ian and me and while that one was not great (it was fuzzy, out of focus, a repercussions of our friend's intoxication), it was proof of our having shared *something*, a cigarette, if nothing else.

Many months later, the friend who took the picture of us ended up in my bed. There exist several photographs of my friend and me together (before and after he was in my bed). He and I talk occasionally still, trade emails, and see each other in person, at readings and such, from time to time. And it seems unfair that I see him; that I am still in contact with him, that there will likely be many more photographs of the two of us taken together in the future; that only the extremity of my feelings for Ian prevent me from seeing him and from having my picture taken with him; the knowledge that if only I felt somehow less, that if only I could successfully corral my feelings, there might again be proof of our friendship (is this friendship?) as well.

Johnny Rotten was all energy and extroversion. He galvanized the kids.
I was the opposite, a sullen forlorn junkie outcast who just wanted to be
left alone, except by admiring girls. — Richard Hell

Once it was apparent Ian wasn't going to return to see me or to allow me
to drive to see him, I began driving my laptop to Jared's house an hour
north. I would leave it there, stuffed under a blanket on a closet shelf,
for five days or two weeks, as long as it took for me to feel the hysteria,
my hysteria, had passed. I would give my son my cell phone to keep in
his room for similar reasons (because I could not trust myself not to text
Ian). My ex husband had not dated anyone since our divorce a decade
earlier. He did not own a computer, was not familiar with the online
world. I told him I could not work with the laptop at my house. I did not,
of course, tell him about Ian. In the early months of our marriage, Jared
would often run from me — once, he ran literally from a gas station in
Minnesota or Idaho, I forget now which, where we had stopped for gas
on our cross country honeymoon, and I did not see him until the next
morning, when he found me at a motel not far from the gas station — but
he always returned.

L. and I were still together the weekend of the party, though he moved
out the week following. It was late May, the start of summer, and he had
just moved all of his belongs back to my house from the university town
in which he was attending graduate school and he had to load everything
back up again five days later. I don't remember seeing him or talking to
him much if at all that weekend and I wonder how much of a difference
might have been made if he had said something to me or to Ian or to in
any way confronted us or tried to stop me. I remember a friend of L.'s, a
poet, on the periphery that weekend, watching me, offering me knowing
looks. I was annoyed by this at the time. I did not want to be reminded
or made aware that what I was doing was wrong, was disrespectful to L.
It is unlikely anything L. could have said or done would have altered the
outcome of that weekend. All of our friends were there as witnesses. My
son, also. I don't think I was in my right mind, if such a mind exists some-

where within me. I was aware of all of these people existing in the shadows and off screen but their chatter was inaudible, as though they were only pretending to speak, moving their mouths open and shut without forcing words through, as background actors in a film are directed to do, and I could only hear Ian, focus on him, think with regard to him, as though morality no longer existed or was a man-made invention, invented by men to prevent their women being taken from them when they could do nothing themselves to prevent it.

I don't think I would have allowed such a thing to happen with L. and another woman. I would have planted myself between them on the porch. I would not have made it so easy for them (to be alone). Why did L. make it so easy? Why didn't he ever once, during the three days Ian was in our house, take me aside, try to talk to me? Why didn't he confront Ian? It was only after Ian left, at the very end of the three days, that L. said anything directly to me, and by then it was too late. By then I did not care what L. had to say.

I remember I had just driven Ian to the bus station an hour before when L. asked to speak to me finally. We were alone in our living room. He tried then to threaten me. To say that if I left the next day, he would be gone when I returned. But I was already gone by then. I was already in another city with Ian. It was not a choice I could make: to stay. L. had let me go three days before, when he didn't intercept on the porch, when he went to sleep in his car.

I am wont to blame L. here as much as myself. As much as Ian. The three of us seem to me equally conspiratorial in what happened.

I got on the bus in the morning. The following evening when I returned, L. was already gone. It was a relief not to have to see him. I could breathe easier knowing he was out of the house. It took six months for this feeling to change.

It is hard not to feel restless without complications. I don't think L. understands this. He was raised in a Mormon household. There was no destruction of property. There were the same two adults all of his eighteen years.

I was late picking up my son the next day; it was a first time being late. Every other soccer practice I sat on the sidelines or if it was particularly windy or cold, in my car, watching. That day, however, we had had to leave almost as soon as we'd arrived, as soon as Eli was out of the car, to take Ian to the bus stop. I had told Eli I would be taking him but that I would be back before the end of practice. Once at the bus stop, however, I quickly lost track of time. For once I was not thinking about Eli, as I always was with L. I could not bring myself to leave Ian before his bus arrived, though in the end I had to, left him sitting cross legged in the grass, pulling blades in a forlorn manner, or in a manner I, leaving him, interpreted as forlorn.

I was fifteen minutes late to pick up my son and while I rushed to make it to him, I did not feel particularly bad about being late. Instead I felt appreciative of those extra minutes alone in my car with Ian. I was behaving uncharacteristically selfish with regard to Eli when typically Eli was the one person I acted in a selfless manner with regard to.

I think I had the sense even then, even as my relationship with Ian was supposed to be beginning, that my interactions with him were temporary, that I could afford to act selfishly, that I could afford to be late to pick my son up this once, because an opportunity to be late would not again present itself.

The reading in New York City was mine. I said I was to go for a friend's reading for reasons of simplicity but really it was my own. I had been asked by a friend to read at a well-known bar in New York, a bar I had wanted to read in since I had wanted to be a writer. I had been excited about the reading. It felt in some small way as though I would be a part of literary history. All these famous writers had read in this bar and now I was going to read there also.

But then Ian came to my house and we said the things we said, and after that I no longer cared so much about reading in the New York bar. I no longer cared about being part of literary history, or I cared about being part of literary history as it pertained to Ian and me only.

I have yet to meet a single person who has been to an apartment or house in which Ian lives, despite having met several musicians and writers who claim to be good friends of his, and two who claim to be "best friends" of Ian's.

Always Ian separates himself a "block or two away" from his home, adding to or creating his own mythology.

THE FIRST TIME I DROVE TO SEE IAN AND HE SAW ME

I left out a crucial part of that scene the first time I wrote it.

I had driven to Ian's city with this woman, the one I mention as being in the hotel room with me — Enid. The first time I wrote this I said she was already in the bedroom with the door shut when Ian arrived but that is not true.

When Ian arrived, Enid and I were in the lobby of the hotel. We had just returned from a reading Enid had given, which had been the original reason for our visit to the city. Enid had been nervous to read and had had a drink or two before the reading and now was having another drink, though I was having only soda. She was in good spirits because of the drinking. She said she was excited to see Ian and I believed her even though she was a good friend of L.'s and I did not think she approved of me leaving L. for Ian.

When Ian arrived he was not feeling well, was likely fevered, as I said in the first telling of this part of the story. He had walked an hour to the hotel and it was raining lightly and he was wet from the rain or from perspiring while walking or from being fevered or all of those things. He seemed sad or quiet or uncomfortable sitting at the table with us, which made the Enid's intoxication seem amplified. Her voice seemed louder, and she seemed to be talking faster, to be saying a lot. She was asking Ian questions. He had not fully sat down before she started and even after it was apparent he was being quiet and did not feel well, she did not let up. She was smiling and asking questions and he was solemn and not answering them and I was caught in the middle of the two of them. One of the questions she was asking, that she kept asking, was about his name. She wanted to know why he used a pseudonym instead of his real name for his music. She wanted to know his real name and when he told her she said she wanted to see his driver's license. She said she didn't believe him. I could tell by his face he was becoming upset, though she was probably too drunk to notice or taking out her annoyance with me for breaking up with L. on him. Either way, she did not seem to care that she was making him uncomfortable. She just kept asking more questions. Finally he said something to offend her — I can't remember what it was, though I remember he said it in a normal tone, normal volume, he did not yell or stand up or becoming anymore visibly upset to passersby — and immediately Enid got up and left the lobby.

Once she was gone, Ian turned to me to ask me what I had said to her to make her act that way. I was as shocked by his question to me as he had been by her questions to him. I didn't like the way his question made me feel, which was accused. I had done nothing. I had had no way of knowing she would act like that or ask those questions. She had said nothing before he arrived about it. She had said simply she was looking forward to seeing him. I told him I had done nothing. That I had been as caught off guard by her line of questioning as he was. That if I had known ahead of time she was going to act like that, I never would have had him around her. He said okay but I could tell he still did not fully believe me. It reminded me of the first year of my marriage to Jared; I had spent those first twelve months convincing him I wasn't going to leave him, that I wasn't cheating on him with my ex or with friends of his or with men who came into the store in which I worked.

We sat there in the lobby of the hotel a while. I had my hand on Ian's arm. This was only our second time seeing each other. It was our first time alone. I wanted to tell him I was willing to wait as long as it took but that seemed like a dumb thing to say our first time alone together and I wasn't sure what it would mean anyway. I remember how vulnerable he looked in that hotel lobby, surrounded by all the loudly laughing people in suits and heels. He was in his boots and army pants and his head was shaved and he had a fever. I took him by the hand and led him through the lobby to the elevator. I wanted to shelter him from all those ugly people. Suddenly the lobby and everyone in it seemed like props in a Kubrick film. It was vaguely nightmarish.

I have seen that same look on his face, the one he had walking through the hotel lobby that night, in photographs and videos online. Most of them are taken after concerts, on tours. He looks exhausted and out of place and melancholy. And I have the same inner response now as I did then. I want to shelter him in the same way I wanted to shelter Kurt Cobain every time I saw him on TV in 1993. In the same way I sheltered Ian that night, up in the hotel room, alone together on the couch, our faces pressed together, his so fevered and warm.

When I wrote the passage about Ian wanting to wash my hair, I had an image in my mind from the movie *Out of Africa* in which Robert Redford washes Meryl Streep's hair. I was sixteen or seventeen when I saw that film in the theater and it had a great influence on what I viewed then as romantic and what I still do. Emma Bovary, after she exhibits bad behavior, infidelity, fevers, . . . is separated (by her mother-in-law) from her novels. The novels are blamed for her ideals of romanticism and passion and her 'insanity' in seeking both. It is at once ludicrous and entirely plausible that novels and films . . . — had I never seen *Sid and Nancy* or *Badlands* or *Raging Bull*, for instance . . . had I never read *Gatsby* or Anaïs Nin or Marguerite Duras . . . had Ian never read Shakespeare . . . had either of us been impervious to plays and fictions depicting anguished separations, . . . had we not fetishized them . . . had my mother-in-law or L. separated me from . . . were I not a writer, myself.

She wanted a son; he would be strong and dark, she would call him Georges; and this idea of having a male child was a sort of hoped for compensation for all her past helplessness. A man, at least, is free; he can explore every passion, every land, overcome obstacles, taste the most distant pleasures. But a woman is continually thwarted. Inert and pliant at the same time, she must struggle against both the softness of her flesh and subjection to the law. Her will, like the veil tied to her hat by a string, flutters with every breeze; there is always some desire luring her on, some convention holding her back. — Gustave Flaubert, Madam Bovary

She hoped she would be a little fool. — F. Scott Fitzgerald, *The Great Gatsby*

"Mainly, I see it as unfair that I would ask you to wait for me, and yet, I know there is only waiting. I am not asking you to wait for me, I can only rely on time." — from an email Ian wrote me in July

"Why are you refusing to accept my (hopefully) graceful withdrawal?" — from another email Ian wrote me fifteen days

By the time I returned home from the hotel in which I had stayed with Ian the second time, L. had left again, gone to another Midwestern city.

Less than a week later I found myself driving E. five hours north to a camp in the middle of a Michigan woods.

Maybe silent hurting is the new Midwest love. — Daniel Bailey

I had arranged the three-week stay six months earlier, when everything about our lives was different. I had envisioned L. and I spending the three weeks working in our offices in the morning and reading outside in the sun in the afternoons, drinking in bed in the evenings. I had envisioned idealism because that is the simplest form of imagining.

I did not want to leave E. now. I stood beside him in line while he signed papers and had his photo taken. I looked around at the young adults who were not much older than he. (One of them briefly mistook me for a camper, seeing me only from the side, my hair long down my back, my legs and back exposed in a short skirt and tank top, not dissimilar from the garb of the thirteen year old female campers.)

On the drive up E. and I had talked about L.'s leaving. He had seemed unaffected or numbed by his departure and I remembered all the men who had left my mother and how, no matter how much I liked or even loved them, secretly happy I was to see them go, to be left alone with my mother, to sit in the front seat of the car again. (I had a similar feeling now, alone with E. This would be a feeling I would have to fight against later when L. and I reunited . . . this feeling of self-isolating with E.)

My instinct was to linger and I stood a while in E.'s cabin before he finally insisted I go. I suppose he was being brave, pushing me out. Or perhaps he did not wish to prolong the anguish of telling me good-bye. (Or maybe I am confusing this goodbye with the one in the hotel a week earlier.)

But, no, this is not right at all. I have forgotten that on this morning, the morning I left E. at camp, I was not thinking of L. at all. I was not thinking of the house as an empty building or of myself returning to it in a lonely state. I had forgotten that I was still that morning under the belief Ian would be coming soon, in a matter of days, immediately upon the return of my short trip to Mexico (also planned long in advance). I was not hurried to leave E., of course. I was never hurried to leave my son. And I did not want him to feel left or to miss me. But I was eager to move forward with the day and the days immediately following to get to the days in which I would be again with Ian in my house.

I remember texting Ian on the drive home. It was another five hours back and I drove at a high speed and rather recklessly, listening to loud, equally fast-paced music, in order to combat fatigue and boredom.

We texted about E. and how much I would miss my son and then once home we texted about what we would do when he came to stay, the Italian dishes he would cook for me, the TV shows we would watch together on the couch, how we would remain in bed for days at a time not showering but allowing the sheets and room to become saturated with our scent, and like that little Fitzgeraldian fool I believed all of it. I cannot remember once questioning it. And partially this is because no one had ever told me they would come to see me and then not come and partially this was because I knew that each of the two times I had said I was going to see him, nothing could have stopped me from going, not L.'s humiliation and heart-sickness, not my want to read in a particular bar in New York City, nothing beyond E.'s sickness would have prohibited me from going to Ian.

It did not occur to me that Ian would not come, that he could resist coming. Not because I considered myself more special than any other woman, but because this had not been my experience with men who had professed an attraction to me in the past. I was accustomed to meeting men and becoming immediately inseparable from them. I did not understand the complexities of dating that I read about in women's magazines because I had never dated. Instead I had found myself transitioning from one long-term monogamous relationship to the other throughout my twenties and thirties.

I did not consider that it would be easier for Ian to have sex with a person living in the same city as him because I did not consider paying a small amount of money, five to twenty dollars, and riding a bus four hours, to be something hard to do. I had done it the first time I had gone to see him. I would do it a hundred times more if he would allow me.

I fell asleep with the phone in my hand as I often did that year. I was not thinking of L. or of E. This was during the time in which it was easy to get Ian to say certain things to me. This was during the time in which I fell asleep mostly relaxed, smiling, contented. Everything was still ahead of us then. This life we never lived.

By then she was sleeping not in the house but out by the pool, on a faded rattan chaise left by a former tenant. There was a jack for a telephone there, and she used beach towels for blankets. The beach towels had a special point. Because she had an uneasy sense that sleeping outside on a rattan chaise could be construed as the first step toward something unnameable (she did not know what it was she feared, but it had to do with empty sardine cans in the sink, vermouth bottles in the wastebaskets, slovenliness past the point of return) she told herself that she was sleeping outside just until it was too cold to sleep beneath beach towels, just until the heat broke, just until the fires stopped burning in the mountains, sleeping outside only because the bedrooms in the house were hot, airless, only because the palms scraped against the screens and there was no one to wake her in the mornings. — Joan Didion, *Play it As It Lays*

My days had a routine to them then, in the early weeks of summer, Eli off at camp six hours north, Ian four hours west in his city (I never realized until now that I was closer to Ian then, physically, than I was to my own son; that a short distance separated us; I wonder how small a distance there could have been that Ian still would not have travailed; if I had been in his city, for example, if he still would have forbidden me to see him . . . I think probably he would have, though of course it is hard to know) . . . I would rise late, ten or eleven or noon, depending on how late Ian and I had stayed up texting the night before, if he had texted me at all . . . I woke and put on a bathing suit and drove to get an iced coffee. I came home and lay out on the deck in the sun all day, emptying gallon sized milk containers of cold water over me, avoiding eye contact with neighbors on all sides. Sometimes Ian would text me that he was looking for a job or to ask what I was wearing or in what manner I had groomed myself.

Sometimes in the mornings, after getting my coffee, or in the early evenings, when it became too chilly to sit outside, I sat at my computer and tried to write. I wrote short stories of a thousand-word length and worked on one longer story, the length of a novella.

In the evenings, at dusk, I went for hour-long drives. At home, after dusk, I drank. I drank wine and bourbon, mostly. Smoked two cigarettes an hour, while listening to music on my headphones in the basement.

I had not drank or smoked much in the years since I had left Eli's father and during my eight year marriage to him I had not drank or smoked at all once I became pregnant with E.

I quickly built up a tolerance for both alcohol and tobacco while at the same time my appetite for food diminished so that I found myself subsisting mostly on dry cereal, fruit, and the occasional children's fast food meal.

My evenings were centered around Ian, waiting to see if he was going to text or email me in reply. In the beginning weeks of summer he almost always did and in the last weeks of summer he did so intermittently, one night texting me for eight hours and then not replying for three days after, and the lack of consistency was the hardest factor to contend with, as there was no real way of training myself emotionally to become accustomed to inconsistency.

I think I failed to realize in 2009 how much this was going to be about class for Ian, because social class was something I did not think about. Class, in this context, was an outdated or old-fashioned notion that did not enter my mind but existed only in old books and films.

For months I was unable to turn on the radio without a certain song by a female artist coming on. This song was just beginning to be played the second time I drove back from seeing Ian. I remember turning the volume on the radio very high and singing along whenever the song came on that day. I was conscious of the fact that Ian would not like the song. It amused me to think of him feigning annoyance with the song and with me for singing along with it. I thought of feigned annoyance as something akin to endearment.

Later that night I told Ian about the song. We were on the phone and he was walking outside his apartment. "I can't believe you, listening to that song!" he teased, and I felt like I had won, like he was endeared to me after all. Like that song would be the song we danced to at our wedding, even if he made fun of me while we danced, even if he whispered "I can't believe this is our fucking song, you dummy," into my ear as our friends and family watched. Now when I hear that song I am reminded that I never met his parents. I never met his brothers. I never met one friend we didn't share in common. Sometimes I wonder if any of them even knew my name, if he ever mentioned me to them, if he ever wrote a single song about me. I listen to his songs and wonder if they are about me or someone else. I want every song he writes to be about me even if every story I write isn't about him.

Once I returned from Mexico I couldn't listen to that song anymore. I did not want to be reminded of how I felt the first time I heard it or of the things I believed to be true at that time. They were the same things the woman in the song believed.

I wanted to believe a great deal of time had passed since the second time I drove back from seeing Ian. I did not like being reminded that not that much time had passed at all.

Before Mexico I had thought about the song the same feelings I thought about Ian which were mostly positive and hopeful. After Mexico the song served only to remind me how little time Ian had given us, and how I'd once believed our relationship would outlast a song's longevity, even a popular song or top forty song, or a song that is ultimately voted "song of the year."

Only recently have I been able to listen to the song again, to enjoy it as I enjoy any other song on the radio, though it will never be any other song on the radio.

– Write about coming home to empty house, spending hours in E.'s room cleaning, going through old papers, photos, toys under the bed . . .

– the time the electric went out

– write about son's friends coming over . . . wait . . . is it better if E. is a daughter? so that the friends coming over are female rather than male?

– bleeding down both legs . . .

Sometimes I wonder, am I writing this to see if Ian is still listening? And if he's listening, what is it I want him to hear?

I paid so little attention to his emails then. I read them only to see if they said what I wanted them to say and if I found that they did not, I disregarded them and acted injured and affronted. It is only five years later that I am studying the following email, looking up the play it references, downloading the play onto my Kindle:

2009, June 10th, (subject line: an excerpt from Miss Julie):

[a statement Jean, a servant, makes to Miss Julie, royalty]

Jean: then i started to run, plunged through a hedge of raspberry bushes, chased right across a strawberry plantation, and came out on the terrace where the roses grew. there i caught sight of a pink dress and pair of white stockings — that was you! i crawled under a pile of weeds — right into it, you know — into the stinging thistles and wet, ill-smelling dirt. and i saw you walking among the roses, and i thought: if it be possible for a robber to get into heaven and dwell with the angels, then it is strange that a cotter's child, here on god's own earth, cannot get into the park and play with the count's daughter... and then i washed myself with soap and hot water, and put on my best clothes, and went to church, where i could see you. i did see you, and went home determined to die. but i wanted to die beautifully and pleasantly, without any pain.

I have left the play excerpt in the font I took from his email and every time I look at it I attribute the font to him, and am charmed by it, as though it were his handwriting on the page or as though he typed it directly into this manuscript himself.

He was reading *Dawn of Day* also, which I had (also) failed to notice when I read the email the first time around (June 11, 2009), so hysterical was I, so self-involved. It was a long email, with the book being mentioned first and things regarding me second and third. I paid attention, I suppose, only to the second and third things, as they related directly to me.

Later I chose to believe that six days — the amount of time I was in Mexico — was all it took for Ian to talk himself out of moving forward with our relationship. Things fell apart quickly after this. Or perhaps they fell apart slowly.

I had developed a very small following in the literary community before Ian and I met and since we met that following had not significantly grown, whereas before we met he had only a single song out and then immediately after we met his first mixtape had begun to sell and by the time I flew to Mexico his name was already beginning to spread on the Internet so that by the time I returned he had a larger musical following than I did a literary one.

After my return from Mexico, he wrote me that he was going to be moving back in with his ex. He told me he would be staying in the "extra room" and I do not remember asking any other questions with regard to that, the day he told me or in the days after. I seemed to almost immediately forget that he had told me, so that when I drove to his city a second time without telling him, six or eight weeks later, I was surprised again that he did not see me.

It helped a great deal, of course, in way of supporting my delusion, that Ian did not mention his ex again either. For instance, the second time I drove to see him and he did not see me, he did not say he couldn't see me because of her or because he was living with her. He did not mention her at all. Instead he said he could not see me because he was working late that night, though I had been unaware until he said this that he was employed.
I am realizing today — while editing this is 2014 — that had he and I simply sat down and had one hour-long conversation at any point in the last four years there would be no need for this book.

(Well, that's not true. This is a book of grief and grief must be worked through in more than one hour-long conversation.)

Again I made a choice not to listen. Though I don't think choice is the right word. I did not sit down and weigh the options of listening to what Ian told me, what little bits of information he afforded me with regard to his life.

She has explained that the feeling I have for her is a mirage. I don't agree.
— Violette Leduc on Simone de Beauvoir

The first time I had driven to see Ian and he had not seen me I had chosen a different hotel from the one in which I normally stayed. It was a more affordable hotel, less opulent. There was no lobby bar, no shops in the basement. I had chosen the hotel with Ian's comfort in mind, and consequently, I was less comfortable. The first room I was given was on the same floor as the pool. I could hear families coming and going. After an hour I asked for another room and was given one at the end of a hall, far from the elevator, three floors up. The room was quiet and I managed to write a bit while waiting for Ian. I had waited to text him until I arrived at the hotel. Two hours had passed and still he had not replied to my text.

We had texted the previous night as usual.

It is hard to remember how our conversations had gone in the two days since my return from Mexico. It would seem likely we had argued over his coming to see me again, as we had before I'd left.

I had gone to the salon to have my hair colored that morning and now I was in a hotel in his city.

There was no mini bar in the room and I had not brought any alcohol with me. I had brought two protein bars, one for Ian and one for me, and I ate the one that was for me while I waited.

I bought a Diet Coke from the vending machine.

I did not turn on the TV or listen to my iPod.

I have no memory of crying though it seems impossible I did not cry. I cried easily then. I cried almost daily in the weeks after Mexico. It is possible I cried daily.

My son was at camp another two weeks. All of my adult friends had moved out of town (except for the one who did not like me anymore). I was alone in my house all day and all night. All of these factors contributed to making it easier for me to drive four hours to a city to see a man who did not want to see me.

It is hard to say if I expected him to come. It is easy now to say I didn't. It is likely I was on some sort of emotional "auto-pilot" then, feeling nothing and everything simultaneously.

After another hour I texted him again.

I don't remember falling asleep or waking up the next morning or packing up my small bag and walking to my car.

I remember only driving back, the feeling of leaving his city.

"I'm sorry, babe," he would say when he texted me a couple hours later. "I wasn't even in the city last night. I hurt my ankle. I couldn't have come to see you if I'd wanted to . . . "

I don't remember being angry or deciding whether or not to "forgive" him. I remember only feeling relieved to hear from him again. I remember feeling excited to be able to go home that evening, to pour a glass of wine and light a cigarette and spend four or five hours texting with him "as usual."

I turned on the radio and sang along, happily, giddily, excited I had what I viewed as a "date" that night, anticipating Ian telling me the words I had longed while in Mexico to hear. It mattered little to me that the words were typed into a phone rather than spoken aloud. They were the same words, weren't they? They held the same meaning. They meant the same either which way they arrived.

I kept waiting for a time in which I would be angry with Ian, as most of my friends seemed to be from the moment I began speaking of him.

It is hard to be angry when you are so overcome with emotion as to be collapsed on your bathroom floor.

A friend convinced me to drive to see her for the Fourth of July. I'd been back from Mexico six days, back from the hotel in which Ian did not see me, four. My friend lived the same distance from me that Ian lived but in an opposite direction.

It was my friend's birthday and we went bowling with other people I did not know. It was hard to be around people but easier to be around people I did not know than to be around those I did. I could not talk about Ian around my friend because my friend had decided she did not like him based on how I was acting. I was not acting like myself, she said. I did not feel like myself or I did not feel like the person she used to know. I did not tell my friend that I felt like a different person entirely. I didn't say aloud that I felt like a person only Ian knew now. I never told my friend I had no nostalgia for the old me, that I preferred this me, the anguished me, because this me felt true in a way the old me never did.

I waited for my friend to go to bed and then sat out on the back stoop to smoke a cigarette and to text Ian. I smoked the cigarette slowly, drawing out the time in which Ian might reply. It was the hardest day since my return from Mexico because it was a holiday and even though I had never cared about the fourth of July, I wanted now to spend every holiday with Ian, and this was the first holiday since we met and already I was not with him.

In the morning I left instead of staying another night, as had been the original plan. Ian had not replied to my text and I could not bear to be around people in Ian's absence. It was easier to be alone with my despair, to drink and smoke alone, to listen to music alone, to wait alone to see if he would text me. It was easier to be alone and cry than it was to be around people knowing I would probably never spend a holiday with Ian.

How am I different from some future person who will write Ian's biography?

It was sunny and warm and I drove with the windows down listening to the radio. I was eager to see Eli, to be distracted by her chatter and laughter in the car, to have someone to watch TV with in the evenings and to go to get coffee with in the mornings. I had spent several hours of the last two weeks in Eli's room, organizing and cleaning. I felt less alone in her room. And, in some inexplicable way, I felt not as far from Ian.

When I arrived, Eli was not in her cabin. I began to gather her belongings, to fold and pack her clothes, to unmake her bed, roll her sleeping bag, rinse and dry her toiletries. It felt good to have another person to care for. I had missed doing Eli's laundry, missed having another bathroom to clean. My household duties had been cut by two thirds after L. and Eli left. I had found myself with too much time in which to think about myself, to think about Ian, to make lists of things he and I were not doing together.

I went into a stall to use the bathroom. I had started my period and the toilet was full of blood. I washed my hands vigorously with another girl's aloe vera soap; dried my hands on a towel that did not belong to my daughter.

A group of girls was entering the cabin when I came out and I saw Eli amongst them. She was thirteen that summer, wearing makeup and ironing her hair and her face had matured into a mix of womanhood and female youth. I wanted to open my arms and have her run into them as she had when she was much younger but I held myself restrictively, patiently. I heard her say to the other girls, "let me go say hi to my mother." And she did not run to me but walked swiftly into my embrace.

"I can't wait to get out of here," she whispered into my ear and I pressed myself to her and told her to get her things then so we could go. It felt conspiratorially, as though we were comrades, rather than mother and daughter. She did not take long saying her goodbyes. We sped off from there as fast as we could. I had made a hotel reservation in a town a few over. There was a strawberry festival, or cherry, I forget which, and Eli had asked in one of the letters she'd written home if we could go. It was a twenty or thirty minute drive and on the way Eli filled me in on everything that had happened to her at camp; the girls in her cabin, the boys in her classes, all the restrictions and rules, the food, the counselors . . . I listened attentively, and did not check my phone or think to check it. I was entertained thoroughly by Eli, enrapt even. I heard myself laughing and asking questions, responding and being responded to . . . It felt good to not be thinking of him.

The hotel was on the water, one of the great lakes, I could never remember which, nor can I now, and I parked in front of it. E. came with me to check in. There was one other person ahead of us, checking in or changing rooms, and they were taking a long time about it, and inordinate amount of time, it seemed to me. I had to use the bathroom, even though I had just done so back at the cabin half an hour before. I had drunk a large iced coffee on the drive. I was wearing a cotton skirt and flip flops and I remember the sensation of drops of water trickling down the insides of each of my thighs and calves as we stood impatiently as the hotel check in desk. I remember looking down and seeing the trail of blood leading into my shoes.

I made a gesture to Eli, pointing anxiously at the blood, handed her my license and credit card and went down the hall to find a bathroom.

Inside I set about making immediate decisions regarding what to address first, the process of cleaning myself, and all the while I was thinking of Ian, of the amusement he would take in my situation. I wanted to photograph the toilet and the blood trail on my inner legs and in my shoes. It was reminiscent of a murder scene in that small, northern Michigan hotel bathroom. Later, the next day or evening, when I did tell Ian what had happened, he was less amused than sexualized. "I would have fucked you and not showered and fucked you again," he said.

Later, in the hotel room, I ran a bath while Eli watched TV and used her cell phone to text her friends, the first time she'd been able to do so in three weeks. I had turned my phone off and left it in my purse. I was purposefully not replying to Ian's texts. I would spend the evening watching Eli talk on the phone and answer texts with the satisfaction of one who has, for twenty-four hours, mastered the art of self-denial. There were few days in which I felt good about myself that summer and this was one of them.

The next day was the same. We walked around the festival, Eli and I, arm in arm, tasting jams and sampling cakes, eating at an outdoor café, standing in the shade watching the parade... My phone was still turned off somewhere at the bottom of my purse. If I could have left it off forever... If I could have spent all my time hooked to Eli's arm...

A week later I was back on my bathroom floor sobbing into a towel so E. would not hear me. It was ten in the morning, already hot, and my face was moist and flush, with tears and perspiration. I had had the a/c unit in the house disassembled when we moved in. I had an aversion to forced air. I cannot recall the conversation Ian and I had had the night before that had prompted the tears but I remember the agreement, suggested by one of us and agreed to by both, that we would not talk to each other anymore as it was too painful and then, very quickly, the not talking became the most painful part.

Finally, prone on my bedroom carpet, I texted Ian.

I said, "Can't stop crying."

I was surprised when my phone buzzed three seconds later. There was our agreement not to talk, Ian's usual steadfastness. I stopped crying to look at my phone. "I know," it said. "I like crying in the shower."

I smiled and cried harder. I tasted the fibers of the carpet. I was constantly torn then between feelings of extreme melancholia and feelings of heightened eroticism. I cried and masturbated and drank with increased frequency. It's hard not to look back at that time now and feel that was when I was most alive but to feel such a thing is to be reductive and unfair to the time in which one is living currently.

Later that morning, E. texted me to see if I wanted to walk downtown. He wanted to get lunch, go to the comic book store. It was a forty-five minute walk each way. I looked at activities as x amount of minutes in which I would not think about (texting) Ian.

I wondered if he had heard me crying. We were halfway downtown. We had just stopped for Italian sodas at a new café. Eli was almost as tall as me now. I neither had to reach up, nor lean down to rest my arm along his shoulder.

"You should have gotten me," he was saying. "I could have helped you. I would have known what to say."

I'd told him about my conversation with Ian the previous night. How it'd all gone wrong. I was looking at a pair of white go-go boots for a reading I was doing soon in Atlantic City. I wanted to look good in the pictures that would be taken at the reading in case Ian saw them. I wanted to give the impression I was carefree even though this had not been the case since he and I met. Even though this had never been the case. My son was coaching me on better ways of speaking with Ian in the future, ways that would not result in me being "the bitch." My son was thirteen and had never had a girlfriend and he was making more sense than I was. Anyone would have made more sense than I did.

I had told Ian that a man, a musician in town, had asked me to dinner. I was presenting it as more than it was. In reality I had texted the man late at night, while drinking, and the man had responded almost immediately, almost assuredly drinking also, asking me to meet him that night. In the morning the man was clearly embarrassed by his directness and no longer seemed to think it a good idea that we meet. I left this part out when telling the story to Ian. I wanted Ian to think I was contemplating going on a date with the man. I wanted to see what Ian's reaction would be if I did. I was struggling to determine how much and what sort of emotion Ian felt with regard to me.

Ian reacted dismissively. He replied that he had no right to request that I did not go. And yet when I told him, a few hours later, that I wasn't going, I received an email from him that simply said, "Thank you."

I did not tell Ian when I slept with L. a week or so later. I was not interested in his reaction to that.

L. was on a reading tour he had planned before our breakup; the last reading of the tour was to take place in my city. I was nervous about housing L. and his tourmates: three women and two men, all strangers to me. I was conscious of them studying L. and me, our small gestures and interactions. The reading coincided with the summer art fair. Half a million people. L. and I walked arm in arm through the streets after the reading. We bought corn dogs from vendors, drank beer on a park bench. Back at the house we were the last two awake. I didn't think then how repetitive the situation was; how two months earlier it'd been Ian and I awake, L. asleep in the backseat of his car in our garage. It'd been seven weeks since Ian had left me alone in a hotel room; since Ian had promised to take the bus to see me. Immediately after sex with L., I felt the need to separate myself from him. I went upstairs to smoke a cigarette on the balcony where earlier in the summer I had made a habit of talking to Ian, swatting away mosquitoes as we talked. I checked my phone for a new text from Ian but there wasn't any. L. came out onto the balcony and sat down across from me.

"Can I have one?" he said.

"You don't smoke," I said.

"I do a lot of things now," he said.

I shrugged and handed him a cigarette. I felt disloyal smoking with L. also. I swatted away mosquitoes and did not talk. I waited for L. to go to bed. I got on my computer to see if Ian had emailed me but he hadn't so I G-chatted with a man who lived in Ian's city — a man I was uninterested in — while drinking whiskey as a pathway to sleep.

The next day I went to a concert with Eli and a female friend of mine and a female friend of Eli's. Before the concert we asked L. to take a photograph of the four of us in the driveway. L. was going to pack the remainder of his belongings while we were at the concert, leave in the morning.

In the driveway Eli began to tell a story I thought inappropriate in L.'s presence. I tried to quietly shush Eli, but Eli didn't understand. Eli yelled out, "What's the big deal? You told Ian yesterday!"

I nudged Eli with my shoulder, looked immediately to L. to see if he'd heard.

"What?" Eli said. "You're broken up. You've moved on."

My child was copying what she perceived as my indifference, she had shut herself off to L. as quickly as I had, willed a non-emotional connection. I had a memory of reacting similarly to my own mother's breakups, to cutting off my emotions for the men I had once loved or for whom I'd at least felt an affection. Once I failed at such an attempt; I sobbed and mouthed the name of my mother's ex while a new man slept in her bed. I sobbed similarly on subsequent nights until I had finally rid myself of any lingering affections.

It was after midnight when we returned from the concert. I went downstairs to see L.; sat on the edge of his bed. I was sweaty from the humid summer night air. I had worn a bathing suit top and cutoffs to the concert. My feet were dirty inside my flip flops. I needed a shower. I leaned into L.; reached for his phone. There was a text from his new girlfriend. I began to read it aloud. L. pulled it away. "You don't get to read that anymore," he said. I looked at his face, even in the dark I could tell he was smiling.

I have some vague memory of him carrying me up to my bed, of him remarking on my sheets, which I had purchased six weeks before.

"It's not like anyone's seen them," I said. I wanted him to know Ian hadn't been here.

In the morning I was woken by L. He was standing over my bed. It was very early. Seven or eight. There was a foggy recollection of a kiss, a foggy awareness of having startled beneath it. I had some feeling of violation, of L. as intruder, as uninvited guest in what I already thought of as "my room."

"I just wanted to say goodbye," L. said.

I waited for L. to leave the room to check my phone, to see if Ian had texted me. Of course Ian hadn't texted me.

During this time my mother was alternately writing me letters, which I neither opened nor read, and ignoring me. One week there would be a package from her — a sweater that was in her taste, not mine — and then I would not hear from her for another month before another letter arrived with her handwriting on the envelope.

I had similar envelopes with similar handwriting from thirty years earlier stuffed in a bin somewhere in the basement. These were envelopes she had written me in my childhood; a series of poems she had written to me in the months leading up to my birth and for my subsequent birthdays until I turned seven, at which point the letters and poems ceased.

It seemed doubtful I was ever going to get over the hurt and anger I felt toward my mother at being left every time she met a new man, at being forced to listen to the sounds of their lovemaking, at being left at home alone so many days and nights. It seemed likely I was going to keep repeating the pattern, the self-sabotage, of pushing away the people who loved me or the people who loved me in a consistent manner or the people with whom I felt a protection that made me uneasy because I was unused to that feeling.

I was having trouble with the Internet. E. was upstairs in his bedroom with a friend who was sleeping over. I had spent an hour taking new photographs of myself. I was leaving for Atlantic City in the morning. I thought a new setting — my bedroom — might encourage a different reaction from Ian. He had been invited to Atlantic City also but he did not fly or he could not afford to go or he was living with his ex girlfriend. I lay on my side and did not smile. The camera was propped on a stack of books. I hadn't read or didn't like any of the books on which the camera was propped.

I got my laptop from the kitchen. I downloaded the photographs, deleted all but three. This was an activity in lieu of dating, in lieu of sex, a way in which to fill my time, to interact with Ian when he wouldn't interact with me. I tried to get online. I didn't have Internet at the house. I used the neighbors' Internet or went to a café or the library. The neighbors' Internet came in better in certain rooms of the house. It came in best in E.'s room. I tried several other rooms but the signal was too weak or something wasn't strong enough.

It was already midnight. I hadn't seen E. in a couple of hours. I packed my laptop into its case and got in my car in the garage. I didn't bother to text E. or to tell him where I was going. I was only going two miles down the street. I would be back in fifteen minutes.

I was wearing boxer shorts and a tank top. I was in my pajamas. I drove two miles to the plaza that holds Whole Foods and CVS and Barnes & Noble. I got out of my car and walked to the bench outside Barnes and sat down. I unzipped my laptop and opened it and tried to get online. There were no cars in the parking lot and I was under the Barnes & Noble lighting and the plaza faced the main road that went through town.

I kept my head down as I got online, signed into my email, began attaching the photographs in an email addressed to Ian. The photographs took a long time to attach. The first one seemed to take five minutes. I lost track of time. I kept my head down. I stopped looking up.

I can't remember if I heard the man approach before he began to speak. I don't think I was aware of a car pulling into the lot. I had attached two photos and was waiting on the third to attach so I could hit 'send.' I had spent a considerable amount of time — twenty or thirty minutes — deciding which photos to send to Ian. In all the rest of the photos I did not like something about myself, either I looked older than I wanted to look or bigger than I wanted to look or some other way I did not want Ian to view me. I did not stop to think that he had already seen me all of the ways before or that if he were here he would see all of the ways again. It was important to me that I presented myself in a certain way even though I was unable to determine what about myself Ian had been attracted to and so I might be presenting myself in a way opposite of what he would like or want or opposite of what he was attracted to.

"Are you okay? Is everything okay?" the man said.

"Yeah," I said. "I'm fine."

I was hoping the man would be satisfied with this answer. I wanted to close my eyes and open them and have the man be gone. The man leaned against the brick wall. He didn't seem to be in any particular hurry to leave.

"I just...I was driving by and saw you out here, alone, at night...I just wanted to make sure you were okay."

"I'm okay," I said. I glanced at the man's face. He looked more like a man from my small Ohio hometown than the university town I lived in presently. He had the earnestness that is indicative of a small Ohio farm town. I had dated a man like him when I was eighteen. The man, Troy, had saved up his truck driving money and bought me a gold necklace with a heart on it that said "I love you" and I had broke things off with him soon after that. I had only dated him because my best friend was dating his brother. The four of us went to see Frank Zappa and to a Monster Truck Rally and drank in a hot tub in their living room. I broke up with him on a pay phone in my dorm in Cincinnati. He'd dropped me there at the end of a weekend on his way south. It was the last time I rode in a semi. I remember he gave me too much money for a taxi because he couldn't drive the semi all the way to my dorm. I think he gave me double what it cost because he'd never taken a taxi before and I didn't correct him when he asked if it was enough.

"I can wait with you," the man said. His voice was similar to Troy's, hushed and sweet.

"Thanks," I said. "But I'm fine. I'm about ready to leave anyway."

I didn't look him in the face but kept my head down. I angled the computer away from him, careful not to allow him a glimpse of my unclothed body.

"Okay, well, bye," the man said. He was backing away but still facing me. It would have been so easy to make him love me.

"Bye," I said.

"You're sure you're okay?"

"I'm sure," I said.

"Be careful."

"I will, thanks."

I felt a great sense of relief as the man got in his car, drove past me and waved. I was glad to see him leave. It made me uncomfortable, how much he seemed to care about my welfare. I realized how easy it would have been to make him love me, and probably this was why I didn't care.

In Atlantic City I felt a sense of lightness. Maybe it was the ocean. Maybe it was being surrounded by people. I thought I would be less likely to notice if Ian didn't text me if I was surrounded by people at all times.

But Ian did text me, with more consistency than he had in weeks. I told myself it felt like the beginning again. Even though I wasn't sure what the beginning felt like anymore.

There was a Southern writer I met there for the first time. He had sent both Ian and me his book around the time we first met. I remember discussing the book cover with Ian at my house, the photograph of the author's uncle. It felt like a connection Ian and I shared: the author who wanted both of us to read his work. A validation that we belonged in the same group of artists, were thought of in the same sentence.

Now I was showing the Southern author a text from Ian as some sort of proof of something. I was bragging, showing off my closeness with the mini musical celebrity, Mr. Elusive, my own private Kurt Cobain. (I had done this the day Ian came to my house; had shown his text to another writer staying with us, the one I would later almost fall in love with. It had been the first text Ian ever sent me. "Finna take the bus.")

The Southern writer smiled (just as the writer at my house had). He was still married to his first wife. Later he would divorce her and marry a friend of mine. He was dressed head to toe in white: a white suit, white shoes, and sweating profusely.

We continued walking through the casino, on our way back to the hotel. There were ten of us staying in six rooms. Earlier we had all read in a park. No one else had come, of course. The organizer of the event didn't know anyone in Atlantic City. None of us did. We were there to drink and to meet and to sleep with one another.

We were there two nights and I remember texting with Ian for hours, sitting out on the hotel steps, smoking, and later, in bed, the covers pulled up over me so I wouldn't keep Enid awake. I didn't want her to know I was texting with Ian even though she was texting with a married man.

I never wanted to leave Atlantic City. Or maybe this is projecting.

Maybe I didn't know then, as I would know at the end of summer in New York City, that when I left the city, when I was back home, Ian would stop texting me.

"Friendship is a good place to start," Ian wrote me in an email when I got back. Which seems like a ludicrous statement to make to a woman who thought you were going to marry her the month you met. Perhaps it was the same email in which he asked me, "I don't know why you have to be so fatal all the time."

Back home after the trip, Ian was once more consistent only in his unreliability. I didn't hear from him for a day or two and then we would email and text all night. In a way I had become accustomed to the inconsistency. It felt normal. It was easier to have no expectations.

The happiness I felt in Atlantic City, texting him so frequently, felt manic by comparison. I had felt unwell. Crazed. This was how I equated happiness then: with feeling sick.

I began to write here, five years after receiving Ian's letter, that it was eerily reminiscent of Rodolphe's 'farewell' letter to Emma. I was reading *Madam Bovary* with E., who had been assigned the novel in a high school class, at the time. I had not read it before. I was intrigued by Emma. My neighbor, when I told her I was going to read the book, had said, "I hated Emma. She's just a materialistic bitch!" Later, midway through the novel, I thought how my life could easily be reduced to such a sentiment. I read Rodolphe's letter with extreme interest. It reminded, I thought, of the letter I had not read in four years. I decided Ian must have shared an inearnestness in writing his letter because it was spelled out for me in *Madam Bovary* that Rodolphe was not earnest when crafting his. I decided many things with regard to the letter Ian had written me in the two days between reading Rodolphe's and rereading Ian's. I began to feel cynically about the letter and about Ian. I made declarations to myself regarding everything I had thought and felt being a lie! I was very dramatic

in my thinking because I was thinking as one does in a novel. I was ready
to dismiss the letter Ian had written me as meaningless because Rodolphe
had put no real meaning into his to Emma and this black and white way
of thinking was far easier to handle or accept than was the greyer version,
the version I have lived with the last five years, the version in which I
don't know what to feel from one day to the next or one year to another . . . It was another shock to me then when I found I was unable to keep
to my cynicism in the face of Ian's actual words. I had thought I would
find exact similarities between Rodolph's letter and his (a part of me even
thought momentarily Ian had plagiarized parts of the letter or unwittingly
emulated it). And at first I did see vague similarities. Both men claiming
they would remember the woman, be it Emma or me, forever (Rodolphe:
"I will never forget you, believe me, and I will continue to be deeply devoted to you." Ian, "and even if absolutely nothing ever materialized, I
would not forget you ever."), both men blaming themselves for the woman's pain (Rodolphe: "I don't want to ruin your life . . . Were you aware
of the abyss into which I was drawing you, my poor angel?" Ian, "but my
ability to no longer feel anything for periods of time is shocking, even to
me still."), both men saying that a lesser woman would have allowed them
to act in a more selfish manner, without regard for the woman's feelings
(Rodolphe: "Oh, if you had been one of those women with a frivolous
heart — who certainly exist — I could have selfishly experimented without
putting you at risk." Ian: "If there were one thing I'd want you to believe,
and given what you say about belief in your letter, this should matter, it's
that from the first night we were at your house, I knew I couldn't let you
feel the agony I have brought to other people. It was a moment that matured me in a strange way..."). But there were less similarities than I had
thought and the overall mood of the letters felt somehow dissimilar . . . or
perhaps, yet again, I was unwilling to view Ian and (more importantly)
his love for me in a negative or cynical light. Even after five years, I still
wanted to believe. And the desire to believe, be it in a god or love, is inexplicable and unjustifiable. I believed because I wanted to believe. And
the next day, perhaps, I would return to disbelief and cynicism. I knew I
would likely continuously change my mind with regard to the past until
I reached a year in which I no longer thought about the past or Ian or a
year in which thinking of him bored me. But in a way, as with any religion,

thinking of him meant thinking of myself also, and so, in that way, I did not expect to become bored soon. My level of interest in myself seemed limitless. And just as some people need to concoct an invisible god to love them, above and beyond their child and spouse, so I concocted Ian.

I sit for a whole hour alone in my writing room staring at his letter. I attempt to memorize the words, to grasp the entirety of their meaning. I want to be the woman he describes at the end of the letter, the one who is "sweet" and "kind-hearted," . . . personality traits I have not felt about myself in a very long time. I fear I have become governed more of late by anxieties and fears and that my foremost characteristic is impatience. I do not like this about myself. I want to blame L. for allowing me to be this person, as though L.'s patience and kindness prohibits my own, as though only one person in a relationship can ever be kind.

Only with Eli have I retained this sweetness and kindness and patience. Only with my son am I capable of extreme acts of selflessness and unselfishness.

I could no more go back and read my letter to Ian, the one he references in his than I could go back and look at the photos I sent him.

As soon as I type this I disagree: looking at the photos would be preferable to reading the letters, a hundredfold.

I could write another whole book about L. and it would not be dissimilar to this. For instance, I wrote L. many letters that year also . . .

During the days or weeks in which my laptop was stored an hour away at my ex-husband's house, I would sometimes drive to the public library to get on one of their computers. There were four or five rows of six or seven computers and I felt a strange foreignness, as I had in the café in Mexico, seated next to people who I imagined could not afford a computer or Internet at their house, who were likely looking for jobs or to further their education. I imagined Ian judging me for thinking this way, for thinking I was better than the other people aside whom I was sitting in the public library on a Tuesday afternoon at two. I knew I was no better; that I was desperate in way I was sure they weren't; that I was behaving desperately, in a fashion my son would find humiliating were he to see me or were one of his friends, who often congregated at this library after school, to see me and to tell him. But I could no more stop myself from going to the library every other day to see if Ian had emailed me than I could burn the library down to prevent myself from doing so.

I remember texting with Ian after E. and I saw *The Godfather* in the old movie theater downtown ...

I remember texting him a photograph of E. and E.'s friend and me at a concert the night after that ... Ian replying to tease us about our taste in music.

I remember everything seeming normal for a while. 'Normal.'

almost feel like it is the best song i have written. tell me what you think.

In late September, or maybe it was early October, Eli brought Saul home with her.

I realize the first three times I wrote this I failed to mention my mental state. It was not something I thought about. I was used to thinking about my mother's mental state (as a child) and my ex husband's mental state (for the eight years we were married) and Ian's (for the year I was talking to him). But it never occurred to me to address or investigate my own. I was used to thinking myself "normal" even though I had had issues in the past with agoraphobia and panic attacks and eating disorders. Even though I dropped out of college and sat inside my apartment for two years as a nineteen and twenty year old. Even though there were nights then I believed myself to be going crazy, hearing voices, when I was afraid for my boyfriend to leave me alone . . . when I sat in a clawed tub in our apartment, telling myself to stop thinking the word "suicide."

On one of those nights, when my boyfriend did leave me alone, when he flew home to White Plains, New York to see his parents, I walked myself to the hospital emergency room on the other side of campus because I couldn't breathe, my throat was closing up, I was afraid of dying alone.

Now when I read back over Ian's emails, when I study my writing from that year, I see that I, too, was in a manic like phase. I was unable to sit still. I didn't eat or sleep much. I drank and smoked more than I was used to drinking and smoking. I drove my car four hours to see Ian four times. I drove my car six hours to see L. the same number. On nights I wasn't driving to see Ian or L. I drove in circles around my city.

I spent most of that year, 2009, feeling restless and frantic.

Maybe I was afraid of dying alone.

When I wasn't driving, I sat on my bathroom floor or curled in a ball on my closet floor.

(In previous years I had been a teetotaler. In previous years, when Eli was young, I had slept eight, nine, ten hours a night.)

I made friends of the teenagers my son brought home from school. Or I allowed them to make a friend of me. I got out of the car when Saul and Darius asked me to the night I'd intended to drop them at the movies. This was in September or October of 2009. It'd been four or five months since I'd seen Ian. I made an attempt at refusing Saul and Darius only once. I said, "No, no, I can't." I was waiting to see what my son would say. But my son did not seem to care. And so I got out of the car.

It was a movie about zombies and I sat next to Saul, eating the candy I'd bought him as he offered it to me from his hand. It was two or three hours I didn't think of Ian. It was two or three hours in which I didn't check my phone.

The second time I drove to see Ian without telling him I did not tell any of my friends either. I was bored of talking about him and embarrassed I had not yet managed to overcome my feelings.

I told my daughter because she did not yet dislike Ian and was not therefore tired of hearing me talk about him. The three of us had spent a small amount of time together. He had gone with me to her riding lesson. He had gone with the two of us to McDonald's. He had been kind with her and listened to her jokes. She was thirteen and he was twenty-six. She did not like the way I behaved with regard to him but she liked the way he behaved with regard to her. I played his songs for her and her friends and he asked for their opinions. He wanted to know if they liked his lyrics or if they thought them phony or forced. He texted her to ask these questions and she texted back. She texted him periodically over the next nine months, as did I, though neither of us would see him again. We did not know that then. She believed we would see him at some point in the future because I believed it.

A week before I stopped communicating with him altogether, he texted E. and asked her to buy me an ice cream and to say it was from him. I had texted him that morning that she and I were going to the mall. This was a year after the last time I had seen him. This was the same week he told me again he loved me. It was the first time he'd said those words in months. He said them in a text because he still refused to talk to me on the phone or to see me in person.

After I stopped communicating with him, I asked my daughter to delete his number from her phone. Or maybe I deleted it for her. It's hard to remember. The last time I checked, his songs were still on her iPod. I have not asked her to delete those. I think they are only painful for me. I think we each have our own relationship to his music. I think this is okay. I do not think we need to be in unity on everything.

By comparison, Ian, in his emails and texts, seems sound. Unshakable. Level headed. He seems, for the most part, unphased by my moods and distractions, my urgings and requests . . .

"You are being disrespectful. I am trying to work." I remember this text he sent me verbatim because it so shocked me at the time I received it, in the days after my return from Mexico. I was unused to being reprimanded. I was unused to being treated as a schoolgirl.

I stared at the words as they appeared in the screen of my phone. I lit a cigarette and went outside. I had been trying to get him to call me.

Later that evening he apologized for his shortness in a text. He did not call me. He was steadfast, unshakable.

Ian responded at some point in the evening to say that he could not see me because he was working late. He had not previously told me he was employed. He did not, of course, say where he was working or what sort of work he was doing.

I was in a hotel room in his city.

I had again driven there without warning.

His only means of controlling me was in keeping information from me.

It is possible I was the reason for his secrecy and privacy, the reason none of our mutual friends knew where he lived.

He kept information from me for seven years. Until I was no longer a threat. Until every cell in my body was new, reshaped, reformed.

no i am definitely ready for you in many ways. sadly, the way i am not ready right now is "entirely."

Once I had titled this book: *Loneliness Is an Addiction Like Any Other*.

I believed Ian equated being alone with some sort of myth of the American male or the Western artist or both.

I wanted to see myself similarly. I pushed people out of my life in a similar fashion. *I want to be Bob Dylan. Sha La La La La La La La La La Yeah.*

Americans like the cowboy . . . who rides all alone into the town, the village, with his horse and nothing else. — Henry Kissenger

I read in an interview conducted by Miranda July that before marrying her husband, she also cultivated this myth of the artist as loner. After another relationship failed she would think to herself, "Well, at least now I can paint at two in the morning again if I want to."

This was my thought, exactly, every time I broke up with L. Though how does the old joke go? Though I never did seem to write at two in the morning.

My writing desk was in my bedroom. I locked my door to keep Saul and the boys from entering. They did not like me to separate myself from them physically.

One afternoon, the boys first knocked then banged on my door. They called my name through the wall that separated my bedroom from the living room. I could not work with such distractions. The boys were jealous of my writing; jealous of the time it took me away from them. I shut down my computer and opened my door. The boys rushed in. Saul jumped on my bed. Darius began opening the drawers beneath it. Inside the drawers were photographs of Ian, letters I'd written him. I yelled at the boys to stop. I yelled sternly, as a mother yells. I had not been stern with them like this before. I had acted maternally toward them without disciplining them.

The boys stopped and ran back out of my room.

I bent down, straightened the stack of photographs and letters. Beneath them were photographs I had taken of myself and sent to Ian. I can't remember how long they remained in the drawer under my bed, how long until I tore them into small pieces and put them in the trash. Three months? Six months? a year?

Once, in early October, I left without telling them. I texted Eli from the freeway to say I was gone.

Earlier I had ordered the boys pizzas and they were eating the pizzas and listening to music and playing pool in the living room. I had felt particularly lonely that afternoon and the presence of the boys had not altered my mood as it usually did. I felt morose and bleak and as though I could not stand to be around anyone, even Darius and Saul and Eli.

I got in my car and drove an hour north on the freeway until I reached the exit of the apple orchard to which I had taken Eli when he was little. I got out of the car and walked around the grounds. There were families there — purchasing apples, walking their children down the small hill to see the goats and sheep and rabbits as I'd once done with Eli. I walked in the grass on the side of the road by the orchard. I was thinking of a song Ian liked about picking apples, how once he had told me it reminded him of me.

Across the street was advertised a corn maze and I crossed over to it, took out my phone and took a picture of the sign to send to Ian. We had been out of contact for two or three days. I don't know why I thought to send him the picture of the sign, what about it reminded me of him or I thought would appeal to him.

I stood at the entrance to the corn maze, wondering what would happen to me if I became lost. L. had led me through a corn maze once, four years earlier. I had kept my eyes closed until L. said we were at the exit.

I wasn't sure if I would close my eyes with Ian.

I can't remember if Ian texted me back about the sign but probably he didn't. I mean, probably I wouldn't.

I remember sometimes relating to the thirteen and fourteen year old girls Eli brought home from school with her. One girl in particular, Mia, was complaining to me about Saul. He was behaving with her in a way that was not dissimilar to how Ian was behaving with me: calling and texting her obsessively for a few days in a row and then not calling or texting her for days after that, and she seemed to be in a somewhat hysterical state because of the stark contrast in his behaviors.

I told her I knew how she felt, that I felt myself at times becoming hysterical too with regard to a man.

Was it cruel then of me later to encourage Saul to break things off with her completely? There was a part of me, I'll admit, that was relieved to watch someone else, someone other than myself, go through the agony of heartbreak. Even if that someone else was thirteen and I was an adult woman who had just turned forty. I think about the cruelty of deriving pleasure from the pain of another but at the same time I think of the pain I saved Mia in encouraging Saul to end it abruptly and soundly, rather than going on encouraging her intermittently, as I would allow Ian to do with me another six months.

L. came to see me in September. Or, he came to see Eli, to take her to a baseball game, and I convinced him to go to dinner with me the night before.

I ordered soup because now I was unused to eating. L. ordered a full meal. He was dating an athlete. He couldn't help rubbing it in my face. He said, "It's nice to date someone who eats."

After dinner we went to the video store. We walked around on a Friday night looking at the New Releases wall with the other couples even though we were no longer a couple. I don't think anyone noticed. I stood close to L., rested my hand on his shoulder.

Eli was spending the night at Alondra's. Saul and Darius kept texting me to ask how my date was going. I looked at my phone but didn't reply.

L. sat on the couch in the basement. The movie theme music played on a loop while I sat facing L., my mouth pushing against his. He said, "I can't kiss you because I have a girlfriend now."

Later, we slept beside one another on the futon in L.'s old office. I kept waking myself up to be in the moment, to place my hand on L.'s chest, to feel L.'s body next to mine.

In the morning I made bacon. I watched as Eli and L. readied to leave for the game. I couldn't push my mouth against L.'s because Eli was watching. I stood solemnly with my arms crossed in front of my chest because Eli was watching. L. didn't come in when he dropped Eli later after the game. She was wearing a new ball cap. My arms were still folded in front of me. I was wearing a shirt L. had left on the futon in the office.

Eli said, "Why are you wearing that shirt."

I texted L. "I love you," I said.

He didn't text back so I sent another text, "I'm wearing your shirt."

I was conflicted like this a good six months. I was actively pursuing both L. and Ian and in love with both but in different ways and for different reasons and with different expected outcomes. I saw only L., but sporadically, once every two months. I was more regularly in conversation with Ian. L. was more cautious with regard to me because with L. there was the possibility of allowing me back into his life. Ian, however, had no intention of ever allowing me into his life and so had no reason to exercise caution, nothing to fear with regard to me.

It was the first Christmas since E. was born that I didn't put up a tree or send out cards. I hadn't spoken to anyone in my family for six months.

On the 23rd of December, Eli and I left the country, flew to the Caribbean where it was 85 degrees and sunny and indistinguishable from summer. I had bought Eli an iPod because it was the easiest thing to fit in my suitcase. On Christmas morning we sat out on the patio of our hotel. I read *The New York Times* on my Kindle and drank my coffee just as I did every Sunday. I had purposely chosen a location where we would have no phone service so I wouldn't feel disappointed when Ian didn't text me. There was a review of a philosophy book in the paper that reminded me of him. It talked about a philosopher he liked and suddenly I found myself wanting to tell him about it. Instead I put on my bathing suit and went to the pool. At the pool it was any day of the year. Eli was listening to his new iPod and I was facing the water.

Later, I wouldn't ask Ian what he had done for Christmas and he wouldn't ask me. I didn't know if he was with his ex or with his family. I didn't know if he ever saw his mother or father.

If he noticed that my complexion was darker in the photographs I sent him after my return, he didn't mention it. Things seemed better between us the less we knew about each other's lives.

The morning we left for the Caribbean I had texted L. (There was no point in texting Ian.)

I had sat on my bedroom floor next to my suitcase at five in the morning. I had texted L. even though I knew he would not text back.

Recently a therapist had told me I had done enough for L., but I knew that I hadn't. I knew I could keep on doing things for years and years and it wouldn't ever be enough.

I stopped seeing the therapist after she said this.

At the end of June, Eli and I went to Peru.

In the days before I left, Ian had told me he loved me again and then a day or two after that he had texted me, "Everything is terrible."

I was at a café in Detroit with a writer friend, Marta, when I received Ian's text. I excused myself and went to the bathroom. I sat on the toilet and written on the stall door across from me were the words, "Everything will be okay."

I think these were the last words I texted Ian.

In Peru, Eli and I stayed with a host family in Cusco. We shared a small, unheated bedroom at the top of the house. Our bathroom was outside on the roof. I slept in long sleeved pajamas and sweaters. Eli slept in a twin bed beside me. There was a small metal wastebasket next to the toilet in which to dispose of toilet paper once it had been used.

Each morning we took a taxi to the other side of the city where the preschool to which we had been assigned was located. Mostly I sat beside four and five year old Peruvian boys, helped them write their alphabet so they could go outside to play. Their noses were often congested and running and I pretended not to notice, just as we pretended not to notice the bathrooms, which the other Americans — another mother and daughter — complained made them nauseous. Eli and I held our urine, ate with the children whatever they ate. The other Americans were vegetarians. They said there were tiny pieces of fish in the sauce on the rice. They said they would throw up if they swallowed any of the tiny pieces of fish. Eli and I were embarrassed and turned away from the other Americans. I asked Eli to throw the ball, to help me push the children on the swings. We were of no real help to the teachers. I knew only a handful of words in Spanish and E. knew only a few more. We could not communicate with the teachers and the teachers stood talking with one another, arms folded in front of them. The children did not talk much outside but used physical gestures that were universal. We were popular on the playground. Back inside the classroom we did our best to feel useful. I broke up fights between boys and held girls' hands. On our last day I handed out stickers and candy I had bought from a cart near our host family's house. I did not know how to ask the teacher if this was okay.

At night the host family made us dinner and left us alone to eat. We drank hot tea and took cold showers and got in our beds. We fell asleep quickly and slept ten or twelve hours. There was no insomnia in Peru. It was something about the elevation. We drank tea made with cacao leaves to counter the effect. We took a bus and then a train to Machu Picchu. People asked Eli and me if we were sisters. I felt fresh faced and clearheaded in a way I hadn't in the U.S. I did not dream in Peru and this seemed like a noticeable change also.

When I returned three weeks later there was a single text from Ian, "Elizabeth, how are you." There may have been more in the time I was out of the country. My cell phone was old and inexpensive. It often lost messages, particularly if my phone was turned off for more than one night. I did not respond to his text, but deleted it and his number from my phone.

There had been some sort of (inexplicable) change that had occurred within me in the twenty days I was gone, similar to the (inexplicable) change that had occurred within him when I had left the country a year earlier.

VOLUME ONE.

I am doing this, setting down words, just to survive, to fight off panic.

 And the picnic table is warm. If I scribble something, I am writing rather than falling apart.

—KATE MILLET,
Sita

To write is to be liberate oneself. Untrue. To write is to change nothing.

—VIOLETTE LEDUC

I was inside a bathroom stall at an art fair today and amongst the pro-lesbian and pro-woman graffiti someone had written, "I still play the things you said to me in my head" and of course I immediately thought of you. I thought to take a photograph of the graffiti and send it to you but then I remembered we haven't spoken in three years . . . I should mention that today is July 18th, 2013, in case that makes a difference.

*With this book I open my campaign against mor*ality. —Frederick Nietzsche, *Dawn of Day*

I was naked each of the last times we parted. I remember the final embraces in a pair of similarly decorated Midwestern hotel rooms, the softness of flannel against skin, the softening of our faces as we said our goodbyes; him fully clothed, backing slowly away from me, a retreat he had begun the day we met and which he now attempted to conclude as I returned to the chore in which I had immersed myself before this final encounter with his mouth: brushing my hair.

The night before I picked my daughter up from camp I took a series of photographs of myself in our kitchen and emailed them to Ian. I wore only a pair of cutoffs; my hands covered my breasts. I was fighting Ian's reduction of me to words typed into a phone or on a computer. I was reminding him I was still a flesh and blood person. I was reminding myself also. (It didn't occur to me that I didn't need reminding, that Ian was very much alive within me and that, therefore, it was likely he didn't need reminding either, that all my acts were vanity acts.)

I had purposefully not washed my hair. Ian had wanted to wash it each of the two times we were together. I was offering him a job; I was providing him an occupation.

"My hair needs washing," I wrote in the email. I was still acting as though I could coax him to me.

Why would you take the most unsympathetic aspect of religion, such as the concept of sin, and let it survive beyond religion. I don't understand this self-hatred. — *Nymphomaniac*, Volume I

There is a Minor Threat album on the wall in my basement. It belonged to Lee but it reminds me of Ian. The man on the cover has a shaved head and his head is in his hands. The man is sitting on a sidewalk or on a step or on pavement. He is wearing boots like Ian's. He is isolating himself from whatever people are outside the frame of the camera. I stare at the album cover while sitting cross-legged on the carpet in the basement where I go to smoke cigarettes and to distract myself from thinking about Ian. But the Minor Threat album, if I manage not to avoid it, continues to remind me of him; of the weekend he was here at the house; of the weekend he slept — without pillow or blanket — on this carpet on which I now sit nightly. That Sunday afternoon a group of us was maneuvering through the downtown area in an effort to find a place to eat. The night before I had found myself in Ian's lap. Now he was so far from me. There were nine or ten of us, standing in a circle on a street corner; no one could make a decision. Ian went and sat alone on the sidewalk, his back against a wall, knees raised in front of him. I remember wanting to go to him, to sit beside him. Lee was in our group also. I don't know if I was more scared of Lee or of Ian that Sunday. Maybe I was afraid of myself. Eli was with us, too — back from her father's — in a denim skirt that matched mine. I remained standing with the rest of the group. It would be another six hours before I was again alone with Ian.

"I am trying to get sober for you," was something Ian wrote me in the beginning. I never asked the obvious question. I never asked, *from what?* I never asked *are you okay? Are you well?*

All I kept asking is *when are you going to come see me? When? When?*

Ian had texted me at some point during the evening that he couldn't see me because he was working late. He had not told me previously that he had a job. I think it was more realistic to assume he couldn't see me for a whole host of other reasons (in addition to the one regarding his working late) including his living with his ex and perhaps most influential of all: the inappropriateness of my driving to see him yet again without telling him, which, at the time did not feel abnormal to me, but which, in retrospect, feels evidence of obsession bordering on a disconnect from reality, of which I have always been slightly prone. Exemplified in my writing letters to TV personalities and rock stars at various points in my life, to my perceived relationship with another author I never met, to my inability to accept that a man who had professed to love me might change his mind.

no i am definitely ready for you in many ways. sadly, the way i am not ready right now is "entirely."

I could make either list. To prove I have more in common with Ian or more in common with L. I think, historically, I have more in common with Ian. But presently my hope is to have more in common with L., though I feel guilty even saying that aloud. I feel guilty either way.

Morality, too, is a question of time, she would say with a malevolent smile, you'll see. — Gabriel Garcia Marquez, *Memories of My Melancholy Whores*

The hotel was not the hotel on the water. I had reserved a room in a less opulent hotel this time. There had been the feeling that the hotel's opulence had been in some indirect manner responsible for the loneliness I felt the last time I was in Ian's city. Consequently, noisy families roamed the hall outside my room. I had been assigned to the floor that housed the pool and, uncharacteristic of me, had gone back down to the lobby, requested to be moved. I tried to write in the new room but found the new room's quietness of equal distraction. I had forgotten to bring or had decided against bringing anything alcoholic. I had a protein bar I had brought for someone who was not I and which I did not eat. I had been unable to locate a mini bar. I sat staring at my phone but there were no new messages, or, there were no new messages of any consequence, only the one about the hurt ankle, the other about not being in the city that evening. I went to sleep as a way of filling an empty itinerary.

In the morning I gathered my belongings. I had not spread them out in the preceding hours, as was my custom when traveling. There was only the protein bar and my phone and the unopened notebook.

On the drive back a message appeared in the small window on my phone: ur crazy!

I pulled off the highway and got a hamburger in a small plastic pail. There was a toy inside. My child was too old now for toys; I disposed of the pail and the toy both at a later exit. I smoked two cigarettes along the highway; the non-menthol kind in a gold box, the kind Kurt Cobain had smoked, though that—Kurt's unintentional endorsement—was not the reason I smoked them.

The house was empty when I arrived. Eli, my child, was away at camp; a month earlier I had given Lee a check for fifty thousand dollars. Or, no, maybe I had given Lee the check two years earlier. At any rate, Lee had moved out.

Another message appeared now on my phone: I want to ravage yr ass w my -----. There was a small crack on the window screen of my phone. I could not make out the last word.

I changed into my bathing suit and went outside. I had bought the house a year before with a portion of the inheritance.

I carried a bottle of wine out with my cigarettes. I took photographs of myself in the pool and on the concrete beside it with a self-timer. Later I would attach the photographs to a message on my computer and email them to a person I had met once or twice in a city to which I did not belong, the city from which I had just returned (to Ian).

I spent the next two weeks alone in a house with panic buttons. The previous owner had installed one in every room. I had not yet decided if I should have them removed. It was possible they were a temptation more than a security.

Everyone was moving to L.A.

My ex — Lee — was dating a wheelchair Olympian.

I could not understand how they had sex. I Googled the possibilities based on a variety of variables unknown to me. I could see that friends of ours thought better of him since we had split. Dating someone with a physical handicap trumped dating a person who had inherited money. Even I understood that.

The pool behind the house was heart-shaped and the shag carpeting in the living room and basement was orange and the kitchen appliances were baby shit green. I found myself on the lookout for creepy-crawlers in the evenings. I stared at the panic buttons in the dark while smoking the cigarettes Kurt had smoked in bed in 1992.

I had loved Lee. I was pretty sure of that. I loved my child, but that was like loving myself. Only I didn't think I loved myself. I thought I loathed myself, but I wasn't sure.

I wanted to be an artist. It had not worked out for me, being a writer.

I had met Ian.

Ian was ~~a writer~~ a musician.

It had not yet worked out for me, meeting Ian.

Ian did not take photographs of himself. Perhaps he did not trust me in the manner in which I trusted him. Maybe he believed in his future notoriety to such a degree, that he was already protecting his future self's anonymity.

I remember Ian commenting on a man looking at me that day, at the restaurant to which we went with Enid for lunch. Ian had been short on cash, unable to find an ATM machine close by, and I had given him the money he had been promised for transportation costs to the festival; money he had previously refused.

"I'll pay you back," he said, though it was money I owed him, not a loan, so I could not understand why he felt the need to reimburse me.

I could see already that money was going to be an issue with Ian in a way it never had been with Lee.

He insisted on paying for my sandwich, which only made me feel worse when I couldn't eat it.

Later, at the house, he commented on the man who had looked at me.

"I didn't like it," he said. "I realized men are always going to be looking at you and I will never like it."

I felt flattered but also a sense of foreboding. I remembered feeling similarly flattered by my first husband's jealousies early on, then feeling confined by them, continuously on trial, accused.

Lee, by contrast, left me feeling unrestricted, in a way that was equally terrifying. None of this would have happened, I don't think, if I hadn't felt so unrestricted.

There is a scene with Cheryl Tiegs in *The Brown Bunny*: Cheryl Tiegs' character sits alone at a rest stop, smoking, in a mini skirt and tank top. An outfit identical to one I wore when Ian came to my house that weekend in 2009. It is easy for me to remember each outfit I have worn in Ian's presence because he allowed us so few interactions together.

– the AC/DC dress I was wearing the day we met in February at the festival in Iowa City (and later the same evening, the grey wool coat worn over a black rain coat, the rain coat unseen by Ian, the wool coat kept on in his presence)

– the denim cutoffs and tank top I wore the first night he was at my house three months later in May, the two of us spending most of the night drinking and smoking cigarettes on my front porch

– the miniskirt and tank top I wore the next day, hung over, walking around town with a large group of people, with L. and E. and Ian

– the jeans the next night, standing sober and quiet together in my driveway

– the miniskirt again the day Ian left, when he complained of a man looking at me in Panera where we went for lunch but were unable, either of us, to eat

– the jeans I wore when we met in a hotel in Ian's city the day after he left mine

– whatever I was wearing when we met at the same hotel a week after that (this is the only outfit I can not picture, perhaps because I was only wearing it such a short time, a matter of minutes); It was Ian's birthday, and the last night I saw him.

– the dress I wore the next morning, though I realize now Ian never saw me in that dress, that when he left me, alone in that hotel room, with a promise to visit me soon, I was still undressed, still brushing my hair, still unclothed.

I think that is all of them.

I think all of our real life interactions could be melded into that one rest stop scene in my head. The moment Vincent Gallo sits down next to Cheryl Tiegs at the picnic table . . . they look at each other but don't speak, or speak in inaudible whispers . . . there is unaccounted for sadness in each of their eyes . . . she holds him or he holds her. It is hard to tell who is comforting whom. There is the sense they know each other from some other time, but at the same time, there is the sense they have just met. And then Vincent gets up; pulls away. He walks with his bottle of Coca-Cola to the van and Cheryl is left alone, as she was when the scene began. After Vincent drives off, it is hard to say what has transpired between them. Just as it is hard to say what transpired between us those early months of 2009.

Maybe it is irrelevant to the rest of the movie. Perhaps it is the most important scene.

Lee did not want Ian at our house. It was three months after the festival in Iowa City at which Ian and I had met and now Lee and I were hosting a festival in ours. Several writers and musicians were going to be staying the weekend with us and I wanted Ian to be one of them. What Lee wanted or did not want did not interest me in the way that it should have. What Lee wanted was easily dismissed, while what I wanted was fought for until gotten.

Three years earlier I had wanted more time alone. I had picked out and paid for an apartment for Lee to live in nearby. Lee and I had lived together two years and now I wanted us each to have our own places to go to on the nights I wanted to be alone. Lee had never expressed a desire to be alone but agreed to stay in the apartment on the nights I decreed and to stay at the house with me the rest of the nights. I did not stop to think of why he agreed to this or if it was fair of me to ask him to do this or what he wanted or needed from me. I had read of male artists (painters and writers and actors) who had procured homes next to or across town from their wives and lovers and I wanted to be like a male artist and wanted to be treated as one. I wanted the respect given a male artist, even if that meant acting selfishly and without regard for my partner, and perhaps subconsciously, this defined what being a male artist was in my mind, and allowed me to act in such a manner I might have otherwise found abhorrent or selfish or mean. I think it's fair to say I was all of those things at the time, with regard to Lee. (And none of those things, at the time, with regard to Ian. It is clear to me now, as it was then, that Ian's wants and needs would take precedence over my own; that within our relationship, Ian would be the dominant figure, the male artist. I cannot say which is better or worse. I can only recognize a difference.)

It was hard to know what to do with a man like Lee, a man so uncomplicated, because my life prior to meeting him had been full of complications. If Lee wasn't going to provide any for me, I was going to create some for myself, out of necessity, out of not knowing how else to live.

Driving back from the hotels each of the times I stayed in Ian's city was the same whether he saw me or not. I no longer cared how I looked or smelled. I was always starving, having not eaten anything the day or night before in anticipation of seeing him. It was a four hour drive back and I would stop at a fast food restaurant an hour outside his city, get back on the highway with a paper bag containing a wrapped hamburger and fries in my lap. I ate them quickly, as I was suddenly hungrier than I'd been in days. (I was subsisting mostly then on a diet of dry cereal and protein bars and an occasional cup of fruit.) I ate everything contained within the bag and then lit a cigarette and smoked it without caring if the smoke went out the window or hovered in my hair and clothing, and smoked another one an hour later.

On the drive to see him I would be incredibly anxious, though I would refrain from eating or smoking. I did not want to smell of anything but the shampoo and soap I had used when we were together. I would pull loose strands of hair from my head instead, a nervous, almost subconscious gesture, so that by the time I arrived in his city, there would be a pile of them on the floor by my feet, and I'd have to stop on the way back to vacuum them at a gas station or car wash, where I would smoke another cigarette before pulling back on the highway, heading in the opposite direction from him, waiting for him to text me, to remind me how good I tasted if he had seen me or how crazy I was if he had not.

A few weeks later my friend Sandrine and I were having coffee in a café in town when she made the statement that she had liked me better when I was with Lee.

I avoided Sandrine for months after this.

I am aware I am not a very likable character, that in this novel Lee is most likeable, that I am only slightly more likeable, maybe, than Ian, though perhaps I am wrong even about this, and perhaps I am the least likable of all of us.

I have said many times I did not know my intentions when I invited Ian to the house. I think whenever I have said this, usually to L., but also to friends who have asked (and once to a therapist), it has felt like an honest answer because I did not know what Ian's intentions were regarding me or regarding coming to the house that weekend. We had not spoken outright of such things in the emails we had traded in the nine or ten weeks since we'd met in Iowa City. We had spoken of a boy E. was friends with who had begun in the weeks since his parents' divorce, to vomit in class. Whenever I had tried to talk about the boy with L., L. had seemed bored, had offered not many words on the subject. I know it is an unfair thing to compare, but Ian had responded with so much empathy, both for the boy and for E. who worried about her friend but also wanted him to like her.

Even after Ian arrived, I did not know his intentions. Even after he left. Especially after he left.

I don't think I ever knew Ian's intentions. And maybe Ian didn't know either. I think it is likely he did not know.

But I knew. My intentions were to make Ian love me. (If I fail at my intentions, do they still count? Do I still need to disclose them? Or can I hold them secret inside me forever?

Can I pretend not to know them when a therapist asks? What about my husband? what about my husband's father?)

Years later I was listening to a man on the radio speak. A man was talking about Lawrence of Arabia. A kindergarten teacher recalled that even as a child of seven, he had shown masochistic tendencies. The teacher said he would deprive himself one week of sleep, the next of food, the next of water. I remember Ian saying he had starved himself in high school, as something to do, to prove to himself he could. I wonder if depriving himself of me was yet another form of masochism. If each time I broke things off with L. it was my own tendencies toward masochism also (to prove to myself that I could).

I only wanted to suggest to you that self-sacrifice is a passion so overwhelming that beside it even lust and hunger are trifling. It whirls its victim to destruction in the highest affirmation of his personality. The object doesn't matter; it may be worthwhile or it may be worthless. No wine is so intoxicating, no love so shattering, no vice so compelling. When he sacrifices himself man for a moment is greater than God, for how can God, infinite and omnipotent, sacrifice himself? At best he can only sacrifice his only begotten son. — W. Somerset Maugham, *The Razor's Edge*

After Ian and I met, I stopped talking to members of my family and stopped seeing them also. At first I was merely too busy being in love with him and talking to him and thinking about him to take the time to talk to or think about anyone else. Later, after it became apparent he was not going to see me again, I lost interest in seeing anyone else as well.

Now things have gotten so returning (to my family, my hometown) would be difficult, there would be explanations and apologies to make. The longer I allow the silence on my end to continue, the harder it will be to ever open my mouth again.

WHAT A STRANGE NIGHT

It was the next night that E. was introduced to Ian. L. was hosting the event at a bar down the street from us where we often hosted such events, mixes of readings and live musical performances. E. had been made to come to them with us before many times. I made her come now to this one also. It was a Sunday night and we drove separately so I would be able to take her home early, get her ready for bed, ready for school in the morning. She had been at her father's the night before; the night I sipped champagne in my bedroom and later ended up in Ian's lap. Ian was getting coffee with another reader (the man with whom I almost fell in love). I sat at a small table with E. L. was on the other side of the bar, setting up the mikes, directing the readers and musicians. I was happy to be left alone with my child. E. had turned thirteen the week before. I was just beginning to become conscious of losing her.

We were taking turns holding the candle, pouring hot wax onto our hands. We sat, waiting for the wax to harden. We knew when we peeled it off our hands would be so soft.

Ian pulled a chair up to our table. "Do you mind if I sit with you?" he said.

I kept waiting for L. to do something, to say something.

L. was always far from me, across a room, across the bar, in the garage where I couldn't see him.

It was Ian's turn to hold the candle. Ian was making balls out of wax.

This feels like the craziest part of the whole story to me now.

It was Ian's turn to perform. We turned our chairs toward the front of the room. I could tell Eli was paying close attention. I could tell she was as enamored with Ian as I was. In a way I was sorry about this, too.

After the event was over, E. and I stood to leave. We did not linger with the others. It was already late for a Sunday evening. I didn't look for Lee. Lee had ceased to be someone I looked for. We started up the stairs. "Do you mind if I come with you?" Ian said. He was only one step behind us.

I drove us to McDonald's, ordered three cheeseburger Happy Meals.

Earlier Ian had bought a pair of plastic Dalmatians from a man on the street. "Two for a dollar."

Ian placed one of the plastic dogs on our bookshelf.

We sat side by side at the kitchen counter eating McDonald's alone in the house.

Much later, the next day or a week after that, Ian told me, "I would have been sad if you had left without me."

I don't know what Ian's intentions were.

My intentions were to make Ian love me.

I never found out what happened to the other plastic dog. 2 for a dollar.

Five years later, Ian emails me to say that this book, the one I am currently editing, the one I began as a way of communicating with Ian when I couldn't communicate with him any other way, showed him how deeply felt my emotions were.

"Even though that's not me," he will say, meaning he is not Ian or Ian is not him. And I will say, "Of course, Ian. It is fiction."

This is not me either.

It only recently occurred to me how odd my childhood was, how isolated, how lonely. I was a child without siblings, without cousins. I was accustomed to being the only child in the room. I was the only child amongst twentysomething hippies in our living room passing pizza and beers and marijuana cigarettes. I was the only child at my grandparents' house, watching adults drink Bloody Mary's and play Euchre or Bridge, talking loudly over one another, refilling glasses at a wet bar off the kitchen.

I was alone in rented farmhouses and urban apartments after school. I made myself pot pies from the freezer, cream of mushroom soup, fish sticks, boxed macaroni and cheese. I was alone in the evenings watching TV in the living room, listening to Broadway show tunes on a record player in a room outside the bathroom. I was alone when our house caught fire on a school night in seventh grade; alone the night my mother and her boyfriend were arrested for public intoxication and assault and battery for a physical fight outside the bar at which they both worked when I was sixteen.

I was alone in an apartment bedroom with a mattress on the floor when my mother came home one night that year and found me on the floor crying in the dark. "You're so weird," she said. "Why can't you be like other teenagers?" We had moved from Ohio to Arizona. I could hear the man in the apartment below us beat his wife. I could hear my mom's boyfriend breaking plant pots and furniture in the living room.

"Stay in here," my mother said, locking my door from the inside and shutting it behind her. I could hear my mother yelling and then sobbing.

Four years earlier I was alone in a bed with my mother in Ohio, her shotgun beside her on the floor by her fingertips, when another man beat at our front door, called my mother's name. I didn't understand then what a luxury it would be to have a sibling. It was always me against everyone, my memory against the memory of every adult in my world. the discounting of memories. The re-assembling of memories to better suit an adult's recollection of the situation.

I never needed an alibi but I never had any witnesses either.

Of course there had been another man, then, too; at the time I asked L. to move out. A mutual friend of L.'s and mine. Our "best friend" if such distinctions warrant clarification here — *Philip*. Nothing much ever materialized between Philip and me. A winter evening spent sitting in our coats drinking beer on my kitchen floor. Another spent drinking in the office basement. I think he may have kissed me there, though I barely remember it, cannot be certain the kiss happened or if I merely wrote it into happening in my fiction.

Soon after, L. and I got back together and Philip and his wife moved out of the country. He had been offered a better job, better pay, at a larger university. I still wrote to him and wrote stories about him for a while, until I met Ian in Iowa City, and then, very swiftly, I did not often think of Philip. I stopped writing stories about him also. Philip took notice of this, emailed me to tell me he was hurt, that he missed being my muse. I cannot recall if I replied to this email. I was fond of Philip, of course, but he had failed to be the sort of romantic figure I needed him to be.

I remember early on, a week or so after he left my house, lying on my bed texting with Ian. I remember being unable to keep up with the volume and swiftness of his texts; barely getting one replied to before another arrived. They arrived so swiftly. I was dizzied by their arrival.

It was mid June and there were screens in our windows because we did not use air conditioning. I was sprawled across my bed in cotton shorts and the top of my bathing suit. I was wiping perspiration from my upper lip with the back of my hand. I was lying on my back with my head over the edge of the bed to free my hair from my neck.

"I am going to woo you forever," Ian texted me. I was lightheaded with the historicalness of Ian's vocabulary. I was caught up in the romance of the outdated words. I did not sit and think about their meaning. I did not yet realize that one does not want to be wooed forever. That at some point what one wants is to be had, to be possessed, to be gotten. I did not know, how could I know, Ian was being quite literal in his declarations. Even in his silence I feel he is wooing me still.

How could I know on that humid June afternoon, Ian's face still clear in my mind, his mouth still a presence on my lips — four, five, six years ago now — that it is the sweetest agony, the cruelest punishment, to be wooed forever?

Lee and I had spent the six months that led up to my meeting Ian trying to decide if we should break up a final time or get married and have a child. Lee was living six hours from me in another university town. On the weekends he came home I felt torn between continuing the routine my daughter and I had established in his absence and altering it to include him. I was remembering all the times my mother had broken up with men and finally it was just she and I alone in the house. I had a hard time understanding how to make more than one person happy.

Things were so much easier the weekends I drove to see Lee. We walked to the used bookstore near his apartment, walked to get sushi.

"I push people out of my life," is something I remember Ian telling me. I took it as a warning of what not to allow him to do to me. I didn't stop to think how I pushed people out of my life, also, how I'd pushed Lee out of our house into an apartment across town. And how later I'd pushed him to apply to graduate schools in other states.

I was in the process of pushing my mother back out of my life also. There were unopened letters from her in a drawer in the kitchen. Unopened cards from my aunt and uncle too.

Twice I drove to see Ian without telling him and twice he did not see me once I arrived. Two times before that I had made the four hour drive to see him with his knowledge and each of those two times he had seen me. The two times he had seen me were a week apart and toward the beginning of our relationship, though in this case phrases such as "in the beginning" and "at the end" feel interchangeable and equally accurate, given that it seemed we were ending almost from the beginning. Even then he was somewhat reluctant to see me the second time. The night before I made the second drive I called him to let him know I was coming. It was a last minute decision on my part. I had made plans to fly to New York City for a friend's reading but had decided for reasons involving my general tiredness, and tiredness when it came to feelings of sociability in particular, not to go. It was merely coincidental that his twenty-sixth birthday fell on the same evening. We were talking on the phone about me coming for a second visit when he made the comment that I was trying to control him. The comment was disguised as a joke and we both laughed but I knew even then there was some truth to it, in his mind, at least, though I did not believe it myself. At the time I attributed a phrase like "trying to control me" as strictly a negative assessment of a situation and since I did not feel that what I was trying to do was negative in anyway, I could not accept that what I was doing was trying to control him. I have thought of this phrase many times since, however, and have come to the conclusion that if by "trying to control me" he meant I was trying to force him to see me again when he felt uncomfortable seeing me and was fearful that seeing me would result in increased feelings of anguish and heartache once we parted, then I admit he was correct in his usage of the word control and I was in fact guilty of trying to control him.

dude dont start acting like i am a criminal now.

I spent the summer driving past cornfields at dusk. I drove for an hour or more every evening. I was restless. I had nowhere to go. Ian had by then forbade me to see him. And so I drove in circles around my small town instead of driving to his much larger one. I smoked cigarettes and tossed them out the window. I wanted to toss my laptop and phone out too but resisted because I had a child. I could not afford to be so irresponsible because I had a child. I could not seriously contemplate suicide because I had a child. I could not move towns for a man because I had a child. I was acutely aware of what I could and could not do because I had a child. I could not tour with Ian or slip beneath the water in a hotel bathtub — as Sadie could — for instance, because I had a child.

Is it possible this was all a clichéd triangle love story? That he never broke things off with his ex?

I want so much more from this story. I have made it so much more in my head.

More than anything, this is a book about obsession. As a small child and young adult I had been obsessed with my mother, in the same manner I was later obsessed with Ian.

I remember a boy in my Speech class my junior year of high school asking me, after listening to the third speech in a row I'd written about my mother, if I were capable of writing about anything else. It seemed a fair, though unanswerable, question.

I'm certain Lee would like to ask a similar question now.

Early on, before I had gone to Mexico, Ian had written me in an email, "I wish you wouldn't view this as 'power.' I feel powerless around you."

It had felt like a gimmick to me then. Ian seemed to have all the power in the world, at least with regard to us, whether or not we saw one another, for instance; whether or not we talked on the phone.

But still I was invested in believing what Ian told me, if what Ian told me sounded vaguely romantic or romantic in the way young men seeming powerless with regard to young women dying of cancer in films I had seen from the '70s seemed romantic. Even though I wasn't dying of cancer.

Even though I was a healthy single mom in suburban Michigan in 2009.

Even though I was no longer what anyone would consider young.

The first time I drove to see Ian without telling him was two days after I got back from Mexico. I think of our relationship now in terms of before Mexico and after. It is the cruelest way to think.

Earlier in the day, when we met, Ian had been quiet and unassuming, taking steps backward from me when a mutual friend introduced us, so that I had to outstretch my hand for him to shake it.

Brought to the center of the train, however, Ian's posture and voice change drastically so that immediately he was in charge, in command, commanding the attention of all of us surrounding him. It was impossible to look away, to think about anything or anyone else.

Ian freestyles two songs and his lyrics seem to be marked with violence and romantic longing, self-deprecation and humor, and I find myself attracted equally to the musician and to the man, so that put together I am completely undone by both.

On the day I am writing this section, I come across this description of Sally Bowles written by Hilton Als in a review of a new production of *Cabaret* in *The New Yorker* (May 5, 2014):

"... Sally moves in with the sympathetic Cliff, then, in what feels like very little time, goes back to Max: his demeaning power over her is easier to take than Cliff's sensitivity."

I wish I could explain to you how much that line means to me. I guess you either get it or you don't: what it's like to be married to someone so sensitive, how much of a monster it can make you feel by comparison.

"i just wish you would hear me, hear me say that i am garbage becoming more garbage, and you are in a different place than me now. and i dont want to jeopardize that for you" — Ian, July, 2009

I wonder if it's true, I didn't listen. I was too caught up in an outcome and anything standing in the way of that outcome (I.e., him), was to be ignored. Only later, after I read his novels, after I read back over his emails four years later, did I begin to listen.

There is this moment in a French film I saw years ago, before I met Ian . . . I don't remember anything else about the film — the title or plot or any of the other actors — just this single moment . . . Johnny Depp is in the scene. Charlotte Gainsbourg is too. In the scene I'm talking about, Charlotte is walking alone through a large music store or bookstore, the kind they had ten or fifteen years ago but which are almost obsolete today. She approaches a listening station at which Johnny Depp is already standing. Or maybe she is there first and he approaches second. It doesn't really matter. At some point one of them is there, alone, headphones on, and then the other comes along, puts on headphones too. And they are both standing there, side by side, or maybe across from one another, listening to Radiohead's "Creep." And Johnny Depp is chewing gum and they have never met but they have this immediate, intense connection. They don't say anything to one another but just stare at each other as the song plays, until it's over. And it's one of the most erotic scenes I've ever seen in a film and it's over fairly quickly and then the two characters have no other interaction, really (until a sort of fantastical sequence at the end), they leave the store separately, go about their ways, and that sort of sums up how I feel about our relationship or love affair or whatever you want to call it, whatever it was that happened between Ian and me, whatever that was, . . .

Something I failed to mention: Lee was on that train also. I was supposed to read my poetry but I was too nervous. I was not a "larger-than-life" personality. I was timid and shy and my voice did not carry. I felt nauseous, sick to my stomach. I convinced Lee to read my poetry for me. One of the poems was about fisting a girl and I flushed when Lee read it. Another man I almost fell in love with — not Lee or Ian but another — read on the train that night also. There is nothing very special about falling in love. It would be another year before I would almost fall in love with this man. By then neither Ian nor Lee would agree to see me so I brought other men to town who would.

I would expect a "normal" person to be devastated by what happened (or didn't happen) next; by Ian's failing to meet me at the hotel that evening. But I do not remember feeling particularly devastated. Or, more accurately, I do not remember my behavior changing afterward, which is how I have come to associate a devastated person.

I remember the next night, back home in my small town, emailing and texting with Ian "as usual," in the usual manner. I don't think that if I had been truly devastated I would have continued to communicate with him in a manner normal for us or continued to communicate with him at all.

I think a devastated person would alter her behavior in such a way as for it to be noticeable to all around her, most noticeably to herself and to the person she was formally in communication with.

After I drove to see Ian and he did not see me the first time, no one noticed any significant change in my behavior, most notably, I did not notice, or Ian.

I have tried to write a physical description of Ian numerous times but each time I do so I think what I have written sounds clichéd and inaccurate and I immediately delete it. I could tell you Ian was tall or well built; how once, in the front seat of my car, I raised a hand to his chest and was surprised to find hardness where I was accustomed to finding softness. I could tell you he had the handsomeness of a 1970's actor. A dark brooding quality. But also a vulnerability, a softness, around the eyes and mouth. I could tell you he looked 'of the streets,' that his boots and clothing were well worn and 'cool.'

That comparatively I was more girl-next-door, more middle class,

It is hard to describe myself, to know how Ian viewed me that day. I think it is likely he viewed me as confident and self-assured, though I considered myself neither of those things. I was uncharacteristically wearing heels that day, which likely gave me an air of confidence I did not normally possess. I had had my hair done the day before also. My hair was uncharacteristically styled.

Years later Ian would jokingly refer to me as uptown, an uptown gossip girl, and when I asked what a tough street guy like him wanted with a soft uptown girl like me, he would say that uptown girls and street guys made the best pairs, and I couldn't help but to laugh, thinking of Billy Joel and Christie Brinkley, and the song he wrote for her. Secretly, though, I agreed with Ian, or wanted to.

Every time I return to this novel, after a week or two months or two years in which I don't work on it, I fall back in love with Ian. Or maybe I fall back in love with the story, our story. Maybe that has always been the pull. The allure. I am in love with this story in the same way I am in love with the story of Elizabeth Taylor and Richard Burton. As I am in love with the story of Marguerite Duras and her Chinese lover. As I am in love with Marilyn Monroe and Joe DiMaggio. Almost from the moment I met him, Ian remained untouchable to me. Consequently, I am always present or waking up in that agony one feels when a puppy is not allowed into your outstretched hands. If anticipation is the purest form of pleasure, I am no longer able to differentiate between agony and pleasure. I only know I am alive with wanting.

For nearly a decade, wanting Ian would be my main source of self-identification.

Later, after the train performances, the large group of us walked around the city in the snow together, and on both occasions, before and after we were on the train, I found myself staring at Ian as one does a person they have met before or seen somewhere before, on a movie screen or in a magazine, as one stares at a celebrity or a semi-famous person.

I remember Ian standing behind my chair in a bookstore later that night at another performance . . . me turning to look up at him, him smiling, making eye contact, though we did not speak to one another. (L. was beside me.) Later still, outside a bar at which a group of us had congregated, we made eye contact again, and again we did not speak to one another. (L. was beside me.) We did not speak, either of us to the other, that evening. (L. was beside me.) I waited three days, until I was back home and L. was at work, to email Ian (under the guise of wanting to interview him for a web magazine L. and I edited) to speak.

For twelve months Ian had me convinced that I was trying to control him, when what I wanted most was to feel as though he was controlling me. Now I see that he was in control all along, from the very beginning, and I had control only at the very end, in deciding the ending, the how and the when, even if it snuck up on me, even if it surprised me as much as it must have him.

Perhaps it was because his forms of control were so subtle that I failed to notice them. He did not, for instance, make outright proclamations, such as, "I do not want to see you." Or, "I am not in love with you." Or, "Stop communicating with me." Instead he said things like, "I can not see you right now." And, "I don't know how I feel." And, "I don't want to hurt you."

I suppose what I mean in saying that what I wanted most was for him to control me, was that I wanted him to take an active role in what I defined as a relationship; to tell me when to call him and when to see him and when he would see me; in other words, I wanted him to act in the manner I wanted him to act — a manner I was accustomed to men acting with regard to me — when instead he was acting in the manner he felt comfortable acting, a manner which made me uncomfortable. What I wanted was the exact opposite of what I claimed to want. I said I wanted to feel controlled by him but I did not actually like the feeling of being controlled.

I wanted to be controlled in an active way, in the way I had seen Mickey Rourke control Kim Basinger in *9½ Weeks*, for example, which was how I thought of the word "control." I wanted to be told when to eat and when to bathe and what to wear, to be blindfolded and made to do things I ostensibly did not want to do, sexually and otherwise.

Instead his form of control was more passive, more about things he didn't want me to do: he didn't want me to come to his concerts or to drive to his city or to interrupt him when he was working or rehearsing. Though, at the same time, he did not want me to stop talking to him altogether or to date other people or to have sex with my ex. He wanted my life in some sort of arrested state of development because that was the state of his life at the time and every time I protested, every time I wanted something different, he accused me of trying to control him, and in this sense maybe we were trying to control each other and both failing or succeeding, depending on how you look at it and when.

At some point that summer I sent Ian a text offering him the spare room in the basement.

He responded by saying, "That is one of the sweetest offers anyone has ever made me, but I couldn't do that. I couldn't stay with you for free."

"But I don't care about the money," I said.

"Well, I do, babe," Ian said. "I could never let you pay for anything."

It had been the same conversation when we discussed the possibility of going to dinner or a movie when he came to visit.

"But I'd rather pay than never see you," I said.

"I'm looking for a job," Ian said. "Just give me some time."

Of course we never did either. Of course Ian never came.

For years I did not look back at the emails Ian wrote me in the initial weeks before and after he came to my house. Even now, seven years later, they are painful to read. I can only read one or two before I must turn my gaze from my computer to the wall, cover my face with my hands. I am newly surprised each time by the enthusiasm contained within them.

Once a friend suggested I read back over the emails in order to remember things Ian said, to include some of those things in this book.

"I think it is important for the reader to see more of Ian on the page," she said.

"Unless the point is the book is about you," she said. "Maybe that should be the point."

Initially I did not include more of Ian on the page because I felt disloyal doing so. I only felt comfortable writing mostly about myself and a little bit about Ian. Now I feel a sense of disloyalty in making this mostly about me and leaving Ian out of it. I am torn between wanting to save all of Ian's words for myself and wanting you to understand Ian better.

Another reason I did not look at the emails for years was the fear that I would reply to them. I had to be very careful with myself, as one is near a guardrail, the fear of heights being more about the fear of wanting to jump than the fear of falling.

It seems our roles were reversed or they reversed upon our meeting. ("Our roles' as far as he who was the self-alleged bi-polar, drug-using, young man, and me the "good girl-next-door," the suburban mother, the stay-at-home mom.) He appears here the sane one, or sane in contrast to me, the one in control of his emotions. Whereas I seem to be madly clinging to him, or to an idea of him. I seem unwilling to let go. I seem a mad woman, the sort I have viewed in films, read about in books: Camille Claudel, Adele Hugo, Frances Farmer . . . with little sense of reality or an unwillingness to accept it.

I think they call this "gas-lighting."

(But who was gas-lighting whom?)

(It is equally possible I was gas-lighting myself.)

(Or is that what someone who has been gas-lighted says?)

Women are the cowards they are because they have been semi-slaves for so long. The number of women prepared to stand up for what they really think, feel, experience with a man they are in love with is still small. Most women will still run like little dogs with stones thrown at them when a man says: You are unfeminine, aggressive, you are unmanning me. It is my belief that any woman who marries or takes seriously in any way at all a man who uses this threat, deserves everything she gets. For such a man is a bully, does not know anything about the world he lives in, or about its history— men and women have taken infinite numbers of roles in the past, and do now, in different societies. So he is ignorant, or fearful about being out of step— a coward. — Doris Lessing, from her Introduction to *The Golden Notebook*, 1971

I began in the weeks after we met, more specifically, in the weeks after Lee and I split up and Ian and I failed to become anything, to drink more and to eat less. Before we met I barely drank. I went out with friends and either didn't drink or had a glass of alcohol and something with caffeine so that I was always balancing everything out. I would have Bailey's and coffee or a shot of whiskey and two Diet Cokes. I hardly ever had more than one drink of anything so that I hardly ever was more than a little tipsy. The only time I ever allowed myself to get beyond tipsy was once or twice a year, alone with Lee, to celebrate an anniversary or my birthday or his. And even then Lee would say he had never seen me really drunk. I never had a hangover. I was never sick. I was just slightly tipsier than I was at any other time.

After I met Ian and there was the break with Lee, I spent most of my time alone. In the evenings I stayed up another five hours after E. went to bed. I drank more than I'd ever drunk and things I had not previously drank in the past. I still did not like to drink around people but people were seldom around. I drank and smoked while emailing or texting Ian, or, in the periods when we were not in communication, I drank while I texted or emailed other people about him or read profiles of him online. I stayed up until two or three in the morning and then slept until seven when I got up to drive E. to school. Some of these mornings I felt myself still intoxicated from the night before. I would stand in the kitchen and eat a handful of dry cereal from the box to settle my stomach. I had never driven E. anywhere in the evenings after drinking. I had never driven myself after a glass of anything alcoholic. But these mornings I somehow felt were different. I had slept two or three or four hours. I didn't think I could technically, legally, be considered drunk. There were only a handful of mornings on which I had to remind myself to sit upright, to mind the line in the center of the road, to take deep breaths to calm my stomach. Then I would drive immediately home and sleep another three or four hours, go out for coffee, start writing. I was never technically hung over. I never vomited. The most I suffered was a slight headache.

This was the closest I came to self-destructive behavior, to aping Ian's behavior, to proving myself as much of a mess as him, even if he was, as he said, "trying to be sober for you."

I saw the ease of being the person "in power" on the few days I was the one of us to stop talking first: During the weeks I took my computer to my ex's or turned my phone off and hid it in a drawer in the back of my closet or E.'s.

I had to explain to friends I would be unable to communicate with them during these times. I would ask them to text E.'s phone if they had something important to tell me. There were only two or three people I bothered about such things. Most of the people I talked to regularly then were thirteen or fourteen years old. Mostly I saw them in the kitchen of my house. I did not need to text them.

E. and I walked through the mall arm in arm that summer and fall. We wore the same mall surf shop cutoffs, the same spaghetti strap tank tops. At home we lay around in the same lingerie store sweatpants. E. ironed my hair while we watched *Gossip Girl* in my bedroom with Saul.

The first time Saul meets me he goes home and tells his parents, "Eli's mom is twenty!"

His parents, as I envision them, are chewing their dinner. One of them, as Saul tells the story, says, "Saul, think about it. Do the math. Eli is thirteen."

I remember late one night waking to a picture Ian had texted me of a freeway overpass he was walking over on his way home from work. I remember smiling in the dark, feeling special, as one would if a rock star were texting them at four in the morning. I had this same feeling the day I met Ian. Every time we made eye contact felt like making eye contact with the lead singer of a band on stage. Every interaction thereafter felt like an interaction I was having with a famous person, even though Ian wasn't famous. I don't think I could feel any more if Ian were famous.

I remember once joking with Ian that if he gave me an address, I would mail him the notebook in which I had written notes about his songs. But for all his talk of trust, he did not trust me in the simple way you trust a person when you give them your mailing address or the names of your brothers or ex girlfriend or mom.

Later, when I showed up twice without telling him in his city, texted him from a hotel in which I was staying, I suppose he felt validated in his decision not to offer me such basic information.

It is hard to say if I would have driven there . . .

I have been tempted even now to . . .

I wish I had never seen your building. It's the things that we admire or want that enslave us, I'm not easy to bring into submission. —Ayn Rand, *The Fountainhead*

In various drafts of this novel I was surprised to find I either had or had not included parts about Lee. At one point in the creation of this novel I had included them and then in another draft I had removed them, deciding that the novel should be about Ian and that the inclusion of L. would confuse the reader or confuse me as the writer. I would not know where to stop talking about Lee, how much of my relationship with L. to offer. Maybe I was mindful of protecting Lee's privacy in the same manner I was, or pretended to be, mindful of protecting Ian's. In both cases there have been definitive times I remember saying, "No, I cannot or will not include that. That is something only between us. That is private. I must save something for real life."

I can't remember if I was talking about L. or Ian when I said that.

I think more than the issue of privacy there was, at one time at least, the under-standing that this novel was a love letter to Ian; that it began as a way of saying to him everything I felt I could not say now that we were not speaking. It was an invitation of sorts to love me (again).

I believe also that I wrote the vast majority of the initial manuscript before my feelings became complicated, when my feelings were solely about Ian, when I was reserving every part of me for him, when I still believed if I kept myself separate from everyone else in the world, he would return to me. Or if he didn't, I didn't care anyway. I would be content to remain alone. Some part of me misses that now, the liberty to be alone, the undiluted romanticism of waiting.

I remember having a conversation with Ian over the phone one night about money, about who would pay for our dinners, our movies, when Ian came to stay with me after my return from Mexico. Ian said he would not let me pay for anything. I laughed and said that was an old-fashioned attitude, outdated, ridiculous. I said I had often been the one to pay with Lee, that it never bothered Lee or me. But Ian didn't see it that way. Ian wanted to take care of me the way he thought a man should take care of a woman and if he couldn't live up to his own high standards, he wouldn't come at all. Or, at least, this is how I have interpreted what happened next.

I think I failed to realize in 2009 how much this was going to be about money or class for Ian.

The part of me that came from privilege, that is, my father's side, is also the part of me that was treated as an illegitimate child.

I was the outsider, who was not invited on family cruises or trips to Europe, about whom it was gossiped I lived in a house with a dirt floor. The reality was I lived with my mother and a succession of her boyfriends and husbands in various farmhouses with wooden floors and wood burning stoves and was the recipient of reduced school lunches. That I came from privilege — that I would one day inherit money left in a generation-skipping trust by my great-grandfather — is not something I knew or realized until I was well into my thirties, until just before I met Ian.

I remember making a point of telling Ian all this, about the reduced school lunch-es and so forth, as though it might make a difference, as though he might love me or love me more if he knew I had grown up poor.

Part of me would be unsurprised to learn Ian came from a background of privilege, that he has doctored or recreated his own back-story in the way Bob Dylan recreated his.

LAUGHING CORPSE

There were various occasions toward the end of summer and into fall in which we — Ian and I — discussed starting a magazine together. A *zine* or press of sorts. If such things still existed. "As a way of alleviating distress," Ian said.

There are mentions of the press in emails surviving from August and November, though we never got farther than naming the thing, a title Ian came up with and to which I readily agreed. I agreed with most things Ian said readily, which is the way in which L. agrees with me.

New Year's Eve I had been texting Ian and he hadn't responded.

"You're probably out at a party," I texted.

I had been down in my shower, taking photographs of myself in a white tank top and cotton underwear. My hair was still wet. I hadn't yet sent Ian the photographs.

"I'm sitting on my couch reading a book, you faggit," he said.

I smiled when I got that text. It didn't occur to me someone might be sitting on the couch reading with him or in the next room or on her way over.

I'm not saying there was.

I'm saying I'll never know.

By mid-January I was lonelier than before or I was bored with my own melancholia. I hadn't heard from Lee since Thanksgiving. Ian's texts were consistent only in the sporadic manner in which I received them. My adult friends had moved away or were acting in avoidance of me now that I was an unlikable person. I went to movies and dinners with fourteen year olds but recently I had realized I was desirous of adult company also. I decided to start a monthly reading series as a way of countering my loneliness with the importing of writers with whom I was already friends or with whom I wished to be.

The first person I invited was the man I almost fell in love with. He had been present the weekend Ian was at my house and the weekend in Iowa City in which I met Ian. He had taken the photograph of Ian and me out on my front porch and he had read on the train in Iowa City in which Ian also performed. He was tall and blond and lanky with a sweet, clumsy, boyish personality. The night of the Iowa City train reading he had come up to L. and me after and asked us to help him find his hotel. He was inebriated and could barely stand. We had walked down the sidewalk with him between us, our arms holding him up, like a threesome in a teen movie. I thought of him as a baby brother then. I continued to think of him as a baby brother in my conscience even after my subconscious had invented new roles for him.

We were at dinner the first night of his visit when he told me he had broken things off with his girlfriend of three years the night before. I was surprised by this news. I felt myself blush. It seemed impossible the news had nothing to do with me.

We had not been alone together in the four years we had known each other. We acted differently now. We were bashful and stumbled in our conversation and smiled too easily.

I drove us home and fixed us drinks. We drank seated across from one another at the table and then after a while we drank standing upright in the kitchen.

I was eating grapes, pulling them one at a time from the bunch, and he told me to stop. It took me a while to finish chewing the last grape. I was conscious of swallowing it, of the trail it was making down my throat.

He was clumsy in the kitchen also. His legs shook against mine. He pulled me like a high school boy onto the pool table. He pulled me into my bedroom, kicking the door closed with his foot, playing out some scene he had watched in movies. We undressed down to our underwear and lay pressed against each other on my bed. It felt like we were both waiting to see if more would happen.

I lay back on the pillow and he rested his cheek on my stomach. I reached down to pet his head, which was sweaty and matted. He said he had broken things off with his girlfriend of four years because she wanted to get married and have babies and he didn't want either of those things. He wanted to be a great writer.

I wanted to lay with him like this the rest of the night but he suddenly stood. His face was that of a child feeling sorry for himself. He announced he was going downstairs to sleep. I worried he would fall down the stairs. I stood and reached for his arm to help him but he shrugged it away, so I stood in my doorway, listening, until I could hear the water running in the bathroom in the basement.

The next night, after the reading and party, there was more of the same. Though because of the party he was even drunker. Earlier in the day, at a used bookstore, I had been sitting on a low stool, hidden I thought from the others, in Biography, texting back and forth with Ian, when he had walked by. He had come up from behind me and I couldn't tell if he had seen with whom I was texting, but I felt a little funny about it. I hadn't been telling Ian anything of relevance, of course, but I felt caught all the same. I had spent the evening looking forward to being alone with him and worried as the night increased that by the time everyone left, he would already be passed out. He was drinking much greater quantities of liquor than he had the previous night. I was drinking more than I usually did also. I wasn't sure what I wanted other than to feel him beneath me again.

Saul was upstairs in E.'s room. They had come to the reading with me, stayed at the party a while also. I climbed the stairs to check on them. Saul was sulking, wounded that my attentions were focused on someone other than him. Later Saul's parents pulled in the drive, and I waved goodbye to Saul from the kitchen, but he didn't see me (or pretended not to).

Finally the writer and I were left alone. This time there was no elongated flirtations or clumsy conversations, we moved right away into each other, in the kitchen, then because there were other people in the guest room, very quickly into my bedroom. It was already almost three in the morning. We were both so drunken and tired. We fell against each other, and though we were where we both wanted to be, there was an almost instant awareness of what wasn't going to happen. We lay together a short while, talking nonsense, knowing tomorrow he would fly home. After he left, I dreamed he came back, that he returned to my bedroom, that he stayed the night.

I relayed this dream to him over breakfast at Denny's the next morning.

"I think I had the same dream," he said, and already I was almost in love with him.

We talked on the way to the airport about his ex-girlfriend and about L. I told him I was trying to get back together with him. I didn't mention Ian. I never mentioned Ian to anyone anymore. I was afraid of sounding like a fool.

Before he got out of the car, he leaned over and kissed me goodbye on the mouth, which surprised me. "You and Lee will end up together," he said.

"We'll see," I said. I wasn't very sure.

I felt a little sad driving home. It's a hard thing to realize that you can't be close with everyone.

Two nights later I made a half-hearted attempt at flirting with him in an email but he did not respond the way Ian or L. would have and I felt embarrassed, slightly, at having made myself vulnerable in this small way. Though I continued to feel something like affection whenever I saw him after that. I still feel that slight sadness with regard to him, but mostly this is my own sense of loss I am feeling. I doubt he feels similarly. Most likely he does not think of me at all.

Because my car was so small, I had to rent a car each month when the writers came to town, to chauffeur them from and to the airport, to chauffeur their luggage. Sometimes I would catch one of my neighbors staring. I had offered them no explanation for Lee's absence and I offered them none now for the new car I drove every month, the strange men who sat in the passenger seat, carried wine and groceries into my house for me.

I was already the eccentric neighbor. Two summers earlier I had yelled at an older woman who lived five houses down to get off my property. Her sons were older, in the military, out of the house, and she had developed a crush of sorts on E. She called his phone and left messages, stood in the middle of the road as he passed down our street on his way home from school. She peered in our windows if we didn't answer the door, walked around the side of the house to our back porch.

In one of her voicemails she said, "It's too bad your parents are keeping us apart." She was another example of what I feared I would become when E. left home for college.

It was still summer, still warm, and the front door was open. There was only a screen door between us. I was hiding in the kitchen with E. and two of his friends; ducked down behind the counter. She rang the doorbell three times.

Suddenly, I was tired of hiding. I was bored of my meekness.

E. said I had a bad habit of steadfast politeness followed by sudden outbursts of rage.

Suddenly I stood. I let go a string of threats and obscenities through the screen door. I closed the heavy front door despite the heat. I backed away from it, rejoining E. and his friends in the kitchen. We smiled, feeling as though a war had been won, slapped palms. Feeling heroic, I opened a can of Diet Coke, leaned on the counter. I could feel my body's adrenaline. How had it manufactured itself so quickly?

Two days later the woman's husband was at my door. I had just gotten out of the shower, had a towel wrapped around my head, fingers held closed another wrapped around my body. I didn't know it was the husband knocking and knocking. I flew out of my bedroom in another outburst of rage, expecting to find his wife again at my door. Her husband was tall and bear-like. He was having his own outburst. I stood in my towels, shaking while he yelled and yelled. I closed the door and backed into by bedroom. I lay on my floor with the towels on the ground around me. I sobbed on my bedroom floor as I later would in the weeks after Ian left. I was alone and vulnerable. This was a valuable life lesson each time.

Two weeks later E. and two of his friends and I drove to Memphis crammed into my VW bug. We went to Graceland and the Civil Rights Museum and to James Dean's hometown in Indiana on the way. We stayed in the hotel with the famous ducks, watched them walk through the lobby into the fountain in the afternoon. At night I was alone in my hotel room. L. wasn't speaking to me and neither was Ian. I cried and drank from the mini bottles in my room when the boys weren't looking and walked around Memphis and joked with them when they were.

They said, "We don't like Lee. We like Ian because he smokes weed." They wanted Ian to teach them how to hot wire a car.

I don't think they liked L. because L. came to town on occasion; took me to dinner. Ian wasn't a real person. Ian was easy for them to like because he was never going to be real. At least some of us realized this.

In February, Ian texted me to ask if I'd received an email from his ex. I remember my phone buzzing and looking at it and being surprised to see his name. It was mid morning and he did not text me mid morning. He did not text me unsolicited. I had not heard from him in days.

"She found some of your pictures on my computer," Ian said. "She said she was going to email you but I doubt if she will. But I wanted to let you know just in case."

I checked my email anticipatorily for a week. I was curious about this person: what her name was, what sort of email she would write, if she would be accusatory or pretend to be looking out for my interest, if we would join forces against Ian . . . I thought I had everything to gain and nothing to lose from any form of communication with her.

It never occurred to me to think how or why she had access to his computer. Why someone who was so strong-willed and in control with me, would allow an "ex" to search his computer in this way.

After a few days I stopped looking for an unknown female name in my inbox. I was disappointed. It was one more piece of Ian I wasn't going to gain access to, another leg of detective work gone bust.

I am shocked to find upon this reading of the manuscript no mention of Thanksgiving and my drive to see Lee. Surely it was included in prior editions. Why then have I removed it here? Perhaps I moved it to Volume Two, thinking Volume One should deal only with my interactions with Ian and not be convoluted by my interactions with both men, sometimes simultaneously. Perhaps I thought the inclusion of scenes with Lee would diminish in your mind my feelings for Ian. Or vice versa. But often, for many months, they did occur simultaneously. And I cannot remember my feelings for either man diminishing.

It's hard to remember talking to Ian in March and April. He had a tendency to vanish in the weeks transitioning from summer to fall and winter to spring.

I saw him only in magazines when I bothered to look at them in bookstores or waiting rooms, an occasional Internet post.

Sometime in the spring, April or May, I was driving back from my ex-husband's house. I had made another trip to drop off my laptop or to retrieve it. Ian and I must have been in one of our more communicative periods. A night earlier I had texted him late while smoking and listening to music in my garage (someone was in my guest room). There was no one else I could text at two in the morning and expect a reply.

Now I was driving and thinking sentimentally of that moment. Ian had responded uncharacteristically swiftly. It had the feeling — that moment — of being the only two people awake on earth. (That's a dangerous thought for a lonely person to have.)

"I guess you're pretty much my best friend now," I texted him as I drove.

Again, as with the previous night in my garage, my phone swiftly alighted with a response.

"Hell yeah," it said.

I smiled and turned up the radio in the car, temporarily satisfied with this relationship I had with a person I had not seen in almost a year and who I had no plans of seeing anytime in the future.

I was supposed to do a reading in Ian's city in April or May (I forget now which). Or maybe he was supposed to do a concert (I forget now which). I remember I was going to be there for some reason. I remember us discussing the possibility of seeing one another again after nearly a year without seeing one another.

"Can you be chill?" he said.

"I don't know," I said.

He wanted to buy me an ice cream.

I was trying to be honest.

The night Ian and I were supposed to see each other I drove back to Michigan instead. I had been at L.'s the night before. I drove from L.'s town to the city in which Ian lived. I was taking someone to the airport. I was tired from the night before, from drinking and from fucking L. I checked into the same hotel I had checked into each of the times Ian had seen me. I lay on the bed coverlet in my bra and underwear and took photos of myself and sent the same photos to L. and to Ian.

I was tired and I missed E.

Philip had stayed the night previous with her so that I could drive to see L.

Ian had texted me that he wasn't feeling well.

I texted him back, "Don't worry. Driving back to Michigan now."

I pictured him staring at his phone. I pictured him eating a plate of chicken.

Two months after Ian and I stopped speaking a final time, Marta saw Ian. She was in his city for a conference. She was with her partner, Lucas, who was in my writing group and who had co-written songs with Ian. (I will never escape the people who connect me to Ian. (I have made sure of this.)) The three of them went to a liquor store and then to a park. It was the middle of summer and warm and they sat outside by the lake. At some point, Marta brought up my name. Or maybe Ian did, I can't remember how the story goes. Marta said Ian wanted to talk about me. She said he told her that everything that had gone wrong between us had been his fault.

Marta said, "Ian said he was the one who had fucked it up. Then he went behind a tree to urinate and Lucas told me not to bring you up again. Lucas was afraid of upsetting Ian or of annoying Ian, but when Ian came back, he still wanted to talk about you."

Marta was whispering as she told me this. We were standing on the back balcony of my house. L. and Lucas were standing at the bottom of the stairs by the fire. It was still summer.

Marta said, "He said there were only two women he ever truly loved, you and his mother."

I rolled my eyes. I was smoking a cigarette. I was sipping whiskey. I imagined Ian saying the same thing to other women he had dated or to their friends.

It was easier to by cynical.

It was easy to think Ian was being manipulative, knowing Marta would come back and tell me what he said.

It was possible he convinced himself of what he was saying each time he said it, like a method actor in a play or movie. Like I do when writing a novel.

Later Marta made a video of Ian and showed it to me. In the video Ian was the outgoing person he was the first night at my house. He was smiling and laughing and making jokes. Marta said she barely recognized him when she and Lucas first arrived at the park. She was expecting the sullen young loner with a mohawk she'd seen in videos and magazine photographs. "He looked more like a frat guy," she said. "His hair was all grown in and he was smiling. I walked right by him."

Ian was a method actor, just like me. Just as I am here.

Or am I lying about that, too?

For years I failed to write the most romantic part of this book because the most romantic part of this book is something that happened with Lee, rather than something that happened with Ian.

The night I drove to see Lee, the night Philip stayed at my house with Eli, I drove with another woman, a female friend of mine, the woman I was once jealous of, thinking Ian in love with her or her in love with Ian, the woman who had gone to the Buffalo conference with me, the woman who drank Bloody Mary's, the woman with breasts larger than mine. She had been at my house also. She had brought with her a Frenchman, her new boyfriend.

The Frenchman kept asking me, "Are you in love?"

I must have answered yes. I must have meant Lee. He insisted we drive to the university town in which Lee lived. He wanted to see Lee for himself, to ask him similar questions.

But Lee wasn't speaking to me. Lee had another girlfriend.

I can no longer remember if this weekend occurred slightly before or slightly after the weekend Lee and I slept together at a writer's conference in Denver.

I can no longer remember if this weekend occurred before or after I got a buffalo tattooed on my ribcage as a way of proving my return to Lee.

We drove—the three of us—myself and my female friend upfront, the Frenchman in back—to Lee's town without telling Lee we were coming.

My friend knocked on his door, convinced him to come out with us for a drink. We had no way of knowing his girlfriend was away, safely on the other side of the Atlantic. Or maybe we did know. Maybe a mutual friend had told me.

We went to the bar closest Lee's house and then to a bar farther away and then to a bar midway between.

I sat closer and closer to Lee.

The Frenchman was too tired to ask questions.

We went back to Lee's. He had invited us to spend the night.

He was helping my friend and the Frenchman inflate an air mattress in his office. I was changing into my pajamas in his bedroom. On the wall opposite the bed were a series of vignettes taped to the wall. The vignettes were pages of Lee's book. The book wasn't yet published. Lee was making edits to the pages on the wall.

I stood brushing my hair, reading the vignettes.

The vignettes seemed mostly to be about me.

The vignettes were tiny time capsules saved from the previous eight years.

After Lee returned from inflating the air mattress, I began to shut the door. Lee placed his hand in the frame. Lee said, "I don't care if they hear." Lee said, "I will never get over this anger." Lee said, "I am going to get the word 'buffalo' tattooed over my heart."

After L. and I got back together, before L. and I went to Jamaica and Vegas and Miami Beach, he broke things off with his girlfriend, a woman he had been seeing for the past year. We had slept together five times while they were dating. We had slept together at his apartment and in Denver and in my basement.

L. was walking around campus after the breakup. One of his ex-girlfriend's friends saw him and walked up to him.

"You're an asshole," she said.

L. told me this later that summer. Maybe we were in Jamaica. Maybe we were in Miami Beach.

"What did you say?" I asked him. Maybe I was standing in a pool or on the bottom of the ocean.

"I didn't say anything," he said. "She walked away."

L. was wearing mirrored sunglasses. I was adjusting my bikini top as he spoke.

He had wanted to fall in love with her.

He told me this many time: *I wanted to fall in love with her.// I don't know if I will ever get over this anger.// I am not going to reply to your texts.// We can fuck but we are not getting back together.*

I liked thinking of L. as an asshole. It is my favorite way to think of him.

VOLUME TWO.

In a sense, the addiction memoir is the simplest form of self-accounting, a grossly distended version of the curve of many people's lives: I sinned repeatedly, my sinning felt beyond my control, I hit something that felt like rock bottom, I realized I wanted to be redeemed, with the help of a divine or earthly love I was redeemed, and now I'm here to declare not only that I'm still around but that I'm better than ever, as proven by the existence of this book. The writer always gives himself some cover by suggesting that he's written this book to help other addicts or recovering addicts or their families, but even if that's obviously true, it's rarely the real point. The real point is that the book itself is the capstone of redemption, and the fact of the book retroactively justifies the addiction—and not only justifies it but renders it, in retrospect, necessary... The more skillful the resulting narrative, the better justified the addiction: the reward for having visited derangement—systematic or not—is the bounty of vital language and deep gratitude one has brought back. The takeaway, though, is that the despond has been safely deposited in the past.

—GIDEON LEWIS-KRAUS,

from a review of *White Out: The Secret Life of Heroin* by
Michael W. Clune in The New Yorker, May 28, 2013

There is no sentimental narrative here... That is both the power of the movie and also what makes it slightly uninteresting. The boring and repetitive drama of the addict, the frustrated meaninglessness of the addict's spiral, its curious lack of drama.

—BRET EASTON ELLIS,

reviewing the Amy Winehouse documentary—*Amy*—on his podcast

I made a note on a scrap of paper last week. "Asserting independence—holding onto Ian or idea of Ian."

I met with Marta yesterday to discuss this book. Or rather, discussing this book was part of why we met. Marta had things she wanted to discuss also: her affair with the married philosopher, for instance. He was the second object philosopher from Texas she had seen in a year.

"I just discovered I am a submissive," she said. "I never knew before."

(I don't immediately think of Ian here but probably I should.)

It's been three years since I've had any contact with Ian.

(Well, that's not an entirely accurate statement.)

It's been three years since I've had any contact with Ian that does not involve reading his blog for indirect messages to me and tailoring my blog accordingly to indirectly message him.

(I read Ian's blog as I imagine Letterman's stalker once watched *Late Night*. Before she broke into his house, before she threw herself in front of a train, I mean.)

But now Marta and I are talking about my manuscript, about this book about Ian. I want her opinion because she is one of the people who told me to publish it. I need to be reminded why. I am in a perpetual state of terror at the thought of publishing it.

"When I first read this book I read it in parts," Marta says. "Remember? S. was in your writing group and bringing it home and I was reading it as he brought it, a new part each month, and I was so enthralled by it and reading it made me love you so much more because before I'd seen you as this very poised, beautiful woman who was strong and intimidating and here you were on the page, so open and vulnerable and raw, and I just loved that. I think a book like this is very necessary for women and I will publicly defend it and champion it."

Even when talking to me Marta is submissive. Why hadn't I noticed before?

"Does L. know about it?"

I glance up and Marta is running a hand through her newly shorn, newly pink hair. Currently she is getting her Ph.D. in something I can't pronounce and don't understand. She has been getting a Ph.D. all the years I have known her: around four.

"No. Of course not."

"I didn't think so."

After this Marta drones on about the latest object philosopher, who she has been meeting in Louisville and New York and Chicago where he is sent to give lectures. I am nodding but not listening. She is talking about the second philosopher and I am still picturing the first. It's hard to differentiate between object philosophers, particularly when both are from Texas and married and nondescript. It is hard to envision being dominated by an academic philosopher (or by an academic, for that matter). She holds her phone out to me and there is a YouTube clip of one of the philosophers speaking on a panel. It's the same Youtube clip she sent me a link to last week that I forgot to watch. I hold the phone in my hand, smile, feign an understanding of wanting to be dominated by this man. I am already in my car driving home. I am rewriting passages of this manuscript in my head as I drive.

When did obsessive thoughts of Ian turn into obsessive thoughts of this book?

It's been three years since I received a text from Ian upon entering the
United States from South America and deleted the text.

A year since I married L...

I am forty-three. Forty-four. (Ask me again when this thing's published.)

This isn't an addiction memoir, per se. I am unwilling to share with you what parts of my life/this book are fact and what parts are fiction. I don't like to make such distinctions even for myself.

This is about this woman, this character, "Elizabeth Ellen," not me. This is what I tell myself. I am constructing a defense for the future. For L.'s parents. And everyone else. For L.

I have already used it on E. "'Elizabeth Ellen' is not me," I told him. We were standing on the curb outside the LAX airport. We were waiting on a Town Car to take us to our hotel. My eyes were hidden behind an oversized pair of sunglasses. It seemed the most opportune time to tell him.

This manuscript is about preferring Chet Baker's face in his later years—ravaged/despaired—to the face he possessed in his earlier years, in the years he was compared to James Dean. (There was so little of interest about his face then, so little to see.)

Marta was showing me YouTube videos of the philosopher speaking on various panels. I stared at them while alternately imagining Ian with a whip in his hand and me with a whip in mine. I never could get a handle on which of us was the masochist, which of us the sadist. I think you could give examples of both for either.

I think you could say my refusal to communicate with him for three years was my greatest act of sadism yet.

I cannot remember how long the period of time lasted in which I didn't think about Ian. I remember making the conscious decision not to talk to him when L. and I got back together but not talking to someone and not thinking about them are two different things.

Recently I spent two hours looking backward at Ian's blog posts and it was clear I had read every one of them going back to the month Ian and I met; going back four years; going back to the initial post in which he mentions my name:

I want Elizabeth Ellen to push me from a moving car!

Something I forgot to mention. Marta referred to this book, to the act of writing it, as "sublimation of desire." I had to look up sublimation when I got home. I was unfamiliar with the word, I had never heard the term.

Sublimation: the channeling of impulses or energies regarded as unacceptable, especially sexual desires, toward activities regarded as more socially acceptable, often creative activities.

I have begun to think of the book obsessively. I can't remember when thoughts of the book became a near constant conversation in my head. (How is this the same/different from having near constant thoughts of Ian?)

The diary taught me that it is in the moments of emotional crisis that human beings reveal themselves most accurately. I learned to choose the heightened moments because they are the moments of revelation. —Anais Nin

I had started Googling Ian's name again, as "research" for this book. I was tempted to show Marta YouTube clips of Ian singing in the same sort of small concert venues in which I had seen bands like Soundgarden and Lou Reed play back in college. He was playing a handful of music festivals over the summer. He was touring the Midwest. Each time I drove on the highway I looked into the windows of busses and vans I passed for signs of Ian.

I can't remember when obsessive thoughts of Ian turned into obsessive thoughts of this book. Or if there is a difference between obsessing over a man and obsessing over a book you're writing about a man. (One seems slightly easier to explain, to your friends/family/in-laws/husband/child.)

It was New Year's Eve 2012 when I broached the subject of the book with L. I had been procrastinating the conversation for a while. The closest I had come was mentioning my friend Enid's problem with her new boyfriend. Enid was the type of writer who wrote about herself and her relationships (in this way we were similar) and the new boyfriend had asked her not to write about him. L. and I discussed her dilemma on our walk one night. I told him Enid had so far appeased the boyfriend, agreeing she wouldn't write about him. I was trying to get a sense of L.'s reaction to the conversation, where he fell on the ethics both of the request and of the act. I was in disagreement with Enid and the new boyfriend. I thought it was a ridiculous request to make of a writer. A ridiculous request to which to adhere.

"Yeah," L. said. "I mean, I guess if he knew she was a writer and the sort of writer she is . . . "

"He told her he'd already read all of her stories before they met."

"Yeah, that's weird then."

"Like, you knew the sort of writer I was when we started talking ten years ago."

"Right."

"And when we got married it was with the agreement I could write about whatever I wanted."

"I know."

"So . . . "

L. looked confused, how I had changed the topic to myself again. He probably sensed the conversation wasn't as out of nowhere as I'd tried to make it seem. That it had been premeditated on my part, a precursor to another conversation, one we would have at some uncomfortable future date. On New Year's Eve, say. Before the start of the new year.

I'm not sure Eli understood me. The Town Car had arrived seconds after my explanation. We'd slid onto the backseat. Eli and then I. Eli had her earbuds in. We were in L.A. to tour colleges. But I wanted also for her to understand me before she left home. I didn't like thinking of my daughter out in the world, misunderstanding me.

PULLQUOTE:

I said to Marta, "My paternal grandmother told me when I was fourteen, 'Get married and have affairs on the side, like the French!'" (But my grandmother was a closeted lesbian so . . .)

When I spoke to Marta, of course, there was no parenthetical (or the parenthetical was implied). (I'm punching up my own script here.)

"I think you should make Ian a musician in Volume One and a writer in Volume Two but that E. should be a daughter throughout," Marta says. "I think the relationship between the narrator and E. is less creepy if E. is a daughter."

But this is what attracts me to alternating Eli's gender. The understanding that readers will be less accepting and "okay" with Eli being one gender than another, due to the intimacy of the relationship, though the roles, that of mother and child, do not change.

L. and I married at a bourbon distillery in Kentucky in the summer of 2011, a year after I stopped talking to Ian. I cannot remember at the time thinking of Ian. In the days leading up to or immediately following my wedding, I mean.

I married L. after nine years of telling him I didn't believe in marriage to prove to him I'd changed. I married L. as a grand gesture of proof I was over Ian even though it is clear (to both myself and to L.) now I was not over Ian. I married L. because L. loved me in the manner I knew I deserved to be loved, even if the way I deserved to be loved was in direct contrast to the way Ian had loved me, which was from a distance and in an inconsistent manner. I married L. because he made it so easy for me to love him.

I married L. and we flew from Kentucky to California, checked into an L.A. hotel made infamous by a film set within it, sat by the pool across from a young sports celebrity and his lingerie fashion model girlfriend. The young sports celebrity spent half his time at the pool standing with his back to us, on the phone with a manager or lawyer, discussing a run in with the police at his home or at a home which he had rented the previous night. The young sports celebrity was in hiding at the hotel pool and L. and I were in hiding also, if a honeymoon is a hiding of sorts, a reprieve from the Internet and the people we know on it.

We ordered food and had it delivered poolside. We ordered food and had it delivered to our room. We ordered an old film to watch on the DVD player in the living room of our hotel room. (It was a strikingly similar, if not the same, hotel room in which the main character of the aforementioned film resides during the duration of the film. The movie poster for the film—which hangs on the wall of my office, which if I turn my head to the right, is within my view currently—is a photo of the two stars of the film reclined in chairs by the pool L. and I sat by on our honeymoon.)

I do not think it was a conscious thought—that Ian would never stay at a hotel like this—but I am thinking this now and may have subconsciously thought it then. (I have fantasized many times about hiding out at a hotel such as this one with Ian even while knowing that if Ian and

I were ever to hide out in a hotel, it would be more of the one story, roadside motel variety. More the Humbert Humbert style motel than the Hollywood celebrity hotel at which L. and I stayed –almost chastely—on our honeymoon.)

Eli overhears me mentioning the manuscript to a friend or I mention it directly to her, I forget which. Either way, she is disgusted with me, with my motivations, my lack of character. "You're not going to publish that, are you?" she says. "Think of what that will do to Lee."

Vincent sits there in a flowered armchair in our living room and winces at the thought that I might put anything sentimental or romantic in the novel. He says that if the novel is about what I say it's about, there shouldn't be any intimate scenes. —Lydia Davis, *The End of the Story*

L. and I did not consummate our marriage on our wedding night. We were too drunk or too tired. Or this was what we told ourselves (I, for one, had sipped half a flute of champagne). I don't remember having sex on our honeymoon either (I know only that we did). I remember other things: driving the west coast in a rental car, touring the Hearst Castle, watching old movies in every hotel room, eating dinner in Napa, holding hands while walking to and from dinner in Napa. Every time Lee and I broke up the sex got good again—unselfconscious, animalistic, liberated—and every time we got back together, the sex was the first thing to go—to turn into a premeditated, fretted upon act, the near constant worry if either of us could get it up for the other.

I remember reading a story by Doris Lessing years ago. E. was very young, two or three. Younger even, maybe. A baby. The story is of a woman whose youngest child has gone off to school. The woman, left alone in the house, begins to feel anxious, distant from her husband. Her husband begins having affairs. The woman begins renting a hotel room in the afternoons. The same room each time. Room 19. She doesn't do anything in the room. She sits and thinks. The husband suspects her of having an affair, and, because an affair is a rational thing, whereas the woman's anxieties and distant state are irrational things, the woman admits to the affair she isn't having. Then the woman commits suicide in the hotel room.

I hated this story when I read it. I hated Doris Lessing for feeling dissatisfied with her family because at the time my family was very young and I could not imagine feeling dissatisfied. Doris Lessing reminded me of my own mother. I did not differentiate between the author of the story and the narrator. Now I see how easy it will be for the reader to hate me. Once, I mentioned to my neighbor that I was reading *Madam Bovary* and she immediately began to shit-talk Emma. She referred to her as materialistic, selfish, greedy, a bitch.

We are not yet ready to accept a dissatisfied woman. A dissatisfied woman is a reflection of all of us. Our mother/wife/sister . . . why can't we satisfy these women? Why are we not enough?

A year earlier, while still in the midst of our breakup, Lee and I had met in Denver for a writers' conference, had sex twice in one morning, had sex the same afternoon. He was seeing another woman then. I was still talking to Ian.

A month after that I was standing with my back against a wall in the early morning hours outside a casino in Vegas, L. on his knees before me, his face covered by my skirt. I had purposely not worn underwear.

A week before we had had sex in the ocean in Jamaica, beneath a common walkway through our hotel grounds, the two of us visible from a bridge overhead, my bathing suit bottoms pushed to the side.

We fucked similarly on vacations in Miami Beach and Champaign, Illinois and on an island off the coast of Washington, during this transitional period, before we officially got back together. Before he broke things off with the other woman. Before I stopped talking to Ian.

These are the last times I can remember not having to think about sex.

I spent five weeks in the fall of 2009 writing twenty-five thousand words, because Ian wasn't talking to me. It was the fastest I've ever written anything. It wasn't even really like writing. It was more like dictating a conversation. It was a conversation I was having with Ian (or with myself in Ian's absence). I entered the words into a Word document and emailed them to four or five of my closest, non-writer friends. For the most part, the response was advice regarding Ian, rather than advice regarding the words themselves. It's hard to say which I required more.

After that I didn't look at the manuscript for three years. I wrote other things: stories, mostly, stories about Ian and stories about L., also.

The summer of 2010, the summer I stopped talking to Ian, I took L. to Maine and to Montana and to Montreal. I sat beside L. on airplanes and held his hand because he refused on principle to hold mine. L. said, "We are never getting back together." L. said, "I don't know if I will ever get over this anger."

But I knew instinctively that L.'s declarations, unlike Ian's, were not to be believed. L. and I had sex in Maine and in Montana and in Montreal. L. could really get it up when he was angry. Or maybe it was that I was more responsive—more naturally seductive—when L. was angry.

I bought L. and I matching gold bands at a Tiffany's in Troy, Michigan that autumn; knelt down in the snow before him the following January on a late night walk with the dogs, pulled the Tiffany's box from my coat pocket.

My German agent says, "Make this more about story, less about reflection." But reflecting is my story.

My friend Scott says, "This is a book about loving the idea of a person."

I say to Scott, "How is that different from your love for your wife, or she for you? How is my love for L. different? how is his love for me?"

As example, of how it is not different, my husband will be surprised by many revelations made in this book, if he decides to read it. Though he has known me for thirteen years. Perhaps for thirteen years he has loved an idea of me. I surprised myself with the revelations I made while writing this book. Perhaps I have known only an idea of myself.

I went on a reading tour with Scott a week after L.'s and my one year anniversary, discussed this idea of loving an idea of a person. I couldn't tell if Scott really believed it. Something told me he did, but only because he wanted to.

I wonder how this book would be different if L. and I weren't married. My goal is to write it as though we aren't.

Oh, have I already said this?

In September a new succession of photos of Ian on tour begin showing up on the Internet, and I study them as I studied photos of Kurt Cobain in 1992.

I think how I could edit this book in a way so that L. would feel less pain also. But I know I won't.

I am writing this book as though I am not married. I am writing this book as though I do not have a father-in-law, a daughter, a son.

In September Marta mentions checking the stat counter on her blog. Marta tells me she can see the words people searched to reach it. Marta says she can see the city the person is in, the type of computer they are using. Under the table I repeatedly pinch the insides of my thighs with my thumb and forefinger while Marta is speaking. When I am home alone in my office, I use my fists to pound the outsides of my legs until the amount of physical discomfort distracts me from the shame of Ian being able to see how many times a day and for how long I look at his blog. I hate Ian for knowing this. And I hate myself for showing him. I hate myself for my weaknesses, in a similar manner to how Enid hated me for my weaknesses in the original novella (Volume One) of this book.

And then three days or a week later I give in to my shamefulness. I begin a new form of communication with Ian via my shame. I search "Ian Kaye ily" and "Ian Kaye faggit" and "Ian Kaye murder you" and click on the link to his blog when it appears. I click on the link as a way of saying hi. I click on the link as a way of saying I hate you and I love you and I wish we'd never met and I wish you were dead and I am sick and I wish I didn't love you. Every time I click on the link to his blog now I am saying each of these things. And I am still holding true to my marital vow not to talk to Ian.

A couple days later, Ian writes a new blog post. He writes, "someone got to this blog by searching the words 'murder you.' All you had to do was ask." I smile knowing Ian knows it is I who searched those words, I who want to murder him.

But no, this is out of order. Chronologically, I mean. I didn't start sending Ian messages until after I thought he was suicidal, which comes later in the book. Thirty pages or so . . . (from here.)

In answer to my father-in-law, Jack, who I know will ask...they are both me. I am both persons. The person you know, married to your son, Lee, mother to your step-grandchild, E., and the person you are reading about here in this book...

Just as some part of you has never left your high school girlfriend, the one you were forbidden, in the end, by both parents—your own and hers—to see, Jack. The one you still bring up almost every time I see you.

In October (of 2012) I send the novella to a female publisher I know. Or maybe I send it to her the previous October (2011), two months after my marriage to L. I can no longer remember . . . The female publisher says she will put it out, but she has a backlog of books. "It won't come out until 2014," she says, the year that is now at its end. Instead I will work on it another three years. Instead I will think of little else but this book and Ian through the summer of 2016.

For Thanksgiving (2012) we fly to Key West—E. and L. and I. We stay at a hotel near my mother's. We walk around the residential area on Thanksgiving morning looking for an open café, somewhere we can buy a Café Con Leche, a crepe, a croissant. E. takes photographs of everything because he is still wanting to be an 'artist.' He takes a photograph of me leaning back in my café chair, my eyes focused somewhere out of the frame.

Later in the evening we go to my mother's, and I approach my mother's husband, Curtis, at the grill, make a stab at amends. Curtis is in ill health. A year earlier he left my wedding before the reception because he was left out of a call and response of family members. All the family members on my side were female. It had never occurred to me to mention Curtis.

"I should have gone with him," my mother said. It had surprised me that she didn't.

"Your mother never put you first and so you always put Eli first, even when it is to the detriment of your relationships," my therapist said the year L. and I were broken up. I knew this was the most obvious cliché a therapist could think of to say to make me feel good about myself and bad about my mom. I knew she was talking about my relationship with L. I also knew that had I not put Eli first, I probably would have moved to the city in which Ian resided, that I still wouldn't have put L. first, that I would still be a shitty person.

A year later Curtis's leg will be amputated at the knee. A year after that he will sign a document that says, "do not resuscitate."

I won't know what to feel when this happens (when no one resuscitates). We will be sitting at a café—L. and E. and I—when E. receives a text from my mother because by my mother and I are not speaking. The fact that I won't know what to feel is the reason Curtis's name wasn't called at my wedding.

It will take years for me to stop wanting to pay my mother back for wanting to have left my wedding with Curtis. Maybe I am still paying her back now. Maybe I am incapable or unwilling of not being a shitty person.

I am listening to the radio in my car and a woman on the radio is talking about choosing between two men fifty years ago. The woman uses phrases like "months of anguish" to describe her decision making process. The woman says one of the men said, "If we don't get married, I'm going to want to go away. I'll probably go to Vietnam." A year later she was married to the other man when she got the news that the man she'd let go had died in Vietnam. 1965.

"It wasn't proper in those days to mourn an old boyfriend," the woman on the radio said. "So I bottled it up. I didn't talk to anyone about it."

Fifty years later, the woman's friend asks her when she fell out of love with Steve, the man who died in Vietnam.

"Oh," the woman told her friend. "I didn't."

I wanted to speak to the woman on the radio, to tell her it's still not proper to mourn an old boyfriend, even one who is still alive.

Lauren doesn't think I should publish this. "You have some interesting ideas in here," she says, after I send her the first hundred pages, "but I think you'll be embarrassed if you publish it. I worry on your behalf." Lauren is a writer and a filmmaker and she is currently at Sundance with another filmmaker and we are Gchatting. "Don't get me wrong," she says. "Parts of it are really compelling, and I like how you show the effects of the Internet and texting and email on modern relationships, how they've transformed this kind of relationship and the exchange of emotion . . . I'm just concerned. Why did you pull this out now? Why publish it now?"

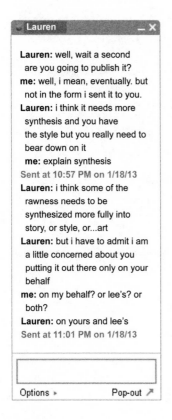

> **Lauren:** well, wait a second
> are you going to publish it?
> **me:** well, i mean, eventually. but
> not in the form i sent it to you.
> **Lauren:** i think it needs more
> synthesis and you have
> the style but you really need to
> bear down on it
> **me:** explain synthesis
> Sent at 10:57 PM on 1/18/13
> **Lauren:** i think some of the
> rawness needs to be
> synthesized more fully into
> story, or style, or...art
> **Lauren:** but i have to admit i am
> a little concerned about you
> putting it out there only on your
> behalf
> **me:** on my behalf? or lee's? or
> both?
> **Lauren:** on yours and lee's
> Sent at 11:01 PM on 1/18/13
>
> Options ▸   Pop-out ↗

I don't have an answer for Lauren but I understand the implication of her question.

I remember forwarding my mother's email to Ian. I deleted the middle section first. I could be as deft at withholding information as he. I was not ready for him to know my age or the manner in which my mother saw me: spoiled, emotionally immature, narcissistic. It was the same way I saw Ian. It seemed ridiculous for the two of us to share characteristics, particularly of the—for lack of a better word—unappealing variety.

I remember adding, "Lol. She thinks I'm stalking you!" above my mother's email and him replying, "Haha. Yeah."

I didn't bother telling my mother Ian liked to be stalked, that he invited such behavior, courted it . . .

I don't think I responded to my mother or to her email for many months after that. I have unopened letters saved somewhere . . . emails I have yet to read.

Lauren says, "What was your goal in sending your mother your book?"

And as with every question Lauren asks I reply, "I don't know."

It made me happy to read of Ian's suffering, the summer L. and I married. The night we arrived home from our honeymoon on the California coast, I poured myself a drink and went straight to Ian's blog. (L. was already in bed.) I couldn't stop smiling. It was extremely encouraging to see him so miserable. This was 2011, a year since Ian and I had last spoken.

Of course it's possible Ian's suffering had nothing to do with me. It's possible I have, like the little egomaniac I am, like the egomaniac Ian is, attached his suffering to me because I had no other attachment to Ian now.

That's not exactly true. I was not made happy by Ian's suffering but clung to it instead as some sort of evidence. I had been on a constant search for evidence of his feelings with regard to me since the day we parted in the second hotel room. I was not made happy by Ian's suffering—I was concerned, separately, about his mental health and well being—but I was made happy by the possibility his suffering was in some way tied to me because for so long I had no or little evidence that any feelings resided within him still with regard to me, and for so long I had felt alone in my suffering for him.

Lauren reiterates, "Why now? What made you take the manuscript out now?"

In July, L. and I celebrate our one year anniversary.

In August, I go on a tour of the west coast with a friend of mine who is a friend of Ian's.

In September, Ian goes on a tour through the Midwest with this same friend, and four or five others. I begin hearing gossip, seeing photographs online.

I have made sure my life is—in so many ways—inescapably tied to Ian's.

Oh, have I already said this, too?

It's hard to remember what I've said aloud, here on the page, and what I've merely repeated in my head as a mantra over the years.

There is a young writer on Ian's tour who worries me. Worries me for her possible interest in Ian as a romantic figure. I do not like sharing interests with this young woman. She is young and wears thick eyeliner and thick bangs and is either a sex addict or a drug addict or bipolar or all of the above. Did I mention she is young?

She is all of the things I am not and she is in a car with Ian.

She is in a fast food restaurant with Ian

She is in a hotel room with Ian.

On the west coast tour with Ian's friend we read in bookstores and cafes and bars. I did not drink or I drank barely. My friend bought a six pack and drank it alone in his room. I was not a lot of fun. I was waiting for our friend to mention Ian. I had disallowed myself to bring him up.

In a city in the Pacific Northwest we had a day off - no reading! My friend was still alone in his hotel room. I had the sense I should not disturb him, by which I mean I had the sense he was enjoying a reprieve from me. I wandered the streets around the hotel until I found the large bookstore for which the city is known. I wandered around the bookstore until I found the section in which Ian's books were shelved. I leaned against a shelf in the bookstore reading one. I flipped through another. There were three or four I had not read. I bought three of Ian's books and sat in the hotel lobby reading them because I could not buy Ian's books when I was with L., and I could not bring Ian's books into the house.

The next morning I left the books in my hotel room when I checked out because I did not know what else to do with them. I left the books in a stack on the desk as though I would be returning for them even though I knew I would not be returning.

I did not remember leaving the books in the room two days later when I remembered leaving my jacket in the room. I asked L. if he would mind calling the hotel about it. I was already in another state with my friend by this time. We were already almost done with our tour.

When L. picked me up at the Detroit airport three days later I asked about my jacket.

"They said they had it," L. said. "They said they found it and a stack of books left in the room."

I quieted at the mention of the books. I kept my gaze straight ahead at the highway as though the traffic and the billboards were the most inter-esting part of the drive.

L. was saying he had asked what books and they had read to him over the phone the titles or the name of the author, which was the same name for all three books. I can't remember which.

I was still quieted.

"The jacket should be here day after tomorrow," L. said. I didn't know if the books would be in the box with the jacket. I was afraid to ask L. for clarification. I imagined L. saying something like, "do what you want with the books," and the hotel person saying, "are you sure you don't want them?"

The whole imagined conversation felt painful in my imagination, for me, I mean, though also, of course, for L.

I thought: should I apologize?

But right then, right as I was wondering if I should say I was sorry, my shame turned suddenly into something more like anger. So what if I'd bought and read Ian's books in a hotel room in the Pacific Northwest? So fucking what?! They were just books, after all. I hadn't fucked Ian. Why was L. acting as though I'd fucked Ian when I'd only read his books.

We sat in silence the rest of the way home not mentioning Ian's name. We never mentioned Ian's name.

Two days later a box arrived with my name written in Sharpie on the outside. Inside was my jacket. No books. I was relieved. I felt unburdened by the removed dilemma of what to do with the books if they arrived. I hung the jacket in the closet. I imagined Ian reading my book while standing alone in a bookstore. My friend had mentioned to me on tour that Ian had a girlfriend now. To be honest, I couldn't imagine my book as something Ian would purchase either way.

I wonder how this book would be different if L. and I weren't married. My goal is to write it as though we aren't.

I'm sorry if I'm repeating myself. I am offering you a glimpse inside my head. The landscape is boring, I'm well aware. The billboards repetitious. It's the same campaign every season, the same six slogans wherever you look.

I spend much of September studying the photographs of this young woman and Ian on the Internet and crying because E. is in his senior year of high school, and soon I will be alone.

I tell myself I will not include Sadie in the book I am writing but all along I know she is already in it, already a part of this and what I am telling myself now is another lie.

Alone with L., but still . . .

I have read of what can happen to a woman when her child or children leave home. The low-level but consistent depression, which is the best case scenario. The madness that can descend like the existential fog of an early twenties breakdown, a worst case imagining.

I have seen both happen first hand.

My mother barely flinched when I left home but my mother was never that attached to me.

Nor did we ever have a 'home,' really but rather a series of rented housing units.

I remember my best friend calling me her second year of college because her mother was in the hospital. I drove my friend back to our hometown. My friend was the youngest of five. I remember standing around my friend's childhood home with my friend and her siblings, being told by one of the older girls that their mother had been unable to stop crying—she had cried nonstop for days, my friend's sister said.

I thought about that for a long time after: how you could be hospitalized for crying. How crying could become an uncontrollable act. How being unable to control your crying was evidence of madness.

My best friend's mother had always been so much more stable and reliable than mine. And look where it'd gotten her.

So far I had been able to keep my crying controlled to private moments in bathrooms and moments alone on my closet floor.

But what if there came a time when I couldn't? What then?

E. was driving now. E. had a car and E. drove herself to and from school and to and from meals with her friends. I barely saw E.'s friends anymore now that E. could drive.

A couple years after my friend's mother was hospitalized, I read of another middle-aged woman's bout with madness in a local newspaper. Or maybe it was a short segment on the local TV news.

The woman had been "found," naked in her front yard, raking rabbits. Except there weren't any rabbits.

I think the woman may have murdered someone also. Her husband or her child. I can never remember that part of the story. I can only remember the rabbits. The imaginary rabbits seemed more emblematic of madness than murder, I guess.

This novel is an attempt at self-preservation. (Have I already said this?)

There are photographs of Ian and Sadie lying across one another in the backseat of a car, sprawled out on a bed with a nineteen year old musician named Sebastian, sitting cross legged on a sidewalk, smoking, while the other members of the tour (my friend) stand behind them, a separate group . . . Sadie and Ian look drunk or high or blacked out in every picture. Sadie looks high or drunk or like she's just had sex in every picture.

I am trying to write this as if I don't have a friend named Ian. I don't know what I have anymore.

I study the photos as they pop up on social media. I bookmark the Twitters of everyone who is on tour even though I am not on Twitter. Even though Ian is not on Twitter.

I had started a new novel at the beginning of summer (one not about Ian). It wasn't going as well as I'd hoped...

Day One of tour, Sadie asks on Twitter if anyone knows where to get Xanax. Day Three Sadies asks if anyone has any Klonopin they want to trade for Xanax. Day Seven Sadie tweets, "will be at the taco bell on high st in col. at 7 if you have oxy for signed books or a blowjob. ian kaye says he will give someone a blowjob for oxy."

I imagine myself making the drive to Columbus. But first I would have to score some oxy from one of E.'s friends. I spend fifteen minutes one afternoon thinking about which one of E.'s friends could get me oxy. I spend thirty minutes thinking about the blowjob Ian Kaye would give.

One night during Ian's tour, L. asks me to play Backgammon. We set up the board in the kitchen and L. makes us Mint Juleps in glasses with etchings of buffalo on the sides—souvenirs of our Kentucky bourbon distillery wedding.

L. and I play three games of Backgammon and I am careful about my mouth during play. I am careful not to transmit my anxieties about Ian's tour to my game-play with my husband.

I turn the radio to the heavy metal station, which the DJ refers to as the "alternative rock station" and dance along to a song by Metallica.

I have won two of the three games.

The third game is unfinished.

"Come on," L. says. "It's your turn."

But I am drunk for the first time in a while and for the first time in a while I feel unconcerned with where Sadie's hands are resting (they are often out of the frame of the photographs she uploads to her blog and to Twitter). Because I am drunk I want to tell L. how unconcerned I am but some other voice that is not mine but is for some reason in my head also says not to and for some reason I giggle but adhere to what the voice is saying.

I giggle and dance around L.'s chair. I pick up my glass with the buffalo etched into the side and upend whatever liquid remains into my mouth.

I am remembering now the time I sat L. blindfolded in a chair in the middle of the kitchen. I am remembering removing articles of clothing and straddling L.'s lap. Jay Z on the radio.

I pull L. from his chair and lead him to the bedroom because E. is still out but she might come home.

I think "Ride the Lightning" but then I think, no, that is the title of an album not a song.

I double back to grab the bottle of whiskey because I want L. to be drunker than he is. We both have to be drunk now.

I feel smug for half a day after this because this is proof we are okay still or I have proven to myself we are still ok. Like getting the oil checked. Like changing the furnace filter. These are things I worry about. I need to make L. and I dental appointments. I have to remember to call about getting one of us a haircut.

I keep remembering I have one more year with E. in the house. *One more year*. The year weighs down on me like a death sentence. The worst part is knowing what is coming. If you're ever given the option, tell them you don't want to know.

I keep trying to save the new novel. I keep adding characters and taking characters away. I add a new dark, sullen teenager. I add an androgynous punk bipolar female who gives me a hard on to write. I keep adding Ian into everything I write even when I'm not writing about Ian. As soon as I recognize this, the illusion no longer works for me. I can no longer get it up for the novel. I keep coming back to this manuscript. One way or another, I keep coming back.

After the tour is over, Sadie posts a "drug video" of herself doing coke in a hotel room with Sebastian and Ian. I begin to see the video reposted on other blogs. My friends text me to tell me they've seen the video linked to on Twitter.

I wait for L. to go to work so I can watch the video while alone in the house. I watch it multiple times, studying Ian's and Sadie's interactions for subtle signs that they were fucking. I study Sadie's and Sebastian's interactions for any signs that they are fucking.

I masturbate while crying while watching the video while L. is at work and E. is at school. I cry while alone in my bathroom thinking of Ian and Sadie doing cocaine and fucking.

I masturbate while watching Ian's face while he watches Sadie snort a line off of Sebastian's stomach. I masturbate while watching Ian adjust his cock while watching Sadie snort a line bent over a toilet lid. I masturbate while watching Sebastian snort a line off Ian's ass. I come, crying, while watching Ian snort a line of cocaine off a plant frond.

I am conscious of my (in)ability to stop crying. I am terrified of losing control with regard to my crying. I stop masturbating if I think there is a chance I won't stop crying. I won't let myself come if I can't stop crying.

I've barely seen E. this week.

I miss the days in which Eli and Saul and I were inseparable.

But, no. Wait. That's not true. I've seen E. every day after school. I had dinner at the mall with E. last night. (But we never see Saul. E. won't let us see Saul for reasons I'll go into later, for reasons which resemble L.'s provision that I not speak with Ian.) We discussed out-of-state tuition. I know I am already projecting onto a time when I won't see E. I am becoming Othello-like in my wish for this whole two year build up to E. leaving to just be over with already. Just leave already! (It is possible this is how Ian felt about me three years ago. Or, more accurately, how he felt about himself with regard to me. Just leave her! Just leave her already! The agony of when he would leave me must have been killing him, which is why ultimately I had to be the one of us to do it.)

In the early evening L. comes home from campus.

"How were classes?" I say. It is Wednesday so I haven't made dinner. I only make dinner on Wednesdays. The rest of the days each of us—L. and E. and I—fend for ourselves from whatever we can find in the refrigerator or freezer, whatever we bring into the house with us from places that assemble food items with slices of bread or tortillas.

L. is unwrapping a cellophane bag inside which is an assembled food item. I take a bite of the assembled food item while waiting for L. to answer. We have been married a year but we have known each other for nine. We have broken up and gotten back together two times in nine years. Breaking up seems like the only healthy way to maintain a long term relationship. People get divorced because they're afraid to break up. We had sex three days ago so we won't have sex tonight.

"They went pretty well," L. says, a bite of assembled bread product in his mouth.

"Would you like a glass of water," I say.

I get glasses of water any day of the week.

"Sure," L. says.

I get L. a glass of water as though I am making him dinner and L. is appropriately appreciative.

"Thank you," L. says, smiling up at me from his cellophane spread meal.

"You're welcome," I say, sitting smugly across from him, waiting to hear more about his day.

A couple days later, Sadie posts another tour video. Ian is in the background of the video and until the last ten seconds he and Sadie do not make eye contact. Until the last ten seconds I feel safe and my breathing is easy. I do not feel like I need ten cigarettes or to fingernail back the skin on my wrist. Then, just before the video ends, Sadie turns back to look at Ian and Ian's face changes, softens, as it did years before when he looked at me in a pair of overpriced hotel rooms. He holds a beer out to her and she reaches to take it and suddenly I feel nauseous. Every time I watch the video I feel sick during the last ten seconds. I think about how I wouldn't be feeling this way if the video had been cut by ten seconds.

I think how I could edit this book in a way so that L. would feel less nauseous also. But I know I won't.

"Who put the Led Zeppelin album in the Nirvana case?" I remember asking Ian after he left my house that weekend in May of 2009. I had been looking for the CD for three days.

"I did," he laughed. It was one of our hours long, nightly phone calls. Before I left for Mexico (and everything changed).

In the videos Sadie made on tour, Ian is not laughing. I left the Led Zeppelin CD in the Nirvana case for a long time. For a long time I left things as they'd been when a man was in my house for three days in May of 2009. I keep searching through Sadie's photos and videos to find an image of Ian laughing. I can't tell if I am happy or sad when I don't find one.

I'm not sure E. believed me. The Town Car had arrived seconds after my explanation. We'd slid onto the backseat. E. and then I. E. had his earbuds in. We were in L.A. to tour colleges together. But I wanted also for him to understand me before he left home. I didn't like thinking of my son out in the world, misunderstanding me.

For a while, E. studies photography. He finds an old camera of mine somewhere in a box in the basement and teaches himself to use it. All summer he is taking photographs of us and his friends and passersby downtown and on campus. I ask him to shoot a series of photographs of me "artistically" mowing the lawn and "artistically" checking the mail, but we fight over every minor detail. He seems unable to capture me in anything but the most unflattering light, the most uncompelling pose.

"Never mind, I'll do it myself later," I say. I don't think before I say this. I rarely think before I say something to L. or to E. Later I wonder if I would be a different person with Ian. Or if I would end up being the same bitch with him too.

I go to the store to buy flowers for E. I leave them in a vase on the desk in her room. I leave a note saying I am sorry. I write, "Sorry your mother is such a B-I-T-C-H!"

I end up saying I'm sorry a lot to E. and to L. Less to E. because she is less likely to accept my apology. By which I mean I try to fuck up less with E. I try to keep my shit together more for her.

A day after Sadie posts the "drug video," Ian writes a blog post that some people interpret as a potential suicide note. I start seeing the post reproduced all over social media and in web articles about Ian. The note reads as if written by someone at the tail end of a weeklong drug binge, because most likely it was written by someone at the end of a drug binge. It does not mention Sadie, thank god. It reads like a confession. It details everything horrible that happened on tour: Ian nodding off at readings, Ian vomiting at readings, Ian hurting people he cares about, Ian being a barely functioning human being. It does not mention Sadie.

Within twelve hours there are over four hundred comments below the post; most are words of encouragement to "keep going;" a couple advocate ending one's life. There are a couple comments from Sadie.

I think about adding a comment "anonymously" but I cannot bring myself to anonymity with regard to Ian.

I consider emailing Ian but there is my implied or stated (I cannot for the life of me remember which and does it matter) marital promise to L. that I won't contact Ian. I cry because I am so worried about Ian but at the same time I am trying to be a better person for L., I am trying to be a good wife. I am trying to be the sort of wife Ian would want me to be.

I study the words I wrote three and a half years ago in a book about Ian. I think about the person I knew and compare it to the one being written about online currently. I consider the fact both are illusions of a person.

I read an article in a weekly magazine about a young woman, a freshman in college, who committed suicide by jumping off a nine story parking structure. She had been an honor's student, a track star, popular, "beloved."

In her suicide note to her family she wrote, "I'm sorry. I'm sorry. I'm sorry. I don't know who I am anymore. I don't know who I am."

I am so committed to L. and to our marriage in this moment that I don't consider Ian's state of mind. Or I don't consider it as something I might have a positive effect on. Or I don't consider it as something worth breaking my (implied or stated) promise to L. to try to positively effect.

I don't know who I am anymore. I don't know who I am ...

Instead I email two or three of my friends who are also friends of Ian's in order to ask if he is okay. Instead I sit alone in a room editing the words I wrote about Ian three and a half years ago. Instead I masturbate while editing words I wrote about Ian three and a half years ago while E. and L. are absent from the house.

Instead I begin to feel in competition with Sadie for which one of us can be more destructive in our personal lives and in our writing (as a way of attracting Ian's attention/proving ourselves to Ian).

(Once Ian said to me, "You are slightly less crazy than I am but it fluctuates depending on the day," and I smiled widely; I chose to interpret this as "the biggest compliment he could give me.")

I was limited due to my role as "mother." I did not have a long list of actions I could take (due to this lifelong role and my dedication to honoring it).

I could not, for instance, lie down in a bathtub in a hotel in Beverly Hills (as was my fantasy version of how I would win).

It was obvious Sadie was without real competition.

Sadie's only real competition was in my head (and here, in my writing, which may or may not be the same thing).

Instead I wait two months and send my book about Ian to a friend of Ian's.

Instead I check Ian's blog twice a day. Check Sadie's social media accounts three or four times a day. Check the social media accounts of anyone else related to Ian or to Sadie twice a day.

Instead I take photographs of myself late at night when no one else is awake and post them to Tumblr for Ian to see. Instead I write Tumblr posts that are seemingly directed to no one but which are obviously/secretly directed to Ian.

I never mention I am married in my Tumblr posts and L. follows and unfollows me on a regular basis over the next nine months because of this (and other reasons).

Instead I go with L. and E. and E.'s new girlfriend Meg (who is the reason we can't see Saul) to cider mills and to haunted houses and to apple festivals, knowing soon E. will no longer be here for such activities. Knowing next year it will be just L. and me in a four bedroom house, that I will preserve E.'s room as he left it in order to tempt him to return. The rest of my life will be dedicated to tempting my son to return home, to preserving a home exactly as he left it. (To wondering when it will be okay again for me to talk to Saul.)

Or I will burn down this house. (Search for Ian.)

It remains to be seen. What path I am yet to take. Lauren asks what path I think I will take. We are Gchatting again and I am talking about the possibility of burning the house down. I am speaking about the possibility of searching for Ian. I am speaking theoretically but Lauren has to take me seriously, like a cop or a psychiatric doctor. Lauren must evaluate everything I tell her as though it is a possible threat I will follow through on.

I wonder how this book would be different if L. ever took himself seriously as an artist or writer.

The more interesting question would seem to be, why does Lauren continue to ask me unanswerable questions.

Another interesting question: why is Lauren always asking me questions about my life while avoiding questions about her own. Why, for instance, did I not know until two months after they had broken up, she was seeing the famous TV actor? It would seem Lauren does not trust me though have I ever been anything but trustworthy with regard to her? I never, for instance, told anyone who her first book was about until after she spurned me . . . and by then, no one really seemed interested anyway. The man had failed to become someone about whom people are willing to gossip. He still has not left his wife. This is either the most interesting or most uninteresting thing about him. I forgot to ask Lauren before we stopped talking.

It just now occurred to me how closely Lauren's lack of trust, lack of transparency with me, resembles Ian's. I had never been invited inside either of their apartments (while each had been in my house), though Lauren had at least given me the address for purpose of me sending her presents and letters.

A couple months after his tour with Ian, our mutual friend sends me a manuscript called *Boys & Drugs* written by a new woman he is seeing. I am reluctant to open it. The title bores me. But also it intrigues me. I worry my friend will expect me to publish this book which is written by a woman he is hoping to fuck or has already fucked and wants to keep fucking. I worry his good sense is colored by his desire. I tell myself I will read the first page only. If that is, in fact, the case; meaning, if my friend's sense is impaired by his carnality. I am in bed when I open the manuscript and I don't get out of bed until I have finished it. I finish it and immediately I begin to sob. I sob because the book is about being young and being in love and being a drug addict and being in love with a drug addict and doing drugs with the person you love. I sob because I cannot be either: young or a drug addict, and I want to be both for Ian.

I sob because Sadie is both of these things.

I cannot be either for Ian and Sadie is both, and so many women are both.

Notes I typed into my phone last night:

In some ways, I am more miserable in my marriage, in my contentment with L., than I was in my misery with Ian; I have issues with anxiety and hypochondria and weight gain and loneliness and melancholia and depression I don't think I had when I was alone and heartbroken in 2009. We need these dramas to distract us from the larger drama that is a lack of meaning in life, a lack of reason for being alive … those of us like L., who are able to not contemplate these questions, do not need distractions; the rest of us need everything. I have too much time now in which to think. In my sobriety. In my inactivity with regard to Ian. In my easiness with L.

Why is repression and quiet discontent equal to 'goodness' or success in modern civilization/culture.—Dan Savage, *Playboy*

Every time I get a voicemail now I am sure Ian is dead. It was the same in the spring of '94, every time a song by Nirvana came on the radio . . .

I send the document to Horatio at three in the afternoon on a Wednesday in late November and the next day at two when I check my email there is already a reply.

Too soon, I think, and I close out of my email. I shut down my computer. I walk around the house seeing what there is that can be cleaned. I consider making a meal for L. even though it is not Wednesday. Even though there is still leftover meatloaf in the fridge.

Horatio publishes books by men, mostly. Young, male writers whose books are labeled by reviewers and critics as nihilistic and masochistic.

I explain to Lauren that I sent Horatio the manuscript "on a whim."

"'On a whim?'" Lauren says. "You sent one of Ian's closest friends—who is a book publisher—your manuscript—which is a book about Ian—'on a whim'?"

I stare at the email but don't open it. I wait until L. has had his drink and we have watched a movie and he has gone to bed. I pour myself a drink and sip it while answering other emails. I go downstairs into the basement and smoke a cigarette while listening to music on my iPod as I once did while texting with Ian. I don't know why I don't drink with L., why I wait to drink alone.

I don't have an answer for Lauren but I understand the implication of her question. (Have I already said this too?)

I come back upstairs, ready to burn the inside of my elbow with the next cigarette if things don't go well for me tonight (as I once did when things didn't go well with Ian).

Horato's email is long. I try to skim it for overall meaning, then give up and return to the top, my comprehension weakened by the whiskey.

"It's been a long time since I've read a book in one evening."

Horatio makes a comparison between my book and *Hunger* by Knut Hamsen, a book Philip gave me once, when I still thought myself in love with him.

Of course I never read the book. Or I skimmed it the day it was presented to me and then very quickly thereafter placed it on a shelf with other books gifted me or recommended to me by Philip.

I wonder what Philip would have to say about the comparison.

I think Ian would say, "Ha ha."

I remember when I was getting married to L. or newly married to L., Philip said to me in an email, "You are about to become a bored housewife."

What I like most about Philip is what I like most about Ian: an uncanny ability to uncover my faults and hypocrisies, a willingness to do so.

"How soon would you be willing to publish this?" Horatio wants to know.

He tells me I have perfectly captured heartache and anguish.

He says, "When can we Skype about our publishing procedures?"

I sit in the basement smoking and listening to music and trying to envision Ian Skyping.

I try to envision Ian doing anything other than coke and Sadie.

I try to imagine myself publishing this while Ian and L. are still alive.

Three weeks after posting the suicide blog post, there was a new post from Ian. I can't remember what it said or what it said was unimportant and the only thing important was that Ian had posted it.

The only thing important was Ian was not dead (yet).

The only thing important was Ian was updating his blog again, which gave my day a purpose, something to look forward to, in the loosest definition of the word: an occupation. I remembered reading a book about heroin; the author stating the best thing about the addiction was knowing how her day would unfold—every day. I think of my days similarly now.

The only thing important was that Ian had not (yet) died not knowing I still loved him.

HAHA! (This is what I imagine Ian saying out loud while reading the above sentence.)

The next afternoon Horatio sends me an email in which he implies knowing who the book is about. Later I will think "but it's about me."

Horatio says he must know if he is to publish the book.

I email him back, confirming his suspicions. I say Ian's name first so he doesn't have to.

"May I send Ian the manuscript?" Horatio asks in a follow up email. Later Lauren will ask me why I was so quick to agree. "I don't know," I will say. (I will get good at this, at not knowing, something I have learned from L.)

For the next two days, everywhere I go, whatever I am doing, I picture Ian reading the book, though the picture is foggy. I cannot envision anything but Ian. Everything surrounding him, his location, the room he is in, whoever else is in the room with him, is out of focus, the same as it was three years ago. The same as it will be next year, the year after that . . .

"Maybe this is why you sent it to Horatio in the first place," Lauren says, meaning so Ian would end up reading it, and I don't disagree. I have changed tactics: gone from repeating the phrase 'I don't know' to remaining silent. Neither seems to have much of an effect on Lauren. Lauren is secure in her theories. She does not seem to need me to confirm or deny them.

But of course she is right. I have said all along that I wrote the book for Ian, as a way of communicating with him when he would not communicate with me. As I way of unburdening myself on the page because he would not allow me to unburden myself onto him.

Lauren says, "Letting go of someone is a lifelong process."

This is my problem . . . I don't know how to let go.

The next few days I sit upstairs in my office with the manuscript open on my computer and stare at the words I wrote three years ago. I try to read them as though for the first time, to read them as Ian will read them.

Maybe I want Ian's approval, is what Lauren is implying, and she is correct, Ian's approval is something I want. I have never sought L's approval because L.'s approval was something always given me. But now I'm not so sure about that, either. I have begun to awake in the night, my stomach worried.

It is impossible for me to predict whether Ian will approve or disapprove. It is impossible for me to predict Ian's reaction in any situation.

I could never figure out if Ian would respond humorously or angrily or romantically or dejectedly to anything I said until I'd said it, and very often his reaction would be the opposite of what I guessed it would be.

By contrast, L. has seemingly one reaction to everything I say and it is something along the lines of "whatever," but in a less sarcastic tone than you are imagining. (But that's not really right, either, or I wouldn't now be waking in the middle of the night with a stomachache, with my mouth dry, with a new sense of dread I lazily refer to as terror.)

Admittedly, I am only offering you the slightest glimpse into my marriage. I am giving you, for the most part, the shit. (I decide what I'm comfortable giving you.) (I'm the villain/hero of this book.)

I remember sending Ian a couple passages of the novel early on; what were once the first two pages. He replied only with suggestions for edits. He said nothing about what I had written in a general sense, or in the sense that it pertained to us or to him.

Salvaged text from another version of this novel:

Ian does not write about women. Ian writes about himself, his self-mythology, himself as loner, as renegade, as drifter.

This is another reason I am conflicted about the writing of this novel, or about the publishing of it, or both. I do not want to add to the canon of books about men authored by women.

Is this a biography (of Ian) in disguise?

Am I now Ian's (unofficial) biographer?

When will men start writing novels about us?

When will I be worthy of being the subject of a novel (or of a poem or of a song)?

I think that if L. wrote a novel about me/us it could be viewed as a biography of sorts. But L. would be even less likely to write a novel about us/me.

Men are ashamed to write such novels. Why aren't we women ashamed?

Why are we not the heroes of our books?

Is it that we do we not deem ourselves interesting enough?

What makes Ian believe he is so interesting?

The same thing that makes me believe it, I suppose.

Hey, I'm the hero here!

Suddenly it is Christmas. I catch E. and his girlfriend Meg having sex in the basement. Meg and all her glorious blonde trusses partially obscuring her perfect size C tits. I was glad L. wasn't the one to find them. Even more so: Ian. (E. was merely the furniture on which Meg was sitting.) (Married to Ian I would fear every teen girl E. brought home in the same way I fear Sadie, in the same way I fear every young woman who considers herself a 'fan,' in the same way I fear the female names who comment on Ian's blog.)

Poor Meg hid in the corner beside the couch. I laughed and pulled her out. E. was unembarrassed; gloating, practically.

Tonight the four of us are at dinner in a downtown restaurant near campus. After which we will pick a tree from the same parking lot in which we have picked a tree for ten years. Meg and E. will decorate it at home and after that we will return to the scene of the crime, sit on the couch on which I found them, Meg astride my son. Meg had misread my emotions. I had been jealous not angry. I could only envision Ian on the floor beneath the coffee table, sleeping. I had no vision of him on the couch beneath me.

L. and I play Gin and sip whiskey as E. drives Meg home. I am thinking of the Norman Mailer quote about affairs occurring when life gets "too safe." I am leaning over L.'s side of the bed, kissing his cheek.

Later there will be a new email from Horatio. "Ian asked me to ask you to email him at your convenience," it will say. It will go on to provide me with an email address, the same email address I used for twelve months to divulge my feelings of attraction and eroticism, worthlessness and despair. The same email address to which I sent photographs of myself nude and in bathing suits and lingerie, with my dogs and cats and E. The same email address I used to attach ten page letters written at four in the morning.

I will sit and stare, dumbfounded, at the email in which Horatio asks me to do this thing I cannot do.

I will sit on the couch in the basement where earlier my son sat, his girlfriend astride him, and cry silently and masturbate silently and feel sorry for myself, while cursing the institution of marriage, while cursing the cultural pressures for monogamy, while cursing myself for going along with a culture of repression and with allowing myself to be made to feel bad about loving more than one person and for allowing myself to listen to Lauren. I will hate L. for not fucking me, and hate Ian for the same reason, and hate myself for being so unfuckable and hate everyone over the age of twenty-one for being similarly unfuckable and/or for not fucking.

But I will not email Ian.

I will not text Saul, either.

It is probable, I hypothesize, Ian wants nothing more than to control my writing. This is what I am thinking two hours later, drink in hand, cigarette burning in my mouth. "He doesn't want to tell me anything of real consequence," I say under my breath, breathing smoke out with the words.

Ian hasn't told me anything of consequence since the day we met in Iowa when he told me his name. And even that turned out to be false, a pseudonym, fake.

I can no longer remember if it is an agreement L. and I made out loud or one that was implicit at our wedding. "I can write what I want, but I will not speak with Ian." I can't understand how anyone—Marta, et al—can choose between sadism and masochism. As if there is ever a choice.

But that's not true, either. That part about Ian not telling me anything of consequence since the day we met. I was angry when I wrote that. Ian has divulged to me numerous things of consequence. Forgive me if I don't feel like listing them for you now. Everything Ian ever told me was something of consequence. Depending on how you define consequence, I suppose.

I don't know how to respond to Horatio so I don't. I don't reply to his email and two days later, three days before Christmas, there is an email from Ian in my inbox. I stare at his name a long time as though he is a celebrity; as though he is the rock star I have turned him into in my mind. The email itself contains five words and no punctuation. "is this still your email." I forward the email to Lauren (masochist!) and Marta, but don't respond in any other way. E. and I are leaving for my grandmother's in Dallas in the morning. For four days we will play Hearts and Canasta and Monopoly and Parcheesi and eat chocolate and drink Tab and go to The Cheesecake Factory and I won't have to think about my book or Horatio or Ian or how I will or won't respond or what I will or won't do. I will call

L. every night from my grandmother's guest room. I will read Hamsun's *Hunger* finally because now it is about me.

The joke is I do, of course, think about Ian in Dallas. I awake one morning from a dream in which I have seen him. I spend the entire day with this vision of he and I together again in my mind. I find five minutes to go and sit in the quiet of a guestroom, to close my eyes and return to the dream. It is the same feeling I once had of remembering the time we spent together in a hotel room in his city, shortly after I had made the return to mine. My mind can make the distinction—between what is real and what is imagined—but my body seems unable to see a difference. My body responds the same way in both cases. To a dream or to a memory.

On New Year's Eve L. and I sat in a parked car outside our friends' house in a nighttime snowfall. I don't remember what sparked the conversation. Maybe I had given myself until January 1st. It was selfish of me to tell him on the way into a party. I see that now. But then there was the midnight deadline and already it was eleven o'clock.

I intimated there was a book I had started three years earlier when we were still separated. I insinuated I had begun working on it again; that I was working on it at present.

This is how our marriage survives: on intimations and insinuations.

What could he say? I didn't have to remind him this time of our martial agreement. But I did anyway.

"Remember, you said when we got married, I could write . . . "

"I know," he said. He reminded me in this moment, in this quiet moment in the front seat of our car, of a Steinbeck character. Someone Henry Fonda might play in a film. His head was all but in his hands . . . *The Winter of Our Discontent*. But, no, that was another actor. Another film.

I could see he did not want to enter the party now. Though I felt better, relieved. I did not want to remain inactively in the car any longer.

I didn't have to say what or whom the book was about.

I could enter the new year with a clear conscience.

I opened the car door and we went inside. We did not again discuss—by either insinuation or intimation—my book for two years.

We still have not really discussed it now

Like a child or emotionally stunted person, I want to tell L. everything, for him to entertain some sort of confessional in our car. I think L. wants to pretend nothing is happening, that he knows nothing, that there is nothing to know. But how can one be certain this is what her spouse wants, without asking? It's another unanswerable question, like the chicken and the egg, like: is Ian a sociopath or isn't he.

The next day, January 1st, I receive a second email from Ian. This one sent to a different email account, the one with which I have been corresponding with Horatio. Again it is a single line, without punctuation—"did you get my other email". Again I stare at it as though a semi-famous rock star or actor has emailed me. I make my mouth say both the first and last name, over-enunciating them. I think about lighting a cigarette, putting it out on my tongue. Something I have always wanted to do. I do not think it would be that hard. I think I would enjoy the taste of the cigarette from the other end also. Again I don't answer.

Something else to consider: How would this book be different if Ian weren't such a complete dysfunctional tool?

I begin to anticipate more emails after this. Like a dog in an experiment of behavior I sign into my email with my mouth moist and open. I look for Ian's name and feel something between disappointment and self-satisfaction when it's not there. I Google his name without adding words of admonishment or debasement. I am punishing him doubly, by not replying to his email and not flirting with him through a popular web search engine either. I am punishing him for not being more driven or committed to contacting me. (Where is his compulsion? His manic, risky behavior, now? Where is his impulsivity? His lack of self-control?) I feel myself justified in not taking him seriously. I have seen movies, read books. If a man wants to talk to you, he'll go to further lengths than this.

I was watching a TV show about a serial killer last night, coincidentally. The serial killer's wife was saying she wished she knew what went on in the mind of their child when their child experienced night terrors. (The serial killer's wife did not know her husband was a serial killer.)

Her husband, the serial killer, said, "We can't ever know what goes on in the mind of someone else. If we did, it would be intolerable."

Her husband had murdered two women by then.

He wasn't pointing directly at me. (I realize now.) It only felt so at the time.

It is shortly after this, a day or two, that Horatio asks me to make changes to the manuscript with regard to the male character. It seems obvious this is Ian's doing. Horatio had said previously he would publish the book 'as is,' sans edits. Now he wants me to alter identifying characteristics, namely, the man's profession.

I feel instantly justified in not replying to Ian's email.

I wonder what it is Ian is worried about, what about the main male character he does not like, if he feels it misrepresents him or if he feels it does not.

Three years ago, when we were still talking, I wrote an essay about another writer, a man with whom I had had a series of comical interactions based on self-deceptions. The man was a literary celebrity of sorts, if such creatures exist, so the essay got a fair amount of attention. I remember the morning it was published, Ian texting me, "you should write an essay about us. that would be interesting!" (That is not a direct quote but a re-membering. That is the general idea of what Ian said.) I wrote an essay in the form of a novella. Then I wrote a novel about writing the novella. I am not saying any of this is non-fiction. If I wanted to write a memoir I would. I have made Ian into a fictional character here for sure. Maybe he never said any of the things I attributed to him. It is possible we never even met. That all of this is based on no one in particular, or is a composite of no ones.

(One thing I have always wanted to know: is *The End of the Story* about Paul Auster or someone else. Is "Paul Auster" a fictional character created by Lydia Davis?)

It is possible "Elizabeth Ellen" is a fictional character also. This is what I have been trying to tell (all of) you for years. I tell myself this every day.

My Brand New Super Professional Psychological Conclusion Based on Nothing:

Of course Ian was not contacting me to tell me anything personal, anything that might service my ego. Of course he was preoccupied with his own.

We are both of us little egotists in that regard.

In every other regard also.

I am, however, surprised, as I open the manuscript on my computer, scan around, that Ian isn't more flattered by my depictions; that he isn't pleased to be the object of so much desire and anguish and longing. What more could a man want from a woman, after all. Was not Paul Auster pleased? If in fact, it was he Lydia Davis based that story on.

"He is your Helen," Marta says, after reading the first draft. I don't know what she means; I have to look that up. I am not very well read. Ian would know. Ian has read everything. I don't understand why Ian isn't more flattered.

I cannot remember how I responded to Horatio initially. If my instinct was to say "yes" or "no." I only know that after a while I made the changes. I changed Ian from a writer to a musician. I grew to like Ian more this way. I enjoyed my creation and the act of creating. I could make Ian say and do whatever I wanted now. His compliance in this form was pleasing to me. I controlled our world—his and mine—for the first time in this manner. For almost two years I controlled Ian in this way. I thought I might control him in this manner forever.

Later Lauren will say, "Why is Horatio's instinct to protect Ian? He is, in this case, your publisher. He should be protecting you."

It did seem a conflict of interest at the very least, one I had instigated, but still.

I begin to wake in the mornings with the sense I have been clenching my teeth. My jaw is often sore. I don't sleep as well. I take an hour, hour and a half, two hours to fall asleep, wake up in the middle of the night . . . Even during the day I catch myself bearing down on my teeth; I look down at my hands and they are fists. L. comes and rubs my shoulders, my cheeks, my scalp. L. makes me drinks and calls people I don't want to call. He doesn't understand this change in me. He is eager to help even when he doesn't understand. Sometimes I resent him for how eager to help he is. Comparatively, what does that make me? is what his eagerness and helpfulness forces me to think.

I sit in my bathroom staring at my teeth in a magnifying mirror. I can't stop staring at the chips, one on the bottom of each of my front teeth...I think one night I will bite down so hard I will break a tooth in half. I will wake up in the morning with a mouthful of broken teeth. I will bite into a sandwich and be chewing on teeth like Harmony Korine.

I take a break from reading dental horror stories to check my email and there is one from Horatio. I haven't heard from him since he asked me to contact Ian. I never replied to that email because I didn't know how. Now Horatio is saying he wants to move up the publication date. He wants to put the book out in May. It is January when I read this. I begin immediately to panic.

When L. gets home he smells my breath—"What are we celebrating."

"Nothing," I say. "I was just thirsty." I pour him a generous drink to distract him. I go and retrieve a bag from the pool table. I hand L. the box inside the bag and start to boil water.

"What is this?" L. says.

"A fifteen dollar night guard," I say. "I need you to help mold it to my teeth."

It's a clumsy act—L.'s hand inside my mouth, the plastic hot, almost burning my tongue and cheeks—and we end up having to do it twice.

I am awake beside L. for two hours before moving upstairs to the guest room. In the guest room I can move as much as I want. I can read with the light on. When I come downstairs in the morning I can tell L. is feeling sorry for himself. This annoys me. How he has made this about him.

"Every time I moved, you moved," I say.

"But I didn't wake up," he says. "You weren't bothering me."

But I was bothering myself. But you were bothering me, I think.

I sleep in my closet the next night. I take my pillow and use a bath towel to cover myself. In the morning he searches the house for me. He looks upstairs in the guest room and downstairs in the basement. He doesn't think to check the closet. When I finally come out to the kitchen he says, "I looked everywhere for you."

"I was in the closet," I say, flatly, as though that is an obvious place for a wife to be.

It's hard to say sometimes which is more shame-inducing, a man who never searches for you or one who never stops.

I don't get online for three days, in avoidance of Horatio. I work on my new novel. I try to stay "in the moment" with L., go for walks with the dogs, watch movies in the basement. I work on relaxing before bed. Go to bed with L. Will myself to stay in bed with L., even if I wake in the night, disallow myself the luxury of my closet.

I make an effort to not think about the novella or Ian. I find myself obsessively thinking about how I am not Googling Ian, how I am not going to Ian's blog, how I am not thinking about Ian.

Lawren: horatio is obviously into shit-disturbing
i'm not saying it's because the book is not good or not of interest but i doubt his intentions
even perfect books need more than four months before publication
me: i thought he liked the book because he knew it was about ian but then he asked me to take all those parts out
Sent at 11:08 PM
Lauren: yeah, that's suspect too
Lauren: he doesn't have your interest at heart
Lauren: he never would have asked you to change those things if he did
he wants to cause the trouble HE wants to cause
Sent at 11:09 PM

me: i think too i am working so
hard on this new novel, so was
tempting to think i had this other
book almost done...

Lauren: i wouldn't be a party
to that
yeah, i totally get that
you want that validation

Lauren: right. that struck me as
wrong and then people talked
me out of thinking it was wrong

Options ▸   Pop-out ↗

I am experiencing high levels of anxiety. I almost don't get on the plane. I sit in the terminal until every other passenger has passed into the runway. I am wearing the wristbands made for seasickness and have eaten four Pepto-Bismol tablets. I have had to leave the gate area three times to shit. I have a hard time flying without E. or L. I am the last person to board.

Enid is against my writing of this book. She told me in an email before the flight to Miami, "I had to stop reading after the first forty pages. I couldn't take how weak you appeared."

I remember but don't mention the impetus of Enid's dislike of Ian. I have the emails saved in which Enid mentions his handsomeness, her single status. She was present the night Ian and I met and the weekend he stayed at my house also. She slept with an unpublished poet that weekend instead. The next day she argued with Ian about his identity while I looked on weakly. I felt smug in my having been chosen. It was only later that I considered the reason why I had been chosen, what characteristics about myself Ian had found appealing.

This is what I am thinking about as I sit in the first class cabin staring out the window trying not to vomit. I keep the sick bag hidden behind a book in my lap just in case.

Somehow I make it to Miami without having to get up to shit again.

I stand outside in the Miami heat and text L. and text E. and text Enid. I am conscious of not texting Ian. I am always conscious of how I am not communicating with Ian.

We are seated on our hotel balcony, smoking. Enid says she has decided to stop writing about herself, to start "making shit up!" She acts as though this is a decision she has come to on her own volition, borne out of some sort of maturation on her part, but I don't believe her. I am pretty sure Virgo, her boyfriend of the past six months, has decided this for her.

"He doesn't want me to write about him or us," Enid told me a month after they started dating. "But I'm so happy I don't care."

Today Enid is less happy. She stares at her phone with a worried look on her face. Virgo hasn't called her since we've been in Miami. He has barely texted her either. I think maybe she is blaming herself, blaming her writing, on things not working out. She is trying to be someone else for Virgo and wants me to be someone else for L. She is in a weakened state. I think she could write an interesting novel in such a state, if she could just let go of Virgo.

"But L. and I had the agreement when we married," I remind her as we lie reclined in rental chairs on the beach. "We agreed I could write whatever I want."

I am prone on my stomach and if I lift up on my elbows and open my eyes I get a straight on shot of several European women in their early twenties, topless. There is a middle-aged man who resembles David Hasselhoff with a slightly younger blonde woman setting up chairs and drinks in the sand a few feet in front of us. They have a portable radio and are listening to popular songs from the '70s and '80s and throwing a Frisbee. They have wine glasses and a cheeseboard. I am thinking that this is where

L. and I should move when E. goes to college, if he holds to his end of the bargain, if I hold to mine, if we make it though the publication of this novel. If, if, if, if!

I wake in the middle of the night, from a nightmare of gnashing teeth, of my tooth broken in half. I reach to feel inside my mouth. I can't catch my breath. I can't tell if I am crying or not.

I barely sleep and when I wake in the morning, I am too anxious to get coffee. I blame my mania on the sun. I am unused to it, I tell Enid. It is winter back home. I don't tell her I have been having trouble sleeping since Horatio said he wanted to move up the publication date to May. I haven't mentioned anything to L. I don't know what I am doing. I have an appointment to see another root canal specialist when I am home. My teeth are cracking. This is all I know.

"I am all into the idea of sacrificing people's feelings for the sake of 'my art.' I think this is important. I think L. will be upset at first but then will come around and understand because he loves you and because he writes too." —Marta writes in an email while I am in Miami with Enid.

"I think you should change him back to being a writer," Enid says, meaning Ian. We are in a taxi on our way to the Miami airport.

"I think it's more honest and relatable if he is a writer," she says.

But I don't care about honesty or being relatable. Changing him back would be a lot of work for me at this point. I have grown used to this myth he has become in my mind, of this myth of me as creator.

On the flight home I order a drink. I say, "I will have a bourbon neat, please," the way I have heard L. say it.

The steward stands, unmoving. Gives me a quizzical look. I start to second-guess myself. This is my first time ordering a drink on a plane.

"What is it you want?"

He seems impatient with me.

"A bourbon, straight up?"

"A glass of bourbon? No ice?"

"Yes, please."

I don't make eye contact with the man seated next to me. Why is everything so hard.

I sip my bourbon; try to act natural. I have consumed only half my drink when the steward returns. "Sorry," he says. "Time for takeoff."

Suddenly I am alone again without my bourbon.

The man seated next to me and I eat our salads in silence. We stare straight ahead and acknowledge only the steward. The man is reading a pop culture magazine and inside there is a small black and white photograph of Ian on a stage with Sadie. I sip water from the bottle I brought on board the plane. Tiny sips so that I will not vomit them back up. Tiny sips to push the bile rising in my throat back down. I decide to tell Horatio I need more time. I try to force my eyes closed but I cannot stop them from going to my periphery, going to the photograph of Ian and Sadie in the pop culture magazine, until finally the man seated next to me turns the page. Immediately after the page is turned, I stand and walk to the bathroom. I walk inside the tiny bathroom, close the door behind me and lock it. I sit on the closed toilet lid staring at the instructions as typed word on objects all around me. I breathe something like relief reading all of the instructions.

I come home from . . . with L. I sit with him while he has a drink, watch . . . I wait for him to go to bed before I make a drink of my own. I don't want to waste my buzz. I act in the manner I acted the year L. and I were broken up. I have not broken any old habits. I bring my drink to my desk and open my computer. I look at Ian's blog, Google Ian's name, read web articles about Ian, watch videos of Ian reading in Cleveland and New York City and Kansas. I drink my drink while searching for Ian on the Internet then go into the basement and smoke a cigarette while listening to songs that remind me of Ian on my headphones. Once I publish this novel my life will become transparent in a way I am uncomfortable with living. I may have to . . .

"Maybe you need closure," Kirstin says. We are texting. I only communi-cate with people through texts. I don't know anyone in my city anymore. Everyone I once knew has moved away, to LA or New York or Canada. For E.'s emergency contact listing at his high school I wrote down the name of a woman I knew when E. was six. The woman lives an hour north, in the town E. and I lived in before I met L. I couldn't think of anyone else. I couldn't imagine an emergency scenario in which I would be unavail-able to E. Kirstin lives in northern California. In some small town I can't remember the name of because it doesn't matter, the same way it didn't matter in 2009 when I didn't know where Ian lived.

"what if closure becomes the opposite of closure, tho," I type.

"what's the opposite of closure."

"idk. that's what i'm trying to figure out."

L. goes to Kentucky for a university reading. They give him $500 and pay for his hotel for the night. L. takes similar trips to similar universities three to five times a year. I spend the evening taking photographs of myself like I used to the year Ian and I were talking, the year L. and I were broken up. I splay myself out on the ground, set the self-timer on my camera. I post the photographs on my Tumblr because I cannot send them to Ian because I am still not talking to Ian. The next day when L. gets home he doesn't mention the photographs and neither do I, even though at this point L. is again following my Tumblr. We ignore it the way we ignore everything else about my unhappiness and his.

I make us drinks and we sit side by side in matching leather chairs watching serial TV and drinking and I don't think about how the chair in which I am sitting is the chair in which Ian sat five years ago, me in his lap, me not wanting to go to bed, Ian's finger tracing the area of my thigh just outside my jean shorts, and for a brief second, the area inside also.

I don't stop to think how L. spent his night in Kentucky; who he may have drank with/flirted with/slept with. I don't think about him watching porn alone in his hotel room, jacking off onto his stomach on the bed. What L. does or doesn't do doesn't interest me in the way what I do or don't do does. Or, what l. does or doesn't do is as much of a disappointment to me as what I do or don't do, so why bother thinking about it?

I sometimes wish I would cease to be a person of interest for L.

"Isn't Connor jealous? Does he know you're not over your ex?"

I am sitting cross legged on my bathroom floor texting again with Kirstin.

.

"I think I'm over him, but not over it," Kirstin says.

I don't understand the difference. It seems a distinction you make for a jealous partner or for yourself when you're feeling guilty about not fitting into society's demands for inner monogamous thinking.

"Connor is 6% jealous," Kirstin says. I think back to an earlier text conversation I had with Kirstin in which she said she believed jealousy was the problem of the person who was jealous. Later she admitted Connor was the person who convinced her of that theory.

"That seems like a good amount," I say. "A not threatening but interesting amount."

"I wish it was a higher percentage," she says.

But I don't think Kirstin means it. I think Kirstin is just being funny.

By the time I took the book back out last fall, I had resigned myself to the fact I would not publish it in my lifetime or in L.'s. This is how women in literature operate: Anais Nin, Simone de Beauvoir...

When Anais Nin died *The New York Times* listed her as married to one man and *The Los Angeles Times* another. She had split her time on opposite coasts with opposite men for years. I don't feel like a horrible person either. No matter what my father-in-law might initiate me into thinking I feel momentarily... (But maybe I am projecting here, too. The Tell-Tale Heart. It is possible my father-in-law doesn't give a shit.)

A year ago, after the publication of my story collection, my father-in-law texted me from the airport in his city to tell me he had just downloaded my book for the plane ride that would bring him (and my mother-in-law) to ours. We were going to spend a week in a cabin together: my in-laws, L., E., me.

"Why worry about things you can't control," L. said when I read him his father's text.

I didn't understand the question. I couldn't fathom the implication that there was an alternative.

Six hours later we were standing in the kitchen: my father-in-law, my mother-in-law, L., E., me.

"I just have a few questions," my father-in-law was saying. I was standing behind the counter; everyone else was in front of it. "Who does she leave Adam for?"

He was referencing a story in my book, one I had based on L., and Ian and me. But he doesn't get to know this. He doesn't get to ask questions like this.

"It's fiction," I said. This was my premeditated, well-rehearsed answer. "I guess you have to decide that for yourself."

(Why didn't I think to answer Horatio similarly?)

Later I asked L. to ask his father to stop reading my collection while we were at the cabin. I was feeling claustrophobic. I was having urban panic attacks in the backwoods of the Upper Peninsula. We hadn't brought any alcohol or cigarettes with us. I couldn't catch my breath.

Later L.'s father told us for the fourth or fifth time about the young woman he had dated for two years in high school.

"In the end, both our parents forbade me to see her."

There was a running list of women L.'s father had dated before meeting L.'s mother: stewardesses, models, beauty pageant queens...

I realized, on the drive to the airport, L.'s father again recounting his time with the stewardess, that I may have misinterpreted L.'s father's questions about my past relationship as judgment rather than as mere curiosity, rather than merely as a way for him to talk about his own past relationships. A commonness between us. L. and L.'s mother sitting quietly, without anything to add to the conversation.

"I am like you," L.'s father may have been saying.

I didn't want necessarily to be like L.'s father.

I don't want to be like myself necessarily either.

We are not always sad, L. and I. For happiness we take our flask to the movie theater and go to the zoo. We are on our way to the latter now. I am unsure if L. or I am happy yet. It is Valentine's Day and the zoo is having a "strolling dinner" and a lecture on the mating life of the zoo's animals. I wore my heaviest coat, thick gloves, a hat, jeans. L. wore a flannel and boots. The first person we see when we park is wearing a dress and heels. The next person is in a nice sweater, wool pants. I think we may have misunderstood the meaning of "strolling dinner."

I leave my gloves and hat in the car. We follow a woman in heels inside; check our coats, retrieve our drink tickets. I give mine to L. so now he has four. Men and women dressed in tuxedos offer us small portions of seafood on trays as we wait in line at the bar. L. orders two drinks as though we will each be drinking one. Then we stand at a small, tall table while he drinks them both, and goes back for another.

I can't remember if it is now that I am thinking today is Ian's (non) official book release (the official release is two days from now, the day E. and I leave for LA.). Earlier in the day I saw a profile of Ian in an online magazine. Every month the magazine asked a different musician or writer to make a playlist. Ian chose songs about love lost and killing an ex's current lover. It was hard not to be egotistical. He had, after all, just read my novella. I made a playlist of my own on my Tumblr. I don't remember what I put on it. That's a lie. The usual dismal stuff.

"You're quiet," L. says.

"So are you."

"Yeah, but I always am."

"I can't talk all of the time," I say. Sometimes I wish he would just ask me outright about Ian so I could say, "I don't know. I never talk to him."

It seems weird to make such a statement unprompted. But I get the feeling he is never sure, that he is always wondering.

L. puts his hand on my knee and I stare at it, place mine on top of his.

"Feels like forever," L. says, and grabs my hand. He means since we met ten years ago. He pulls me over beside him and gives me a kiss and it is almost time for the lecture on the mating habits of zoo animals and we finish eating and file inside the hall with the rest of the couples. I think, maybe I only love one man. (meaning L.) I think, obsession isn't love. Addiction isn't love. (meaning Ian.)

On the drive home we are recounting everything we learned in the lecture and laughing. We need to remember all these stories to tell E. tomorrow, we say. After a while we are quieter; L. is falling asleep in the passenger seat. All those free bourbon cocktails. I turn on the radio, hunting for a song that will remind me of Ian.

But obsession and addiction win out every time . . .

You live like this, sheltered, in a delicate world, and you believe you are living ... The symptoms of hibernating are easily detectable: first, restlessness. The second symptom (when hibernating becomes dangerous and might degenerate into death): absence of pleasure. That is all. It appears like an innocuous illness. Monotony, boredom, death ... I am aware of being in a beautiful prison, from which I can only escape by writing. —Anais Nin, *Diary: Volume One*

At home I sit on the side of the tub removing my makeup and talk to L. while he brushes his teeth. I pull back both sides of the bed and turn on both bedside lamps. I turn on the sound machine, adjust the volume of the ocean. Tell my husband goodnight.

I go into the kitchen and pour myself a drink. I turn on my laptop, sip the whiskey, straight, while I wait. I check my email and there is nothing new. I check my Tumblr. I go to Ian's blog. I sit in shock, smiling; my hand held over my mouth; captive.

There is my name—"Elizabeth Ellen"—on Ian's blog; the first time in six years. It is (ostensibly) a post about my cat but it also a post about me.

I go and stand in my bathroom with the door closed, smile into a towel in the dark. Five years earlier I stood similarly in my bathroom with my face in a towel when I couldn't stop crying and didn't want E. to hear. I'm pretty sure E. heard.

I don't want L. to hear me smiling . . .

I brush my teeth, smiling, and get in bed, smiling. I stare at my open book but don't connect any of the words. I turn off my light and I am still smiling in the dark. I can't stop smiling and I wonder if I should be concerned, if an inability to stop smiling is a mark of a mental instability, a mark of mental illness, in the same manner as the inability to stop crying.

Of course it doesn't last. The happiness or mania or lunacy or whatever it is you want to call it, is short-lived. It dissipates, slowly at first, over the next day, with the realization I still cannot communicate with Ian, that I'll probably never be able to communicate with Ian again...because I am trying to be a good wife for L.

I can't tell anyone about this, Ian's blog post, my subsequent happiness and return now to something like despair...

It is only now, as I type this, that I hear an outsider say, "why didn't you leave L., if you were so unhappy?"

And I want to say, "Because I loved L." I love L.

Maybe that isn't coming across here. Maybe it's only coming across that L. loved/loves me.

There was always the half-conscious awareness, the self-analysis, that told me I was crazy/obsessed/ungrateful/selfish/narcissistic . . . that I was happy and didn't know it. That I was happy and refused to be so.

Once I had accused Ian of the same thing: a refusal to be happy.

We could each of us blame our childhoods . . . but I won't let either of us off that easy. (Sorry, Ian!)

Ian's new book came out the day E. and I left for LA. I downloaded it onto my Kindle as we sat in the airport terminal in Detroit. I planned to read it in LA, delete it before our return.

"Is L. okay with you reading that?" E. asked. She had glanced at the screen as it was sent to my Kindle.

"No," I said. Or maybe I said, "I don't know."

E. looked uncomfortable and put her earbuds into her ears. We were seated beside each other rather than across from one another so neither of us had to decide to look away.

At the front of the book was an 800 number to text if you wanted the author to text you back. It was part of the book's promotion.

The number was good for the first day of the book's release only.

I sat staring at the 800 number in the bathtub at the hotel in LA. I had my phone beside me on the ledge. E. was watching a reality show on the TV in the other room. I kept thinking how easy it would be to sink under the water and not return to the surface. How Ian's face would soften when he heard. How I would beat Sadie at her own game. But I couldn't be that cruel to E. I kept coming up for air.

The flight, for once, had been "fine." E. and I had sat together in first class.

"I don't have a fear of flying, I have a fear of strangers," I told her. "Of strange men, in particular."

I thought I might have some form of PTSD based on this one guy my mom dated for six years. I would wait in a longer line at the grocery store if the cashier was a woman. I would hang up if the person who answered the 800 number on the back of my credit card was a man. I felt like I was going to throw up if I had to sit next to a middle aged white man on a plane.

"Weird," she said.

"Yeah," I said.

During hour three we had shared a pair of earbuds and watched a fashion designer reality show on my iPod. We had put our hands in the basket that was passed around, pulled out small candy bars and unwrapped them while we watch.

We had already discussed Enid's dilemma with her boyfriend, the ultimatum he gave her: writing about him or him.

"I would never write anything that would hurt someone I love," E. had said.

"You have an aversion to the truth in art?" I'd said. It was an asshole thing to say but I'd said it with a smile on my face to show I was joking even though I was dead serious also. She didn't yet understand how incredibly easy it is to hurt people. How hurting people was easier than anything else you could do.

"That's why I don't want to be an artist anymore," she had said. Or maybe she doesn't say that (then). Maybe she says that later. When we are lying on our hotel balcony in the sun or running through the Chateau Marmont as a prank, taxi running, or eating room service off a tray in front of our television.

I don't think I have ever told E. I am writing this book. I would say "surprise!" here but I don't think she'll ever read it. I think she's too smart to read her mother's writing. I wish L. and his father and my mother were as smart as E.

E. had been concerned it was the same Beverly Hills hotel in which the singer had recently drowned in a bathtub. We had been in Ft. Lauderdale when her funeral aired on TV. The man giving the eulogy was one of E.'s favorite actors. He'd been in a famous movie with the singer. But he hadn't been able to "save her in real life." That's what the tabloids said.

"I'm not staying in that hotel," E. had said.

"It's not the same one," I told her. "I double checked."

I hadn't told my mother we were in Florida. Anyway, it was a large state. I couldn't stop thinking of the singer's daughter, checked into the hotel room next door to her mom's ... how they'd rushed her to the hospital the same night, how she was the same age E. is currently ...

The point is, I couldn't stop thinking of the singer's daughter. Or maybe I can't stop thinking of the temptation to fill my lungs with water. (Narcissist!)

On the patio of our L.A. hotel I imagined the young women who texted the 800 number instead of me. There would be samples of Ian's texts to them on his website when I got home. That they were not strikingly dissimilar to the ones I remembered him texting me four years earlier ...

He has a talent for ...

E. no longer wants to be a writer or filmmaker.

"I want to work with animals," he says. "I don't want to do anything 'artistic.'"

We are still in L.A.; we are touring UCLA and USC because two months ago he still wanted to be a screenwriter or director. The weather is abnormally below temperature. I remove my oversized sunglasses. I feel unlike myself wearing them and maybe that is the point. We had spent the previous summer watching movies in our basement: Hitchcock and Capra and Lynch.

"I'm sorry, guys," the UCLA tour guide says. "This is our one day a year of rain. I don't even know how to turn on the windshield wipers in my car."

I keep bracing, my arms wrapped around my chest.

"That's good," I say to E. I decide not to take it as a jab to my profession. "But why the hell are we in L.A. then."

I'd ended up reading the entire book on the flight to L.A. I try but I can't remember what I read. I don't mean that as a slight to the book or to the book's author—don't take this as a book review, Ian—I just have a problem with comprehension currently, is what I'm saying. (I couldn't find me anywhere on the page, is what I mean.)

I remember Ian's first three books with extreme clarity. I see whole pages of text in my mind. What I remember of the new book is flying to L.A. I remember sitting next to E. I remember wanting a ginger ale but ordering a club soda instead.

We are in the LAX airport, waiting to fly home. E. is flipping through a copy of *Rolling Stone*. Lil' Wayne is on the cover. She hands it to me, opened; there is a one-page feature on Ian, a photograph of him sitting, disheveled, in an unmade bed. I do not recognize the shirt he is wearing or the bed. There is a cigarette burning in an ashtray beside him and I wonder if it is his or someone else's. I try to discern who else is in the room based on photographic clues. I search the background for human form shadows, cheap heels, lingerie . . . I search for some evidence of Sadie: fishnets, razor blades, e-cigs, piles of cocaine or heroin, bloodstains on the sheets or on Ian . . .

The article does not mention a woman. Ian talks only about himself: his music, his writing, his influences, without divulging any personal or private information. There are no mentions of family or friends. No mentions of schools attended, current books read or music listened to. In four thousand words you will learn nothing new about Ian.

I glance back at E. and she is rolling her eyes.

According to E.: no. According to Eli, I should "know" better.

"Not to read a book?"

"I don't know," she said. "It just seems wrong. And look what happened last time," she says. "You hurt L."

I am actually ecstatic E. doesn't want to be an artist; overjoyed. I am not being sarcastic. I am telling him this.

"I think I would be so much happier sitting quietly in the bushes of Africa observing gorillas seventeen hours a day."

See, this is what I mean. I cannot make one statement about E. without turning it back to me.

E. will be so much happier. Or happiness will not be a word E. will use. If he is lucky. The second you ask yourself the question, you've already lost the battle.

I never ended up texting the 800 number.

It seemed like a bad idea in that it could only go one way and I would have wanted it to go several (or none at all).

This isn't an addiction memoir, per se. I am unwilling to share with you what parts of my life//this book are fact and what parts are fiction. I don't like to make such distinctions even for myself (and certainly not for those I love).

Oh, have I already said this?

I could write another 100 k words and you still wouldn't know anything about me (either).

I moved L. into an apartment across town, for instance. This was right after the inheritance. This was right after I bought my house (this was how I referred to things then). I was feeling independent. (I sounded like a bitch.) I was feeling like Jack Nicholson/Diego Rivera/Jean-Paul Sartre. Whatever. (Fill in whatever bitchy things you can think to say about me here. I want to say, "they are probably all true." I want to say also, "you have no idea.") It was a tall, dormlike building that mostly attracted foreign grad students. There was a large fitness room on the first floor and a long, rectangular pool out back by the river in which L. and I stood holding paperbacks that summer. I remember staring into the reflective lenses of L.'s sunglasses, admiring my breasts, which were firm from the cool water.

I paid the year's rent upfront. Wrote a check for whatever it was . . . fifteen thousand. Twenty. I gave L. an additional check also. I wanted to be fair, after all.

"Think of it as your studio," I said.

I thought of it as an interesting place to fuck.

(It became interesting in a different way after L. and I got back together. After Philip and his wife moved back to Mexico. After Philip and I didn't end up having sex like I thought we would.)

This, I see now, is precisely the treatment Ian was wary of, that he avoided. He was smart to run from me . . . from my money . . . is this me "being controlling"? Maybe some people just like being controlled, Ian.

As L. says now, "I can't believe I didn't just take the money and run."

I think but don't say, "I can't believe I gave you fifty thousand dollars."

I didn't owe him anything.

I want to be submissive to someone and the only person I am currently submissive to is E. and soon E. will be gone.

I found this out of context statement in an earlier Word doc. I don't know why I wrote "someone" when I clearly meant "Ian."

This has probably been a larger issue than I have cared to consider in my marriage: Everyone likes L.

L. is an extremely likable person.

I like to think I am doing L. a favor here.

L. tells me a dream he has in which we break up. In the dream he starts seeing a new woman and excitedly tells his dad about her. He uses words like "cute" and "cool" to describe her.

"I don't care if she's 'cute' or 'cool,'" his father says. "'Cute' and 'cool' are what got you depressed all these years."

I keep forgetting it is just a dream. I keep remembering the dream dialogue as if L.'s father actually said it. It fits so easily with my idea of how his father views me. It fits too easily with my idea of how I view myself. (Narcissistic/Sadist/Bitch)

Of course there's another side of me I'm not showing you. I don't know why I keep doing this. I feel more vulnerable (or less interesting—is there a difference?) showing you my sweet, affectionate side, showing you the side L. comes back to, showing you the side that wants L. back, over and over and over again. I haven't shown you me curled onto L.'s lap on a Sunday morning as he reads the paper, my cheek pressed somewhere south of his collarbone, my fingers grasping the collar of his pajama shirt. I haven't shown you the two of us walking hand in hand downtown, seated across from one another in a corner booth, deep in conversation, clinking glasses, toasting each other, my foot on his lap under the table, my shoe abandoned on the floor. (Are you bored yet? Should I keep going? Should I describe for you our shared laughter? Is this enough?)

Marta doesn't ask "why now", what made me pull the manuscript out now. Which is probably why I keep talking to Marta.

I have, for the most part, stopped talking to Lauren.

I agreed in the moment with Lauren and immediately after I discounted everything she said with Marta.

Yesterday Marta and Sabine were here. L. was still out of town and it was warm enough for the first time this spring to sit out on the balcony. We stood outside, smoking cigarettes and talking.

Marta said she'd been asked to do a reading in Ian's city.

"Is there anything you want me to say to him if I see him," Marta said.

I felt unable to answer such a question. I suggested we smoke another cigarette. I felt inhibited by Sabine's presence. I had not known her long. She gave off a moral vibe. She seemed happily married, for instance . . . She seemed to have no complaints.

"I'll tell you later," I said, to Marta. My back was to Sabine, who emitted now some sort of small noise from her mouth. I turned to look at her. She seemed visibly distressed by my exclusion of her from the conversation.

"I'm sorry," I said. "I didn't know how you felt, how much you wanted to be made privy to."

Sabine began to tell us a story about the man she had dated before she married James, how things between them had ended vaguely, how they had continued to see each other and be in touch with one another, while living in separate cities, for months after. She told us they would meet up every once in a while to talk and have sex. And then one time when they met up he revealed that he had had a girlfriend all along, or for many of the months, and Sabine had been shocked by this information. "I had thought we would just go on like this indefinitely . . . talking and seeing each other periodically."

I still didn't know what I wanted Marta to tell Ian. But I felt closer to Sabine. I felt I could include her in a select number of my thoughts.

"I don't know," I said, when the conversation had come back around to me. "I don't know what I want you to say or ask. Maybe nothing. Maybe just..."

"You never had closure," Marta said.

"That's right," I agreed, though closure was not a word I would have used. "Is it selfish of me to want him to know I care? That I didn't...abandon him...that I still think of him. I just...because of L...or because of myself...(I did not want always to blame L. for how things were), I can't speak with him."

"No," Marta said. "That's not selfish." (Though I wasn't sure how much I could invest in Marta's opinion, given that it seemed she would always support me, even if I proposed an affair or murder, in the same way I would support E. if she killed a person; I would not question E.'s judgment. I would assume she had been justified.)

"I don't think it's selfish," Sabine mimicked, but I was unsure she believed what she was saying. Part of me thought she merely wanted to be included in our conversation and so was pretending to have no moral objections. Part of me thought she merely wanted to be my friend and the only way to be friends with me was to feign an ignorance of morality and ethics as a whole.

In the end it didn't matter. Ian didn't show up to the reading.

A week later L. and I are at a party at Sabine's. L. has consumed six glasses of some sort of rum punch...we are talking to two different couples...I am sober...drinking club soda...keeping a distance...retaining control...I come in from standing with Sabine while she smokes and L. motions me over. He is standing in front of Sabine's bookcase with another writer he has just met, a friend of Sabine's from out of town, Milan. Milan is gesticulating toward the books, asking which we would put on our writing table, read over and over...reminding me of the first night Ian was at my house, only Milan lacks charisma, Milan lacks charm; only Milan seems "coked up" or...at one point he begins naming contemporary authors not represented on Sabine's bookshelf, asking L.

and me for our opinions regarding them, "For instance, Ian Kaye. Have you read Ian Kaye? Everyone is always telling me how great Ian Kaye is, but no one can tell me why. I think you should be able to say why you like a particular author ... "

L. and I stand still, silent, shaking our heads "no."

No, we haven't read Ian Kaye.

At least one of us is lying.

Half an hour later I drive us home. It is only nine o'clock. We leash the dogs, set out on our walk. Almost immediately L. falls behind with the female. I turn around with the male. There is a "recognizable" pained look on L.'s face. I can't tell if it is recognizable as something belonging to L. or to me.

The male wants to walk ahead and I allow him. I turn back around, disassociating myself from L.'s look and from what he is trying to tell me with it.

Too easy, I tell him inside my head.

I tell myself I bear no responsibility in the absence of direct address. (This is a new rule I have determined for us without disclosing it to L.)

I blame L. for drinking too many rum punches.

"It wouldn't have come as such a shock if you hadn't drank so many punches," I mumble so only the male dog can hear me.

I knew it was unfair how much we were both thinking of Ian, but I didn't see a way out of it. Not while I was writing this book. Not while Ian was alive. Not after he was dead either . . .

I remember someone telling me they worked with aged people in a retirement home and once asked an elderly woman if the young man in the photograph by her bed was the woman's recently deceased husband of fifty odd years and the woman replying, "Oh, God no. That's Benny, the love of my life. He died in WWII."

If only Ian were a dead soldier.

At least then (L. and) I would be haunted by a ghost proper.

L. and I meet at a hotel in Iowa for a wedding. He has come from a writers' conference in St. Paul or Minneapolis. I make the six hour drive alone. I smoke cigarettes and listen to songs from Ian's playlist. I feel around the car to see if L. has had it bugged. I cannot find anything resembling a microphone but I feel not entirely alone either.

The second night at the hotel I bring up some thread of conversation that leads L. to pontificate upon why it is he does not like a particular movement of writers. I do not point out that I have been identified at times with said movement. I am thinking but don't say aloud that Ian also has been identified with this movement. L. has not said Ian's name in four years. We do not speak his name, nor the name of the woman L. dated for a full year when we were broken up. During the conversation, or, argument—I did not think of it as the latter until Ian's name was spoken aloud—I was not conscious of leading it to a place in which L. might say his name... but then, L. feeling I've somehow backed him in a corner, I suppose, or dared him without knowing it, says it, says Ian's name, for the first time in... since...? Says his name not once, but twice. Maybe more?

I feel immediately as though... I have been punched? Is that what people say in this instance? I do not know what I feel but I am surprised how much I feel it.

Immediately, I turn away from the conversation.

"Now I just want to go home," I say. It is an hour and a half before the wedding we have come to the city to attend. Or is it more? Is this before or after we had sex for the second time that weekend? (Back to back days... an unusual sequence of events for us in this, our tenth year, of our relationship.)

The night before we had unprotected sex. It was the only time in ten years I allowed L. to ejaculate inside me without protection. I had decided this was to be our one "stab" at procreation. This one allowance. If we were meant to have a child it would be because of this weekend. This hotel in Iowa. The city in which Ian lives. The city in which I once wanted to become impregnated by Ian.

(Spoiler alert: we weren't!) ("Meant to have a child," I mean.) (L. and I, I mean.) (Ian and I also, I suppose.)

The second time we have sex in the hotel I tell L. to ejaculate on my back. He has entered me from behind and I say, "I want you to cum all over my back. I want you to shoot your cum all over my ass. I want you to lick your cum off my ass." This is more customary for us, now that I no longer have an IUD. Now that we are not using any form of birth control. Now that is increasingly hard to make my husband come. Now that I have to pretend to be someone I am not, so my husband can ejaculate on me. Or I could just turn porn on.

But in the moment I still just want to go home. Something about hearing L. say Ian's name aloud has . . . broken me? Saddened me? Why? Why should L. be disallowed to say Ian's name?

"I would never say the name of the woman you dated when we were broken up," I tell L. I try to sound serious, try to make the two seem comparable in emotional damage. For L.'s sake. Though I doubt L. has given much thought to the young woman he dated while we were broken up. Then I remember I am his Ian. I am the asshole in L.'s life.

We make up, L. and I., somehow. Change the channel on the TV, perhaps. This is when we have sex for the second time. A man ejaculating on a woman's face on the TV screen so my husband can ejaculate on me while pretending he is ejaculating on her.

We take a taxi to the wedding. I have chosen the shortest of my dresses. The higher heels. I have not been to a Jewish wedding. I have no idea the customs, what to wear, how to openly mourn without seeming like a dick.

The first person I see when we enter the hotel in which the wedding is to take place is Philip. Philip is with a new woman, a younger Mexican woman, a woman much younger than his ex-wife, Martha: Ana. (I see her name—"Ana"—written—on a card at our dinner table later.) Perhaps he does not want to lose his fluency of the language. I have always thought (and still feel) he fears American women (me).

He smiles, nods. I wave. L. is already engaged in conversation with some-one else.

I have no more romantic (or sexual; why use the word "romantic" to mean sexual?) feelings for this man, but there is a fondness still. I feel fond of so few people anymore ... I want to walk with Philip, to become engaged in hushed conversation with him, to feel his hand on my back. But there is L ... And there is Ana anyway ...

I seem to have retained a memory of Philip's finger inside me, though I cannot remember anything else, not even so much as a kiss (though surely there must have been at least one). This was so long ago, after L. and I broke up for the first time, before I met Ian and became a truly horrible person.

I wrote a few stories for Philip but they were always less serious, more whimsical in nature, in keeping with my feelings for him (though I told myself they were quite serious for two weeks in the middle of the winter of 2005/2006, in a series of evenings spent talking in the front seat of Philip's car in a bowling alley parking lot and on the kitchen floor of my house and from the second row of a strip club in which Philip was preoccupied with the fear of seeing one of his students to the point of annoying me/not having sex with me).

Later we find ourselves, L. and I, seated at a small round table with Philip and Ana and three other people we do not know. Everyone else in the wedding hall seems to be engaged in conversation. L. and I sit silent. I feel an overwhelming sadness come on. Like, I may have to sob if we stay here much longer. "I want to go home," I whisper to L. for the second or third time this evening. I avoid eye contact with Philip. Even more so I avoid any kind of contact with Ana. I actively avoid a reprisal of Ana's weak handshake.

As soon as I say this the woman seated to my right turns and begins a conversation with me about German translations of English books and vice versa. She is from Germany. Teaches at Columbia. Is going through a divorce. Her husband: the ugly American. Two small children. Her younger, she says, is five, which surprises me, because I had thought her 50 or 55, someone much older than myself. But she cannot be that old. She is a sad lonely heart. Who will love her now? Her husband wants to keep the large Manhattan apartment, she says, move her and their two small children to a smaller two bedroom somewhere farther away... Brooklyn or Jersey.

Her husband, I think but don't say, sounds like a schmuck, like me.

And then the wedding ceremony is beginning and we all stand in a circle around the...

Philip and Ana are standing behind the bride and groom. I feel as though I am staring at them. All I can see is Philip's drunken face, that familiar grin.

As I recall there was only a solitary kiss.

A finger inside of me ten seconds; the only penetration.

Not even my breast was kissed? Or was it? I don't recall if it was.

I remained clothed, wearing a dress.

This was in my basement. Which is now L.'s office.

"All right, tonight is the night," Philip had said earlier in the day, indicating some event that never came to fruition, which ended the possibility of future sexual encounters. Which rendered our relations platonic ever after.

Why do none of my extramarital affairs end in copulation? This cannot be coincidental.

I have a new theory based on a story I heard a man tell on the radio earlier this evening. The man telling the story had attempted to commit suicide some years ago by jumping off a bridge. "Only, the second my hand left the railing, I knew I had made a terrible mistake," the man said. "I saw my daughter's face and my wife's face and I knew it was the worst decision I had ever made."

I wonder if each time I have attempted to finally separate myself from L., by consummating a relationship with another man, I have had the subconscious realization that I have made a terrible mistake.

I have no memory of seeing L.'s face in those moments.

To be honest, I think it was the man I was with each time who decided it would be a terrible mistake for us to have sex.

But isn't it prettier to think it was I?

If only L. knew how unromantic my encounters with Philip were, maybe we could all be friends again. Though there would still be the problem of this Ana, who might be twenty-four, who gives a weak handshake and seems of severely limited personality, who makes me yearn for Martha. Martha, who was sturdy, hearty, who may have liked me more than Philip. For the most part, Martha was hardly ever around.

The dancing is over and Philip is standing behind our chairs, inviting L. and me to a party in November. "I'm turning forty," he says. "I'm throwing a big bash. You fuckers better come."

Later I ask L, "Are you going to go?" as though Philip has invited only him.

He smiles, laughs. "Of course not."

We are friendly here, at the wedding. But we are not friends.

"Don't be ridiculous," L. says.

I think it is at this point that I feel like leaving the wedding. Something about the finality of the end of our friendship with Philip . . . I am thinking also of Ian . . . of how he would empathize with my feelings of isolation and loneliness here amidst this large wedding party to which I do not fit, this larger traditional literary community, people here who have been in *The New Yorker*, *The Paris Review*, who have had books published by HarperCollins and Harper Perennial and Knopf . . . I, who am known to them, if I am known at all, for an essay about "stalking" one of their fellow authors, someone who has also been in *The New Yorker* and has had books published on big presses . . . I feel on the verge of weeping . . . L. knows some of these men, has a familiarity with them at least . . . I have nothing to say . . . feel inept . . . feel like running . . . I am wearing the wrong dress. An older Jewish gentlemen, somebody's grandfather, the groom's? Lets me know this with a series of disapproving looks. I keep reaching to pull down my dress. Earlier in the hotel room, L. had said, "You cannot bend over."

I fear I will be dragged into the circle of dancing people I do not know. L. seems fine with the possibility. Inviting, even.

I am exhausted from making forced conversations with people I barely know.

My thoughts, as always begin: If Ian were here with me . . . (would he ever attend such an event with me? Most likely not, but if he did,) he would say, yes, let's leave.

He would not hesitate. But would grab my hand, lead me out.

Then I remember: Ian isn't here. Ian never came back.

(I did leave the wedding that evening. I found a bathroom down the hall. I sat on the toilet, waiting to cry . . . I waited a while . . . fifteen or twenty minutes. I smoked an illicit cigarette. I waited for someone to complain but no one did. L. said, "Where were you? Are you okay" when I found him at the bar. "Yes," I said. "Can we leave now?" And we did; left without saying goodbye to Philip or the others; the woman at our table whose American husband was leaving her, the ones who have been published in *The New Yorker*, the ones who knew great American authors or were great American authors, or soon would be . . .)

Days later there is an email from Philip. "You and L. were real dicks that night at the wedding . . . " This surprises me. I had thought . . . He mentions he is teaching at a different university, a prestigious one in the northeast. He will modestly state he does not know how he got such a prestigious job.

"This is all very apprapros, tomorrow I'm teaching *The End of the Affair*," he writes in one of five emails he sends me that evening.

Dialogue:

Philip: "We should have at least had sex, if I was going to lose two of my best friends."

Me: "You know as well as I do it probably wouldn't have been very good."

Philip: "But it might have been great."

Me: "Now you're just being sentimental."

I am aware even as I type my response that I sound like a character in a novel. Something by Graham Greene or Hemingway. Philip is fond of quoting from *The Sun Also Rises*. That last line, something about it being pretty to think so.

Of course, I want to say, it is always pretty to think.

Sometimes all I do is think.

I return from the wedding feeling similar to how I felt each of the times I returned home from Ian's city in years past: emotional, neurotic, on the verge of tears, in tears, entertaining obsessive thoughts of Ian, and now obsessive thoughts of Sadie too...

I go to Sadie's social media accounts...she has a new Twitter account: "Sadie Unedited," in which she manically writes her every thought and activity throughout the day/night. I have already found Ian's name three times, randomly thrown in thoughts of him amidst tales of snorting and shooting heroin, amidst tales of eating pasta and vomiting, amidst tales of sex with some ex who is not Ian...shitting in the street...stealing yeast infection medication from a drugstore...contemplating suicide...planning a reunion with Ian in New York City the following month...planning the procuring of drugs for the reunion with Ian...talking to Ian via his blog, emailing with Ian, posting more photographs from her last tour with Ian...

Ian, Ian, Ian...

I am supposed to go to New York City also. Not the same week as Ian, a couple weeks before. Next week.

To read with some of the same people...

To read with Kirstin who is flying in from LA...

I don't know... I just...

It's so hard to know.

I awoke three times in the night, panicked, jaw sore, clothing soaked. Each time I got up from bed, walked silently into the bathroom, toweled my back and chest, drank water...I was unusually thirsty, also. I sat cross legged on my bathroom floor drinking big gulps of water.

I woke this morning before my alarm, the decision not to fly to New York having already been made at some point in the night. I tell L. before we've gotten out of bed. I am sobbing a bit, quietly. I am naked, also; my sweated-through bedclothes on the bathroom floor where I removed them the last time I woke at four or five.

"What about Kirstin?" L. says.

"I don't know," I say.

I will wait until I know her flight has left California to make the call. I don't want her to cancel her trip. Kirstin is the funniest person I know, my little sister; Kirstin was on tour with me and our friend who knows Ian. I don't know why I didn't write her into those scenes. I am writing her in now. I am letting you know I abandoned her also. My little sister. The funniest person I know.

An hour later, L. calls the hotel in New York, makes sure the room is pre-paid for Kirstin. I am washing my drenched clothing, changing the sheets on our bed.

Things I could no longer envision myself enduring: the departure airport, the flight, sitting next to a stranger, trying not to vomit while sitting next to a stranger, the arrival airport, the taxi ride, the city, the reading, people at the reading, people who asked us to do the reading, the possibility of Sadie being at the reading, the possibility of other young women who may or may not have fucked or tried to fuck Ian being at the reading, the possibility of other young women who may or may not have done drugs with Ian being at the reading, the physical act of reading, of standing in front of these people who may or may not have fucked or done drugs with Ian, of having to make small talk with them after, of being asked to do drugs with them after, of being the person who won't do drugs with them after, of being written about in blog posts or on social media as being the one who won't do drugs with them after.

"I think I need to go away for a little while," I hear myself say to L. in the same manner I once made a similar declaration to Ian.

I begin searching hotels on the Internet. I am in a separate room from L. I cannot see his face.

"What do you mean?" he says. His voice has a worried tone to it. I don't think he has ever gotten used to me. I think he is always a little on edge in my presence.

I tell him I want to check into a hotel an hour or two from here, for a week or two, three tops, to work on or to finish my novel. I know it is unclear to him if I mean the novel about the teens I began last fall or the one whose existence I disclosed to him on New Year's Eve (this one). I don't clarify. I don't bother telling him that until I finish this novel I will be unable to stop thinking about Ian. That all my thoughts revolve around Ian, this novel, my book now.

I am looking up a hotel in which L. and I stayed on a Valentine's Day weekend years ago. I am packing my bags for a two week stay. I am so relieved not to be packing for New York. I am so relieved not to be getting on a plane, not to have to do another reading, not to have to explain that I don't do drugs, not to have to pretend that I don't know Ian.

I pass the bathroom mirror and am surprised to see that I am smiling. I am surprised to find that I am experiencing a sort of weightlessness. I have to stop and lean on the counter. I make sure to stop smiling before I leave my room. It is important to present myself to L. (and to E.) as a person in control of her emotions. (I have not, for instance, allowed myself to smile again while thinking of the post Ian made with my name in it.)

My son is at school. My son is busy in his junior year is busy in his senior year is busying with his girlfriend/part time job/college preparations/SATs/ACTs/night life/teen life/fucking his girlfriend. My son will barely notice my absence from the house. I am not having a pity party here. I am not complaining. I am justifying my running away.

I text my son before I leave, tell him where I'll be, how long.

My son is in class. I receive a text from him forty minutes later.

"OK," the text says.

We are on our way to the hotel, L. and I. I am unsure even in the moment how we end up having this conversation; what precedes it. I am only cognizant once we are fully engaged in dialogue, once the words are escaping my mouth, the same ones I have been both guarding against and trying to emit for months.

"I mean, you knew I was working on this. You knew I was working on two novels," I hear myself saying. I am incredulous but unstoppable.

"I didn't know you were working on this," L. says, and all I am thinking of is proving him wrong, of being right, because I know I am right in this instance.

"Yes, you did. I know you did." And here I pause, and for a second it might seem to an impartial observer I have finally retained a minute amount of dignity or civility or empathy, but then I catch my breath and without an ounce of introspection, continue forward. "I know you did because I took notes on it . . . the conversation we had on New Year's Eve, on our way to the party at Matt and Shelly's."

"No, you told me about 'finding' the novella. You told me you were thinking about publishing it."

"And I was . . . but then I decided to add to it, to add another part. To make it as much about the writing and publishing of such a book as the book itself; about the effect it has on the writer's spouse and child and family and friends . . . it's now about being a female writer/artist and being married/a mother and the repercussions of both/all."

After this last . . . confession or admission . . . after this final damning detail, there is only silence. I glance sideways in the car and L. is staring out the window, looking wounded as he always does anytime the conversation has any remote thing to do with Ian, without either of us ever mentioning or even alluding to Ian. Immediately I realize how horrible the "notes" were, the admitting of taking them. There is the awkward and painful unspoken awareness like a presence in the car that anything more said on the subject, and everything said up until now, will also be recorded by me, will be noted in a journal or in a Word document, will be used also in my book, my novel, whatever I am calling it. Here.

"And now you're being quiet because you don't want me taking more notes on . . . this," I say and L. nods, turns his head to the side window.

"It's not as though I rushed home that evening and wrote everything down in a notebook," I say, as though the distinction will make a difference, as though what I am saying is true. I honestly can't recall now if I made notes on our dialogue that evening or the next. Or if I wrote it from memory weeks later. (Does it matter?)

Now all I can think of is Arthur Miller and how much I hated him, how his work, all of it, was ruined for me by watching a scene in a made-for-TV movie about Marilyn that depicted Miller taking notes on his wife, of her finding them and feeling betrayed and destroyed. I could not believe anyone could be so cruel to Marilyn, to his own wife, so inhuman and unfeeling, such a monster.

I was not a writer then.

We are in the backseat of a Town Car. We are listening to E.'s iPod. She keeps picking songs by Eminem. There is an earbud in each of our ears. We are riding through Beverly Hills. (I no longer have to pretend I'm someone I'm not.) We are on our way to the highway. People are afraid to merge. This is what the driver tells us. I'm afraid of my daughter leaving home. I don't say this aloud.

E. says, "Eminem is the most personal rapper."

She turns down the volume, says, "Other rappers rap about their cars and dicks and money. Eminem raps about his childhood and his mom and Kim and Hailie."

"Yeah," I say. "That's how some writers are. They don't want to write about themselves or their lives. They want their privacy. They want awards."

"That's why they'll never write anything very good," E. says.

I turn my head to look out the window. I am wearing oversized sunglasses even though it's overcast. I turn my head so E. can't see that I am smiling.

For a moment, it feels like she is on my side.

You have to be willing to give part of your life away. Comics don't worry about people in the audience. They worry about people they have to be around after they leave that stage—the people trying to help them, the people in a relationship with them. The audience doesn't know the extent of Pryor's drug use; maybe they think he's making it up. They don't know his personal life. They haven't been in bed with him. They haven't raised him. They haven't done anything with him other than watch him on TV and on stage. But someone in his life didn't know all those details yet, so that's a whole different thing to give up.

—JB SMOOVE

on Richard Pryor on freebasing, *Playboy*, July/August 2016

These are the questions I sent via e-mail to Ms. Davis after Ms. Davis was agreeable to taking part in a short interview conducted via e-mail. The fact that Ms. Davis never responded once the questions were sent her leaves me to believe one of two things may have occurred: a) Ms. Davis got busy and forgot about my e-mail/never opened the Word document in which the questions were posed b) Ms. Davis showed "Vincent[4]" my questions and "Vincent"—who is probably happier living in a world in which *The End of the Story* and questions pertaining it don't exist—deleted my e-mail or asked Ms. Davis to delete my e-mail. At any rate, here are the questions, which I still find interesting to consider, as *TEOTS*—along with *AHWOSG*—has had such a large impact on me as a writer.

—e.e.

–*The End of the Story* seems to be as much about what's left off the page as what is included. Did you remove a significant amount of text before publication or did you write *TEOTS* with the intent of retaining a distance or of being less direct perhaps than you could have been?

---

[3] *If Ms. Davis is reading this and has changed her mind about answering these questions, please e-mail me. My e-mail, in case you have "lost"—or in case "Vincent" has "lost"—it, is ee@hobartpulp.com. Thank you, Ms. Davis.*

[4] ***some randomly chosen passages from* TEOTS *in which the character of "Vincent" is mentioned:*

"There is a creek not far away, so wide I used to call it a river before Vincent corrected me."

"I told Vincent I was writing less than a page a week, and he laughed because he thought I was joking."

"Vincent asked me why I didn't show it to him."

"Vincent happens to be reading a novel that includes the same sorts of things he hopes I will leave out. He doesn't think they belong in that novel either —he describes to me how the woman lusts for the man until she can hardly bear it, and how he consents to satisfy her, though he deserts her again after only a few hours. I don't think Vincent likes the book enough to go on with it."

"As Vincent says, I often want more than is possible."

—One could make assumptions about your life during the writing of *The End of the Story*, based on what one reads in *TEOTS*. If assumptions are correct, and you were with a longtime partner during the creative process, did that relationship ("VINCENT") affect what you left in the story and what you left out?

—Do you think a writer or an artist can ever be truthful, to herself and the events of the story she is trying to tell, if she is engaged in a romantic relationship during the creative process? In, say, the way she would be if she were single?

—You said in your *New Yorker* profile that children are "off limits," as far as being the subjects of one's writing. And I wonder why you think this (you are not alone, obviously; the majority of my female friends feel similarly). Why one often has no problem writing about one's parents, say, or one's siblings, neither of whom asked to have a relative who is an author either . . . can one ethically explore through one's writing the relationship of being a parent, of having a child?

—Do you think female writers concern themselves more with the "ethics" of writing than their male counterparts?

—If we women concern ourselves with "ethics" (with not hurting friends/ family) when writing fiction (or nonfiction), can we possibly be truthful or reveal new truths about ourselves or others?

—Is there anything you left in *The End of the Story* you wish you had taken out or vice versa, something you removed that you now wish you had included?

—Did your agent/publisher seem to understand the novel from the beginning? Or was it, as they say, a "hard sell?"

—Did the novel change much from the first draft you showed the publisher to its final form that we read today? If it changed, in what way did it change?

Thank you for this nice note — I'm always glad to hear that the "orphan"
among my books has not been overlooked.

I'd be able to do an interview, though the coming weeks are going to be
pretty busy. Best for me, probably, would be by email and limited to no
more than ten questions, no hydra-headed ones — if that would suit, then
that would be fine.

All best,

Lydia (Davis)

VOLUME THREE.

Is that what you meant when you said you think of yourself as evil?

— *THE PARIS REVIEW*
interviewer to the poet Anne Carson

I stopped watching.

I forgot about Nudes.

I lived my life,

Which felt like a switched off TV.

— ANNE CARSON,
"The Glass Essay"

Ian is a phantom, at this point; a ghost, a myth.

Or maybe I am. It is so hard to tell.

The night before I go to the hotel, I watch *The Fountainhead* with Lee. (Earlier I watched *Requiem for a Dream* and *Jesus' Son* with him and felt similarly.)

I see similarities between the main characters and Ian and me (I have made a quiet habit of comparing Ian and me to couples in movies and novels and history because Ian is not a real person either).

Afterward I try to have a discussion with Lee about the film, the philosophy, etc.

"I don't think about it. I don't think about anything," he says.

"But don't you want to be a great writer? Don't you have personal goals?" I say.

"No," he says. "I don't want to be great at anything. I don't want to question anything. I just want to enjoy my life. I don't like using my brain."

This is what attracts me to Lee and what frustrates me simultaneously.

(He is playing devil's advocate to an extent but still . . .)

I want someone with whom I can debate ethics, philosophies, our roles in life.

(or do I?)

I want someone who will fight for me, for himself, for what he believes in. I think how Ian never would have allowed another man to come to our house, to talk to me for hours alone on our front porch . . . to sit with my son and I at a reading the next day; to leave with us, go to McDonald's with us, go to my son's soccer game with us . . . how I wouldn't have allowed a woman to come to our house and talk to Lee . . . how I would have sat myself down on the front porch with them, sat at the table with them, left the bar with them . . . I begin to blame Lee for everything subsequent that has happened, or to assign fifty percent responsibility. Which is in direct contrast to the percent responsibility I previously attributed to him: 0.

Then I remember: Ian isn't here. Ian never came back.

Ian was always arguing with me, challenging me, my opinions, my judgments. Ian was impossible for me to control. I remember complaining to him that Lee had never had a differing opinion from me—that Lee was always in agreement with me or easily swayed to my views regarding books and films and people. I see now this was a form of laziness on Lee's part. This was the easiest way for Lee to end a conversation with me or to avoid one.

I don't want to hurt Lee but hurting Lee seems inevitable.

It's an hour drive to the hotel. Lee is gracious, complimentary. Lee says, "I'm so proud of you," squeezes my hand. I am a monster. That's the implication. That's what you are thinking. It's what I am thinking also.

Lee uses the card to unlock my door and we go inside. There are two rooms, a bedroom and a living room, a couch and a desk and a mini bar.

Lee goes out to the car to retrieve the rest of my things and I stay in the hotel and begin to unpack. During our breakup, I had to do everything myself. Now I am an emotional cripple who has become so accustomed to Lee doing things for me I hardly do anything myself. I haven't been to a grocery store by myself in months. I have Lee take the car in for an oil change because I am afraid of the men who work there. I have Lee call and ask about our taxes, call the bank, call the New York hotel to cancel my reservation, in case a man answers, because I don't want to talk to a man, because I have some irrational fear of men. Or maybe it's rational. I can't remember.

Or maybe this is Lee's way of keeping me; his way of ensuring I stay, by encouraging my fears and inability to leave the house alone, without him.

I walk Lee by the hand into the bedroom. I sit him on the bed, get down on hands and knees. I am thinking about how all the most significant and irrelevant moments of my life seem to occur within overpriced hotel rooms. I am thinking how I owe my husband for all the misery I have put him through and all the misery I am about to put him through. I am rating hotel mattresses in my head. I am thinking about how I was never on my hands and knees with Ian, how many hotel rooms I have stayed in since leaving those in which I did and didn't see Ian.

If Lee knew the frequency with which I think of Ian; when and where . . . I swallow my husband's ejaculate to prove I am not a monster and all the while I am thinking of Ian. I never stop to think who Lee might be thinking of—an image memorized from photographs of young naked women on his phone, maybe. Or a woman he had sex with during our breakup. Or a woman he would like to have sex with if we break up again. Of course it is narcissistic and naïve of me to think my husband is not also thinking of someone else in these moments. Maybe I'm not the only monster in the room, is what I'm trying to say. Maybe I'm just the most egotistical monster.

I feel like abdicating as a writer. It suddenly seems monstrous to me to expose the feelings one has, even those in the past, even the dead ones.
—Anais Nin

As soon as Lee is gone I begin to panic. I have wanted for weeks months to be alone and now that I am, I am terrified. I walk from room to room, opening drawers, reading brochures. I am unsure what I am looking for. I have stayed in similar hotel rooms with both Lee and Ian. I cover each of the two TVs with the extra blankets I find in the closet. I pull back the curtain and stare down at the street. I am directly over the entrance to the hotel. One of the bellhops looks up and I let go of the curtain, take a step back. Twice Ian did not show . . .

It's five thirty or six by the time I am done unpacking. I sit in front of my computer, open my novel in Word... I don't get up again for seven hours. That first night I sleep soundly. The blankets are heavy and I pull them to my chin. I lie awake in the dark at nine o'clock. I turn the clock toward the wall.

(I fall asleep almost instantly and don't wake up until ten in the morning.) The last night I will sleep more than six consecutive hours. Soon I will not average more than four.

The next few days I don't leave my room.

For four days I make do with the foods I have brought with me; protein bars, water bottles, pretzels. I eat the occasional snack from the mini bar (cashews, potato chips) but since I am not leaving my room, there is no way for housekeeping to come in and refill what I have eaten. Soon there is little left. A jar of gummy bears I have been eyeing, some sort of oriental mix I'll never eat, airplane sized bottles of alcohol, and a pack of gum.

I call down to room service every morning, have them bring up a large pot of coffee and cream. A young man in a bowtie named Devon delivers my coffee, places it on the table, removes the plastic wrap from the creamer, pours a cup. For five days, Devon is my only connection with the outside world. I find myself thinking about Devon after he's left my room. I wonder where he lives, if he's in school, if he has a girlfriend, what he thinks of me.

I sit at the desk where Lee placed my computer. I stare at the screen, type words into a document I began several months ago. I have no memory of the writing of most of these sentences. I read them as though reading the work of another writer. I feel strangely untied to them. Most of them seem to be about Ian.

I sit on the floor away from the window and read the newspaper. I read about a man in Florida whose bed fell into a sinkhole and a teacher who baked his semen into cookies and fed them to kindergartners in California.

I receive texts from people I have met on the Internet; young writers who have emailed me their work or to say they have read my books. Most of them live in states I have never been. I take comfort in my own ignorance, my lack of travel.

I open my phone and there are three new texts from a twenty-two year old in Arkansas. She has published only one poem, but it is memorable in the way most books of poetry are not. Mostly the young woman texts me about sex she is having with my peers, male writers I know or have known.

I keep waiting for her to mention Ian. As long as she doesn't mention Ian this will all be okay.

For almost two hours she studied an old issue of Vogue she picked up in the poolhouse, her attention fixed particularly on the details of the life led in New York and Rome by the wife of an Italian industrialist. The Italian seemed to find a great deal of purpose in her life, seemed to make decisions and stick by them, and Maria studied the photographs as if a key might be found among them. —Joan Didion, *Play It As It Lays*

After we had watched *The Fountainhead*, Lee had gone up to bed and I had sat in the basement smoking with the window open.

Once when I had still been mired inside of this thing with Ian, I had texted him (Ian), asking him to call me.

"You are being disrespectful. I am trying to work," he had texted back.

I am still wrestling with the sort of assuredness Ian possessed four years ago.

By the fifth day I have not overcome my fear of leaving the room. I stand with my ear pressed against the door.

I have written over twenty thousand words.

I have fit all of the newspapers Devon has brought me neatly inside the trashcan under my desk. There are two more trashcans just like this one, leather-bound and lined with plastic, and I carry them into the living room, sit all three side by side. I stick my tray in the hall at one in the morning. I still have several rolls of toilet paper from the stash I brought with me to the hotel. There is an assortment of cards on the coffee table written to me from various members of the housekeeping staff: Wanda and Tracy and Lenora. Wanda and Tracy and Lenora have asked me to dial the housekeeping extension should I require their services. Every day around two pm there is a new card slipped under the door. Every day I turn my head toward it, acknowledge its existence, return back to whatever I am doing: typing or reading the newspaper, texting young women in New Mexico, Arkansas.

It is 2013 and I don't have a smart phone. Marta says it is important for you to know this.

In an attempt at alleviating existential panic I stare into the magnified mirror bolted to the bathroom wall at random hours of the day and night, pluck tiny hairs from my cheeks and from the tender area over my eyes. I have concerns about my teeth. I wake sometimes to the sound of them gnashing together. I get out of bed to see if they are all still intact. I stare at the new chips along the bottom ridges of my teeth. I remember watching the movie *Betty Blue* as a nineteen year old who experienced panic attacks every time I left my apartment. I remember Betty Blue popping out her own eye at the end of the movie. After that Betty was committed to the mental ward of a hospital. After that her lover snuck in and suffocated her with a pillow when no one was watching at the hospital.

I remember feeling terrified of Betty Blue, of becoming like her. I remember wondering if I would ever have a lover who would care enough about me to kill me with a pillow.

I open the newspaper, read a story about a young man in Oregon who hasn't left his apartment in months due to his near constant state of nausea. Two years ago the young man was diagnosed with cancer and now the cancer is gone but so are parts of his vital organs, the ones that keep him from vomiting several times a day, without warning. I think about his isolation, compare it to mine . . . I think about writing him a letter, comparing our isolation (I am a monster); don't.

Don't confuse the monster on the page with the monster here in front of you. —Donald Barthelme

It may or may not be worth mentioning that Betty Blue's lover was a writer also.

I sit, naked on the edge of the tub, plucking hairs from my lower abdominal region. I press the flesh of this region flat with the palm of one hand and use the other to navigate the tweezers. I only wince the first couple of times. A small pile of hair forms on the floor at my feet. I cannot decide what to do with it, how to properly dispose of its contents. I step over and around it on my way to the toilet and shower until a decision can be reached.

I read a newspaper article about the decline in the youngest generation's rate of acquiring driver's licenses. The economy is one factor, the newspaper says. Also more urban living. But another factor, perhaps the greatest factor, is the increase in online socialization . . . less young people going out to socialize. The socialization via phones and computers.

I open a magazine. There is an interview with a young woman, 19 or 20. She says her real friends are those she knows online. She says the weekend before she went to a club as "research," but the whole time she just wanted to get back home to talk to her real friends on the internet.

I wonder—as I wondered three years earlier—if I could not have continued to have a similar relationship with Ian. If the relationship we were sustaining via text messages and emails could not have continued on indefinitely.

By the sixth day I am becoming restless. I am still terrified of leaving my room but the terror is no longer enough to keep me in it. I am bored too. I call Lee and tell him: today is the day. I am going out.

I find myself standing in the middle of the lobby. There are guests seated on couches and in chairs having drinks to my left.

It feels as though everyone is aware my presence in the room; that they have either turned to look at me or are consciously not looking in my direction.

I hesitate a second, then raise my right forefinger in front of me. I feel lightheaded, anxious, nauseous. I press the button for the elevator. Perhaps it has not yet left the floor since I exited it.

I pass a man in the hall on my floor but I am so close to being back safely inside my room I don't flinch. The Do Not Disturb sign is still hanging from my door. I use my key to enter. I close and lock the door. I walk immediately into the bathroom. I do not stop to pick up my phone, though I can see I have a new message. I stand in front of the magnification mirror, begin to pluck my eyebrows. I sit on the edge of the tub; remove my pants.

Lee will be here Saturday. I will wait for Saturday to leave my room with Lee.

IN MY ABSENCE LEE AND ELI BOND

I run a bath and lay in the water reading E.'s last ten texts. They are all about school and Meg and all the things he and L. are doing together in my absence: eating at the bar in town I like the least, playing Frisbee golf, watching a new TV show about zombies. I am happy for them; that they are bonding in my absence in a way they haven't in the previous nine years with me around. This is another pro for my staying gone: L. and E.'s relationship. I reply to E.'s texts as routinely as I can. I tell him I am happy he is getting a part-time job, happy he thinks he has made a decision about college, happy L. and he are spending so much time together.

I am sorry, I say, I can't be there with him.

But I'm not sure I mean it. It was difficult being around E. now that I realized he would soon be leaving. I found it agonizing doing each seasonal activity together, as we'd always done, knowing it was unlikely we would have an opportunity to do it again the following year or any year thereafter, for that matter. It was like an extended, painful breakup. I had found myself in tears more in the past six months than I had in four years. I was exhausted from feeling so much as I'd been exhausted five years earlier, the summer I met Ian.

During the second week I stop sleeping regularly. I call down for a second pot of coffee in the evening. I read and write and answer texts from people I barely know most of the night, until no one else is awake. I have lost my appetite also. I open one of the mini bottles of whiskey in the bar, and change my mind, pour it into the sink. There is a mirror at the back of the bar, which I avoid. I avoid all mirrors except the ones that are magnified. I cast my gaze downward while brushing my teeth. I stare into the sink.

I put on the red strapless dress I wore at my wedding reception and take photographs of myself on the bed with a self-timer. I change into a bathing suit I wore on my honeymoon and take photographs sprawled on the couch and draped over a chair. I pass three hours taking photographs of myself before I realize I have no way of showing them to Ian. I stare into my camera deleting photographs. I can only look at myself in pictures I manipulate for good lighting and posture. I never photograph myself in daylight, for instance. I find the shadows in a room, move into them. I can't tell if I am a true narcissist or my own best company and what does it matter.

[Years later Eli will say, "I told you not to write this book. I told you it would make you obsessed with him again." We will be standing beside one another in a candle store. Eli will be holding a candle out for me to smell: Ocean Breeze or Fresh Linen. What does it matter.]

Something about taking photographs for Ian makes me sentimental. I write five new pages of sentiment that I immediately delete in the morning. I sit staring at the pages I have written. I don't realize I am crying until the tears pool in my collarbone. I get my Kindle, search Ian's name in the online 'store' as though I am searching for Ian in a room at a party.

By morning I have finished one of Ian's novels and am midway through a second. There is a part about anal sex. When Devon comes in the room to deliver my pot of coffee I wonder if he can tell I have been masturbating while reading the part in Ian's book about anal sex.

I stay inside my room another three days; write another nine thousand words; continue to read Ian's books. I realize my obsession with Ian is increasing due to isolation and a lack of distractions. I remember E. telling me that Eminem didn't start doing drugs until after he rapped about doing drugs. It's hard to know what came first in my case because almost from the beginning I was both obsessed with Ian and writing about Ian.

I read a review of a book about Gandhi in *The New York Times*. The review talks about a sister of a friend whose "apparent infatuation with Gandhi led her to chase him from England to South Africa. 'She cannot tear herself away from me,' Gandhi wrote in one letter to Henry."

I read a new review of an old film in *The New Yorker*. The movie is Truffaut's *The Story of Adele H.*, a semi-fictionalized account of Victor Hugo's daughter's obsession with a "handsome but entirely worthless officer" with whom she has a brief affair and then follows from Europe to Halifax to the Caribbean. Of Adele, the reviewer, David Denby writes, "[she] is a liar, a voyeur, a blackmailer—despite moments of manipulative lucidity, she's mad, and the movie is devoted to her simultaneous self-creation and self-annihilation."

I am interested in the reviewer's portrayal of Adele as having 'moments of manipulative lucidity,' in his wanting to hold her accountable for her actions while also glorifying her madness. I am interested in his description of the officer as 'handsome but worthless.' I want to know what makes one man worthy of obsession and another unworthy.

"And I just hope I am worthy of all this," Ian wrote me in an email three years earlier.

LEE COMES TO SEE ME

I've been at the hotel nine or ten or eleven days, it's hard to remember, when Lee comes to see me. I shower and pick up the room, put away my notebooks, turn off the computer, shove my camera and Kindle in my suitcase. I am careful not to expose evidences of disloyalty. I comb my hair, practice making shapes and noises with my mouth, as one is taught to do before a musical performance or before giving a blowjob.

It's been so long since I said anything aloud. The only person I have spoken to is Devon and the young woman who stands in for Devon on Devon's day off. The only words I have uttered aloud are, "Yes, thank you."

I want to appear as normal as possible, to not give off any "funny" vibes. I am thinking of my best friend's mother and of Betty Blue. I am conscious of not wanting to end up like either one of them: alone in a hospital room.

I sit on the couch and wait with my hands in my lap. I straighten the hotel magazines on the coffee table. I get up, check my lipstick and teeth. I sit back down with the knowledge Lee would not suffocate me with a pillow. Lee does not understand the concept of mercy or how he could be a participant in it.

My phone buzzes with a text. I stand and walk halfway to the door, run my hands over my hair, practice smiling again, feeling with my fingers the way my cheeks push out. I stand in stillness four minutes. I am mentally preparing for a visit with my husband like a patient in a mental hospital, like someone who has been granted visitation after a suicide attempt, after taking too many pills, after having a very heady emotional affair three years earlier from which she has yet to recover.

Eli would do it, I am thinking. E. would suffocate me with a pillow if it came to that, I am fairly confident.

There is a knock and I walk carefully to the door. I feel the tension leave my body. I pull Lee inside, feel his arms wrap instinctively around me. He is carrying bags of protein bars and Diet Cokes and cigarettes and pretzels. He is carrying a bottle of whiskey, which he sets on the bar by the mirror.

"I missed you," I hear myself say, surprising myself with the genuineness of the sentiment.

"I missed you, too, silly," he says, and he sits down on the couch. "You really did miss me," he says, laughing, making a nod at my hands wrapped tightly around his arm.

I get up, walk to the bar, make Lee a drink. I can't remember if it is

Lee or I who suggest we watch porn. It is an old crutch. It could have been either one of us.

We had been talking about Eli, I remember, just before.

"I barely see him," Lee had told me. "He's so busy with the end of the school year and everything." And by 'everything' I knew Lee meant Eli's girlfriend. I wondered if Lee had a crush on her, if she was someone he thought of during sex with me.

Lee had removed the blanket from the TV in the bedroom, folded it neatly and set it in the closet. I positioned myself so I didn't have to look at the screen if I didn't feel like it. Maybe it was drinking on an empty stomach, but I was starting to feel nauseous.

I had begun recently to resent porn, or to resent Lee's dependence on it. I didn't understand what happened to his tenderness, why it seemed to vanish at the most crucial times. Maybe I just needed to drink more. I seemed to want only to be held now. Lee, for his part, seemed uncharacteristically aloof and unreachable. It was hard for me to feel anything, while watching actors on TV. I felt like an actor also, but not a very good one. Lee must not have been paying attention, because I didn't think I was very convincing.

At dinner in a diner I asked him if he thought he was addicted to porn, if he thought porn would be hard to give up. I asked how many times a week he watched it. He said two or three times a week and he didn't know but probably.

I sat mushing fries around my plate and in my mouth. I still felt slightly nauseous. Lee had gone to a doctor to get pills to take for when we had sex without porn. It all seemed pretty awful if you thought about it so I tried not to think about it. Lee didn't like to think about it either. He had that look on his face now like an adolescent boy gets after a scolding. Talking about it just made us both feel like shit so I decided not to talk about it.

We had planned to see a movie. There was a giant multiplex around the corner from the diner and hotel. Everything about this town reminded me of The Truman Show. I thought how easy it would be for a person living here to develop the psychological disorder they'd named for the film. The streets were lined with corporate coffee shops and retail stores like a fancy mall but all outdoors. But there was hardly anyone on the street.

There was no trash or animals either. A lone actor stood here and there, on a newly painted bench or on a street corner. I thought if you could pan far enough back, you could see the tops of the sets, how there'd be no back ends to the stores.

The giant movie multiplex was empty also. Big surprise. We rode the escalator up to the second floor where you bought tickets. I didn't understand the purpose of the first floor. The woman in the glass booth who sold us our tickets seemed like an actor, too. Her Midwestern accent seemed inauthentic. I wanted to engage her in a dialogue that would encourage her to say the words "follow" or 'dollar" to test her, but I couldn't think of how that dialogue would feel natural so I let it go.

Lee wanted to see two films, back to back, like we'd done when we'd first started dating. I was trying to be accommodating. Lee didn't ask for much. The first film wasn't too long and was a comedy, though I couldn't recall laughing. Lee bought M&M's and I tried letting them melt on my tongue like I usually did but I had to quietly spit them on the floor during a loud scene so Lee wouldn't notice because I was having trouble swallowing again.

Twelve minutes into the second film I started to get a headache. Or I'd started to be unable to distract myself from the headache that had probably started at some point during the first film. It was a gripping, throbbing sort of headache and I wanted to lie down on a bathroom floor but I was concerned the bathroom in the theater wasn't really a bathroom in the same way the ticket seller wasn't really Midwestern.

The second film was set in space and 3D and watching it I had the feeling I was undulating, which would have made more sense if the film had been set on a boat. I took off my 3D glasses and sat watching the movie without them a while. Lee didn't seem to notice, and I felt relieved and annoyed about that at the same time. I knew from past conversations that Lee had trained himself not to notice things. How much of what transpired between Ian and I could I pin on Lee having trained himself not to notice things? How much of seeking out Ian or of allowing myself to be sought by Ian could be attributed to my feeling unnoticed by Lee?

My head was really throbbing now and staring at the screen without the 3D glasses was just making me dizzier. I grabbed my purse and leaned over to Lee.

"Don't follow me," I said. I said it as a whisper even though there didn't appear to be anyone else in the theater. Just in case. I had meant it as a generosity—I didn't want Lee to miss the rest of the film just because I wasn't feeling well—but it came out more as a threat. Still, I was somewhat surprised when I turned around in the hall that led to the exit and Lee wasn't behind me. I felt the same mixture of relief and annoyance I'd felt when he hadn't noticed I'd removed my 3D glasses.

When I got to the end of the hall I was unsure what to do or where to go so I just kept walking. I kept walking down the escalator and out the front of the multiplex and down the street to the hotel. I walked through the lobby to the elevator and from the elevator down the hall to my room. It seemed like once I had the idea the town was populated with actors, it was easier to pass by them. I no longer had to worry about them talking to me, or how I would respond if they talked to me. Dialogue was someone else's concern, not mine.

I looked at my phone to see if Lee had texted me and there was a text from the young woman in Arkansas. There was a photograph attached to the text. I could barely make it out on the small screen of my cellphone but I was pretty sure it was a picture of Sadie and Ian. I replied with question mark and five seconds later there was a new text that said, "from sadie's twitter. she and ian kaye were in nyc." A second text came through while I was still reading the first. "probly on molly," it said. I didn't know what to say in reply. The young woman didn't know anything about my experiences with Ian. I sat staring at my phone waiting for something to happen, for Lee to text me or for the young woman in Arkansas to tell me more or for Ian to text me, even though the last of the three seemed almost an impossibility. Somehow it seemed as plausible a next step as any other in that moment.

Finally I typed "lol" into my phone and hit send.

I was sitting on the floor of the bathroom. I sat there a while waiting to see what would happen next.

For a long while nothing happened at all.

For a long while—an hour or ninety minutes—I lost track of time, I lay reclined against the bathtub waiting for something to happen next.

Finally there was a knock at the door.

I remained still. I wasn't sure if I was going to answer it or not. I had decided it might be Lenora or Devon.

"It's me," I heard someone say. I couldn't be sure of its origins.

"It's Lee," the voice said.

I got up and walked to the door. I looked through the peephole and it was Lee, just as he'd said.

"I hate when you leave the theater," he said. He was still standing in the hall.

"Do you want another drink?" I said. I was standing in the doorway but I was facing away from Lee. Something had distracted me on my way to the door. I was suddenly concerned about the TV. Lee had forgotten to drape it with the blanket. The blanket was still neatly folded in the closet.

"I have to drive home," Lee said. I stared at his face, realizing I had been thinking of Sadie and Ian this whole time.

"What now? What should we do now?" I said.

"I don't know," Lee said. "People don't really change."

I knew I should feel bad in this moment, about the distance I was putting between Lee and me. Instead, I was thinking about how as soon as Lee left, I could go to the business center and see for myself what Sadie's Twitter said. I could look at other people's Twitters. I could search Ian's name.

I decided not to say anything, to resist making a counter argument to Lee's claim. I didn't want to extend his stay. Instead I moved closer to him, waited for him to embrace me. I was picturing him alone in his office in the basement, masturbating to moving images on his phone. I wondered how he pictured me when I wasn't around. If he bothered to imagine me.

I didn't have a counter argument to make anyway.

None of us was changing. We were each of us treading water in our own isolation.

[Once, a long time ago, the title of this book was *The Isolationists*.]

AFTER LEE LEAVES

After Lee leaves I walk to the bar in my room, pour a drink. I am making a conscious decision to get drunk. I haven't been drunk in twenty years. I am giving myself permission to be sick. I pour more whiskey in my glass. It's sometime after midnight, one or two in the morning. The hall is quiet. I have changed into sweats and a t-shirt. I am wrapped in the hotel robe because earlier I was freezing. But now, suddenly, I am sweltering. My cheeks are flush. I slip out of the robe, leave it on the floor where I will lie down when I return.

I walk down the hallway in my socks with my key in one hand, a bar glass in the other. Surprisingly, despite my drunkenness, I remember the way. I don't get lost or have to double back. I don't encounter any businessmen or their female counterparts. I feel lucky. The business center and fitness rooms are empty. I key into the fitness center feeling cocky in my drunkenness. I stand on a treadmill and walk, placing my cup of bourbon in the hole meant for water bottles. I walk for five minutes, changing channels on the wall mounted TV. I consider shaving my head. I consider the signal that would send to Ian. Look at me! I am like you now! I am batshit crazy! I am ready to be batshit crazy with you! I consider running away from my life, going on a mad spending spree in New York or LA or Paris. How long would it take me to spend all the money that separates us? Six months? A year? Staying in five star hotels, ordering room service, top shelf bottles of liquor, a wardrobe of clothes worn by rappers and young movie stars. I would come to you, finally, with gold chains around my neck, leather pants and six inch stilettos and furs. I want to look glamorous for you, for the next decade of years living in filth. I will retain my sense of style while losing my dignity (or is that something that was long ago lost, the day we met?). I will succumb in a bathtub more Gummo than Beverly Hills. I want you to be in the next room nodding out or out looking for more drugs. I want you to climb in the bathtub beside me when you return fully clothed. Remove one of the chains from my neck and put it around yours. Never take it off. Overdose with my chain around your neck. I picture you dead wearing that ridiculous chain.

Overdosing doesn't seem so bad. When you consider the other possibilities. ("Most men lead lives of quiet desperation."—for instance.)

This is the most fucked up, inebriated version of a fantasy. Ian would hate it. Ian would tell me it is bullshit. "This is not me," he would say. "I don't even recognize myself in this anymore."

Maybe that is the point. (I don't know if I'm telling him this or you.)

I don't recognize myself either, Ian.

I stop walking, sit on the floor with an orange and my bourbon. I eat three segments of the orange, leave the rest on the floor. I want the hotel staff to think there are squatters. I leave an opened water bottle on the floor too. Take another one with me. Take a towel too. Why not? I want to take everything available to me now.

I key into the business center, go straight to Ian's blog. While I am waiting for it to load I swallow another mouthful of bourbon. I think about how the two times we slept together, neither of us drank. I think of sobriety now as being with Ian. I tell myself he avoids being sober because it reminds him of me. I am less cynical, more romantic when I am drinking. This is what he doesn't realize. The first night I curled into his lap I was drunk. I needed the false sense of courage. I didn't know how he felt about me. I wasn't sick in the morning but I didn't get out of bed all day. I'm unsure if I was hung over from the alcohol or overcome with (the idea of) him. The next night we didn't drink and I didn't curl up in his lap. I stood an appropriate distance from him in the driveway. Maybe we were both still in shock from what had transpired the night before. We were clueless where to go next. Everything hereafter, I am realizing as I type this, has been about the both of us being clueless about where to go next. The now what. We could never figure out the now what of our situation, of this predicament we found ourselves in, of us.

I do a search for Sadie's name and when I don't find it I smile.

I am comforted by Ian's latest suicidal rant. There are photos of him bent over, vomiting on stage. He is a barely functioning human being. Something about this awareness (perhaps it is only my own drunkenness) makes me smile a second time. (Let's be barely functioning human beings together!)

But then I remember he likes me because of my ability to function and to (his perspective:) function "well." He likes me because I am the opposite of Sadie. (It's a hard thing for me to remember in the face of so much video and photographic evidence to the contrary!)

There are links to music sites and magazines, reporting on the tour, on Ian's moods. There are photographs there of Sadie and they are imprinted forever in my mind.

I imagine standing in a bathroom mirror, watching the hair fall to the floor in soft waves.

I imagine walking to CVS in my hotel robe, purchasing a pair of pliers, pulling the teeth in need of root canals from my mouth.

In my drunkenness I lose all sense of hopefulness or perspective.

I have a tendency to forget about Lee, to focus solely on my obsessions, which amount to my teeth and errant hairs and Ian.

I go to my email. I don't read anything in my inbox. I write emails to mutual friends. I tell them I'm worried about Ian. I say I just want to know if he's okay.

I don't tell them I am worried about Sadie.

I don't email Ian.

I still, even in my drunkenness and despair, have my promise to Lee.

Of course I know no one will reply to me about Ian. It feels like a conspiracy at times.

The next day L. calls to tell me about a documentary he watched about a contemporary female performance artist. In the documentary, he says, the artist sits in a museum, staring into the eyes of anyone willing to wait in line.

"One of her old lovers waited in line," L. says.

I know about the artist and the man because I have read articles about the documentary. I know the man who waited in line is an artist also, and that they once came close to marrying. I don't mention this to L. I let L. tell me about it in his own words. I am curious what those words will be.

"They didn't speak but there were tears visible in both their eyes," L. says.

Immediately I think of Ian, as I have whenever I have read about the documentary, about the two artists—one male, one female; old lovers.

I think of how this couldn't have been L.'s intent, inciting in me an image of Ian, but that I cannot figure out another intent either.

Later I realize this was probably an attempt on L.'s part to draw me in closer to him, to take an interest in something he knew would interest me.

At the time, however, all I could think to ask was, "But what about either of their current lovers? Is this not disrespectful to them?"

I was always trying to validate my own artistic choices with L. I was always attempting to make or combat a moral point.

E. calls me later the same day. I suspect L. has put him up to it. It is the last time I will talk to my son for a long while (though of course I do not know this or maybe I do and what does it matter). E. tells me about plans he is making for his senior prom and plans he is making for his graduation party. We talk about Greece, a trip we have planned to take together later in the summer. Our final trip together, before my son reaches adulthood.

"There are so many places I want to show you," he says. "The Parthenon and the Coliseum and Ithaca and the islands . . . "

It felt harder saying goodbye to him than normal, though I tried not to let on. I tried to sound cheerful, anticipatory and excited about the future.

The night before I had read a passage in one of Ian's books about the future. It was a philosophical narrative, written in first person. An argument against the future. An argument for living without fears or problems.

For abolishing the need for either by living in the present, without looking backward or ahead.

I was considering if it were possible to live like that. So much of my life felt like planning. So much of raising a child was about assembling a future for that child and by extension, for oneself. It felt almost impossible to let go of this habit. But I began to look around me. Here was my life now in this hotel room. Here were my books and my writing. Here was my present self. Not some self worried about a future with L. or with Ian. Not some self concerned with the past, either. Here was a self that existed only in this room, concerned only with these words on this page. I allowed myself to feel liberated by this way of thinking—by the lack of a need for morals it implied, even while some "other" part of me viewed this way of thinking as selfish and resented the author for thinking selfishly. That other part was the part of me that still felt rejected by Ian. I didn't know if it was possible for me to let go of that part, even in this new way of thinking. Even in this viewing of myself only as I existed on this day, in this room.

I spend a succession of overnights in the business center, doing Google image searches of Ian and Sadie, reading blog posts. I stop my daytime routine. I sleep from six in the morning until three in the afternoon. Someone else brings my coffee. I instruct them over the phone to leave it outside my door. I wait until I am sure they are gone to open it. Occasionally I sit in front of my computer but I don't move the manuscript forward. I add sentences that I delete the next day or an hour later.

I walk to Starbucks and CVS. I buy caffeinated drinks in cans, buy nicotine gum and lozenges and cigarettes, buy cold medicine and sip it from the bottle.

I keep a growing stack of printed out blog posts on the coffee table and the table beside my bed where I read but do not sleep. When I am not in the business center I sit on the floor or lie in bed and read them.

I tape the photographs around the room. Pictures of Sadie in a hotel bed with Ian and Ian's drummer, Ian and Sadie in the backseat of a car, Ian slumped on her shoulder, a cigarette burning in her red mouth, Sadie playing guitar on stage, Ian visible in the wings.

I take long baths, smoke in the tub. I have stopped worrying that hotel management will contact me. I have been smoking in my room for seven days now without incident, without so much as a phone ringing or a note slid under the door.

I think how easy it would be to slip under the bath water like a pop star in Beverly Hills; how beautiful a last image this would be for Ian. I upend the bottle of cold medicine.

I text Saul from the water.

I imagine him standing next to my son in the school cafeteria when he receives my text.

I text the young woman in Arkansas while waiting for Saul to text back.

I text a young man in Austin. Another in California. Another in New York City.

I text the people with whom I am the least intimate in the same manner in which I once texted Ian.

I climb out of the tub, wrap myself in the robe, lie on the bed, looking backward through my texts. My eyes are heavy with an inability to sleep and I close them reading backward through old texts I've saved with Saul. There is always in the back of my mind this idea that I could run away with him now that he is eighteen.

Or that I could catch the bed on fire with my carelessness with a cigarette.

These are only a couple of my ideas.

I have others.

I call L. I don't want to worry him. I am afraid he will show up at the hotel. I try my best to act normal, to speak normally on the phone.

"I'm getting a lot of work done," I tell him. I've been telling him the same thing for two weeks. Only now it has changed, now it is no longer true.

"When are you coming home?" he asks.

"I don't know," I say.

I don't have a timeframe for him. I don't know myself.

"I miss you," he says.

"I miss you, too," I say. I am chewing nicotine gum and smoking a cigarette. I feel sick but the kind of sick that reminds you you're awake, you're not yet dead.

STAT COUNTER

Once I allow myself to check Ian's blog that initial evening, I very quickly begin to check it in an obsessive manner. I start checking it twice a day and then four times a day and then eight or nine or ten. I find every reason to leave my room. I need ice, I tell myself, stopping in the business center with the empty bucket in my lap, even though I never use the ice once it has been procured. I get a second or third cup of coffee from Starbucks, cigarettes and bottles of 5 Hour Energy from CVS, stop in the business center before and after. I begin using the treadmill multiple times a day, for shorter amounts of time, ten minutes, five, waiting for the business center to empty...

Ian, in turn, begins updating his blog more regularly, sometimes multiple times a day.

LIVEBLOG

I go to Sadie's blog. There are three hundred photographs from tour and I scan them all quickly looking for Ian. He is in at least half of them. In some he is standing backstage with women I don't recognize and in others he is onstage and he looks lost or vacant. There are photographs taken in hotels of Ian and Sadie and other members of both bands and extra people I don't recognize, splayed out on beds, sitting on floors, drugs and bottles of alcohol visible around them, young women naked and in bikinis. And the one I pause on, the one I can't get out of my head, is the one in which Sadie is lying on her back in a satin nightgown and under one arm is Ian and under another is a guy I don't recognize and the three of them appear to be sleeping, though Sadie has a burning cigarette in one hand, in the hand cradling Ian's head. I look at another hundred photographs and stop on one of Sadie and Ian in the backseat of someone's car, Sadie again cradling Ian, Ian leaning up against the side of her body, eyes shut, mouth open. These photographs, combined with Sadie's description of the tour as "life changing" and of Ian as "one of the most special persons I have ever known...," sours my stomach. Suddenly I feel genuinely sick. I throw the cup of coffee I've been refilling for twelve hours in the garbage and open the bottle of water I took from the fitness room. I swallow as much as I can and wait to see if it will stay. I am leaning toward the trashcan just in case. I wait a minute and nothing happens and I go back to looking at Sadie's blog because I can't stop now.

CRACK VIDEO

There is a link to a video titled "crack" and I click on the link and soon I am watching a video of five people—Sadie and Ian and a guy I recognize from Ian's band and a guy and a girl I don't recognize but who look young, like eighteen, maybe—in a room together, and Sadie tells us, tells the camera, they are about to smoke crack. One of the people I don't recognize, the male, lights a pipe and takes a long drag and coughs and takes another before passing the pipe to the person, the young female, next to him. The pipe gets passed around the room. Ian is all the way in the back, on a couch by himself, wearing a pair of shorts and boots. He has a moustache and his hair is grown out and he barely resembles the person I met four years ago, the young, angry man with a shaved head. Then he looked like a young de Niro. He looked capable of killing a person. Now he looks indistinguishable from people I pass on the street. He looks soft and hollow-eyed and apathetic. I want him to look angrier. Four years ago when I met him he could have been the world's strongest man. He was young and angry and there was a solidness about him, like a thousand pound bull couldn't have knocked him down; which made the anguished look on his face all the more affecting.

I pause the video, stare into his face. I look around to see if anyone is in the fitness center, to see if there are cameras in the ceiling.

I want to be alone with Ian.

It was already crushing to read about a time on tour in which Sadie and Ian locked themselves in a hotel room for the night, ostensibly to do drugs . . .

All this stalking of Sadie is really only filler because there is so little of Ian to stalk.

I turn on my computer, look at the thirteen hundred words I wrote last night. I don't recognize the voice. Do not remember typing these words.

I light a cigarette, ash in the tub. I have turned my entire life into cinema. This is what I have always wanted.

I return to my room, work on my novel, stare at a photograph of Ian I printed the night before, taped to the wall, stare at a photograph of Sadie and Ian in the back of a car, stare at a blog post Ian wrote in 2009 after we met before he came to my house, think about what it would feel like to cut the inside of my arm, consider what it would feel like to use a baseball bat to shatter each one of the computers in the business center.

There is something I want. I cannot articulate what it is, even to myself. (Tell me.)

I write some more. Listen to Ian's voice in my head. Place my face in my hands. Or my hands over my face.

(I feel too much.)

I am thinking now of Lee's and my conversation from the other night. I feel strangely liberated by it. By Lee's unwillingness to change. By his willful surrender to his own inertia, to his addictions.

I am beginning to understand my restlessness. The first time I wrote this section I wrote it in third person. I felt safer writing about masturbation

from a distance. I masturbated on the floor of my hotel bedroom and immediately after I wrote about it. I wrote about the song I listened to on repeat
while masturbating, how Ian had mentioned the song on his blog before I'd
left for the hotel. How it was a love song, a song sung by a woman. How I
masturbated in an elongated, romantic manner while thinking of Ian and I
in a dark hotel room listening to that song. I wrote in an ugly, cheap way, using words I would cut from any other writer's prose, words I am too embarrassed to name here. I wrote about how I was worried I had injured myself,
injured internal parts of me, while masturbating; how I had introduced a
common grooming item inside myself. I said I had never masturbated anally before. I was getting myself off a second time by writing about it. I was
overcome by years of sexual frustration and repression. I was overcome with
thoughts of Ian and Sadie locking themselves in a hotel room on tour. I was
as jealous of their shared drug use as I was of anything else that occurred
inside of a locked room. Their was an intimacy and an eroticism to sharing
and taking drugs together I would never know with Ian, and I felt that absence as keenly as I felt the absence of our sex, as keenly as I felt the absence
of either of us on our knees on a dingy, treaded carpet.

Overnight I wrote two thousand words and this morning I wrote another
nine hundred. I am writing more than I have ever written in my life, though
I am unsure if any of it is usable. I am unsure this book is publishable. I tell
myself I just have to finish it; that I don't ever have to publish it. "You can
publish it posthumously," I tell myself. I think maybe all books should be
published posthumously, for reasons of honesty and authenticity. I imagine
The New York Times Book Review if all the books reviewed in it were posthumously published books. I imagine how this book would be different if I
knew for certain it would not be published in my lifetime (or Ian's or Lee's).
I honestly can't imagine it being much different. (I am a monster.)

Lee wants to come visit but I dissuade him from making the trip. I tell him
I am engulfed in research, manically writing, that soon I will have finished
my manuscript, soon I will be home. Eli is graduating in six weeks. I have
stopped wondering what will become of us, Lee and me, when Eli goes to
college in the fall.

I have been wondering for months how it would happen, my crack-up, my unraveling.

JAMES FRANCO, OR, THE NEXT BIG SEX SYMBOL

I go to see a movie. I have to get out of this hotel room, out of this hotel, away from my novel, thoughts of Ian, thoughts of myself.

In the movie, a woman goes to see the man she is in love with to tell him another man has proposed marriage to her. When she tells him, the man she is in love with barely reacts; says nothing.

"But what do you think I should do?" she says.

"You couldn't do better than [man who has proposed to her]," he tells her. "He's a good man."

"You could be a good man, if you wanted to," she tells the man she is in love with.

"But that's the thing," the man she is in love with says. "I don't want to be."

I leave the theater after twenty minutes. I am having a harder and harder time remaining in one place. I am chewing three pieces of nicotine gum. I have drank half of a concession stand large Diet Coke.

I stop at CVS to buy a razor. On the magazine rack by the counter is the current issue of a men's magazine and on the cover is an actor who resembles Ian. The actor is British and new to the U.S. and being touted as "the next big sex symbol" and I reach to turn the magazine over so I don't have to look at the next big sex symbol/Ian.

I am unsure whether my stay at the hotel is an attempt to overcome my obsession with Ian or to surrender to it.

Once, shortly after I'd driven to see him for the second time, Ian told me in an email that someone—one of his roommates? one of his brothers? He was consistently nonspecific about his life when speaking with me—had left a sports magazine on the coffee table and that the woman on the cover—a blonde tennis player—had so reminded him of me that he'd had to turn the magazine upside down. I thought for a moment I had won at something.

When I get back to the hotel I have a voicemail from Lee. There is an underlying sadness in his voice. Before hanging up he says quietly, "I think I'm just too sensitive."

The problem with mixing fiction with nonfiction is that people can't tell the difference. That was supposed to be the upside. Hiding bits of truths inside of lies.

I LOVE MY DOG

The next day and the day after and four or five days after that I stay in my room. I work and take baths and listen to podcasts. I listen repeatedly to a podcast in which Ian is interviewed about his life. It's an hour long and Ian reveals almost nothing but I am enamored with his voice. I had become unfamiliar with it. I listen to the podcast while eating yogurt on the bathroom floor and while crying in the shower and while masturbating while writing. At the end of the podcast the interview asks Ian if he loves his girlfriend and Ian says, "I don't know." "You don't know?" the interviewer says. "I love my dog," Ian says. "I know I love my dog."

I wanna be Bob Dylan. Sha La La La La La La La La Yeah.

Dylan: Do you think it would bother me one little bit if you dislike me? I've got my friends . . . I'm well situated.

Interviewer: But what about before you had any friends, were you worried?

Dylan: Was I worried? I wasn't worried about it, no. I was lucky, weren't you? Weren't you lucky when you didn't have any friends?

Dylan: I'm a guitar player. That's all.

Interviewer: When you meet somebody, what is your attitude toward them?

Dylan: I don't like them.

Interviewer: You don't like them?

Dylan: No!

Interviewer: I mean, I come in here, what's your attitude toward me?

Dylan: I don't have any attitude towards you at all. Why should I have an attitude toward you? I don't know you.

Interviewer: No, but, I mean, that's what I'm asking. If you wanted to know or didn't want to know me.

Dylan: But why should I want to know you?

Interviewer: I don't know. That's why I'm asking.

Dylan: Well, I don't know. Ask me another question.

—Bob Dylan, interviewed in *Don't Look Back*

LIVETWEET

Sadie says she is listening to a live recording of Ian singing reading on their tour while she writes. (I wonder sometimes if Sadie and I are the same person, if I have created another personality, like in *Fight Club*, like Tyler Durden.)

MORE NEWSPAPER CLIPPINGS:

—in Ohio a couple who has owned a black bear named Archie for 30 yrs is afraid he'll be taken from them when new laws regarding exotic animals go into effect

—in Pennsylvania a man is awaiting trial in the shooting death of a gun shop owner

—in Oregon a woman is sentenced to two years in prison for pouring hot bacon grease on her ex bf who was asleep on her couch. "It was time for him to go," she said.

STARTING TO NOT BELIEVE

I sat back down at the computer. I wanted to finish this book but I didn't know how.

I think of Elizabeth Wurtzel: *just let me finish my book, then I'll go to rehab.*

I was starting not to believe in it. I had begun at some point, unwittingly, to despise it. The writing of it, the author, the book itself. I was beginning to develop a disdain for literature in general. For any book or author who referred to their work as such.

HOTEL HORROR STORY/ Get *Lunar Park* On It

They somehow know when I leave my room. If I am gone a half an hour or an hour—to Starbucks or to CVS or to the business center or to get ice—my room is always cleaned when I return. I look for cameras in the hallway. It feels as though people are constantly hovering in the hall outside my door. I hear footsteps all day and night, people breathing when I press my ear to the door.

At night I hear sounds coming from the room above mine. The sounds are like mini bowling balls being rolled over a marble floor, though every floor except the bathroom is carpeted. I hear these sounds all night long and at five or six in the morning I wake to sounds of a shower running.

During the day it sounds as though the same room over me is being worked on, remodeled. I hear the sounds of construction: hammers and drills and saws. I take the elevator up a floor, walk the hall outside the room above mine. I can't hear anything abnormal. Part of me expected the room above mine to be a laundry room or closet. I see no evidence of anyone staying in the room. I check on it periodically. I check it for the Do Not Disturb sign on the door, for room service trays in the hall. I listen for voices on the other side of the door. I never hear anything until I'm back downstairs. I sleep with a pillow over my head. I sleep on the floor of the closet like I do at home.

Marta texts me. Marta says, "You're suffering for your art! It's glorious! You're an artistic genius!"

I thought she just felt guilty because she had been the one to tell me about Ian doing the reading with whats-her-face.

"It makes sense you're feeling this way because you're writing a book about obsession and he is the basis of the book."

I didn't want it to make sense.

I am exhausted from suffering; bored by my own obsession.

Perhaps he just prefers the imagery of love made familiar by fashion magazines: images of the subject exhausted by "feeling," undone by a crush, recuperating in an atmosphere of glamour and allure. —Hilton Als, *White Girls*—Andre Leon Talley section: "The Only One"

I got out of the bathtub, slipped back into my robe. I was falling easily into the role of hotel recluse. I ordered up a pot of tea and a bowl of oatmeal. I had to plead with the woman who answered in the kitchen for the oatmeal because it was late in the evening and they only served oatmeal before noon.

I walked toward my phone at the same time a knock was heard on the door. I reached for the phone and stuck it down in my robe pocket. A young man I didn't recognize asked to come in and I stepped aside so that he could pass by me and set my tray on the table. I was as far from being the sort of woman Ian would date in this hotel than I'd ever been. Or maybe I was closer. I couldn't decide which. It was so hard to tell. I signed the bill with what I hoped came out a smile and thanked the young man and closed the door. I removed the lids from both the oatmeal and the tea in order to hasten the cooling process, then removed my phone from my pocket, opened it to read the text that had come through while I was at my desk.

The text was from Saul. I had not heard from him in months.

The text said, "I'm back in town. Dinner?"

"I'm not at home," I texted back.

"Where are you?"

"I'm at a hotel in ----. Writing," I said.

"The next great American novel?"

"Something like that." ("Not even close.")

It was fifteen minutes before another text came through from Saul. I was having a hard time figuring out how to fit each person into my life.

"I could come over there," Saul finally texted. "We could have dinner over there."

I had forgotten Saul could drive, that he was now eighteen. I didn't know if this made it better or worse. I didn't know what "it" was.

"I don't know," I said.

I could never figure out how I felt about Saul. There was no cultural precedent for what we were to each other. There were no labels either. Far as I could tell, we weren't supposed to talk even.

"Please," Saul texted. "Come on. For old time's sake."

"I don't know," I said. I was planning on drinking more cough syrup with my tea. I was smoking a cigarette while eating my oatmeal. "Maybe tomorrow. Text me tomorrow, ok?"

"K," Saul said.

I got up and set my dinner tray outside the door in the hallway. A woman walked by and smiled and I didn't know how to react.

I opened a new bottle of cough syrup. Considered how it might help me deal with my unknowable feelings for Saul, my unknowable feelings for myself, and everyone surrounding me.

Were I truly a liberated individual living in the moment, I would have allowed Saul to come over, to eat dinner with me, and whatever else.

But I have never been truly liberated.

It is only now that I am contemplating being a true individual.

BLOG POST

In the morning I go to Ian's blog first, as is my habit. There are several new posts since last I checked, four or five or six hours ago. I am unsure how long I slept. I read them fast, skimming them first, knowing I will return to the top, read them slow a second time. Or print them and take them with me to read at my leisure in the privacy of my room, where I may engage in activities not fitting for a public area, if I so choose.

I skim down to the last post, retch into the wastebasket beside me. I haven't yet eaten anything and only coffee comes up. It looks less like vomit than like someone threw her coffee cup into the trashcan without a lid.

I use the sleeve of my robe to wipe my mouth.

The last post is a direct statement to me, a request for me to email him. He doesn't use my name. Instead he says, "I emailed someone three months ago. I have not heard back from this person. I don't wish to bother you. I just want to talk if you're willing." He ends the post with his email. The same email Horatio gave me, the same email that is at the top of the blog under 'contact info.'

I sit, unmoving, staring at the screen. I feel as though Ian is watching me. I am panicked. I realize I have forgotten my cough syrup. I am having a hard time catching my breath. I need a cigarette, a nicotine lozenge. Any distractionary activity.

I hit print and watch the blog post flow out as if by magic, as if Ian has sent me a letter in the mail.

I carry it back to my room, nauseated. I have left the coffee cup on the table by the computer. I have left my vomit in the trashcan.

For twelve hours I sit in my hotel room contemplating the situation, Ian's request. I read his blog post until I am no longer looking at the words on the paper but performing a recitation of my own memory, as though I have written the words or as if I am forming them into sentences as I speak. I stare, under the haze of Benadryl, at the photographs I have hung on the walls of Ian and Sadie; smoke cigarettes with my hand held in imitation of hers.

I text Lee and E. under the guise of normalcy. I do not text anyone else. I tell no one about the blog post. I no longer trust any of my friends. I have detected something ... artificial in their natures, something untrustworthy. I sense they do not have my—or Ian's—best interests at heart.

I believe there is a conspiracy—of which I am unsure the motivation or means of execution—to keep he and I apart.

I may be part of this conspiracy, unwittingly.

I don't know who I am anymore. I don't know who I am.

Suddenly I remember that the young woman who committed suicide wrote those words not in the suicide note she left atop the parking garage from which she jumped, but "hidden" in a drawer in her dorm room. The note left on top of the parking garage—along with presents for every member of her family—was the note of a perfectionist. Only later did her family discover there was another note. A less perfect version of their daughter ...

AN APOLOGY (OF SORTS)

I wonder if this novel will read to members of my immediate family (and to L.'s) like the second found suicide note of the young woman.
I'm sorry ...

I am not who you think.

I am not what you believed me to be.

I'm sorry. I'm sorry. I'm sorry. I don't know who I am anymore. I don't know who I am.

Or, maybe, I do know who I am. But it is not who you want me to be. (It is not necessarily what I want either...)

I DON'T WANT TO HURT LEE BUT HURTING LEE SEEMS INEVITABLE/HOW WILL I KNOW MY "REAL PERSONALITY" WHEN IT APPEARS?

I remember reading in the back of *The Bell Jar*, in the section in which they give the casual reader a bit in the way of biography of Sylvia, a long quote from her mother. It was from a letter her mother wrote to an American editor a few years after Sylvia's death, in 1970, upon the first American publication of her daughter's novel. I remember it saying that the novel represented "the basest ingratitude" and how that ingratitude was uncharacteristic of Sylvia's real personality. The letter continued to say that this (the incongruity of Sylvia's narrator's personality and her own) was the reason Sylvia had been so frightened when the novel had been published in England to more than moderate success. The letter alleged Sylvia had written her brother to say the novel "must never be published in the United States..."

I wonder if Lauren has figured out by now that the true purpose of this novel is self-destruction. (The destruction—or deconstruction—of self as the only true means of liberation, Lauren.)

WAS IT JUST AFTER THE (ENGLISH) SUCCESS OF *THE BELL JAR* THAT SYLVIA STUCK HER HEAD IN THE OVEN?

How many times do I have to tell you people I don't have the options of the rest of you? I cannot seriously contemplate things like suicide or drug abuse or madness because I am a mother, because of E., because only one parent is allowed the luxury of escapism and in this case E.'s father claimed such escape long ago...before E.'s conception even...I should have known then...I should have been more careful about limiting my options.

My German agent, upon reading parts of this novel asked, are you ready for the fallout?

I don't know, I said.

Things I didn't say:

Is one ever ready?

Should I build a shelter in my backyard?

What should I put in my fallout shelter? What provisions? Cigarettes? Razor blades? A rope? How does that old Dorothy Parker poem go? *Might as well live*?

Hours later, Saul texts me again. I don't know why, but I have the instinct to trust Saul. I am back in the business center, otherwise occupied with the task of printing more blog posts and emails. I do not have time to text Saul back at the moment. But I fully intend to text Saul.

I am less certain about emailing Ian. I tell myself, maybe when I finish this novel . . .

I ask myself, Why doesn't Ian email me again, explaining what he wants?

I worry it will be my unraveling, if I do.

I worry if I say anything, anything at all, I will never stop speaking.

I can't stop thinking about how I began this volume: then I remember: Ian isn't here. Ian never came back.

Then I remember it's been somewhere in the vicinity of four to six hours, or, close enough. I take a sip from my bottle of Benadryl.

The printer doing its job makes a pleasant sound.

I curl up on the carpet beneath the computer where I will wait until the printer is silent again. I think this will be another two hours. Maybe three. I think about Ian sleeping under the poker table in my basement six years earlier.

571

I never went down into the basement either of the nights Ian slept there/ at my house.

I have never fully been an individual.

I'm not sure, but I think I might be becoming one now. (Too soon to tell. But I no longer feel like a monster. I have forgotten, until now, in fact, that I ever believed myself to be one.)

I would think most Americans learn in junior high to differentiate between the writer and the character he is writing about. People seem to insist I'm a monster. —Bret Easton Ellis

(THE) BEGINNING OF THE END (OF IAN'S BLOG, ETC.)

Two nights later I receive a text from a number I don't recognize, asking me if I am aware Ian has killed his blog.

It has been five hours since I was last in the business center.

I am on the floor assembling blog posts and emails chronologically.
    Scotch-taping them together.
    Forming one long inchworm of Ian's words over the floor between living room and bedroom.

Who is this, I begin to type in response.
    I look up at a photograph of Sadie I have taped to the door separating the rooms. My inspiration.
(Yesterday I had begun to truly believe I was going mad. I had first lost the blog post in which Ian asked me, indirectly, to contact him. It had been prominently displayed on the coffee table when I stepped out momentarily to retrieve an energy drink from the vending machine on the fifth floor. When I returned it was no longer there. I searched under the coffee table, under the couch, under my desk, on and under my bed... I searched

the entirety of my hotel suite...I began to suspect someone had taken it...I had called first housekeeping to inquire if someone had been in my room during my brief absence and when they had assured me they hadn't, I called down to the front desk as I suspected them of lying...the person at the front desk, in obvious alliance with her staff members, of which, housekeeping is one, offered me her assurance as well that no one had been in my room in my brief absence...I then left my room again, after first gathering and securing all remaining blog posts and emails in a location I felt was well hidden, and went back to the business center to reprint the blog post...however, when I went to Ian's blog, I could no longer find it. I scrolled down and there were the blog posts I remembered coming just before and just after it, but not the blog post in which he had asked me to contact him! I didn't know if he had changed his mind and deleted it, either because he no longer wanted me to contact him or because he was embarrassed because I hadn't yet contacted him...or if I had conjured the post entirely from my own wanton desires, my own need to be continually contacted, nee, stalked, by him...I returned to my room with great uncertainty...for a few hours I had believed Ian wanted me, again, to pursue him, and now I was unsure if he did or didn't want to talk to me...I had come to the conclusion that I would email him, soon, tomorrow (which was now 'today', meaning yesterday)...but now I didn't know...what was the right thing to do...back in my room there was a phone call from L...he was pleading to see me, saying he was worried about me, that he was going to come soon whether I wanted him to or not...and I got off the phone as quick as I could...looked again for the blog post...until I was wrung out from looking...until a swig of cough syrup sipped while inside a hot bath relaxed me enough that I could, if not sleep, lie motionless for a period of time...)

I have a change of mind. I leave my phone open, the message unsent.

I swallow another mouthful of Benadryl, swallow it with water I drink direct from the bar tap. I forget to avoid the mirror at the back of the bar. I make eye contact with myself. Or with someone who resembles an idea of myself. I flinch when I see her. Glance quickly in another direction.

The hall outside my room is quiet.

I feel my way down with my fingertips touching the walls on either side.

I think momentarily about the cameras, but do nothing to alter my behavior.

I feel somnambulistic.

I can't figure out when this vision quest began—before I entered the hotel or after.

There is no indication of when it will be over.

Or of when the visions will cease. (When the quest will be concluded.)

I key into the business center as one keys into his/her home. The computers are always on, waiting. I pat the one I sit down in front of. Good boy, I say.

My hand is warmed.

I am always cold and the computers are always warm.

More human than human, I think. (When did I cease being human? I ask of no one. I ask of an inanimate object. I ask the camera overhead.)

I type Ian's name. I speak his first and last name breathlessly aloud as though speaking it into a microphone or telephone for an audience of one or a thousand. As though Ian can hear me. Ian Kaye.

And though I have been forewarned, it is a shock when I click on the link and it leads nowhere. When I fail to see the familiar font, the familiar colors.

I have driven to a house that no longer exits.

I sit in my car staring at a square patch of dirt.

I scratch at the back of my throat by swallowing over and over many times in quick succession.

I scratch at my arms and legs until they are visible entries in my journal.

I realize I now have no way of contacting him.

Suddenly I am angry, retaliatory, spoiled.

I go to my Tumblr, find the deactivation section.
    Click "yes" thinking "fuck you."
    Thinking, This is not fair. You cannot watch me if I cannot watch you.

Immediately after my anger veers toward despair.
    My anger veers toward frantic worry.
    I am suddenly overcome with ideas for what has happened to Ian.
    My face is in my hands, secretions from my eyes and nose stream through my fingers.

I stumble back down the hallway, my hands flattened on either wall of the hall; holding myself upright, steady.

I gather what remains of the loose emails and blog posts in my hands, carry them with me into the bathroom. I sit down inside the bathtub, clothed, the blog posts and emails covering me; light a cigarette (hoping to catch them or myself on fire?), swallow a mouthful of 5 Hour Energy, read an email from 2009. Read a blog post from 2011. Read until my eyes blur with characters I no longer recognize. Read until I no longer understand where I am, what year it is. Light another cigarette. It does not matter what year it is or my location. I am a participant in an activity that transcends time and space. I watch the smoke fill the air above me. I relax downward; sink backwards into a warm rush of water that isn't here. Feel the weight of Ian atop me. My knees widen to let him in. I exhale one last long puff . . .

The only reason I remembered this play was because it had a mad person in it, and everything I had ever read about mad people stuck in my mind, while everything else flew out. —Sylvia Plath, *The Bell Jar*

THIRD PERSON/PSH, RIP/END HOTEL

Perhaps if it'd been summer . . . but the dismal days . . . one after another of grey skies and snow, unwalkable sidewalks, . . . added to the feelings of . . .

Combined with the actor's overdose . . . she had read about it in the daily delivered newspapers all that week . . . leaving always a feeling of darkness and melancholy, exhaustion . . . reading about the actor's "last days" . . . the things he had said to bystanders, re his inevitable succumbing to death . . . he knew he could not last much longer, going as he was, and he could not stop going . . .

The addict's tiredness affected her.

She thought of herself in third person now; saw herself driving to . . .

She was a fictional character now as much as Ian; this freed her in a way, freed her of the guilt of being a real person.

She could barely get out of bed, out of the bathtub; barely sit upright at the computer . . .

She only felt awake when in the artificial lighting of the business center, Googling Ian's name.

Desperate for him, two likeminded people, both dark . . . [Sabine says she doesn't buy this, when reading this part of the novel; writes comments in the margins saying she doesn't believe it. Perhaps Sabine is correct, to disbelieve, or perhaps Sabine is in denial when it comes to the author; perhaps Sabine likes an idea of the author, in the same way the author likes an idea of Ian.]

The actor had talked in recent interviews of the requirements of acting, which she realized were not dissimilar to the requirements of writing: the long hours of introspection and self-awareness.

"Most people don't think about . . . they go about their days, but actors have to constantly evaluate."

The actor had been sober—"recovered"—for years. Had taken a wife, had produced children. The actor had been a mentor to other former drug addicts. Before he succumbed. Before taking an apartment near his family's. Before going to an ATM, taking out enough money to purchase enough heroin to kill himself.

She remembered back to another interview the actor had done. How when asked by the interviewer about his sobriety, about the possibility of drinking a single glass of wine with a meal, he had replied, "But who wants one glass of wine when there is the whole bottle?"

She is thinking, even if she manages to be a good wife now, to separate herself from Ian, to give up reading his blog, to stop staying up later than her husband, to promise not to read Ian's books, to try to keep her mind straight, to discipline her mind from going to him . . . how long can it last? How long did the actor's sobriety last? Thirteen years? Fifteen? More? And how long did it take, this last round of use, before he was dead? Two months? Six weeks? Less?

It's hard to love an artist whose primary emotional register is shame.
—David Salle, *Town & Country* article about the Detroit artist Mike Kelley who committed suicide in 2012

IAN'S OVERDOSE

I remembered dreaming of Ian's death once. I woke after the dream in a hotel with Lee. We were out of town for a university tour. E. had stayed in a dorm with other incoming freshman. In the dream I was standing outside Ian's apartment with a group of friends, other writers and fans of Ian's. I don't know how we suddenly knew his address. I remember thinking—or possibly asking a female friend who was there with me—if I should contact Ian's mother, to ask her for our emails—his and mine, the ones he hadn't deleted from his computer. I had deleted some years ago and regretted it now. I wanted to put together a book of our correspondences. In the dream, I mean. This was what I was thinking of while mourning Ian's death in my dream.

But . . .

For now Ian was still alive so there was still the possibility we could die together.

LAST DAYS

I wake in the afternoon, order a cheeseburger I do not eat. I am out of 5 Hour Energy. I call down for coffee. I don't leave my hotel room. There is commotion in the hallway, a large party or family of people sharing neighboring rooms.

Before midnight I text Lee, because I have forgotten to call him and now it is too late.

I open my mini fridge and look inside. I am down to one yogurt, which is expired, and a mini Diet Coke.

I run a brush over my hair, slip on a jacket. I have reached a state beyond nervousness. I take the elevator to the first floor and walk straight out of the hotel. The cold is unexpected. I don't have the sense to button my coat. I wrap my arms around myself and keep walking. I am unaware of my mouth changing in response to the men standing outside the hotel. I seem to have heard myself telling them I am a writer. But that seems impossible and I think probably I have daydreamed it instead (somnambulist!). I cannot remember speaking outside my head or in a volume anyone but myself would detect in days.

I walk into the artificial light of the drugstore, conscious of the cameras on the ceiling. I grab several small bottles from the energy drink aisle and several larger bottles from the cold medicine aisle and find my way to the part of the store that sells shampoo and hair dye and nail polish. I fill my plastic basket with items and walk with assuredness to the register by the door. I am unsure if it is me or another customer who is making small talk. I had been unaware there were any other shoppers in the store until now. I must have asked for a pack of cigarettes for I am smoking one on the walk back to the hotel. I stub it out on the sidewalk while the bellhops and valets watch. I seem to remember a nodding of some sort from them or I, though I cannot with certainty say which of us it was.

Upstairs in my room I do not think of the men. I spread my goods out on the bed, light another cigarette, walk around the room with it like a 1930's chorus girl; stub it out artfully in the sink. I use my teeth to open the packaging, stand in the bathroom mirror. It is like mowing a lawn, I say, making the first pass over my ear. I make several more passes and a quarter of my hair is now in soft piles on the faux marble floor. I will let them be, I think. I unplug the razor, run three fingers over the sides of my shorn scalp. I turn my head and stare closely in the mirror at the silver glints that are now visible and caught by the light.

I return to the bedroom, select my next purchase from the bed. My phone alights with a new text. "8 new messages" it says on the screen. I turn it upside down on the bed. In the bathroom I wrap a towel around my neck, squeeze the bottle in unequal bursts over my head. I light another cigarette and watch the ink-like liquid stream down the sides of my face into the towel. I realize that in my haste for transformation I have forgotten the assortment of caffeinated beverages I have purchased and spread out neatly on my bed. I go and retrieve one, drink from it while I watch the clock.

When it is time I stand in the shower —a cigarette burning in the soap dish—until the water at my feet runs clear.

I stand in front of the mirror blow-drying my hair.

I want nothing about myself to be recognizable.

I think of Sadie as I press the cherry of the cigarette to the exposed scalp behind my ear. I think of them as native markings, rites of passage, spiritual calligraphy. I think, stupid fucking shit.

In the business center I upload my novel to the computer, email it to Horatio. I think, Who gives a fuck.

Back in my room I gather Ian's emails and blog posts and shove them in a suitcase. I rip Sadie's and Ian's photos off the walls and shove them in too. I shove what clothes will fit, my camera, the bottles of liquid energy and liquid cold medicines on the bed.

I leave everything else in the room: my computer, the books I have brought with me, the clothes I can't fit, extra shoes.

My hair is still damp. I lost patience with blowing it dry. My face looks pale against the backdrop of another woman's hair color. I am certain the men outside the hotel do not recognize me as I pull my suitcase along. It is almost dawn. I ask which way to Hertz or Avis, whichever is closer. I ask the time even though I have my phone in the pocket of my jacket. One of the men says it is six thirty. Avis doesn't open until seven, the other man says. I say thank you and keep strolling. I buy a coffee at Starbucks and drink it on the sidewalk while smoking a cigarette.

At seven, I am standing before a middle-aged man with the affected speech of a man much more affluent than his standing. Perhaps it is from interacting with wealthy people on a daily basis. He has confused himself with them. I must look comparatively pauperish in my appearance; easily dismissible. I provide a credit card and driver's license and he studies the latter, but there is no way out and ten minutes later I am holding the keys to a car I cannot correctly pronounce.

The first thing I do is light a cigarette and the second thing I do is send a text to Lee. "Up early!" I say. "The writing is going well this morning!"

I pull out onto the street and take the first onramp onto the freeway. When the man at Avis or Hertz, I have already forgotten which, asked me how long I needed the car I felt unable or unprepared to answer such a question. He possessed an odd posture, reminiscent of an elevator operator or doorman in an old film, perhaps. Maybe it was his hat. Finally I heard myself answer "one week." I felt satisfied with the answer then, thought it very clever, even, though now I am unsure.

I drive seemingly without navigation. I have not made up my mind about anything. I keep reaching up to graze the left side of my head. I seem surprised four hours later when I arrive in the city in which I arrive, when I pull before the hotel in which I will spend one night, at least. Perhaps more. The valet seems familiar to me. Also the man who handles my luggage. Something in their sideburns or jackets, maybe. My phone alights with a text from Lee as I am standing at the counter. "Call me," it says. "We should talk soon."

The man behind the counter hands me my key, points me to the elevator. Normally this is Lee's occupation, navigating hotel hallways and elevators. I have to keep paying attention to directions now in his absence. I have to make or avoid eye contact with people speaking directly to me. I have to make decisions I would prefer not to make.

I go for a walk, the train whizzing overhead. I smoke cigarettes and shuffle by storefronts, the mannequins and I appraising one another. I am dressed less fashionably, of course, but I have the cigarettes. Still there is a certain chicness in their uprightness. In the reflection of the window I can see that I am slouched. I think that if I had a more active occupation . . . if I were always on stage, for instance, traveling in a private bus.

I remember Ian saying I was not a novelist and I think, as much as it pained me at the time to hear this, he was correct.

Though I am more of a novelist than Lee, as biting as that may sound. As much as it doesn't fucking matter.

Suddenly it is imperative I get back in time to call my husband. I make my final selection from the table. Hand the salesclerk the hosiery, five satin undergarments, a silk eye mask. I have had trouble sleeping of late. I am unsure how many hours . . . It seems I am always awake, waiting for sleep to begin.

In my room I remove my bottles of cold medicines —pretty reds and greens and blues—from the inside compartment of my suitcase, line them with my facial astringent and lotion on the bathroom counter. I slump in the bathtub, cover myself with a towel. The bathroom is oddly familiar, designed and decorated similarly to the one I left earlier this morning, a sameness to the arrangement of the toilet and shower and sinks, so that I already know where I am in relation to everything else. So that I could walk through with my eyes closed in the dark late at night without bruising a shin.

"Hello, Lee," I say, my voice hinting at a slur, a byproduct of the green syrup I have been ingesting since my return to the room. "How is Eli?"

I do not wish Eli to be angry with me but it seems an inevitability, an inevitable outcome.

"Is Saul with him?" I ask, lighting a cigarette. I have not yet consulted the hotel handbook to apprise myself of its various guidelines, nee rules, nee impositions. It is possible I am violating many. Quite a matter of fact.

"Yes, the writing is going well . . . I don't know. . . Not too much longer . . . I know, I know . . . well, when is it?"

I turn my wrist as if to look at a watch, though I have not worn a watch in years. I glance around the room, expecting to find the time somewhere on the walls, though Lee is talking days not hours, and so things like minutes and a.m./p.m. seem to matter less . . .

It is my son's graduation of which we are speaking, which is Saul's graduation also. I had calculated the age I would be at this ceremony the moment I discovered I was pregnant. I could never decide if that made me young or old, and I suspect no one but I would care. Certainly not Eli. Perhaps Saul . . . .who can tell.

Outside on the street earlier I passed a man who resembled Ian in dress and stance. I would say with almost extreme assuredness, in fact, that it was Ian except for the fact that I knew it wasn't. He was standing outside the door of a club where I last knew Ian to work. That is, in the part of the city I knew Ian to work. I could not say with any certainty which club it was in which he worked for the name was never told me. I avoided making eye contact with the man just in case and I am not sure if the man saw me though he did seem to make a gesture toward someone in my vicinity and I darted away swiftly just in case.

The phone is still in my hand though no longer pressed to my ear and I wonder when it was I hung up with Lee and what more was said. There are new messages and one is from Saul. None of them are from Eli, of course, and I think to myself, "He already knows and is avoiding you self-protectively." I envy and applaud my son's sense of self-protection. If only I had possessed any in my childhood or five years ago with Ian.

I am so tired. I am exhausted from having to make decisions. I tell myself as long as I remain in this hotel room I will not have to make any more. I close my eyes beneath the silk eye mask and when I open them again I am unable to tell if I have been asleep one minute or ten hours. I feel neither refreshed nor fatigued. It is possible I am sleepwalking as I make my way into the second room. I am wanting to sit upright at a desk. I think this action will aid me in determining my physical capabilities in this moment. As I approach the window, which provides the only light in the mostly darkened room, I am aware of an object on the desk. It is familiar to me in size and shape. It is familiar to me in a way that terrorizes me. I do not know how it could have gotten here, who could have brought it. Certainly not Lee. Just as certainly not Eli or Saul. And yet here is, my computer, facing me as it has for several weeks, though I said goodbye to it just this morning, though I have no need for it now that I have finished my manuscript.

I wish for a drink in my hand. I feel unsteady in my ambling backward toward the bathroom. I reach my hand downward in my pocket for a cigarette then find that I have no matches. I open drawers, searching. I upend my purse onto the floor. I consider picking up the phone but am unsure who I would dial, what extension matches my personal predicament. I cannot demand a book of matches be left outside the door like a pot of coffee. I try and remember other means of igniting flame.

There is a knock on the door and as long as I don't answer it I won't have to make a decision regarding the person standing on the other side, their possible motivations or inquisitions. I shuffle back into the bathroom . . .

On the bathtub edge is my lighter. I shake it near my ear. There may or may not be repeated knocking. I am too distant, too far removed. I can only speculate as to what noises may or may not be coming from the other room.

I open my suitcase to remove the emails and blog posts I printed earlier this day or the last or a week ago, I can no longer remember where one day or week bled into another. But when I unzip the suitcase, I find it empty. All of my clothes have been hung in the closet, placed neatly inside of bureau drawers. There is no sign of the emails or blog posts I spent hours or days printing. I sit down on the carpet, light the cigarette I have been carrying with me from room to room. I consider searching the hotel for its business center, printing the emails and blog posts and photographs all over again. But I am too concerned about the knocking to leave my room. But Ian has killed his blog. I tiptoe from one carpet edge to another, silently blowing smoke through my nose as I have seen Sadie do in videos.

I stand completely still before the door. I stand until I am sure five minutes have passed. Then I stand still for five more. The waiting is what I imagine the inside of meditation to be like. I feel calmer than I have in days. The cigarette is still in my hand though it is no longer burning. I look down and there is a pile of ash on the carpet near my feet. I think I may have been in a trance. I cannot remember the cigarette expiring.

I begin my approach of the door. It has been half an hour, maybe more, since the last knock. I cannot imagine anyone persistent enough to outwait me. I slowly bring my right eye level with the small glass hole. I am afraid of what I will find inside of it. I tell myself to expect nothing, no one. I tell myself I will see only an empty hallway, an expanse of carpet.

Instead there is a young woman standing, in boxers and a t-shirt. Her hair is platinum and cropped but otherwise she resembles Sadie, who, like me, is a natural brunette. I study her, forgetting momentarily to breathe. I compare the image I see now through this tiny piece of glass with the image in my mind of Sadie in the back of a car with Ian. I run through all of the images I have stored in my memory of Sadie: Sadie, naked, with a paper bag over her head, Sadie experiencing hallucinogens, Sadie cutting her inner thigh on stage, Sadie barfing on a sidewalk...

The young woman (who is not Sadie) looks distraught. I wonder if she is on the wrong floor. If her room is one floor above or below mine. I take my eye away, blink, return it. She resembles the DJ girlfriend of a famous actor. I have seen photographs of them together online and in movie magazines.

"You are obsessed with movie stars," Ian told me once, after I had compared him to an actor I held in high regard. I had thought I was being complimentary. Lee would have been appreciative. Lee held the actor in high regard also.

I don't want to open the door or to let the young woman in. She is, after all, a stranger. But I cannot bring myself to walk away from her either. Some part of me wants to hold her, to sleep beside her in my bed. I leave the doorway only momentarily, retrieve my cigarettes, my green and red and blue bottles and my phone, and lay them all out before me on the carpet. I sit with my back to the door and pass the time as I would in a chair at home. Every now and then I rise to put my eye to the glass. I expect at some point the young woman will be gone, and then I will have to think about what to do in her absence... But for the moment she is here so I sit back down and light another cigarette, tongue the outside of the green bottle for its stickiness. I am finished making decisions for the time being. I no longer feel so ambitious. I am feeling more like Lee every day. Or is it Ian. Maybe I am feeling more like me. Or the young woman on the other side of the door. It is so hard to tell. Too soon to tell...

I must have blacked out. When I wake it is dusk again. There are ten new texts on my phone. I use my foot to kick it across the room without checking them. I start to stand; my bladder is full. I must locate the bathroom. But before I do I remember the girl on the other side of the door. I hold my breath and tiptoe toward the peephole. I can't tell if I will be disappointed if she is or isn't there. I look out; don't see her. It is possible, I reason, she has lied down along the wall, out of sight; that she is asleep. I am too afraid to open the door to see if this is the case. I tiptoe to the bathroom instead; light a cigarette as I urinate.

I walk back into the living room with a towel; use the towel to cover the computer. I don't want to think about how it got here. I don't want to think about Ian's emails and where they have gone; who might have taken them; who could possibly be reading them. I locate the hotel welcome manual; search the table of contents for information about the business center. I go back to the bathroom, run my hand over my hair; pat it down smooth. I am getting used to not recognizing myself. I can't find my toothbrush. I squirt a line of toothpaste on my finger and rub it around my teeth.

I open the door to my room slowly, in case the girl is still in front of it. I cannot detect any resistance and so I open the door further. It appears the coast, as they say, is clear. I walk the hallway to the elevator; take the elevator to the fourth floor. I already forget which floor the business center was on in the last hotel. I have little sense of time or location. I ignore the fitness center, go straight for the computer; take a seat "like I own the place," like this place is my office, like I own the building. Light a cigarette. If I had sleeves I would roll them up. I do a search for Ian's blog out of habit or maybe out of hope. Still missing. I go to Sadie's blog. Nothing new, slow night. I go to my email. Search Ian's name. Start printing. Lean back, "like I own the place." Exhale "like I own the place." A man enters the business center, waving his arms; waving his hands, more specifically.

"Where's the fire?" he says. I cannot tell by the way this man is dressed if he works for the hotel or if he is a run of the mill businessman, the kind I am normally afraid of. For some reason, so far, I am not afraid. Maybe it will come later, I think. The "fear." In the next thirty seconds or so. We will see.

"What? Where?" I say, looking around, confused.

"The smoke?" the man says, gesticulating. "Where's the fire?"

"Oh, right," I say, remembering now to ash in the trashcan. "Smoke."

The man looks confused. I feel confused. I have no sense of time or location. I don't know this man, or do I? Do I know you, I think to say, though nothing but smoke is emitted from my mouth when I open it. I gather my papers, officially, as though they are official papers; sign out of my email.

"Have a good night," I say, though I am unsure the time of day. I am unsure the time of evening. I am unsure.

I have Ian's emails in my arms, my cigarette in my mouth. It is still burning. Long-burning, these modern day cigarettes. I don't look back to see if the man is following me. I see a sign for the stairs. I take the stairs: perfect. I am an escape artist. No one can find me now. Not Lee or E. or Saul or Ian.

Wait. I am trying to find Ian not hide from him. Or am I? It is so hard to tell anymore. I think I am trying to find him but I feel unsure. I walk-run down the hallway to my room. Check under my door for the girl. No girl. Maybe I am hiding from the girl or the girl is hiding from me. It's hard to tell. Too soon to tell.

The phone is ringing when I open the door to my room. It rings five more times. I am counting along: one, two, three, four, five. I am standing completely still staring at the phone. I didn't even realize there was a phone in my room. I see my cell phone on the floor under the desk where earlier I kicked it. I wait to see if the message light lights up on the hotel room phone. I don't want it to light up. Please don't light up. I don't want there to be more new texts on my cell phone. I think about the last time Ian texted me four years ago. "Elizabeth, how are you." Always so polite. Haha.

I can see the message light is flashing now. Fuck. I have to make a decision. Two decisions, maybe. I have to decide whether to listen to the message and then I have to decide whether to look at my cell phone. Or maybe that is one decision. I decide it is one and grab my purse. I decide to walk around the city. I decide I am hiding from Ian but also I am trying to find him too. I will find you first!, I think. I will find you, but you won't know I have found you.

It appears it is "late." I don't know the hour, specifically, but the sky is dark and women appear intoxicated and are wearing heels. Their makeup is smudged. They wobble.

I have never taken the train before but I follow behind a pair of young women, watch what they do, mimic it, and now I am taking the train!

I get off a stop after the young women so as not to terrify them. It is not my goal to terrorize young women. Even Sadie. (I like Sadie. I want to hold Sadie, to sleep beside Sadie, to gather every thought and memory of Ian from Sadie's brain.)

I walk down the street at this stop. There are more young women in heels but the heels seem trashier, dented, worn down. I start toward a bar with the idea of entering it. I look down at my own garb. I am wearing my new lingerie under an old dress, the same heels I had on the night Ian and I met. I am a sentimentalist. Among other things. (I am a monster!) I pull out a mirror, investigate my face. My eyeliner is smudged, my mouth also. Ian will never recognize me. I am no longer "uptown." I am barely "Elizabeth Ellen." (Or am I more "Elizabeth Ellen" than ever before?)

I walk toward the front of the first bar, expecting to find Ian. I hold out my I.D. Feel stupid. I am so far over 21. The man has his hood up (like Ian). I cannot immediately discern his face. His posturing is like Ian also.

I enter four bars this way. Only the entering/initial part is exciting. The part where there is the potential to encounter Ian. After that I am just inside another loud annoying bar filled with loud annoying people. After that I am figuring out a way to dodge loud annoying men while imbibing one drink in case Ian is somewhere just out of sight, on his break, or attending to a problem inside the bar or fucking a woman anally in the backroom or politely escorting a prostitute out onto the street.

After that I take the train back to the hotel and consider going to the business center but I am tired. Suddenly I am falling asleep or blacking out. I ignore the blinking red light on the phone. I ignore the knock on the door. I ignore the sad vast emptiness inside me. (I am a monster.) I light a cigarette and fall asleep.

I awake to the taste of ash in my mouth. I awake to the sound of the phone ringing (again—I think I have heard it multiple times this morning or this afternoon or whatever time of day it is).

"People are worried," L. says. I smile; I have beaten Sadie at her own game.

"I'm fine,' I say. It doesn't occur to me that by people he might mean E., that he might mean my son, rather than random people on the Internet, rather than Sadie or Ian.

"I'm going to be home soon," I say.

"I just need a little more time, more research, another week or so, to finish my book," I say
      L. is silent.

"Look," I say, "I have to catch the train"

"The train?" Lee starts to say, but I have already hung up.

I take my phone with me this time; hold onto it in my pocket until I reach the tracks. I stand along them a while, peering down. I am waiting for the train, just like I told Lee. As the train approaches, I pull the phone from my pocket, drop it down. I wait for the train to whiz by.

I decide on a train stop at random. Enter five more bars. It is late afternoon/early evening. I don't know what time of day Ian works. I have to cover all my bases.

At the fifth bar I order a burger. I can't help but wonder if Ian is making it. I want to ask the name of the cook. I want to ask for a tour of the kitchen. I can't rule anything out; any of the various bar occupations, any shifts of the day or night, any sort of drinking establishment: sports bar or hipster bar or college student bar...

"Can you tell me the name of the cook?" I ask my server.
"His name?" she says, bringing me a second glass of water.

"Yeah."

"P.J.," she says.

And I remember I don't know Ian's name.

I pass a bookstore down the road. I backtrack; go inside. I search the fiction section, search the K's. There is a handmade sign I failed to notice recommending Ian's books, noting Ian is a "local author." I look around for indication I am being watched, looked around for anyone who might know me, a bookstore employee or another writer, Ian . . . I look around for indication I am being watched, slip two of Ian's books into my purse, walk a different aisle, feign an interest in other authors. "My interests are singular," I think, a cheesy line of dialogue I remember from a movie I have forgotten.

I sit on the train skimming Ian's books. They are the ones I read in Portland. I use a lipstick to mark pages in which Ian indicates places he goes. There are street names given; train stops, crossroads, intersections. It is as though he was offering me clues all along and I didn't realize it. Ian is helping me narrow my search.

I buy a map of the city in the hotel gift shop; sit on the floor of the lobby marking the streets mentioned in Ian's books. (I am rejoicing in my lack of freedom! I feel liberated with the realization I am needed! It has occurred to me almost at the same time that Lee has never needed me, and that perhaps that has been our greatest undoing; that E. no longer does.)

When I get back to my room the phone is ringing again (or maybe it never stopped). I realize it will always be ringing.

I gather my things back into my suitcase; my bottles and clothes, Ian's emails, Sadie's photographs . . .

I don't pack my computer.

I leave the hotel without officially checking out. I get my car from the garage and drive toward one of the areas I have marked on the map. I think maybe I will see Ian walking down a random street. I think how you usually find people when you're not looking for them. I don't think about how I am actively looking. I don't bother with imagining what I would say or do if I found him.

I remembered something Eli had said about Gatsby. "Gatsby spent five years pursuing Daisy, and then when they finally met again, it was a disappointment. She couldn't live up to his fantasy of her. She didn't say the right things."

I remembered Adele H. walking right by the object of her obsession on an island in the Caribbean after years of searching for him.

I see several young men walking with their hoods up. I see a couple men running along the lake. I see a handful of men who upon first notice could be Ian.

I drive around smoking and looking for Ian for an hour or more. I stop the car near a liquor store; go inside for a bottle of beer. There are young men on the corner and young men inside and they each turn to look at me but none of them are Ian.

I consider asking them if they have seen Ian but I don't know how I would ask. I remember I don't know his name.

One of them asks me for a light and I stop and hold out my lighter to him.

"You live 'round here?" he says.

"Not currently," I say, lighting my own cigarette after him.

"I didn't think so," he says. "I know just 'bout everyone 'round here and I haven't seen you 'round here so that's what I figured."

I consider asking this young man what bars he goes to, if I can go to them with him. I think about asking him back to my hotel to drink but I remember I don't have a hotel right now. Instead I study the sign over the liquor store; memorize it, in case I want to come back; in case I want to talk to this guy again.

"Well, see ya," I say.

"Yeah," he says, and he starts making his way over to another young guy on the wall.

I glance back—consider standing on the wall beside them (another new occupation!)—get in my car. I don't open the bottle until I'm down the road. I don't stop at another hotel until I've emptied the bottle.

The hotel interior is similar to the last two hotel interiors. The hotel room layout is not discernibly different from the last two hotel room layouts.

The phone is already ringing but no one knows I am here so I unplug it, set it on a shelf in the closet. I see my computer here again too. I set it in the closet next to the phone; shut the door.

I change my clothes, fix my hair with my hands, brush my teeth with my finger.

I get on the blue train and this is my job now. I have an occupation now. My job is looking for Ian. My occupation is riding the train and entering bars and asking unanswerable questions.

"What's the opposite of closure?"

My job is the opposite of closure.

Hobart: Have you talked to Liz lately?

Salvador Plasencia: I talk to everybody in that book because we're all friends.

Hobart: Any responses?

S.P.: She won't read it, but whatever.

Hobart: She won't read it?

S.P.: She refuses to read it. We're friends, we're amicable. It's not . . . you gotta look at the novel as a time capsule. It's not this intensified feeling forever. Also, the book is not real. Except when it is. The reality and the made-up and the fantasy—what's the better narrative? That's what matters.

—From a 2006 interview in *Hobart*, issue 6, conducted by
George Ducker, re Salvador's novel, *The People of Paper*

And even as Farrow, [Sinatra's] third wife, was frozen out, his second wife, Ava Gardner, continued to occupy a dark and complicated corner of his emotional landscape, and would do so until his death in 1990.

—BEN YAGODA,

New York Times Book Review, Sunday, December 4, 2015

VOLUME FOUR.

... another way of describing the dissatisfaction of a writer when [a novel] is finished: 'How little I have managed to say of the truth, how little I have caught of all that complexity; how can this small neat thing be true when what I experienced was so rough and apparently formless and unshaped.'

—DORIS LESSING,

from her Introduction to *The Golden Notebook*, 1971

The entirety of my life has been built upon books and movies and personas of women who go mad with love. Who must be hospitalized with their madness. Who walk the streets of cities in search of their lovers, in their madness. Truly I couldn't even manage that. In real life I could manage only to ruin my marriage and to ruin a novel and to ruin my reputation and the reputation of my husband, and to glorify a man I chose to call "Ian" because I did not know his real name.

I never left that hotel alone, as I said I did at the end of Volume Three. I wrote that ending because I did not know how to end the book and because I believed in the disguise of fiction. I want the reader (i.e., my father-in-law, my husband, my daughter, you) to be unable to decipher what is real and what is unreal. I chose this ending because this was my fantasy ending. And I failed at that, too.

I left the hotel ten days after I entered it, with Lee. I watched as Lee carried my computer and suitcase down to the car the same way he had carried them in. I sat helplessly watching. I sat, knowing I had failed, as a writer and as a wife and as a woman trying to make a man love me.

I had not managed to finish my novel nor had I managed to rid myself of this obsession with Ian, for the good of my marriage and for the good of my mental health.

I went home and continued to work, off and on, on this novel for the next three years.

I went home and continued to stay up late, after my husband had gone to bed, to drink and smoke alone, to look at Ian's blog, to think of Ian as a fantastical and heroic figure, in part because I had never gotten over him and in part as a way of dealing with the uncomfortableness of domestic life, the stillness and uncertainty and immobility.

I did see Ian again.

I was on a reading tour with four other writers in the fall of 2015. By this time Ian and I were friends again, or, of this he had temporarily convinced me. By this time we had started and stopped talking three or four times in a twelve-month period. By this time my husband and I had separated, living in separate residences across town from one another, living in some sort of limbo on account of Ian or on account of my feelings for Ian, which I could never quite make sense of or which I refused, even while in therapy with my husband, to give up. I wasn't ready to let go of my marriage but I wasn't ready to let go of (the idea of) Ian, either.

I had lived my life in limbo for six years, since the day I met Ian, and I (told myself I) didn't know how to live it any other way. (The truth is more that I didn't want to live it any other way.)

I had spent the winter of 2014/2015 talking to Ian on a daily, if melodramatic, basis. I suppose I invited the melodrama, sought it out. In contrast to the quietness of my marriage.

It's funny how undone you can feel via text message. How wounded. How submissive. How undead.

I remember, as an example, one morning making the hour drive to see Eli, to see my daughter, to have lunch with her at her university. I remember "fighting" with Ian (via text message) on the drive.

I had stopped at a rest area ten minutes from Eli's dorm to text with Ian because Ian was angry with me. There were the remains of a dead animal on the pavement near where I parked. I took a photograph of the dead animal with my phone and sent it to Ian as a gesture of goodwill, as an apology of sorts. He ignored the photo. He retained his anger with me. He was not ready to give it up.

I got back on the freeway five more miles, got off at the exit with the Dunkin' Donuts and the Cracker Barrel and the Dairy Queen. I drove another three miles and pulled into the parking lot of a church a mile and a half from Eli's dorm to argue more with Ian.

As I sat in my car, parked in the church parking lot, writing text after text to Ian, a text came through from my daughter.

"Where are you?" it said.

"Almost there!" I said.

"You said that fifteen minutes ago," she said.

"Five more minutes!" I said.

This was the sort of distraction I needed in my life at that time—Eli's first year away at college, my first year alone in the house, having found myself embroiled in a literary scandal, the focus of banning and boycotting for an essay I'd written, for something I'd said.

I needed Ian to argue with me, to distract me from myself, from a life I couldn't make sense of, about which I was uncertain.

I needed Ian because he was the one person—other than my daughter—who called me on my shit, but also because he was the one person—other than my daughter—who made me feel partnered with, against the world, against anyone who hated me, because the world hated him, too; because he understood feeling alone and despondent and uncertain of his future.

But nothing was ever easy between Ian and me, either.

In January and February we talked about moving together to New Orleans or to Texas or to Florida, of purchasing a bar together, of living in a trailer on a beach or on a sand lot. Plans I never believed in because I didn't think Ian believed in them. Plans I didn't believe in because we spoke only in emails and text messages. We talked off and on for a year without either of us asking to meet in person. I didn't ask because I had asked numerous times five years earlier and I wanted Ian to be the one to ask this time.

By early summer (of 2015) we had stopped talking again. There had been another petty fight, a stand in for a real conversation about the futility of our talking. Neither of us could ever figure out the "now what" of our situation. We didn't talk until late August and then we didn't talk all of September. By mid-October we were again talking, but sporadically. Ian had started seeing someone, in real life, someone with whom he would soon move to Texas, making good on our plans.

"Hey, put me on that reading," he texted me, meaning the reading we were doing in his city at the beginning of November. I took this demand as an implication he wanted to see me. *Finally.*

It'd been six years since we'd last parted in a hotel room in his city.

I asked Ian not to bring the woman he was seeing. I asked him how he would feel if I brought Lee.

In the meantime, my husband wouldn't talk to me.

I asked my friends about the ethics of making plans to see Ian at the expense of my husband's feelings.

I asked my friends about the ethics of publishing a book about Ian.

I couldn't get a clear-cut answer in either case. In both cases, my friends seemed to support the idea that art cannot be moral or immoral. No one seemed sure about what I could or couldn't be.

The afternoon we pulled into Ian's city, I texted Ian. I said, "It's so hot. I can barely breathe."

He said, "haha. What?"

I said, "Nothing. Never mind."

It was still early when we got to the bookstore. It was a small bookstore, divided in half by a wall of books above which you could not see without standing on a chair or ladder. On one side of the wall was a row of chairs, set up for the reading. On the other was the entrance to the bookstore, the cashier.

Kirstin and I stood near the entrance. I was turned toward Kirstin and Kirstin was turned toward the front door. I saw Kirstin's face change. She was saying hi to someone. I turned and the someone she was saying hi to was Ian. Ian was walking into the store and when he saw us he froze. He took a step or two back. I had said hi as he approached. I had smiled. He did not return the greeting nor did he smile. He seemed surprised, stepping back and saying, more to Kirstin than to me, "Hey, I'm going to grab something to eat. Does anyone want anything?"

I think Kirstin said, "No, no, thanks." Maybe I did or we both did.

A little later I saw Ian on his phone outside the bookstore and then I didn't see him again until he was called up by an employee of the bookstore to read.

I was sitting in the audience with Sabine, who had moved to the city a year earlier.

I had purposely not been put on the list of readers, had gotten someone from the bookstore to host.

This way I was able to sit on the floor with the audience, on one side of the bookstore, while Ian and my tourmates were standing on the other side, where I couldn't see them until they read.

After the reading I stood in line for the bathroom with Sabine. When I came out I saw Ian standing with two young women. I recognized one of the young women, the one who was talking, as a writer who lived in Ian's city. I did not recognize the other one.

I walked outside and stood on the sidewalk in front of the bookstore with Kirstin and two of my other tourmates. It suddenly occurred to me that the young woman I didn't recognize was the woman Ian was seeing.

Kirstin went to ask him if he was going to come out with us for a drink. A large group of us were going to a nearby bar. She came back and took her place in our circle. She told us he said he couldn't go.

Then Ian and the young woman walked out of the bookstore, passed us on the sidewalk and kept walking. He didn't say goodbye to me or to Kirstin or to our other tourmates, with whom he was also friends.

I turned and watched Ian walk down the sidewalk with a young woman none of us knew.

Now that it was finally over I didn't feel much of anything or I didn't know how to feel.

I walked with Kirstin and Sabine and the other people on my tour to a bar down the street. I sat at a picnic table and ate a burger. I went into the bathroom and a song that I could easily have made significant was playing and I chose to ignore its significance. We went back to the hotel and I ordered a whiskey and smoked a cigarette on the sidewalk outside the hotel and then went to bed.

We had two more cities on our tour.

And then I went home to Lee. And then I went home to my husband.

Words have their own meanings, they have different meanings, and then all those words change their meaning. Words that meant something ten years ago, don't mean that now; they mean something else.

—BOB DYLAN,
No Direction Home

Jane Lynch: We were brought up with these notions: "Let It Please Be Him" and "I Won't Last a Day Without You" ... you know, romantic relationships are basically bullshit ... I had a renaissance in terms of thinking and I'm done with the romance; It's stupid.

Marc Maron: So what do you look for now?

JL: Nothing. I'm a happy girl, right here, right now.

MM: Right?

JL: I love it. I love the now.

MM: The romantic thing, like, if somebody has romantic notions that you're with, you start to feel the pressure of that.

JL: Oh yeah. It's crazy. It's so odd. You start to change. They start to ... And you're both acting artificially.

MM: Right. They start getting disappointed by their idea of what you should be.

JL: Right, and then you're like, "Oh, I've got to rise to what their idea is of me."

MM: That's right. Oh, it's crazy.

JL: It's the biggest lie in the word.

MM: It's exhausting. And then you end up resenting the reality of them.

JL: Exactly. It's crazy, isn't it?

MM: Like, "Lower your expectations, I'm not who you think I am."

JL: Whoa, Nelly, relax.

[Laughter]

> —*WTF* podcast with Marc Maron and Jane Lynch, Episode 727,
> listened to by Elizabeth Ellen on Friday, September 16th, 2016,
> as she finished edits on this novel

[Chelsea Martin, Chloe Caldwell, Tao Lin, Amanda Goldblatt, Scott McClanahan, Sean Kilpatrick, Juliet Escoria, Mira Gonzalez, Victor Freeze, Donora Hillard, Steve Anwyll, Leesa Cross-Smith, Elle Nash, Amanda McNeil, Ben Gross, Shannon McLeod]

ELIZABETH ELLEN is the author of the story collections *Fast Machine* and *Saul Stories* and the poetry collections *Bridget Fonda* and *Elizabeth Ellen*. This is her first novel. She lives in Ann Arbor, Michigan and is deputy editor of the literary journal *Hobart*. A long time ago she won a Pushcart Prize.